Therapy
apy
Mam-
mals

A Barnacle Book | Rare Bird Books
Los Angeles, Calif.

Therapy Mammals

JON METHVEN

This is a Genuine Barnacle Book

A Barnacle Book | Rare Bird Books
453 South Spring Street, Suite 302
Los Angeles, CA 90013
rarebirdbooks.com

Copyright © 2018 by Jon Methven

FIRST TRADE PAPERBACK ORIGINAL EDITION

All rights reserved, including the right to reproduce this book or portions thereof in any form whatsoever, including but not limited to print, audio, and electronic. For more information, address:

A Barnacle Book | Rare Bird Books Subsidiary Rights Department,
453 South Spring Street, Suite 302,
Los Angeles, CA 90013.

Set in Warnock
Printed in the United States.

10 9 8 7 6 5 4 3 2 1

Publisher's Cataloging-in-Publication data
Names: Methven, Jon, author.
Title: Therapy mammals / Jon Methven.
Description: First Trade Paperback Original Edition | A Genuine Barnacle Book | New York, NY; Los Angeles, CA: Rare Bird Books, 2018.
Identifiers: ISBN 9781945572999
Subjects: LCSH Rich people—Fiction. | Private schools—Fiction. | Businesspeople—Fiction. | Parenthood—Fiction. | Animals—Therapeutic use—Fiction. | Manhattan (New York, NY)—Fiction. | Black humor (Literature.) | Humorous fiction. | BISAC FICTION / Humorous | FICTION / Satire
Classification: LCC PS3613.E885 T54 2018 | DDC 813.6--dc23

For Lib

Part One

Morning Drop-off

"Teachable moments, Toby," I say. "The fundamental component of progress."

The things we do for our children. This is my predicament as I come out of the darkness to find my hands wrapped around Toby Dalton's warm neck. The notion is residue from an earlier blog post on the Gopa website on the topic of sacrifice and commitment, my knuckled fingers a demonstration that our words as parents translate into actionable guardianship. Everyone likes Toby. He is popular, handsome. Like much of the student body, he comes from wealth, which gives him an optimistic sheen, a glorious yelp that privilege has its merits, nice hair, immaculate teeth, a dapper glow. His neck is bronzed and soft, a teenager who understands the benefits of luxury moisturizers and can afford them. I feel the restorative properties from his skin surge through my fingers as I shove his head against the cement wall. Captain of the Gopa lacrosse team in his junior year, Toby is going places.

The restroom is located toward the rear of the school's lobby. On the far side of the door I listen for the morning arrival, the familiar prattle of students and parents and nannies and the security guards hired to prevent this exact lawsuit, the viscera of the Gifted and Purposed Academy, Gopa for short. According to the website, we are "a premier private school on Manhattan's Lower East Side devoted to the growth and accomplishment of its student body." Toby would mark the building's first homicide.

A Wednesday morning in April. I do not remember following him into the bathroom. I am just coming to terms with my strategy. Perhaps a discussion about the unbecoming pictures of my daughter I am told he possesses. An understanding of whether they exist and, if so, what is it they show of Iliza, and how such images might impact all of our futures. An apology, a handshake. Instead Toby stares me down too emphatically, tips his chiseled chin at an unbecoming angle, *What can you do about it, old man?*

I have the little shit pinned against the paper towel dispenser, his jaw pressed hurriedly upward as the motion sensor incorrectly perceives dampness and litters the floor with napkin, a subtle iniquity to my position on the Gopa Parents Think Recycle committee. A light flickers. Snot drips, balances on my lip, and pirouettes to the tile. My body is freezing, unable to control the shakes, my hands blue with struggle. Toby underestimates my pear physique, my suit and tie civility, thinking that I value my standing in the Gopa community, my career as a meteorologist. He has allowed me to strangle him with a detached coolness, that not even confused murder can deter his divinity. But he has come to terms with the rage a father feels for his children, wholly immersed in defending them against a creeping wickedness beset on the world. I am incoherent as I squeeze, a bystander to my misanthropic diligence. Blackouts, a doctor calls them in my personal infomercial, side effect of my medication along with dry mouth, dizziness, forgetfulness, and erections. The medicine mixes with the adrenaline and my inner voices causing something to break inside, pipes bursting and scattering liquids of me that I secretly loath: docility, understanding, nonpartisan approval. Let it drip.

He swings meekly at my shoulders, his sneakers grasping for tile, his voice a whisper over the squeaking rubber. "Pisser, stop."

"What is it, Toby?" My pocket buzzes. I cannot take the call.

"Listen to me." His voice is desperate breath.

"You see, Toby, you have come to a point of incalculable danger, what weather nerds call the storm surge." I shiver out these words, arms shaking. "A man will go some lengths to protect a daughter, abiding by societal rules, of course, principle, logic, the gist of the whole if you follow. But a creature, Toby. A tribe of creatures. Things that reside in the indentations of our bosom. They know not comfortable rules of kinship. They know only starvation and repercussion and survival."

Enter Doug Whorley, all-league defenseman of the lacrosse team and *deus ex machina* from the lobby. His morning dump, of all things, will preserve Toby's life and rescue me from what would be a well-publicized jail sentence. If a grown man is strangling you in a bathroom, Doug is the friend to have. He sees our embrace, the growing hill of paper on the floor, and his fists intrinsically clench. Six foot something, the benefits of steroid use come to mind, he resembles an upright bulldog awaiting a meal. Suddenly he demonstrates his "go team" attitude when he realizes his captain is fading, punching me squarely in the forehead. I fall to the floor, cold and snot and laughter.

About the medication. It has been suggested that failure, in both my marriage and career, is due to a deficiency in playfulness. Not happiness, but rather an innate frolicsome that children demonstrate, an ability to cavort in spite of age and social fatigue and unpaid bills. Because of this I lack qualities that would make me a better husband and weatherman: humor, personality, a firm grasp of the female demographic. I contracted with an independent pharmaceutical representative for trial pills of Luderica intended to tap into my psyche and locate my playful aura. Side effects also include uncontrollable laughter.

My body is silly with the chortling, the slate tile crisp against my heavy face, the dispenser a paper waterfall of recycled efficiency. Toby coughs, wanders the restroom massaging his soft neck.

"Mister Pistilini," Doug says. "I didn't mean to—"

"Fuck, Pisser." Toby spits and clenches, wanders with distance, judging whether he can safely kick me in my head now that Doug is here to protect him. "What are you smiling about?"

In fact, I am not smiling. I am laughing, hard and urgent so that I cannot catch breath or halt considerable drool, my body repressing vomit. When I try to stop laughing it comes in lavish bursts, the dizziness from Doug's fist, the bruise I feel welting on my forehead. A foreign cell phone lies beneath the sinks, buzzing and spinning and drawing attention. It is not my phone. My phone does not work. I need to order a new model, which I cannot do without my old one because my deft retail provider demands all purchases be made by mobile contraption. I place the contraband item in my pocket. The sound of my retching has carried into the lobby until the bathroom is filled with Gopa dads, younger kids enthralled at the massive pile of paper, a five-year-old leaping into the joy as his guardian senses filth, recycling material, parental engagement.

"Now, David, was that a good choice?"

Someone helps me to my feet. Toby and Doug have fled, leaving me to explain the laughter to the hovering parents. They are smartly dressed for morning drop-off, soldiers of a foreign campaign over a fallen comrade, everyone armed with hand sanitizer and cell phone. It takes a moment to transform from tribe into Tom Pistilini, failing husband, father of two, homeowner, semi-known meteorologist. A face I recognize is beside me, Josey Mateo, an administrative assistant who volunteers with the drama department.

She resets the dispenser. "What's happened, Mister Pistilini?"

"Nothing," I say. "Just a dizzy spell."

"You need a doctor." I am the victim, not the aggressor. She holds my arms, standing on her toes to peak into my dilated eyes, bony hand on my forehead, her skin littered with pen drawings of animal totems: a stick tortoise on a forearm trampoline, two emaciated pigs wrestling or fucking near a bra strap. "You're freezing. And sweating."

"I'm fine, Josey, really."

"Your face." She tries to hold my stare. "It's all scratched. Let me call the nurse."

"That's not necessary. A silly misstep is all."

I should mention that Josey Mateo, twenty-seven, has an unhealthy affinity for the weather, and what I believe is an innocent crush on me.

Thirty-one days. That is how long she claims my consecutive streak has grown of successfully predicting the weather for Channel Fourteen, neither Manhattan's go-to nor relevant source of news and climate condition, a stroke of wily luck that began in the throes of March and now grips Manhattan's unpredictable April. I am an average weatherman at best, though Josey claims to watch me each morning and plan her wardrobe on my prognostications. She suggests I have the flu, more questions, a water bottle is placed in my hand as she re-rolls the towels. She studies me thoroughly, more questions, and leaves it with a whisper.

"I'm a friend, Mister P. I know something happened with the little fuck."

Gopa Lobby

I AM USHERED BACK into the lobby now swollen with pre-enlightenment vigor. No one acknowledges there was an attempted murder in the bathroom, a falling out between myself and the lacrosse team that will have implications for the remainder of the season. The Gopa Worthy is favored to win New York's private school league championship and knock off some impressive out-of-district schools from Long Island and New Jersey. Had I murdered the captain and best faceoff man in Gopa history, it would have been a blow to the offense, though possibly a good thing for team unity. Nothing coalesces a republic like tragedy, a fledgling band of athletes engaged in a righteous mission for the fallen.

Everything is normal, the lobby entrance predictably cheery; I am reluctant to believe my morning dispute ever occurred. Perhaps it was another episode brought on by the medication, which our family therapist, Devin Brenner, has cautioned can be dangerous. The lacrosse coach and my business associate, Russ Haverly, is also my dealer. I will have to decide whether to mention my morning when I see him as I know he is fond of Toby and would look unfavorably on my strangling the boy. I search the room for a platoon of lacrosse meatheads or security guards mobilizing toward me, but everything is calm.

Toby is a friend of Iliza, an ex-boyfriend perhaps, although I have been cut out of my daughter's romantic entanglements. He is arrogant but maybe someone I do not hate the way I thought I did moments earlier. The photograph rumors likely originated with the nannies, known locally as our nanny chain, but they do not always get it right. They once conjured an affair between Howard Willis and Monica Rhimes, a rumor that was untrue until it brought the two families together to discuss it, which initiated the actual affair.

We have been without a nanny since the accident in January, which gives Laura and I a disadvantage when it comes to gossip. All our friends have domestic help. Nannies guard their employers' children against malicious gossip. They offer up overheard rumors about other families without being prodded. If there was any truth that Toby Dalton possessed photographs of Iliza, we could validate the news much faster if we had an insider on the payroll. As it is, I may have murdered our nanny with a claw-tooth hammer in the backyard, staging it to look as though she tripped and slammed her head into the stone patio before drowning in the Jacuzzi lagoon. The 16-ounce titanium claw-tooth hammer retails for a $189 on VillageShop.com. Our former nanny was stealing from us. It is conceivable she made off with my hammer prior to her accident.

I feel better now that I am among my people—a stinging in my forehead that I could be imagining. I enjoy the morning drop-offs, the coming together of the Gopa community as we bid our children goodbye and greet one another with tender affinity that is somewhat fake and bearably genuine and maniacally envious. We share similar habits, what might have passed for smoke breaks in another era—hand sanitizers, eye drops, moisturizer, hair gel, sunscreen, bottled water, a series of liquids with which we douse our children so they are disinfected and hydrated following the morning commute. We barely listen to one another, the same conversations, all of us communicating our own agendas and feigning interest in other families' plights.

"Yes history and Bushel nearly took her first step the Hamptons this weekend did you know about Tuesday the kids have homework I hate your son irrationally."

The line of SUVs and taxies is orderly today. The Gopa flag floats haughtily, drifting in a persistent waft so I am never able to read the Latin wording. We bask in the heavily armed security that covers the front entrance governed by Lieutenant Misch, former NYPD who oversees bygone soldiers and SWAT officers and one Navy SEAL, trained killers lured into the private sector of defending children of wealth while they learn arithmetic and yoga. There is free coffee near the elevators. A dog barks toward the southeast, from where we can expect a mild breeze for much of the morning and into the evening commute.

Our community fosters a fairly intense population of animals—therapy dogs, security dogs, remedy Chihuahuas riding inside handbags not to be confused with miniature dogs that ride in handbags as accessories and not for their healing value. They all hate me. A rough estimate, forty percent of Gopa families own therapy creatures; the rest get their therapy in inorganic form. I represent the human version of fireworks, distractions that spook bestial sensibilities. When I am near an animal they yip and pant and cause their owners anxiety, which is why I stand off to the side and watch the morning activity.

All the kids, even the parents, are on phones catching up on text correspondence and the popular website, Lustfizzle. Iliza and her best friend, Tungsten Sedlock, hover over devices. In her junior year, my daughter is an aspiring actress, starring in the spring production of *Our Town*. Tungsten, her understudy, sports a bandage on her left hand that I do not recall from a week ago but could be a fashion statement instead of a compression. I wave to Iliza but she ignores me. This morning she is playing the part of cunty teenager who does not know the lengths her father will go to protect her innocence. Gus, my twelve-year-old, chats up a security guard. Foreseeably, he is dressed as an elderly woman, Millicent, fallout from the January death of our Tilly.

Since the accident Gus has taken it upon himself to cover the former nanny's chores, doing the laundry, cooking, even shopping for decorative pillows he claims complete a room, one of Tilly's signature skills. Gopa is the type of community to foster my son's strange identity crisis and help him through a failed set of standard tests, which via the nannies has become widespread banter with the other parents. Everyone here is politically correct. Everyone is progressive and understanding and has experienced the fortune in life that they do not pass judgment on another family's tribulations.

Like any community, we have our cliques—and within those, sub-cliques, and within those, tighter cliques, and within those, two-person cliques, husband and wife—battling for the limited resources we believe life affords. One resource, in particular, has hung over our dealings the entire school year, the Extended Cultural Immersion, or ECI, a pilot program that has taken hundreds of hours and dozens of applications and is open for the first time to next year's senior class. There are eighteen spots available for a class of a hundred and fifty. We all wish it for our children, which indirectly means we do not wish it for other children. We care about each other and loathe each other. We are on our best behavior, still sharing hand sanitizer but in ever-smaller squeezes.

Our community is broken into three tribes: Manhattan parents, typically the wealthiest; Westchester and Brooklyn and New Jersey, who commute to Manhattan for jobs and Gopa; and myself and other parents from Slancy, a manmade island off the coast of Brooklyn's Red Hook neighborhood, who view the Westchester-Brooklyn-Jersey clan as the true imposters. We Slancy inhabitants bond on the shuttlebus, which leaves each morning at a quarter past seven. The only exception being Ray McClutchen, who bikes through Red Hook and over the Brooklyn Bridge, just to make a point about global warming and exercise.

Gopa is not all cliques and walls. In the end we want the best for our children. We appreciate the camaraderie. We support our impressive drama department and sports teams. We volunteer for inconsequential committees. We have a growing Asian community of which we are proud. We even have one mother, Sharon Li, who dons a prosthetic leg that none of us think is strange or creepy or stare at too long as it taps away during morning drop-off. She is peppier than most moms, playful and sprightly in a way I find irritating and impossible to maintain. She has a son, Whisper, also a junior, captain of the chess club, which I have forced Gus to join. Whisper's ethnicity and nerd power ensure he is a shoe-in for ECI.

"Hey there, Pisser." It's Grant Wheeler, father of Crenshaw, eighth grade, and Amen, whose gender I cannot recall. "What's on tap for today?"

Death. Agony. Some fetid hell the most imaginative Hollywood scriptwriters have not thought up yet. I shove my hand into his sweaty, unsanitized palm. "Nippy this morning but should give way to a beautiful afternoon. Some fair clouds out of the south will resemble vapor trails from missiles our government will launch at our enemies, and our enemies' children, so that our children can grow up without the constant worry of foreign terrorism. None of that will make the news to bother you."

"Like to hear it. Good day for a round."

"It'll be a cold round. Still only April. People are starving right here in this country, some just down the street. I think I've come down with the flu, but I'm playing this afternoon because I'm avoiding going home to see my family. See you there?"

"Might happen. Sorry to hear about the test trouble Gusser's having." He slaps my shoulder. The nannies? The comment section of the Gopa website? "Anxiety's a bitch. He'll get his head around it. Don't worry."

"I'm not worried. Say, Grant, did I hear Amen had similar test anxiety?"

"I wouldn't know."

"How's that?"

"We don't talk about it."

"Why not?"

Grant has located his hand sanitizer and is scrubbing away my aura. "Might give the impression there's something to talk about, something wrong with Amen, which there isn't. Amen is an excellent test taker. Always has been as far as we're concerned."

This is how we communicate. "But can you confirm that some kids do have test anxiety. Maybe not your Amen," I say, hands up, letting him know that Amen's testing ability is off the table. "And that with a sympathetic tutor and proper confidence instilled, they get better at test taking?"

He shrugs uncontrollably. "Wouldn't know, partner." He slaps my chest. "See you on the course. By the way, you look like shit, Pisser."

This morning everyone talks around the typical issues. Some parents would like the children to have thirty minutes of phone time in the middle of the day. Otherwise they are gluttonous when they get home. A rumor that the ground beef served during last week's Burger Day was not sourced locally has sparked a gathering of concerned moms, a potential committee that none of us believe in but would do well to join since we could take partial credit for locally sourced meat. The big lacrosse game is approaching, as is the spring play. The bunny epidemic has worsened. During a yearlong lesson of the life cycle for the first graders, the science department bred two Angora rabbits. Angoras being tiny fur balls, everyone fell in love with the photographs that were circulated (pre-breeding) on the Gopa website. The actual bunnies were born different. Aggressive was mentioned. Mentally challenged was bandied. They are constantly turning up dead, or fucking uncontrollably when it's time for the six-year-olds to nurture them. A decision has to be made—euthanize, allow the sophomore biology classes to dissect. No one can agree and the longer the rabbits await judgment, the faster they breed, increasing the problem.

"Morning, Pisser." Someone I do not recognize slaps my shoulder. Without thinking I offer him sanitizer, which he accepts expectantly. "Heard about Gus. We've got a great tutor. Have Laura call Janie. We should do dinner. Go see a doctor."

"Definitely," I say, bumping fists.

Dead Chipmunks And Wine

TONIGHT IS A WINE tasting for Gopa Parents for Trees. It is a sign of social standing to sit on a Gopa committee board, and because I am a meteorologist people think I know more about global warming and tree preservation, which I do not. But it feels important to be involved, to have a hand in the four large, potted trees, which were assembled in the ballroom, and into which we have deposited members of the Gopa administration. It was my idea to harness them to the structures to prevent injuries since they also are consuming wine, the fundraiser an invitation to get slightly tipsy without judgment. Each time we raise $10,000, a ladder is procured and we hoist down one of the administrators. For now, Heather Pace, head of the school, and the others sip and wave to constituents. I consider how pleasant it would be to watch someone plummet to the floor and splatter, a giant bag of pinot.

Parents kiss and reintroduce themselves and sanitize. Like marbles of different sizes shaken through suitable perforations, soon we wander the ballroom until we are among our preferred sect. I grip hands and triple kiss cheeks of my fellow Slancyites, a tight-knit group of four households: me and my wife, Laura; Ray and Olivia McClutchen, who I only pretend to like; Jason and Jackson, our next door neighbors; and Harry and Allie Sedlock, who look perfect and behave perfect, whose children are also perfect, and who because of their perfection have raised the profile of Slancy families within the Gopa community.

Together we are inhabitants of the city's first, fully functional artificial borough, which when we are not present everyone describes as gaudy and stripmall-ish. We know each other's children. We socialize together. We have invested our savings into the Sedlocks' startup, and one day we will all be wealthy together. These are my people and I love them. Except for Ray McClutchen, who I believe fakes his optimism to sell motivational books. This evening they stare, pitying me, preparing to make jokes at my expense, which serves as our bonding ritual.

"What happened to your face?" Olivia McClutchen is Indian, jeweled, attractive skin if not always bunched into a judgmental scowl. She has a fake accent she did not learn growing up in Long Island, which disappears when she experiences emotion. "You look like you're dying."

"We're all dying." I touch my face to feel the numbness. "I'm not well, no."

"It was a dog, wasn't it?" Jason references the scratches, the welt on my forehead. "They shouldn't be permitted anywhere. It's unsanitary."

"It wasn't a dog," I say.

Harry Sedlock steps forward, commandeering the examination. "You need to put something on that, Pisser."

My wife stays out of it. Laura is tired of me, tired of my grumpiness and insomnia, tired of everyone feeling badly for me ever since I returned from the retreat in February. I have conjured a reputation of perpetual injury, a man forever on the cusp of destruction. Somehow, impossibly, she knows as I do that the conversation will turn to the chipmunks and the steps I have taken to keep the little fuckers out of our backyard. They all think it—that I lost a fight with a chipmunk—and any minute…

"It was a chipmunk, wasn't it?" Olivia brightens, the accent fading as she delights in this misfortune. "One finally fought back."

"It wasn't a chipmunk. A stray cat got me."

"It's in the homeowners agreement. You cannot kill the wildlife. The land belongs to them."

In fact, the land belongs to Laura and I, an insurmountable monthly mortgage that makes us nostalgic for our West Village days and the tiny one-bedroom above the bakery that smelled of warmth and poverty. Specific to the claim of chipmunk ownership, the actual land consists of tons of dredged material arranged into ninety-five acres of artificial real estate that crooked developers learned too late could not support skyscrapers, onto which an ecosystem was introduced of earthworms and warblers and picturesque chipmunks that were bred in a laboratory with immaculate features. They were placed in Slancy by our homeowners association that thought they would drive up property values, which they might. But they are impossibly stupid or brave, venturing into my Jacuzzi lagoon as if it is their own water source. Our chipmunks have no history. They have no parents or children, which means they have nothing to worry about but swimming and drowning and getting stuck in my filter.

"A cat, geezus," Jason says. "In the neighborhood?"

"Near work. An alley cat," I guess.

Olivia again, "And stop feeding them nuts. Our chipmunks have nut allergies. You've already desecrated their hibernation routine with that lagoon. They think they can stay awake all year and be warm next to your deathtrap."

That Olivia McClutchen has researched the life cycle of laboratory-grown chipmunks strikes me as pretentious. She chairs Slancy's preservation committee, which includes two men who only joined so they can take photographs of the warblers in neighbors' backyards without seeming odd. I concentrate on not smiling which makes it impossible. I burp out a laugh and think of Gus and the standardized tests and the old woman glasses and I cannot control myself.

"It's not funny, Pisser." She pronounces it *Pissah* as the accent wanes. "I found a sick one last week. Wandering, drowsy. I know it was poisoned."

I laugh into my glass. "Now, dear," Ray says. He rode his bicycle to the event, a tricycle actually, which folds into an efficient carry-on, a nifty product that retails for $600 at VillageShop. Ray wears his fold-up trike on a strap over his shoulder as he sips wine. I have a deep need to crush his cheek with a wine bottle.

"How do you know it was poisoned?" asks Jackson, coming to my defense. "Unless you ran it over and then performed an autopsy?"

"Olivia, you cannot run over chipmunks and cut them open to see why they're not sleeping." We all pretend to laugh at Harry's joke, which diffuses the tension.

Olivia again, no hint of inflection, the accent gone. "It isn't funny."

"Seriously, Pisser, stop killing them," Harry says. "Allie found one on the doorstep the other day."

Allie Sedlock, flawless and sensitive, smiling innocently that the dead carcass was no bother, no bother at all. She is dressed seductively for a parent event, makeup on and hair pulled back in a graceful ponytail. She gives a fast curtsy and shrug, which means nothing, though we all come out of our shoes at this gesture.

A waiter pours more wine. "What about the gun?" Olivia asks.

"Let's just drink wine and stop being dramatic." Laura takes my side, finally says something, anything in defense of her idiot husband who is only protecting their property from the creeping sophistication of Designer Rodentia. "It's a BB gun. And he couldn't hit a moving car much less a tiny rodent."

I am somehow grateful for my wife's attack on my manhood, the insult to my innate frontiersman, the evening has turned into a coming together of our marriage. Everyone knows about the BB gun, but not about the crossbow, nor the scythe, and certainly not the titanium-handled hammers or the chainsaw. Jason and Jackson know about the bow because it was delivered accidentally to their house after it was delivered accidentally to the Hendersons. When you have a rodent problem like I have, you never know how much firepower you might need. My intention is only to scare the chipmunks, not have the BB projectiles lodged in their fur and kidneys and soft brains, which could lead to blood clots or slow bleeds. I would use a high powered air rifle if I wanted clean kills, or the crossbow that sits in its packaging in the attic.

"I only fire warning shots so they don't get close to the water. Otherwise, they drown." I perform a public service for the chipmunks, I say. "Imagine a chipmunk paddling its tiny paws for hours, trying to stay afloat. Eventually it gives out to exhaustion, drowns, and gets caught in the filter. That's the problem—the filters are expensive."

"You should have thought of that before you installed a Jacuzzi in their habitat."

"For chrissakes." Laura again. "It's our property."

"You all enjoy taking a dip," I say, to which Jackson clinks my glass.

"Not since," Ray says.

"Nor ever again," Olivia says. Everyone finds something else in the room to watch.

"It's lovely," Allie says, and so is Allie when she slips out of a fluffy bathrobe to reveal a charming, red one-piece that accentuates her symmetrical breasts, dips a toe in the fiery Jacuzzi as the steam rises over a drunken end to a community picnic. That was six months ago. No one but Jackson has joined me in the Jacuzzi since the nanny drowned. In fact, it's not even a Jacuzzi. It's a backyard lagoon with water jet propulsion, the entire infrastructure purchased on VillageShop for a small fortune.

Despite the verbal attack on my backyard oasis, and the suggestion I have been murdering the wildlife, I enjoy these rituals. They offer purpose to my life, a bedrock affirmation that I come from somewhere, belong to some people, that their concerns are my concerns. I am happy. I think I am happy. Happy is not really the point. Rather, I am not unhappy most of the time. I am content. I am glad to know we are raising good children in an evil world with the camaraderie of neighbors.

"Sort of probably maybe definitely not sure unlikely improbably no, we have plans on Saturday and there's a meditation seminar for the kids we want to attend..."

I catch a glimpse of my reflection in the window, slightly chubbier than I expect, rounder in places that need chiseling. I try to remember if the principles of appearing overweight on camera also apply to anonymous windows at charity wine tastings. I look like the other fathers, pleasant, well fed, with places to be. Except I have a tribe of savages that have taken refuge inside of me and are clawing their way into the future, creatures I believe were released by my trial medication and will not retreat back to their caverns even if I stop taking it, which I cannot. At first look, I am Tom Pistilini, Channel Fourteen weatherman. But a closer observation indicates they have moved in beneath my eyelids, around the tension in my mouth, in the manner I hold my hands into fists when discussing committees and sanitizer and school plays. I do not want them to leave. No one calls the savages Pisser, even when I have told them I prefer Pistol as a nickname version of Pistilini, or just Tom.

"Pisser?"

"Tom!" Laura shouts, shaking me back to the ballroom. I blacked out again. I never know how long I am gone, but when I reappear everyone watches my hand that shakes, scattering red wine on my sleeve and the floor.

Jackson rubs my neck. "You okay, Pisser?"

"Sorry about that." A waiter arrives to assist. "Daydreaming."

"You were talking and then you weren't talking. You were here and then you were gone." Laura awaits an explanation. Everyone else has drifted into their phones, though I cannot tell if it is legitimate communication or they are just being kind, allowing Laura and I a private moment to adjust our cohabitation oversights.

"Yes, well," I inform everyone. "Better recheck those harnesses. They were my idea," I remind them.

Tom Pistilini With The Weather

THE CHANNEL FOURTEEN NEWS team is neither a winner nor a loser in the twenty-four-hour dispatch bonanza. Rather we are a solid band of broadcast junkies who hate what we do and are too old and well paid to do anything else. There are three main news segments—nine in the morning, one and four in the afternoon—a schedule that ensures we do not have to compete with the larger, better-funded teams, which get up earlier and stay later and race around this metropolis in teched-out vans as if their contributions mean anything more than a whiff from the shit pile of inanity our industry spews onto an insatiable public. We have no news-copter. We rarely go live to the scene. We are the stay-behind team that gathers happenings over coffee.

We have managed a respectable following without ever inquiring into social media, until recently. Instead we owe our success to camaraderie: Charles Kreb and Alisson Lovato, our anchors; Melanie Trotter on traffic; and myself, Tom Pistilini, with the weather. We have been together for seventeen years. Viewers appreciate hearing about the world from the same faces, incrementally fatter and more tired and unable to secure jobs at stations for which our younger selves yearned. We are a safe bet for local advertisers wanting to sell cars or furniture or insurance, and who want to avoid major network costs.

I record the late night and early morning weather reports each afternoon, and we run the segments whenever there is something to say about the skies. I am in by nine, out before five. The past month or so, I have been suspiciously accurate in my prognostications. I am nowhere near as popular as other meteorologists. But when it comes to making conjectures about our atmosphere, as if we can predict anything so inconstant and wild, my instincts have honed.

We would go on this way, Charles and Ally and Trotter and Tom. But our tiny station was purchased by Lustfizzle Media, a pop culture company that runs a website backed by venture capital, wanting to add a television arm to its programming aimed at the millennial demographic. They have made few changes, but in the past month fresh faces roam the building, well dressed, smiling, watching. They have given their word they will not fire us—"Why would we break up the news team? It's the reason we bought the station"—but we can smell the end, the way old dogs know when to take one last jaunt into the woods.

This morning I am joined in the studio by my producer, the little shit Whitman, a twenty-something wunderkind in charge of Lustfizzle's innovative programming. Innovation includes blowing up a watermelon live on the Internet using only rubber bands, an event seen by nearly a million viewers. It includes dressing up interns in mascot garb and livestreaming them fishing in the East River, viewers wagering bets on who will catch the largest smelt; 1.7 million watched. I do not know if Whitman is the first or last name. Like Madonna or Prince or God, he just is.

"Over to Tom Pistilini with the weather," says Allison Lovato. "Morning, Tom."

"Good morning, Allison. And a chilly morning for New Yorkers. Sun's peeking out over the East River, and we're seeing temperatures slightly above average for this time of year. Expect some late-afternoon sunshine that'll have folks rushing for the doors early. Guys, get those golf clubs ready. As long as you don't mind a nippy round, this afternoon might be perfect for some warmup swings. Cold front moving in from Canada, but we're not expecting too much rain since..." And on and on, seventeen years of atmosphere and precipitation, of telling people what hovers just outside their windows. I am sick today, wheezing and sweating, my report a congested failure. "Melanie Trotter! Good morning to you, and how's the traffic?"

Whitman slaps my back, as if I have just completed broadcast history. He never pays attention to the Trotter Traffic Report, coming around me with a fist bump and passive aggressive flattery.

"Great job, Pisser." We bump fists again and he produces sanitizer that he squeezes into both of our hands. I sneeze. A napkin is procured. He smiles, a pink mouth, teeth so white they seem like cartoon kittens. "That was momentous. The way you set up the sun. That thing about Canada. Working in the golf. So, so real. Like I could feel myself out there getting ready to pound one down the fairway. Dig?"

I sniffle. "Sure, dig."

"You said, 'Guys, get those clubs ready.'" He mocks my voice and the impersonation is superb, everything from my nasal delivery to the unintentional neck jiggle. My pocket buzzes. I ignore it. "Kind of sexist, don't you think? Half the audience is female but you're only talking to the men, people like you. Dig?"

It is early April. The only assholes on the golf course are men like me. Specifically, I am thinking of only one golf course, the seven holes that occupy Slancy's western terrain just over the tree line in my backyard, where literally only assholes like me will pound balls down fairways until the weather warms. "Dig."

"And the rain. You never mentioned it until the middle of the segment. Work that in early." Again with the impersonation. "'We got a stormy weekend ahead so make sure that rain gear is rocking.'"

"It probably won't rain."

"You said rain. Higgins, he say rain?"

"Rain," calls Higgins, whoever Higgins is.

"All the other stations are forecasting a wet weekend."

"There might be a passing shower, but in order for a storm we would need a cold front pushing under a warm front, which then releases moisture."

Whitman watches me like I am a blathering idiot, a snot-spewing geriatric speaking a language unintelligible to his demographic distracted only by what is next. Up close, he can see what the makeup team covered, my splotchy skin, swollen eyes, the cut on my cheek, and bruised forehead. "You need catch phrases. Buzzwords. Teeth-chattering. Cold surge. Sweltering."

"It's just a mild weather day, Whit."

"Whitman. Earthquakes, sinkholes, hurricane season. That's the stuff that gets ratings. Give them what they want to hear. But be sensitive. Always remember, people are scared. I'm not trying to tell you your business, but work with me, Pisser."

"You want me to talk about earthquakes? As in," and now he's got me impersonating myself, "The region will see a passing shower on Sunday but likely no earthquakes. In fact, we're well below our earthquake quota for this time of year."

Whitman claps on one leg, howls into a fist, delighted. He interrupted the Trotter Traffic Report, which will have to be redone. "That's the shit." He wraps an arm around my fat neck and tugs me down the hall. "You know what you're missing, the one thing that would make the weather report thrive?"

"A death toll in the corner of the screen?" I know the answer because he told me already.

"Playfulness." That word again, the bane of my pain in the ass life. He does a thing with his hands and then taps each side of his forehead. "If we can somehow get more playfulness into the weather report." Hands over his head, spirit fingers. "Wow."

I have to say this. Otherwise I am closed-minded, set in my ways, not willing to evolve, a curmudgeon. "I've got some ideas," I lie.

"I need to hear those." Another fist bump, he buttons a jacket, checks his phone, a call. "I got to take this, but your office in one and a half. We need to rap."

I hate fist bumps. I hate sensitivity and delivering the news with a playful tone to make the rain and earthquakes seem less jarring. The good news is Whitman is too busy, too fast, his thoughts so entwined with digital domination that he has already forgotten our chat. I crumble into my office, hoping for a nap, only to discover Whitman already seated in my chair, staring at me with disturbing intensity.

I reach into my jacket and scatter a pill onto the table, wash it down with cold coffee. A few seconds pass and I feel no different, so I try another pill.

"Easy, Pisser. Those make you weird."

Along with the erections and laughter, the blackouts are the major side effect. But there is also dry mouth, sleepy eye, a loss of hearing, intense concentration, improved lip reading, better association with the struggles of the disenfranchised. I have to defecate constantly. My nose occasionally bleeds. Luderica is currently being tested but does not have FDA approval. It contains chemicals used in pesticides, synthetic opioid, and dideoxyclosanide—a crucial ingredient in dandruff shampoo and gunpowder. Because it cannot be prescribed, I have no choice but to purchase the pills through backchannels. An anti-psychotic, anti-depressive, anti-everything, if Whitman had any idea his weatherman relied on trial pills to stay vertical, I would already be out of a job.

"How are things at home?" he says.

"Same. Iliza hates me. Gus is flunking out."

"Laura?"

That's Missus Pistilini to you. I shake my head. I still have two more weather reports and cannot discuss my marriage with Whitman, that I have doomed us with my negativity and failure, driven her into an emotional friendship, whatever that means.

He smiles, loves this part of our mornings, the mythic imposter and his suburbia woes. "Let's talk chipmunk. You get rid of the rats yet?"

"Still working on it."

"I told you already. Get a cat. Cats are smart, territorial, ruthless. They don't take shit from items lower on the food chain."

"I tried that." Acting on Whitman's advice, I went to a pet store and inquired if they sold hunting cats. The woman phoned security, informing me that pet stores now have security. "All the pets have these cards on the cages describing their personalities. Friendly, snuggly, napper, frisky. I want a cat that likes to kill things that trespass."

"Thousands of cats nobody wants and you're the only guy who can't find one." Whitman slaps the table. "Twenty strays within a block of this place."

"Tried that, too." I show him the scratch. He's bent over again until we tire of each other's small talk. And then, "Listen, Pisser, about those pages you gave me."

Sitting in front of him on my desk, the folder open, is the new investment outline for Moveable Museums, my neighbors' tourism company. Did I leave it on my desk? Or did I give it to Whitman, as he suggests? Laura is the intelligent branch of our family tree and reviews the fine print of financial arrangements. But Whitman is dependable, in ways I cannot quite place, and I occasionally fish for his thoughts on mortgage questions. This document, however, is extremely private. I don't think I would have showed him.

He kicks up a leg, looks longingly into the wall to consider the question. "Why do you think you left them for me to read over?"

"This is confidential." Standing, I push the pages into the envelope, scattering some on the floor. "You have no right to go through my affairs."

"I think you did it on purpose." He reopens the folder to find a segment he earmarked. "Have you read through this yet?"

"A little bit." I was planning to read it all, which is why I brought it to work, although I am fairly certain I intended to keep it private. Whitman has me curious. "Something catch your eye?"

He seems a decade older than me as he considers the question. "You're strange, Pisser. But you're not strange evil." He taps the folder. "This is diabolic."

He turns to a page that covers the lifeblood of the new venture into novel tourism. The business plan outlines former locations of mass shootings, some of them schools. Familiar names: Newtown, Connecticut, and Columbine, Colorado. Historic locales: Bath Township, Michigan, and Austin, Texas. I know the broad strokes of the proposal. If I have left them here, open on my desk for Whitman's perusal, I am likely hoping he will validate my belief that we are no guiltier than employees with 401ks who invest in the gaming industry, or companies that build weapons or engage in environmentally unethical industries.

"A tourism business centered around visiting sites of mass shootings." Whitman says it aloud for our mutual consideration. "And more specifically, many of the sites are schools. This hits me as..." he pauses, wrangles that millennial mind for just the right phrase, and then unleashes, "primordial indecency." Nailed it.

"The Sedlocks are friends," I say, as if it matters.

"You realize how fucked this is. It could go badly for you."

"You can't say anything. Attorney-client privilege."

"I'm not your attorney."

"Well, friend-friend privilege then."

"I'm not your friend, Pisser." He is scolding me now. "But if I were your friend, I'd tell you to put some proper thought into whether or not this is worth it."

I am sniffling and tired, my skin chilly and preposterously warm all at once. Part of me expects this rebuke. He tosses the pages on the desk, slaps down a hand that seems all knuckle. "Another item for your Doppler."

He stands, stretches, insinuates a transition. I am approaching a cataclysm of something once righteous, but also time-consuming and ordinary, a career that has girded me into the being I am, lower member of the caste system to Whitman and his kind. A different, better version of me would have torn up the Sedlocks' proposal instantly, would have ordered Whitman out of my seat.

"Lovato," he says. "Her contract isn't being renewed."

"Allison?" It disappoints me to hear her name instead of my own. Allison Lovato, as honorable a news desk sidekick as there ever was. Trotter is the perfect name for a traffic reporter, so I knew Melanie would not be first. I just assumed it would be Charles or me, the two white guys. "You're firing her?"

"Technically, no. Just not renewing her contract."

"Seventeen years." I do not have to ask the reason. Lustfizzle wants to bring an element of hip-hop into the newscast, which means asking

Allison Lovato, a fifty-four-year-old mother of three, to occasionally rap the news. I would rather hear she was being canned than listen to even a minute of her attempt at relevance. "That's how this works—I refuse to rhyme about tornadoes and flashfloods and I'm out?"

"I'd have fought for Allison. She chose the severance. I have to respect it." The severance package is not an option for me. I have too many expenses, and two too many kids in need of private school and college. "So long as I got a breath in my body, Pisser, you'll have a job. That's a promise." He takes a seat and leans into the desk to focus on my eyes, the frown, and holds up the folder. "But ask yourself something—why did you really leave this folder here for me? What do you need from me, Pisser?"

Kidnapping An Emotional Support Animal

THE WEATHER IS BRISK, temperate, just like the sweaty man on Channel Fourteen promised. A cold sun takes one last breath, tiptoes over New Jersey, and casts chilly shadows across the metropolis. Whitman sent me home. I should have gone straight to bed but I am avoiding my house, instead arriving at the golf course for a quick round. It is an abomination, swinging recklessly into sand and water and the small patch of woods that separates the course from our residential neighborhood. I am sick with the flu, my body aching with each wobble of a club. My four-iron is bent at an impossible angle, the arc a noted reminder that I do not belong among these hobbyists, where institutions such as patience and grace equate to athletic prowess.

I wait for Russ Haverly in the clubhouse. There is a matter we must discuss, although the Luderica and the illness make me forgetful and I have lost track of the content, assuming it must be my morning dispute with Toby Dalton. Russ keeps a boat in Manhattan and docks in the Slancy Harbor, which is a quick walk to the clubhouse. Some nights after lacrosse practice, we meet for golf and a drink, which is a cultured method of exchanging money for drugs. He missed our round so I sit alone at the bar, cold and raw, lonelier because I do not have a phone to check the Gopa website. Parents can post anonymously if they choose, from as many usernames as they care to enlist, which allows us to bicker and casually insult one another. My handle is ndr_cnstrctn, which is only new this week since my last username (Gopadad4) was banned for suggesting the cafeteria be segregated. I was misunderstood. What I actually wrote was the Spanish immersion students (Iliza among them) be separated from the Mandarin and French immersion students so they can practice their language skills while they eat.

Without a phone I cannot involve myself in parental disputes. I still have the device that does not belong to me, and which is no use because it is an older model. Each time my pocket buzzes I check the caller but do not recognize the numbers. After several beers it appears Russ will be a no-show. I take a walk across the fairways for home.

When I come to I am somewhere in Brooklyn. I locate my coordinates from the missing Manhattan skyline and the relative size of the buildings. It is the southern end of Greenwood Cemetery, no one wandering the streets, which suggests I am moments away from being murdered, or mistaken for a murderer. A cage at my feet is less surprising than the articles I hold: a net in one hand, the BB gun in the other. I assimilate to the situation. This is not my first trip to the cemetery. I have my heart set on a particular tabby, a large, splotchy brown feline that makes its home in the headstones, that will not appreciate chipmunks sharing its resources. This is how I got the scratch on my face, a longer one on my neck and down my back. The net will do nothing against a feral cat this fat and angry. The gun is not meant to injure the animal, but rather to protect me if things go wrong.

I have brought along catnip, bags of it, and I shake some into the grass, placing a larger pile in the cage. Moments pass before the first cat appears, and then another, but they can see from my demeanor no catnip high is worth a confrontation. My therapy animal appears, climbing from the cemetery and stepping closer than the others, eyeing me cautiously to see how much fight I am worth. It knows what it has done, chased me from its world the past two weeks, and now it must decide whether to attack or accept my offering. Tonight it seems exhausted, chubbier somehow. It wants no fight, arching its back and creeping hastily toward my feet and into the cage. The animal is larger than I remember, its paws the size of blueberry muffins. I close the cage, trapping my beast as it claws at the bag.

I lean down and watch him watch me, either indifferent to whether I have trapped him or he has agreed to the journey, both of us accepting that the universe has melded us.

"Your name," I tell my new pet, "is Clint Eastwood. I have work for you."

How To Build Suburbs

IN THE LATE EIGHTIES, Theodore Slancy had a vision to create an island off the coast of Manhattan and charge real estate moguls billions to develop the property. Known as Teddy Tantrums, he also had a drinking problem and a reputation of being stubborn, believing he could defeat erosion and looking upon everyone who pointed out flaws in his plans as naysayers. An entrepreneur and somewhat shady businessman, years earlier Slancy had pioneered the Finger Lakes Dredging Company. In its heyday, it handled most of the dredging from Maine to the Carolinas. Anytime a beach eroded or a Herculean storm made landfall, Teddy Tantrums was the man to call.

When he could not find developers to invest in his vision, he began using his personal fortune to fund the island. Finding enough dredged sediment to build the property was the easy part. It was the politics, lawyers, payoffs, permits, city and state and maritime ordinances that had to be filed, the environmental groups protesting every grain of sand he ripped from the harbor or shipped in on a barge. Building the island was killing Slancy, both financially and mentally, right up until it finally killed him, a sinkhole near what is now the fourth fairway of the Slancy Golf Course. One story claims he was sucked into the crevice and workers were unable to reach him. Another that he owed so much money to crooked politicians and the longshoremen, that someone decided to make the island six inches thicker with his body. His remains were never recovered. Golf balls take strange flops on the fourth.

His successors at the dredging company wanted little to do with a pile of sand that held the stigma of Theodore Slancy's stubbornness. With no one to claim the project, it was left to the city to solve ninety-five acres of what became known in the newspapers as Slancy's Shambles. Structural engineers determined if something were not done, it would drift into the harbor, blocking the shipping channels. Urban engineers tested the soil, deciding it was too soft to support skyscrapers or casinos, which scared off the larger developers. Years passed while politicians bickered over how to wrestle nickels out of it. What is now Slancy was the brainchild of Duffy O'Neal, a then banker who wanted a place to play golf without wandering too far from his native Manhattan. He put together the plans, along with the lawyers and investors: a gated community of thirty single-family homes would occupy the eastern half of the island, with a seven-hole golf course carving out the western side, a slice of Americana for people like Duffy and his friends who could afford $3 million properties in the priciest real estate market in the country. When newspapers got wind of the Eden being erected to the south, editorials were heavy with accusations of elitism and privilege that nearly killed the project. That was when Duffy got the idea to make half the properties available by lottery to lucky Americans who wished to give island living a shot—under the guise the lottery entrants could afford the mortgages—which allowed people like us, and several of our neighbors, to become homeowners.

Duffy left out of his plans everything he hated about New York City living. There are no apartment buildings or public transportation other than a ferry that leaves every hour for Manhattan and the shuttle bus on weekdays. There are no vehicles, except for the utility crews, a security car, twice-a-week sanitation, the constant delivery trucks because we have no stores, ordering everything online and shipping it to our front doors. Homeowners with cars park them in a lot near the East Bridge that connects the island to Brooklyn, and from there we can be in Manhattan in minutes. We have our own harbor where neighbors dock boats. When prompted as to my lack of maritime aspirations, I claim a dislike of water instead of admitting we exist in a habitual state of near bankruptcy.

Most of the homes are separated from the western side by a few hundred sugar maples and junipers, patches of trees that conceal a hiking path that we proudly and adorably refer to as "the woods." Intermingled in the timber are cell phone towers disguised as trees, which look exactly like cell phone towers disguised as trees, a feature that I loathe. There are cameras everywhere, which helps our one-man security detail patrol the island. We have little crime, other than the occasional trespasser wanting a look at our world, and the several cameras that have been destroyed, most likely caused by the wind. On the far side of the woods is the local economy, a 7-hole golf course occupying a tight 45 acres that is free to residents and which busy Manhattanites pay $200 per round, reachable only by ferry. The ride out and cost does not deter them, the course packed each morning beginning at six and every afternoon until the island blends ominously into the dark secretions of the Hudson River.

There are weddings every weekend, sometimes three squeezed into a holiday period, which pays for the golf course and clubhouse and assists with the constant upkeep of the shore. We have a tougher immigration policy than most nations. If you are not coming to Slancy to golf or celebrate nuptials then you are not welcome. When there is a house for sale, which happens rarely, the homeowners association has full jurisdiction over who is eligible to purchase the property. It is not limited to solely white bankers, like Duffy and his friends. The association has accepted buyers of all racial and sexual orientation, so long as they agree to upkeep the property, and pay the annual greens fees, and adore exclusivity.

We bike and barbecue and smack golf balls. Those of us who employ them speak highly of our nannies. We take twilight cruises when boating neighbors invite us and sip prosecco and gaze upon New Jersey and Brooklyn and the byzantine skyline. We wink at each other, knowing pretentious Manhattanites still refer to our utopia as Slancy's Shambles. We built suburbs out of sand, in the periphery of their urban hipness, and for that they despise our existence. We relish how much the view of their overcrowded metropolis inflates our property value, though none of us would ever consider selling. I sit in my backyard paradise listening to the sound of children, the distant hum of plentiful worlds, listening as Allie Sedlock peddles past, her blonde hair waltzing in the musty breeze, her long legs working the peddles, a smile and a wave, and I contemplate—if I cannot obtain a playfulness for life in this environment, and I seem to be unable to do so, then it may never exist for me.

Neighbors Just Other Friendly Tribes

LIKE ANY SET OF residential blocks in Kansas or Idaho or Pennsylvania, we are a community of parents invested in each other's dramas. I know my neighbors' concerns. I care about their security systems and the direction their cameras point, capturing the shadows that mine neglect. It pleases me to hear their lawns are not infested with bugs, or that the rodent problem that haunts me is a passing concern to them because they chose not to invest thousands of dollars transforming their backyards into lagoons. I am engrained in their children, as I am my own. Love is not the proper sentiment. Devotion isn't the best affiliation. I do not want their children to die or suffer cataclysmic diseases, or scrape their knees or fall out of trees, or fear the distant lights that glow over our tranquil dusks. But I also do not wish for them more success than my own children deserve. I refer specifically to Gopa's ECI program, an opportunity I fear because it will mean my daughter traveling abroad for much of the year and not fighting with me each morning and evening over cell phone use, skirt length, curfew. Instead ECI will expose her to architecture, museums, history, cuisines, opportunities that most high school children can never access, stops in fifty countries, and it lurks over our lives with offers of fortune and intellect and elitism. I want it for Iliza because there are only eighteen spots. What I mean to say is—I want it for all the eligible children in the world, and since they all cannot have it, for all the kids in my neighborhood, so long as my daughter is highest on that list.

I want it for Todd McClutchen whose parents, Ray and Olivia, were once our dearest friends and who have descended into that band of people I must exist beside until our children no longer occupy the same zip code. Olivia is a stay at home mother, an animal lover, and the coldest human being I can name. Ray is a bastard. Everyone calls him Clutch, a far better nickname than Pisser, even though he never participated in sports outside of Ultimate Frisbee. An author of inspirational books for working parents, he is most likely sleeping with my wife. Their youngest, Madison, age two, is allergic to everything from nuts to cotton fabric to actual hand sanitizer, a constant challenge at potluck dinners as to what will bother her first. Todd is in Iliza's junior class, a member of the Gopa lacrosse team, a somber boy who does his best to live up to the fairytale image his father forecasts for the future in his books, which sell well enough to keep the McClutchens optimistic.

I want it for the twins, Damian and Rhythm. Jackson and Jason Ferris, known to all of us as the Jays, are our main claim to diversity in Slancy, the homeowners association checking off two multicultural boxes with their mortgage. Jason is a slim poetry teacher at Gopa who wants six children, although adoption rates for interracial gay couples suggest this is unlikely. Jackson makes up the larger component of their surreal alliance, a bulky, Southern man, my friend, and a musician who writes for Broadway shows, the breadwinner of his tribe. They went into the adoption process with open minds and, according to Jason, were placed on a bigoted list for parents who fell into the category

Other. In the meantime, they were rewarded with having teenage delinquency in their family, a relative of a relative on Jason's side with a pregnant sixteen-year-old and no idea who the father was, and who for a price was willing to be called a surrogate.

After costly negotiations with attorneys and the parents of the girl and a crooked social worker, they became proud guardians of Rhythm. It was not until the girl turned four that the adoption agency contacted them with news of a Rwandan boy, also age four. We all politely refer to them as the twins, though their differences do not stop at skin pigmentation. Damian is an honors student, a tutor for fellow Gopa classmates in need of assistance, and a shoe-in for ECI. Rhythm is slightly chubby with a gothic vibe, an average student and an exhibitionist. Jason believes she will be excluded from ECI due to her white skin color, and while there exists no polite way to tell this to a neighbor, it is her white trash DNA that differentiates her from Gopa's elite students. Still I adore Rhythm for her giant heart, that like me she does not belong on this sterilized island, and I find myself wanting ECI for her the most, relatively speaking.

I want it for Tungsten, Iliza's savvy best friend. Harry and Allie Sedlock are the understood leaders of our Slancy crew and we unanimously respect them as parents and business associates. Along with the Jays and McClutchens and Russ Haverly, we are seed investors in their remarkably successful tourism company, Moveable Museums. Harry is an excellent golfer and a connoisseur of fine wines. His wife is one of the leaders of the Gopa moms and a genuine piece of ass. Together with a majority of Gopa parents, we voted both Sedlocks onto the PTA Committee, on which they have represented our interests for years. Tungsten is Iliza's understudy in the school play and a constant fixture in my home. Their son, Rhenium, is a freshman on the lacrosse team. At age fourteen it is clear Rhen will move through life like his father, a mechanical triumph, with a refined confidence that will make it easy to grant him conveniences for which others will be expected to achieve through careers they do not care for, performing tasks that will whittle down their happiness to a brittle sprig.

I never cared about children before fatherhood. Now they consume me—constant paranoia that my scions are doomed, thoroughness to my worry that I am doing something incorrect that will render Iliza and Gus anxious adults and incompetent lovers and irritating citizens who fluctuate between default complaint and victimhood. What are they thinking? Do they hate me? Why do I fail at loving them completely? Are they scared, and what do they fear? Whenever I click across stories of sick kids in hospitals, or dying of malnutrition, or suffering through genocide in remote parts of the world, I spend hours scanning the photographs, making myself look: reverse pornography. I pray to an irrelevant source, thankful that mine are enrolled in private school and only a phone call away on smartphones I reluctantly purchased them.

I pushed them into soccer and piano at early ages, and when that did not take, swimming lessons and karate, T-ball and ballet, violin and basketball and more soccer and gymnastics, and then wrestling for Gus and kickboxing for Iliza. Music classes before they could crawl. Classes to paint their feelings, test their intelligence, kickball, tennis, volleyball, anything with a net; cooking classes, gardening, crocheting, how to build wind turbines, origami, summer camps, pottery. I drink copious amounts of wine at charity events where I eavesdrop on other parenting styles and adjust accordingly. If I read about a study that stresses exercise over listening skills, or overhear a parent talking about a life skills one-day workshop in Greenpoint, the Pistilinis are there.

We are a household that awakens early on Saturdays and has breakfast on the run as we race from activity to activity, molding their minds, building them into better human beings, returning home exhausted from our own evolution, too tired to enjoy one another's company. I look forward to the workweek in the way voyagers squint toward a sliver of horizon, anything to climb out of the shitshow of parenthood into an existence that does not require chores.

Despite the years of investment and molding, one child is captivated with boys and escaping home, and the other is experiencing an identity crisis that one university offered to pay us to study. Iliza is well rounded in mathematics and theater and hoping to attend Brown or Dartmouth in two years, assuming I can afford either. She has worked hard to earn a starring role as Emily Webb in the spring production of *Our Town*. A penchant for the spotlight and the fame that comes with it, boys have begun to notice both her and Tungsten. I have preached about the dangers of sex, of social media, how once either has infiltrated their lives it can have drastic effects. My daughter's eyes exist in a ceaseless, rolling motion in my presence.

Gus is failing mathematics and leadership, an outcast on the wrestling and chess squads. We are told he shows no interest in free play and did not take to a therapy hamster the school suggested. In the past year, he has enrolled in a writing program he seems to enjoy, although he is behind in his complex sentence structure skills. Only thirteen, twice a month we are called in for conferences with the principals and school psychologists and Heather Pace. It has been suggested that perhaps Gopa is not the best environment for a child with his needs. Parents have asked that their sons not be paired with him during wrestling practice. Moms have posted anonymous petitions on the Gopa website calling for his dismissal from the chess club. It all began with the nanny.

The Sedlocks have a nanny. The McClutchens have two nannies, one for Maddie, the other for Todd, though both essentially assist Olivia with her lifestyle upkeep. The Jays have a nanny they fire every few months for some minor infraction. Our nanny perished in a terrible backyard accident. Gus dresses like an elderly woman, Millicent, wandering the school complaining about cold drafts, snuggling beneath an afghan he wears over his shoulders, asking about the bunnies, inquiring of the front door security. He awakens in the middle of the night to do laundry, de-grout the bathtub, and order the glasses into perfect stillness. He has the shakes and the gait down, but every once in a while I see his back straighten, his eyesight pivot to wonders that infatuate teenage boys, and I know my son is in there. Transgeneration. That's what our therapist, Devin Brenner, calls it, which is different than transgender or non-binary gender. Transgeneration is a term for people whose self-identity does not conform to the generation in which they live. It used to be "old soul," a term of endearment.

"He never asked about wheelchair ramps," Laura hollered several months ago in a meeting. "Don't invent crap that isn't happening. Let's concentrate on facts."

Laura is the one who speaks up during conferences. She purses her lips, often for entire meetings, and then issues a scathing critique that punishes prides with neutering punctuation. I sit beside her and nod complacently, reach over and fraudulently place a supportive hand on hers, occasionally loft magnanimous and spineless verses that mean nothing: "It is what it is" and "We want what's best for the school even if it doesn't include Gus." All lies. Whereas Laura's demands are terse, full of conviction: Gus is fine, it's a phase, we will figure it out, and until that time, we spend a fucking fortune for you people to teach him to read and add. Out on the sidewalk, we fight over our plan going in and what ends up spewing out of my mouth, my wife admonishing me for passing security guards and nannies to enjoy.

Now even the fights are fleeting. What I once adored about my wife, the fire and candidness, have coursed into subtle apology. The wit that turned intelligent people to shambles has been corrupted by pop-psychology melody, a feel-good falsehood to her methodology. The language crept slowly into the meetings with school officials, an amber rust that sullies a copper ladle, buzzwords like manifestation, emotional scale, vibrational energy, positive reinforcement, with school administrators nodding, understanding, loving her for coming to the middle. Where once my wife scoffed at inefficient pandering, at some point she began talking like them, the Ray McClutchens of the world, sending out positive energy for Gus, visualizing success, demanding her husband find his playful nature. All of which is my fault. I am the one that could not handle the stress of twenty-first century parenting and had to go away to remedy myself, returning to less of us. Where is the fire? Where is the rage? Where is my wife?

Laura is a brilliant mind, a visionary mother and entrepreneur who has assembled a respectable standing pancake business that may turn its first profit this year. I never cheated on Laura, but I failed her in thousands of insignificant ways that no one tells you are crucial to marriage. Showing up. Taking risks. Making decisions. Kissing goodnight. Listening to mundane complaints about household chores and motherhood. I put all my worries into raising adults and neglected to raise a family. Go too long as roommates occupying the same terrain, paying off the mortgage, and one day you wake up to realize you need therapy. You go find yourself, and you can never come home.

I have a memory of our first year together, a tiny one-bedroom in the West Village with a window that faced the back of several buildings, a kitchen so cozy we had to rub against one another as we experimented with her pancake idea. Awoken at four in the morning, a car alarm, a stifling heat, we knew we would not sleep. I led her naked onto the fire escape. The metal was cold beneath the sheet, a slight wind leftover from nighttime shade, nothing moving but the sound of blind creatures foraging for existence in the rubbish below. We made love under the slumbering dwellers—no, that is not the memory that cradles my nostalgia. We fucked there, giggling at our deed, not needing the proper mattress or higher thread count, only the chaos and mess of youth. I think how I got from there to here, a ruined marriage, a dying career, a contemptible investment, and I know I am missing something vital that Laura and the children can sense each time I force my presence upon them.

Backyard Lagoon Killing Fields

FOR ITS SIZE AND pull-power, the Manman twelve-gallon Shop-Vac is the best in market, by far the most efficient Father's Day present I have ever received. It is an item I would recommend to every homeowner. It has a powerful motor and comes with several extensions. I use it this evening to vacuum up dead chipmunk bodies, parts really, that upon returning from the office I found scattered across the lawn and back deck. It is unclear how many designer rodents perished in Clint Eastwood's inaugural rampage because he tore apart a few to reach the meaty center. Anywhere between seven and twelve, a purge that would take me weeks to achieve as I lack the ferocity and agility I knew Clint Eastwood maintained the first time I laid eyes on this therapeutic creature. Doing a fast estimate of how much it costs to repair the lagoon versus the cost of the cat trapping equipment, it appears my investment has paid off. The body parts disappear into the Shop-Vac with a thumping gulp, the horsepower surging up my arm causing me to laugh miserably into a weep. The pills dig out a playful vibe and I am helpless to silence my painful laughter. My pocket buzzes. I ignore it, choosing to sneeze instead, the persistent cold or the pills causing my dizzy state.

  I have successfully predicted the weather for thirty-three days, though outside Josey Mateo, the Gopa secretary, no one is counting, the Luderica a key component of my science. Gloomy clouds silhouette a desperate skyline with light winds off the coast, a chillier end to a day that saw two separate suicide bombings, one in a German train station, the other in a Shiite shrine in Baghdad, the deaths highlighting an otherwise dull day in global murder. My major accomplishment of the week is that I purchased a new phone to replace my broken one. It is a sleek model for which I rewarded myself with a minor shopping spree. I am not a shopping addict. I am a mobile shopping addict. While I enjoy new possessions, and the fresh dust that a ripped box emits, it is only comforting, strangely, if the merchandise is purchased via phone.

  Trending on Lustfizzle is a quiz guaranteed to give male readers erections and make female readers hungry. From my new phone, I argued with several moms for three hours on the Gopa website over my idea to turn the library into a telekinesis center. My argument, that moving objects with the mind was invaluable whereas reading books is outdated, was meant to be ironic in response to Pinkgopamom's suggestion that we need a culinary program to rival the Benedict Academy's. I buckled down on the side of telekinesis when the moms grew irate, and then as they slowly realized I was talking about concepts similar to the dreaded law of karma, many became convinced at my argument. That was when I swapped allegiance in support of a world-renowned reading program instead of feel good nonsense, and they grew confused and preachy. Once the moms stopped arguing, I doubled back on my support of the mind-reading laboratory and inquired if anyone had seriously considered suicide in the past school year.

Friday night, the end of the workweek, when neighbors gather for dinner and wine. It is our night to host. We are planning the first barbecue of the season, chicken drumsticks and a pork tenderloin Laura marinated overnight while I stared into the refrigerator at the gray, dead meat after everyone went to bed. My insomnia has worsened with my latest battle with the flu. Laura is inside handling preparations. I was dispatched to the backyard to clean and prepare the grill and make sure there are no chipmunks floating in the Jacuzzi, or lying slain, having heroically attempted to storm the side patio. It puts Olivia in a nasty mood, complaining about the chipmunks' nut allergies and accusing me of purposefully scattering a thirty-two-ounce container of mixed nuts onto the lawn, of which I am guilty.

My backyard is the envy of all island homeowners and a feat that deserves to be photographed for décor magazines. I hired a three-dimensional design firm to lay out the blueprints and did all the work myself over two years. The landscaping begins at the tree line and cascades toward our back deck, bushes so full and ordered they look professionally manicured. When the weather warms, I will fill the banks with tomato plants and marigolds and petunias, and neighbors taking a soak will feel they are bathing inside a controlled jungle, the base of which is a fire pit that we gather around when the temperatures cool. The faucet is hidden in a crevice of ferns, spouting a waterfall that meanders through the yard, eventually plummeting over a lighting source I can change to set the mood. Red, silver, yellow, blue, or just put the lights on shuffle and watch them pirouette across the lawn and woods.

The centerpiece is a twelve-person, concrete floor Jacuzzi with a gentle slope toward the middle that stands four feet deep. I keep it heated year-round, the invigoration of emerging into the winter as the steam rises over the yard, snow dusting the earth, and disappearing into the warm acceptance. Even neighbors like Olivia McClutchen, who claim I have built a death trap for woodland creatures, are forced to admit that my backyard exists as an example to other property owners. I have mounted a screen and rigged up a digital projector to shine movies or concert videos overhead, which gives the yard a cinematic vibe. Tonight, I show a music concert, *Jason Isbell: Live at Austin City Limits*, a gift from Jackson who knows good music, the lyrics poetic as I hose blood from the patio. The backdoor opens. I suppress a chuckle. The bushes above rustle. I catch sight of Clint Eastwood escaping into the woods and I cannot help but feel an affable intimacy with the universe.

Iliza has been sent to check on me, a task she was begrudged to fulfill even as I notice something in her posture, an eagerness to seek out her father. She is barefoot in April, staring at her phone.

"Mom said you need to get ready. The Sedlocks are here."

"Thanks, honey. I'll be right in."

"What's so funny?"

"Nothing."

"When I came out you were laughing."

"Thinking about work. Just getting the grill ready."

"With the hose?"

Iliza loved the Jacuzzi until we found Tilly floating in it, two gallons of industrial red dye sitting on the deck, only one of which was emptied. She has heard the macabre rumors of her father's involvement, which she dismisses as nonsense, though she knows about my chipmunk purge. While she ignores the tactics I must take to keep our yard rodent-free, she is quietly supportive of me in this endeavor, the creatures born in a laboratory that do not know to fear the food chain, who cannot offer primal affection to other creatures because their instincts are chemically augmented. They will wander within inches of a human foot and sniff the fabric to see if there is anything worth foraging, a point Iliza and I agree earns suspicion.

Our collusion on the bloody remains makes headway in the silence that has existed between us. I should let it drop, enjoy the one, small victory of her smile. But I cannot do that, of course. I am a father and an egomaniac when it comes to her fondness, and I must know she loves me a percentage of how much I love her.

"How was school today?"

She taps the phone. "Fine."

"Ready for the big play?"

"I guess." I know preparations are going well because I've been spying on Iliza. Josey Mateo updates me regularly.

"You're going to be great, Iliza. I know it."

"You have to say that." She shuffles her toes on the cold wood. "Thanks."

It is something, a nicety in times of struggle, and I should be content. But I am furious at my daughter, for reasons that are not entirely clear, the patterns of my discontent cloaked inside the sleeplessness and Luderica. The anger comes in fits. One moment she is my innocent Iliza, the next guilty of some transgression I cannot discover. And if she is guilty, I am guiltier.

"Something else. I spoke to Toby," I say, shifting the mood. Jason Isbell is singing about an encounter with a girl, and I do not know if he struck her or if she fell of her own indecency, but there is a strong hint that they are pushing on in spite of their past and I love the grit of this musical relationship, and I think of something Whitman said today about primordial indecency and how beautiful he can sound, and I wonder if the Sedlocks are my friends or my destruction and if Russ will be at the dinner party because I am low on pills. The hose has caught something hard in its stream. A tiny paw, an esophagus maybe. Iliza types into her phone. "Did you hear me?"

"I know, Dad. Everyone knows."

It's concerning to hear. "Who's everyone?"

"The nannies." She glances from the phone to catch my stare. "What did he say?"

"Never mind." Never mind because I do not remember. Never mind because I was not sure I actually spoke to him until you just confirmed it. The nannies do not always get the story right, but they get the story.

"If it's something about me, I deserve to know. Unlike most of the shit that goes on in this fucked up family."

"Watch your mouth," I say.

Iliza has no interest in chatting with her old man. This is a reconnaissance mission. There is movement from the side yard, which at first I mistake for Clint Eastwood until I see Jackson leading Rhythm and Damian. Jason carries a dish.

I grab Iliza's arm before she can escape. "It's between Toby and me," I whisper. "But I can promise you—" Promise what? Happiness? Innocence? Life in prison if anyone so much as harms a particle of your anatomical wonder? "So help me, Iliza, if I find out..."

I do not finish. She wrenches her arm loose as the Jays hug hello, the usual niceties as they follow Iliza inside. I think I am alone until I notice Tungsten, who has materialized like a blanched specter out of the mist from my hose. She is leading her tiny therapy dog, Muggly, to take a shit on my newly washed lawn. A bandage on her wrist I think to ask about. "Hey, Mister P. How's it hanging?"

I want to believe she refers to existence itself, or the hose, and not my cock. A clever girl, Tungsten is aware that Laura and I are trying to conceive without the actual act of copulation. Science these days. I masturbate several times a week and deliver the sample to a sperm bank, which will eventually be used to inseminate my wife's egg. The painful erections arrive at the wrong time, caused by the pills, none of which is any of Tungsten Sedlock's business.

"Fine, Tungsten. How is school?" She lets Muggly scratch at my grass and nose away at the pavement, likely smelling blood. The rat glances up at me and barks. With the wide mouth extension I could Shop-Vac Muggly in seconds, a conquering *whoomph* when his body left this plane and disappeared into the twelve-gallon mausoleum. The thought warms me until I'm chuckling again.

"What's so funny?"

"Just thinking about work."

"Weather. That's funny." She checks her phone to see if she missed anything in the last seventeen seconds. Tungsten is not nearly as beautiful as her mother, though she pretends to be with makeup and expensive clothes. She dresses too provocatively, which I have complained about to Laura. "Just warning you. Allie found another dead chipmunk on the front stoop." She refers to her parents by their first names, suggesting my kids refer to me as "Pisser" behind my back. "Thinks you put it there intentionally."

"Why would I do that?"

"I don't know. A warning maybe."

"Warn your mother about what?"

"I was talking about me, Mister P." Tungsten picks up the dog and moves toward the door. "Maybe you left it there to warn me."

I take out my pills and shake another Luderica into my mouth. My pocket buzzes, the old phone that is not mine, and on which, oddly, I feel someone is trying to reach me.

Giveth Us Our Daily Bread

WINTER'S TREACHERY GIVING WAY to the embers of spring is not complete until scorched animal flesh cascades across neighborhood yards. There are no buds but the trees have straightened after a long hibernation, ready to fill the world with life and pollen and dust mites and other treatable maladies that will drive Maddie McClutchen into an early grave. Existing in a perpetual state of phlegm and rash, the child's main food group consists of my wife's pancakes, a recipe that is non-allergenic, gluten-free, nut-free, dairy-free, non-GMO, corn-free and egg-free, skinny morsels of ethical perfection that, unlike regular pancakes, stand upright and ensconced with decadent uniforms that can be applied to any social function. I am not sure what holds the pancakes vertical, or how she first thought to cleverly decorate them as little pancake people. At first decapitation they taste like putty, but the more torso one eats the more one craves. Despite the financial shambles we find ourselves converging toward, Standcake—Laura's disruptive innovation to the breakfast and dessert industry—is destined for success.

She provides pancakes free for all the lacrosse game tailgates, a marketing ploy that has paid off with exorbitant orders. Parents love them. Even the players snack on them at halftime. She is expanding to other sports that host tailgates in the autumn, soccer and football, and partnering with Gopa to purchase the delicacies for events.

The children gather around the table chatting and ignoring the age difference as a bathrobed Gus cleans up after them. Most stare down at cell phones. There is quiet talk of Gopa and a stray cat in the neighborhood, and Jason does that gay thing where he grasps his chest, appalled, and we all react with indignation. Russ Haverly did not show for dinner. While it is possible I knew this, it comes as unfamiliar information that Russ has missed lacrosse practice all week and no one has been able to locate him. I am concerned about his whereabouts but also my refill, which I have been awaiting since last week. I mostly listen at these dinners, lobbing questions or insults that are drowned out by the cacophony of mutual conversations. I am ill. I take a fast nap with my eyes open.

"The big concern," Olivia says, "is tomorrow's game in Montclair. Will Russ show?"

"People disappear. They have other lives going on that we don't know about. One day they are dining with us," I say, half asleep, no one listening. "The next they've been ripped open by a chainsaw, their insides splattered along a remote corridor of I-eighty-seven, dozens of counties and hundreds of man hours just to find the parts."

"Could just be a personal issue back home," Harry Sedlock mentions.

"...the madman driving past the crime scene. So many cars..."

"Though it's not like Russ to not answer his phone."

"...a throat near Glen Falls, part of an ankle in Chestertown." I pour more wine. "Anyone know how far it is to Montreal?"

No one has brought up the chipmunks and the wine flows, Allie Sedlock accepts a second glass. This is substantial because keeping up with the Sedlocks drives our semen storage initiative. If Allie is not pregnant, it implies there will be less pressure to masturbate into a jar, which should open up my weekend. Even Laura notices the second glass and compliments me on the perfectly cooked tenderloin that I stared at vigorously last night, imagining how it got from there to my plate. What did it yearn for? Did it trust the farmers that kept it fed? Did it enjoy life? I chuckle as the meal finishes and we fall into the nightcap and small talk about Gopa, which is typically a rerun for those of us who spend our free time on phones browsing the school message boards for much of the day.

The Sedlocks coax Jason into petting Muggly, although he is squeamish about just sitting near the dog. Laura talks with the McClutchens and I tap my jacket pocket to know it is there, the BB gun. I should be the bigger person and wander over to my wife's side, but pride prevents me and I disappear into the backyard where Jason Isbell sings about cancer and sex. Jackson, too, has snuck out of the small talk. He has the fire pit roaring. No one has brought swim gear, which means I will not be able to take a dip until they leave. A chilly night, we pull chairs close and sip scotch, and Jackson leans to check that we are alone.

"Anything you want to get off your chest?"

"I don't think so. Is there?"

"It's just us." I am fond of Jackson. At age forty-five I am proud to be young enough to appreciate the multicultural pandemic of our society. I do not consider myself a bigot, but he is my first and only gay friend. That he is also a black man makes me feel progressive because I do enjoy people of all racial and sexual natures, even if I look predominantly white and closed up during newscasts. I am not friendly with his husband, Jason, who does not care for me. "Tell me everything."

"Not much to say. It happened rather fast," I guess.

"But it's true?"

"Depends what the nannies got wrong. Some of it probably."

He slaps my knee. "Self-entitled little fuck. Good for you, Pisser. Not that I condone strangulation. Russ will have something to say about it, sure. And you're lucky you didn't get arrested. But hot damn."

Damian is one of Gopa's top students and earns a small stipend tutoring the lacrosse team. He has relayed stories of cruel upperclassmen, and Jackson and Jason have complained to the administration, which is reluctant to get involved. The athletes have parents every bit as protective of their princes as we are of our brood, and it has been agreed to keep a teacher in the room at all times. But it is the things people cannot see that ruin our faith. And no one knows it better than a gay, black man.

We are joined around the fire by Harry and Ray and Jason. Harry and Ray have sons on the lacrosse team and are aware of the strangling rumors. I am an accomplished weatherman, a member of their investment club, and have a reputation of being an out-of-shape weenie. They know the nannies tend to exaggerate. The wives congregate inside around the breakfast bar. Some of the children have departed for home or to their phones. I pop a pill and am blithe and ornery and content and drunk, and I smile at what it would be like to carve open Ray McClutchen's stomach with a serrated knife and barbecue him over a spit. Someone tells a joke and I laugh in contemplative wonder if optimists burn as awkwardly as the rest of us.

I am aware of the passage of time. Everyone is gone and the lights inside have dimmed. Jackson hugs me goodbye, tells me to see a doctor. I am alone with the fire pit, the Jacuzzi gurgling. Not alone, exactly. I have my phones and Clint Eastwood, who occupies one of the chaise lounges, staring into the embers catatonic, a chilly night. I pull up the Gopa website and, using my third handle in as many weeks, Feralocity, I post a picture of third graders dining in our cafeteria, a professionally staged shot, along with a photo of Liberian children starving, a photo of buzzards picking at a raccoon corpse. My other pocket buzzes. It's time to deal with my seeker.

Tug Doppelganger

FOR SEVERAL DAYS I have been carrying an extra phone that does not belong to me. It is an older model with a small screen, a faulty camera apparatus, none of the bells and whistles that keep humans living inside our palms. When it buzzes, only numbers appear, no names. I answer it but say nothing. I listen to decide what is happening on the other end but it is always a standoff, two parties breathing, waiting.

I know nothing about the owner. It belongs to a man named Tug Reynolds, although in this day I suppose that could be a woman. I keep it charged in case the owner calls and asks for his or her phone, at which point I will be eager to assist, but they must speak first, a rule I am certain means something. Occasionally someone asks for the owner. "Tug, you there?"

The phone has buzzed several times, Friday night, a busy evening. I push the cool aluminum alloy against my cheek. Someone chews on the other side, a small mouth, fast rhythm. The caller is nervous, multitasking, ambitious for something.

"Is this Tug Reynolds?" I say nothing. "I'm calling about some items you ordered from VillageShop."

VillageShop.com is an online retailer and the main supplier of all consumer products for the Gopa community. If every family orders all their needs through our communal VillageShop account, we get discounted items and special gifts and free shipping and vacation vouchers. Our materialism will also help fund a school in remote parts of South America or the Middle East, I cannot remember where exactly, but that is not the main impetus to shop. It is the deals, the membership advantages, our lifestyle shipped free in neat boxes so that every day is Christmas morning. Most of the items in my backyard were purchased via VillageShop at a discount: the grill, the fire pit, the blue rape lights that line the northern walk so that guests are not inconvenienced by accidentally stepping in damp grass while creeping through my darkness. Based on the amount I have spent in the past decade, I have achieved Zenith Member at VillageShop.

"I hear you breathing. I'm going to continue," the voice says. "Your items shipped to a residential address not affiliated with your account." It is the address of the Hendersons, my neighbors to the south who are retired and travel for much of the year. "We're aware some of the items are pet-related and might be important. Can I read you the items?"

I keep silent but do not hang up.

"A luxury two-door, two-tier cat cage, four twelve-ounce canisters of organic catnip, some…" I do the math. The items I shopped for to trap the cat staring at my fire pit were purchased using this phone, but how did I access the account? Credit card theft is certainly a possibility. I could probably claim it was an accident, except "…an elite series combo air rifle with scope, a 250-count of double-point air pellets, the 825 self-cocking tactical crossbow—these last items did not ship because we're not permitted to ship more than one weapon to a residence in the New York City area. Are you there, Mister Reynolds? Legally we're required to notify the authorities."

She waits. "I hear you breathing," she tells me again.

"I'm here. It's probably a mistake."

"It happens. Let me ask, Mister Reynolds…"

"Tug is fine."

"Were you planning to hurt animals with the weapons?"

"Of course not. I'm an animal lover." Despite the Shop-Vac full of chipmunk parts, I really do enjoy animals. "This sounds like a big misunderstanding. Any chance we can leave the authorities out of it?"

"Well…" I hear her type on her side. This is a minimum wage task, calling in the middle of the night to check on retail fraud. Most people just hang up, but I have been cordial. "Probably a computer glitch. I can go ahead and make the adjustments."

"I appreciate that very much, Miss…"

"Angela. Have a good evening, Mister Reynolds."

Saturday Morning Chores

I AWAKEN IN FRONT of a hapless fire, daybreak not yet cresting my house, BB gun in hand. Clint Eastwood is gone. I am slightly hung over and my eyes do not adjust in time, but I have the strangest sensation there is a naked creature running through the woods. It is slightly bulkier than Iliza, its breasts swinging in the chilly air as it dashes behind a tree. It could be the flu, or the pills, but this would be the first occurrence of hallucinations. Mostly it has been blackouts until now.

The backdoor opens and my estranged wife appears with coffee. She is dressed in a white blouse, a skirt that stops just below the knee and articulates beauty and decisiveness and order but also vulgarity. I would give anything to hike it over her back and fuck her obscenely in the flowerbed, her knees scratching into the fresh mulch. I am lying on a chaise, covered in a blanket, and clutching the gun. Laura is disappointed, but not enough to have come out the night prior to fetch me. Saturday is our busy time, activities and seminars and classes and school events and practices and chores and later, once the children are in bed, discovering little projects to avoid each other. There is a lacrosse game in Montclair, which most parents attend, though I will not be one of them. My wife has Standcake deliveries and will be gone for the day, handing me coffee along with a list.

"You didn't forget?"

"I didn't forget."

"What am I talking about, Tom?"

I should know the answer. Considering the hour, I require caffeine.

"The semen sample," she says. "It has to be at the clinic by ten. You forgot."

The Manhattan Cryobank is our storage unit for a kid we may or may not bring into this world to obsess over, depending on what the Sedlocks do. Because I have been erratic lately, going on two years depending on the source, Laura wants to stockpile some inventory. It is not important that she have *my* baby. Instead, she wants the children to share the same DNA, which studies show will give them a firm sense of camaraderie once we are gone.

"Of course I didn't forget." I assumed since Allie Sedlock left tipsy, there would be a reprieve in the semen collection.

"So you'll do it?"

"As soon as I finish my coffee."

"I'll call shortly to make sure it's done."

"You don't have to call," I say loudly, the start of a fight.

"Another thing," she says. "I overheard something last night. I have to ask. But I want to be clear. I cannot hear answers. Standcake," she says, which is how she distances herself from all my failures. "The business cannot be compromised. Understood?"

"Okay then."

"Toby Dalton. Did something happen the other day?"

"Well, it had to do with the thing we spoke about—"

"Don't answer. You know these lacrosse tailgates are important for business. We need this. Don't fuck it up, Tom." She watches me sadly, feels badly for me, then feels badly that she must always feel badly. "Is that how you got all scratched up?"

"I didn't want to—"

"Don't answer." Irate replaces sympathy. "He's a child, for fucksake. We have to be careful. Do you remember why? Did he injure you?"

"He didn't really injure—"

"Stop talking." She turns angrily. A book escapes her bag, a Ray McClutchen title, *Rescuing Your Inner Wolf*. She bends to retrieve it, embarrassing both of us. "Oh, Tom," she says. "What happened to you? Where did you go?"

Is she referencing last night, how I ended up asleep on a chaise in the backyard, holding a BB gun? Or is it a metaphor of my life, something I think about in front of the mirror now and again? Where did I go? What happened to us? What happened to me? To where did Laura disappear, my hard, exotic, intelligent woman now brandishing self-help manuals and vegan batter recipes? I sip the coffee and review the list, not eager for the first task: drop off sample. It sounds easy enough, but what it does not include is that I first have to obtain the sample, which means finding a suitable website to energize myself and maintain an erection long enough to finish the chore. I swallow the rest of the coffee and review my Saturday.

- Drop off sample (by 10!)
- Groceries (list on counter)

- Drive Gus: therapy, piano, wrestling, chess, thrift store
- Make sure Iliza has a ride to kickboxing this morning, theater this afternoon
- Fix the bathroom faucet
- Get rid of the cat. It trapped the Rotchfords in their garage this morning. Three calls about this shit, Tom. Deal with it!

What Happened To Us

ALL THE SHITTY, INSIGNIFICANT episodes that occur in wedlock become harmless plaque. One day, suddenly, the marriage clutches its chest, cardiac arrest; everyone is surprised even as the signs of poor health are present for years. I was less than Laura deserved and more than she could throw away. We had two children, a Gopa news network that thrived on misfortune and countless studies that insisted divorce would rob their innocence and tarnish their happiness. The catalyst arrives, the life-affirming or altering or crippling event from which good marriages have difficulty surviving, much less people not having regular intercourse, or even talking that much. Dead kid. Affair. The holidays. Cancer. In our case, the catalyst was Tilly, our nanny.

I left work early on January 12, hoping to take a long soak. I found the body floating in the lagoon and calculated the logistics: our nanny of ten years, deceased, I would have to drain the tub to remove the now-red water, have the interior specially treated, and most likely wait for warmer weather to refill it if I wanted to prevent cracking. Tilly was likely drunk, an afternoon problem that became a morning problem, that turned into her showing up to occupy our couch each day. It was bad form, among the other nannies, to fire one of them for the sins we all practiced. I had been on Luderica for a month at the time.

The death was not ruled suspicious, the gallon sized buckets too heavy for her frame, toppling her into the water with the girth. There was no evidence that supported foul play, but there were suspicions in the Gopa community, mostly from me. Initially I found nothing strange about the two blood smears on the concrete that were an awkward distance apart. Blood marks were what occurred during death, and if the authorities did not spread tape and check arithmetic and call in technicians, who was I to question their conclusions? Even so I began bringing it up at school events and on the Gopa website.

"Why two blood smears?" I wrote, the first comment in a blog that I posted alluding to overheard suspicions. "Did she fall, smack her head, get up, and fall again? Highly unlikely."

"I didn't use the word suspicious," I told the nannies one morning, eight of us sequestered near the free coffee. "But now that you bring it up, two blood stains, five feet apart, one a streak much smaller than the other. Yes, I'd say suspicious is fair."

"I think she was probably murdered," I offered to Laura during a wrestling meet, when a kid from Bay Ridge dragged Gus around the mat in a legalized lynching, eventually pinning his lifeless body and invoking applause. Laura went to sit with the other parents.

Four weeks later, neuroses that had been building steam for a decade left me bedbound. What used to be referred to as a nervous breakdown, Devin Brenner diagnosed as CRCB, or complex regional chakra blockage. Whitman ordered me to take sick leave. Laura threatened to move out if I did not stop talking about the death as though someone, myself perhaps, was responsible. Iliza refused to be in the same room with me. Gus made it worse, dressing in Tilly's old clothes and dusting the house, the early stages of his Transgeneration. Devin offered prescriptions. Instead I stuck with what Russ Haverly turned me on to, the new wonder drug still in the testing phase, though completely safe, that some of the other parents found successful to cope with marital disputes, long-term depression, the dreaded weekends when we schlepped our brood from enlightenment to enlightenment. According to Russ, once it got FDA approval, the Luderica would replace Ritalin and Xanax as parents' preferred remedy.

"One day people will pop these like aspirin. Helps rough out the edges, dig out whatever is missing from your personality," Russ explained. "It's perfectly safe in small doses. I hear the teenagers love it," a comment that would later haunt me.

It was my good buddy, Ray McClutchen, who suggested I sign up for one of those retreats people who read Ray McClutchen books attend. Laura thought it would be good for us. Ray told me he would maintain the property, that Michelin star chefs cooked the meals. I went to Malibu looking for God or one of its neighbors.

Taking a sabbatical from work to find oneself at a resort with other like-minded answer seekers is not a white privilege thing. It's a wealth privilege thing, an American thing. Ray got me a discount. There was yoga at sunrise. Coffee at dawn. Breakfast seminars during which motivational speakers told us about vibrations and erogenous zones. We napped. We played volleyball on the beach. We lunched on catamarans and discussed our feelings, or lack thereof. We sipped cocktails free of judgement and smoked marijuana as part of the recuperation. We ate fish and stews, drank wine, talked late into the evenings about divine missions. I should have been there vacationing with my wife. Instead I was there with my fears and other cowards who could not handle the pressure of showing up each day.

I was discharged with a peculiar thrill that there was nothing in the universe to hope for or know, just skin and grit and lack and luck. I learned something. I was a man, am a man, who does not do the right thing most of the time, unless it is for my own needs, for my children and wife and possessions. There exists duty in that role, but duty that comes with regret: treating my privileges like they are something I earned, taking more than my share, neglecting my fellow human, not doing good. It's who I am.

Three weeks later, everything was different. I was twenty pounds heavier still with no God and no more playful about my world. Laura had been left to manage the farm, pay the bills, worry over the finances, truck two kids to school and theater and therapy and kickboxing and chess and wrestling and dentist appointments. Iliza had aged seven years in a month. Gus was a full-on geriatric crossdresser. Ray had gotten Laura hooked on the worst type of drug, his self-help books—all the furniture rearranged into Feng Shui mazes, healing candles in every room, the kids each had their own crystal, Laura in a karmic daze, hibernating from her ruthless self. I did not know about her and Ray until I was told by Olivia, who enjoyed breaking the news of the Cooperative Marriage. I laughed in her miserable face at the suggestion a woman like Laura would ever be interested in a weenie like Ray until I saw the way my children looked at me. They were sorry for me.

I did not feel rage or jealousy. I did not punch anything, the natural reflex a man in love should display. I shrugged, nodded, promised to be open-minded about my friend stealing my wife while I was in God rehab. It was me; I made her weak. Marriage does not always end with domestic violence; more often tiny patronizing glimpses into our eerie failures, subliminal battle fatigue that wages on for years. I pushed her into a cloying, sentimental creature visualizing solutions, meditating on positivity and abundance, waiting for a wilted hand to sprinkle goodness on bills and dead nannies and worn-out husbands.

Navigating A Cooperative Marriage

THE NEWS OUT OF the Gopa website is that Russ Haverly did not show for Saturday's game. Outside of the occasional girlfriend, he is a lone wolf, no family in the area, no siblings or cousins, no one to phone. Along with local authorities, the school is doing all it can to find answers. The immediate answer is Assistant Coach Hunter Herman, who made several rookie mistakes on Saturday pandering to the referees over calls that should not have gone our way, when he could have been concentrating on the first midfield line, starring Toby Dalton, that was dogging it on defense all afternoon. We were still able to eke out a three-goal win, but we were easily ten goals better than Montclair.

Hunter Herman is young, wants what's best for the team. He does not have the clout to handle the complexity of private school parents, nor the rapport to order kids like Toby Dalton and Rhen Sedlock into his system, especially this year. The private school title is within reach. A state title is not out of the question. And I suppose everyone is concerned about Russ's wellbeing.

Seventeen. That's how many tablets of Luderica I have left. I never call Russ since I see him so often, a pattern I do not intend to break. There are other drug dealers I could contact. The nannies probably know someone, but Russ is safe. He plays golf at the club. He dines with us some Fridays. He invests in the Sedlocks' start-up. He sits on the ECI committee, which the Slancy parents admire and never discuss. He is one of us.

Russ's second occupation began as a weed dealer to friends. One of the nannies was a customer, which is how word spread. He supplies pharmaceuticals for other parents in the Gopa community, a few teachers, even Heather Pace—the head of school—is a regular client and occasional sexual liaison, a detail Russ spilled over beers. OxyContin, Adderall, Klonopin, Ritalin for parents who do not want the paper trail, the newest drugs awaiting FDA approval. I do not ask where he gets the stuff nor do I care. Although I will care in another month, when my supply runs out—me and the rest of the Gopa dependents.

Once Sunday arrives I like to put my mind on cruise control until about Wednesday. Every other Monday is when our group's investment club meets and Harry updates us on progress. Tuesday I pick up Gus, and Iliza if she'll allow it, and have a father-kids dinner. Wednesday means the weekend is in sight, which is when I feel I can be at my best. Not that I am my best at this stage in life. But if I am able to overcome some general flaws, weekends in the backyard will be my glorious time. Unfortunately, my domestic situation prevents me from overlooking Sunday, when we meet to strategize marriage with the McClutchens.

I have been reluctant to rage about what is happening between Ray McClutchen and Laura, mostly because they have been so upfront about it, so goddamned honorable and thoughtful. If they snuck around I would have cause for jealousy. Ray being the bigger person, and relying on his pop psychobabble to be forthcoming, when my wife and neighbor were discovered, they sat down Olivia and me and explained how it could work. They even brought in Devin Brenner, a Manhattan counselor who both Gus and I see biweekly, to proctor our sessions.

Devin calls it a Cooperative Marriage, a polite, sophisticated, politically correct term for what used to be referred to as swingers. We are so PC that in the first meeting I was bullied into admitting it was okay, in this age, for wives to initiate affairs, and to believe otherwise painted me as a misogynist. When members of two families fall in lust, rather than get a costly divorce that causes anxiety in children, they can all agree on a Cooperative Marriage. Instead of leaping into the sex, we phase-in the affair. Once a week, Tuesdays in our case, Ray and Laura get together for dinner and whatever else. Olivia is fine with it, happy to share Ray with another woman, wanting never to have sex with him again. Like a marathoner's knee tissue that becomes eroded to the bone, Olivia's sex drive is neutered, having heard more inspirational talk than any sane person can absorb in a lifetime. She is eager to spend the money from his books and lectures without having to fellate him a few times each year.

Me, I am in love with my wife, something I realized just after I was informed about the Coop. But the alternative is divorce, and I would never put my kids through it. Studies show—and the Gopa message boards are rife with data—that children raised in a single parent home, or in separate households, grow up with higher addictions to alcohol, drugs, pornography, and typically blame the father for their failure as adults.

Laura is in agreement. Like many of the Gopa moms, she has become addicted to self-help manuals and whatever the daily horoscope thinks about marriage. "Namaste momming," we call it. She has read all of Ray's books. She will not leave me because she worries about the karma. I paid for her graduate school. I supported us when she had no job and in the early going I funded Standcake. We have two wonderful children. Always determined and confident, her zest for life faltered with home ownership and parenting and waiting for me to be better. If spending time with Ray makes her happy, I am on board. Another reason to have Devin Brenner in attendance: we are reluctantly trying for a third kid so that Gus and Iliza will be accepting of their blood-related brother, Abraham—we already named it, this child of a strange wedlock, born of artificial insemination because his parents have not made love in two years.

There is no agenda at these Sunday meetings. Todd, the McClutchens' son, is upstairs with Gus because Iliza locks herself in her room, refusing to entertain her classmate. They left Maddie home with a nanny. Devin Brenner begins by reminding the group each week to go easy on Olivia and I, that we are making a mature decision about complicated emotional matters, that we deserve recognition for our presence. We sip prosecco and discuss whichever topics arise organically. Tonight we have done the weather. We grouse through the political spectrum. We discuss Gopa and I refill glasses, mostly my own, opening two more bottles and washing down a pill. I notice that Devin Brenner and I are the only ones drinking, despite my flu. Ray never touches his. Laura has tea. Olivia gives up after a sip. Suddenly everyone laughs and enjoys the banter, I believe sex is the topic, and I realize I have sat down holding the bottle of prosecco, without my glass.

"What about you, Tom?" Devin asks.

It is my turn to talk. Laura knows from the dumb pant of my expression that I have drifted again. She watches with deprecation and fear, wondering what stupidity will seep out of my mouth. "Olivia caught Todd masturbating," she says, updating me on the conversation.

"Ah, yes." I pretend to care about stupid Todd McClutchen's hermetic sex life. Todd is on the lacrosse team because his parents made him. Shy and homely, he will never touch a teenage breast with that attitude, reduced to wanking it in the privacy of his bedroom where his parents should damn well leave him be. "Embarrassing for sure. We've all been there."

This irks Olivia, who explains in perfect Indian royalty, "No, Pisser." *Pissah*. "We have not *all* been there."

"I think what Tom is trying to say is that he's familiar with Todd's emotional response from his own experiences of being caught." This excites everyone. Had I been paying attention, I would have understood we were not sharing experiences, rather critiquing the ritual of masturbation via forced loneliness as a response to paternalistic oppression. I do not know how much the McClutchens and Devin Brenner know about my sex life, but it is *all* masturbation at this point. And not out of enjoyment. We are doomsday preppers stockpiling semen for marital Armageddon. I am the resident expert on the topic. "Care to share your views?" Devin asks.

"It's disgusting." Olivia generally vents disgust, her emotional constant.

"From my understanding, it's probably a shameful moment," Ray says. "Is that about it, Pisser?"

"Not really, Clutchster. I've never experienced shame because there's nothing shameful about it, whereas there is something tremendously upsetting about you dating my wife." The phrase "getting caught" is subjective. Laura leaves me chore lists, reminding me to drop off my sample at the cryobank, which is the same thing as reminding me to masturbate. Has she caught me? She has walked through the room while I was crossing items off my chore list. "It's efficient sex," I conclude. "Better Todd take care of things in his room than forcing himself on an unwilling girl."

"That'll be all of that," Ray says.

"You really are an asshole," Olivia points out. *Osshole.*

"Are you a magazine or video man?" Devin asks, genuinely interested. He has a pad of paper and a pencil.

"Strictly video." I have a nasty cold and just want to be in bed, which is why I am dressed in sweatpants and a bathrobe, medicating with prosecco. I uncross my legs, get into the spirit of the evening, and begin lying about matters I know will bother my neighbor. "I was thinking the other day during a video segment: you know who would like this? Olivia McClutchen would like this. It's unemotional, fake props, detached existence. The men have large penises, which Olivia has never experienced."

Ray settles his shoulders as if I hit him in the sternum. Laura smiles, but then catches herself and rolls her eyes at my immature barb. Olivia abruptly inches forward on the couch, stares at Ray, and then Devin. "Is that even allowed? I don't want Pisser thinking about me while he's doing...that."

Devin starts to speak, and Laura interrupts, and they have a dignified discussion about the rules of pleasuring oneself. Can we, in fact, masturbate to each other, or do we need permission, or is that a Cooperative Marriage boundary we should all respect? I mention that every heterosexual Gopa father has masturbated to Allie Sedlock, but no one listens to me during these discussions, which I enjoy. Ray says it does not bother him who masturbates to him, so long as it is not me, and Laura conceals a chuckle. In other times she and I would wait until we were alone and relive the best moments of this absurdity, but now we are on separate couches.

Olivia is near tears, sans accent, explaining how this is a violation of their agreement, that she did not expect to be masturbated to during the Cooperative Marriage. Devin calms her and Ray moves to sit next to her and no one pays attention when I speak.

"I'd like to rip off Olivia's head and punt it into the kitchen. What would you all think if I stood up and did just that?" I am trying to explain, in my own way, that a tribe of miscreants has invaded my terrain and we do not harbor feelings for Olivia and would never involve her in our imaginings. During the course of the discussion, I have developed a violent erection, a product of the Luderica. "I would never fuck Olivia. Unless she was headless, and I was responsible for the headless-ness. The blood stains would go well with the new kismet throw rug."

Devin takes over, a calm voice and soft lips I would like to bludgeon with a tire iron, suggesting it is my aggressiveness that upsets Olivia, that if I had introduced the prospect of passionate feelings for Olivia in a gentler manner it might have been less dramatic.

"But I don't feel passion toward her." Now I am the insulted. "I totally get why Ray is sick of fucking her."

"See?" Olivia is shouting. "It's the same with the chipmunks."

"Fuck, Olivia," Laura says. Along with the erection, I feel a grin. "Again with the chipmunks?"

Olivia places a hand on her chest and tries to talk down to Laura who is not having it. "I feel Pisser's solution for everything is aggression. Why does he have to murder sentient creatures? Why does he own a gun?"

"It's the cat that's the bigger concern," Ray says. "Went after a golfer yesterday. That won't fly with the homeowners association, Pisser, I can tell you right now."

"Dad?"

When did the gun appear? Olivia is yelling and I am pointing the gun and explaining why the weapon is a necessity. I am at war, I hear myself shout. Sure, it is a war against designer chipmunks, but a war all the same, and it is a violation of my second amendment rights to suggest I disarm. If the chipmunks knew we were not permitted to arm ourselves, they would behave any way they damn well pleased.

"Our children play in this neighborhood and he's walking around with a loaded weapon. I just don't feel I need to be part of his sexual fantasies. I've been very collaborative through all this. Haven't I been collaborative?"

"You've been a true adult," Ray says, patting her knee.

"You've been wonderful," Devin adds, patting the other knee.

"That's my one request. That Pisser not wank off to me." She laughs, crazy. "Is that what it's called—wanking off?" The size of my erection right now, the gun's handle. They all wait for me to address it. "Look at him. He thinks this is a big joke."

I cannot do anything about the smile, like drool to an invalid, the hardness and humor and dry mouth and blackouts. Sex with Olivia and the chipmunks and Clint Eastwood hunting golfers in their plaid pants and collared shirts—it has all formed a treasure chest of playful imagery. This is what Laura wants, what Whitman at work has asked for: a man who can face hardship and find the playful, sappy center. Devin is saying something about giving him the weapon and my head is shaking no, which is hilariously making Olivia weep and laugh harder and Laura hide her face in her hands. They do not know I have a backup BB gun hidden in my upstairs closet, nor the crossbow that was accidentally delivered to the Hendersons and then the Jays, and now sits securely in my shed.

"Dad?"

"What's up, kiddo?" It's Gus, rescuing me. He has been standing there for several minutes. Dressed in a floral housecoat we picked up at the thrift shop, he walks with a cane fashioned out of a lacrosse stick. It's a hilarious costume. Not so much if your thirteen-year-old son is planning to wear it to school in the morning.

"There's an officer at the door," he says.

Olivia smiles. Laura's eyes are wide, though I cannot decipher if she is upset or trying to convey strategy. Ray snickers. "Bill's outside?" I ask.

Bill Chuck runs security for the Slancy community, quiet and decent and possibly mean if provoked, retired NYPD officer forced to take this job because it pays better than bank security and he's too old to guard celebrities. I often wonder how Bill Chuck feels, after patrolling the city for so long, that his retirement career finds him protecting a gated, predominantly white community. He likes to talk to me about the weather and professional wrestling and I think we enjoy each other.

"Not just Mister Chuck," Gus says. "The man from school is with him."

Lieutenant Misch

THE TWO MEN ON my front stoop take a look at Gus and I and assume they have interrupted a game, which distracts them from the bulge in my pants. They are too decent to address my son's outfit, or that I am dressed exactly the same. Devin and the others eavesdrop: why would the head of Gopa's security detail travel out to Slancy on a Sunday? I escort the officers to the den.

"Sorry to bother you, Tom. You know Lieutenant Misch, I believe."

His name is Reginald Misch. Everyone calls him Lieutenant. Like Bill Chuck, he is former NYPD and now oversees the small band of mercenaries who protect our children through daily education. I run through the arsenal of infractions that might render me onto his radar: Toby, chipmunks, Clint Eastwood, the BB gun uncomfortably shoved into my waistband above my fleeting erection.

I jangle my wrists, a horrible sense of humor when nervous. "You got me. Go ahead and cuff me."

Bill laughs, I laugh, Lieutenant Misch does not. He has an intimidating lack of facial hair, a man who respects detail. He does not want to be here, a tiredness to him that reaches back years. If he recognizes me from the lobby, he is not impressed. "You're familiar with a Russ Haverly?"

"Yes, of course."

"I was notified he hasn't been to lacrosse practice since Tuesday."

The two men stare. I shake my head. "It's awful. This waiting."

"What happened to your face?"

"Yardwork," I say. "Accident."

He stares at my outfit. "You have a cold?"

"The flu maybe." Paranoia strikes. "What does that have to do with Russ?"

"Your nose," Misch says. "It's running into your mouth."

I wipe the back of my hand across my face and rub that into the bathrobe, suddenly aware of how hot my skin is.

"Anything you can tell us, Mister Pistilini."

"Call me, Tom."

"I'm better with last names." Misch checks a notebook, looks at my face, sighs. "You golfed with him on Tuesday."

"Let me think." We do not always golf this time of year, but there's a driving range where some of the locals hit balls into huge nets, an excuse to drink beer and avoid home. It was cold on Tuesday. "I don't recall."

"This past Tuesday, Mister Pistilini. Days ago. Can you tell us where you were?"

"Tuesday." The word seems exotic. I was at work. I forgot to pick up the kids and had to call Laura. It was her night to have dinner with Ray, but they canceled and retrieved Iliza and Gus. I drank a few beers at the clubhouse. I wandered through backyards, smashing out security cameras. I drove out to Brooklyn to kidnap a feral cat from a cemetery, failed miserably, my face scratched to hell.

"You were last seen leaving the clubhouse bar with Mister Haverly."

The accusation embarrasses Bill, who monitors the island by camera and provided this information to his colleague. I have seen enough police shows to understand this is trouble. "You think I did it?"

"Did what exactly?" Misch's hairless face is crinkling and red, a small animal burrowing. His eyes should be on my eyes, staring me down, but they wander across my face and clothes and lies.

"I don't think I like your tone." I turn to Bill. "I don't like his tone."

"This is a school matter," Misch says. "No one's accusing you of anything."

"Settle down, Tom. Whole thing has folks spooked. Mischy just has a few questions." *Mischy.* These two are pals. Bill pats my shoulder. "Russ has a boat I've seen a few times. That's gone as well. Thought you could tell us if he left in the boat Tuesday."

I am rattled and nervous, which triggers the anxiety, the giggles, my head so hot. I am one bad moment away from blacking out, struggling to remember. "He would have taken the boat out here on Tuesday," I say. "There were other people in the clubhouse. And, like I said, I didn't golf on Tuesday."

"You didn't say that, Mister Pistilini. You said you couldn't recall."

"It snowed on Tuesday." The voice comes from behind me. I turn to Laura, arms crossed, frowning. "Tom wouldn't have golfed in the snow because he isn't an idiot. He's a weatherman."

"I'm aware of your husband's occupation, ma'am. We spoke to his employer. But he was at the clubhouse Tuesday. So was Mister Haverly."

"Along with dozens of other members," Laura says.

"Your husband was seen leaving with Mister Haverly"—he checks the notebook, the two discussing me like I'm no longer present—"between seven and nine o'clock."

"That's an awfully big window."

"Yes, ma'am."

"Tom was home just after seven. We had dinner." Lieutenant Misch is dubious of this information. "Fish and asparagus. Cod that I bought and breaded myself." Laura's voice is stern and getting louder. "Would you like to see the receipt, Lieutenant?"

"That won't be necessary."

I think Misch would not mind getting a look at that receipt, which does not exist. I do not remember where I was, but I know I was not eating fish with Laura.

Misch is tense, angry. "I have a few more questions for your husband."

"You have a few more questions for both of us."

Misch frowns. "What is the nature of your relationship with Mister Haverly?"

"Friends," I say. "Golf, dinners, drinks. That sort of thing."

"You're in business together," Misch says.

I am surprised how much a school security officer knows about my life. "More of an investment club. Moveable Museums." When this does not click, "Bike tours through wine country, Native American civilizations, rugged terrain if you're into it."

"Bike tours. That's what you call it?" Misch closes the notebook, frowns. Bill seems disturbed.

"That's what Tom calls it because that's what it is," Laura says.

"Odd way to make money if you ask me."

"I didn't ask you, Mister Misch." Laura has recrossed her arms, seems ready to lawyer up or call in backup. "Why are you asking questions about our affairs?"

"It's an investment club," I say. "Bill?"

Misch mumbles but loud enough that we all hear, something about yuppies and boats and a lack of decency. Suddenly it matters that he spoke with my employer. The only person I discussed Moveable Museums with was Whitman. We occasionally encounter bigotry in the form of mainlanders who hate the concept of artificial islands popping up in waterways. Lieutenant Misch strikes me as a bigot, which is troubling since he's in charge of my children's safety and believes I am possibly involved in a missing person investigation. He wants to know how we can live with ourselves. He mentions Tilly and if I would be willing to discuss it.

"We're done," Laura says. "Bill, show Lieutenant Misch off our property." She stares him down. "Don't come back unannounced."

Bill has a hand on his shoulder, turning him to the street. "Good luck with your investment club," Misch calls. "I hope you people are proud of yourselves."

Another Blackout

THERE IS EXCITEMENT IN the living room as Laura relays Misch accosting us at our front door, bringing up both the investment club and deceased nanny, Ray coming to her aid and patting a knee. That's his thing, the knee-pat, which is analogous to the ass-pat in professional sports—keep everyone's mood up when the storm waters crest. The McClutchens are investors as well. We have forgotten the Cooperative Marriage and our missing friend, and instead we are aghast that our way of life is under attack. We volley the possibility of taking this encounter to the Gopa administration, see if we can get Misch fired. Laura opens another bottle of prosecco.

"Pisser, a moment." Devin pulls me back into the den. "I didn't want to say anything in front of the others." He shoves a bulky envelope at me. There's a dead chipmunk inside. "It was mailed to my office."

It looks like a stuffed animal. I feel the giggles build. "I didn't send this."

He opens the envelope and points out the evidence. "It has a bullet wound, right there in the neck."

I peer closer. "It's a BB gun wound."

"It's a projectile wound," Devin says. "You're the only one on this island carrying a weapon to a marriage counseling meeting. Also, I noticed the erection when you stood up." He mentions it the way he might alert someone to food on a lip.

I scratch my head. Part of me is relieved that my aim is not as bad as I assumed, although I do not remember mailing roadkill to my therapist. "I'm sorry, Devin. I honestly don't know what to say."

"It's okay. It can't happen again." He pats my shoulder, which transforms into a neck rub. We close up the envelope and decide it probably belongs to me now. "Blackouts can be dangerous, Pisser. Still taking the Luderica? I warned you about that. It hasn't been approved."

"I feel like they're working."

"It gives you a euphoric high, screws up your chemicals. You need to be careful."

This jogs my memory of Russ snorting the stuff. There is a rumor that high school kids are doing the same with Luderica for the high, although my experience is much different. The drug never brought me blissful moments, but rather the understanding I bear a primitive horde that has been dormant.

"Blackouts, psychotic episodes, suicides," Devin continues. "From what I know about it, Luderica may one day work wonders, but it is extremely dangerous. Where are you getting it, may I ask?" I consider telling him about Russ, who he knows, and then realize I could have mentioned to Misch and Bill that their missing person was involved in narcotics. "Don't answer that," Devin says. "Let me put you on a more manageable prescription, something I've had success with."

He begins writing a prescription. He has wandered into a bad domestic situation, and I loathe him for trying to make the Cooperative Marriage work between the McClutchens and us. But Devin is just trying to help.

"I appreciate it. But once these are gone, I'm going cold turkey."

"I don't recommend it. Everyone needs a little help, especially you. Say." He hands me the prescription and leans close. "I heard some talk." Devin meets with many faculty members and Gopa families. I know before he asks. "The Dalton kid. You really strangle him in the bathroom?"

"Where did you hear that?"

"Nannies were talking. You know his father? GPS mogul, owns a bunch of satellites? He nearly disowned Toby when he was kicked out of his last school." Devin smiles, another neck rub. "How does his neck feel?"

"Soft. He has great skin, Toby."

"Pictures of your daughter, right?" He slaps my shoulder. "You may have done the right thing. Too early to say for sure. Don't let anyone tell you different, Pisser."

"Thanks, Devin."

He holds up a finger. "But that cat. You need to get rid of it. It's shitting in the bunker over on seven. And we cannot have that."

Polyethylene Living With Fiberglass Poles

WINE TASTINGS AND COCKTAIL hours are how the nanny chain thrives. Olivia will mention it near her nanny—a rumor that Tom Pistilini was the last person seen with Russ Haverly, according to school security—and the nanny will understand it is part of her domestic duties to spread the slander. By the time I reach the backyard, there is already a blog post on the Gopa website suggesting as much. The guests left long ago. I light a fire, pitch my Moonwhisper Four-Person Tent between the Jacuzzi and the retaining wall, just beneath the water dropping toward my lagoon. After a while Laura checks on me, leaves disgusted, and returns with a blanket.

"What's wrong with the den?"

I tell her about the chipmunk I mailed to our marriage counselor. I mention the blackouts again, which she already knows about. I explain that during tonight's meeting I imagined a scenario of punting Olivia's head across the room, though I do not mention the sex with the corpse. "It's not safe if I sleep inside. For you or the kids."

"You're being dramatic."

"I don't think so. The blackouts are getting more frequent. And we really don't know for certain what happened to Tilly."

"Don't start that shit again, Tom. You may have wanted to kill her, but you didn't do it. The police are certain it was an accident. Drop it."

I drop it. I am carrying a BB gun to Gopa and work. I do not tell this to Laura because this is the closest we will come to being a married couple: hunkering down, talking low, strategizing our lives.

"I'll be fine. I have reading material," I say, showing her the Sedlocks' fundraising pamphlets. "Have you gone through this?"

"Yes, several times."

"What Misch was saying?"

"He was an asshole, Tom."

"But he knows. You heard him. He was disgusted. Whitman said the same thing. Maybe we need to rethink things."

"You hate Whitman. Why are you discussing this with him?" She sighs, hopefully infers I have no one else in my life to discuss important matters with other than my sniveling, younger boss. If we bothered to speak anymore, we would have had this discussion weeks ago. "What's there to rethink? We invested the money a year ago."

"We just received the new material. Whitman says it's borderline illegal."

"It's not illegal. They've had the attorney look it over. Besides," she stands now, shivers. "School security has no right to address it. I have a good mind to speak with Heather about it tomorrow."

"We're not allowed to discuss it. Say anything to Heather Pace, it'll be in Allie's ear in an hour." Laura knows I'm right. I fumble the pages and reposition myself. "I want to read through this tonight."

Laura is anxious, tired, the bane of her existence camped out in the backyard. "Good night, Tom."

"Goodnight, Laura. I love you."

Harry and Allie Sedlock conceived Moveable Museums five years ago, a concept that married exercise with tourism. Bike trips through historic regions, hiking through preserved lands, adventures through uninhabitable terrain that proved thrilling for vacation goers. The costs were titanic: equipment, personnel, permits, insurance concerns that made a bank loan difficult. Instead they came to their closest neighbors for seed funding, and along with the Jays, McClutchens, and Russ Haverly, Laura and I dumped a portion of our savings into the venture. The return was impressive, enough to renovate the backyard and expand Laura's pancake business, and even put a little away for college.

A year ago, the Sedlocks came back for another round of funding. This time they promised a larger return, and though Laura and I do not have the money to spare, we believe in Moveable Museums, in how well it paid out the first time. We tripled our earlier offering, taking loans against both the house and the business, I even cashed in half of my 401K, with ludicrous penalties. If the venture fails, we will be ruined financially.

Clint Eastwood has curled up near the tent, enjoying the fire. My pants buzz, a familiar number.

"Mister Reynolds?"

"Angela, how are you?"

"I'm well. How are you this evening, sir?"

"Just Tug, not Mister Reynolds."

"There was another order placed to your credit card from this phone. It's still going to the wrong address, the Hendersons."

"My neighbors." The first time can be dismissed as a mistake. Angela knows this is no mistake, and because I feel like we know each other, I am slightly embarrassed at what I may have ordered. "What are the items again?"

Angela reads. A twenty-inch gas-powered chain saw, wire cutters, goggles, ten eighty-pound bags of concrete mix, and a gas canister. What am I planning to do now? "I'm doing some work around the house."

Angela types it on her side. "The thing is, Tug, you're purchasing these items through a community school account."

"And these items might raise a red flag if the wrong person sees."

"That's my position, yes."

Angela is an accomplice in this caper, having already made disappear the weapons I purchased. I sense she is willing to do it again, a strange friend the internet has bestowed on me. "Just some basic landscaping, Angela. Perhaps the easiest thing is to delete these from that account, as well."

"Possibly." She taps away on her side, not hanging up, not entirely sure if I am a nice guy or a serial killer masquerading as a confused customer. If she has access to the Gopa community VillageShop information, she would know everything we order. The groceries we eat, the chlorine granules and mineral sanitizers I use to treat the Jacuzzi, our brand of toothpaste. "Your cat. What's its name?"

"Clint Eastwood."

"It's a boy?"

"I haven't any idea, Angela."

A hesitation, maybe a smile. "No more guns, Tug."

Mornings Are For Fistfights

THE MULTICOPTER POWER TREE Pruner retails at VillageShop for just over $2,000, an item we cannot afford and do not need. It is a drone with dual eight-amp power saws attached to the bow and stern, maneuvered from the ground by remote control. Lately, I fly the Multicopter through the Gopa lobby during drop-off and trim out some of the undesirable objects I have noticed taking up space and desecrating what should be the better portion of my morning. Some of the men wear the collars up on their jackets and shirts, as if their necks are cold, and I trim these off, along with most of the unnecessary winter boots the moms feel are stylish. Therapy puppies annoy me with their size and yipping, and because they despise me, I cut them out of designer handbags like a do-it-yourself cesarean, their moist and trembling bodies spilling onto the world to self-mobilize like the rest of us mammals.

Occasionally, I fly the Multicopter in too tight, it is a crowded lobby after all, and I nick an ear lobe or jugular. I have killed Ray McCrutchen seven times this spring. I have watched nannies bleed out. The dean of recruitment, who suggested a portable web-cam for Gus so we know what he's doing at all times, was accidentally disemboweled by the Multicopter. Harry and Allie Sedlock suffered massive contusions to their faces this morning when emotions steered the drone, pummeling them over what I feel is an unethical use of my life savings. Many of the moms rehearsing math cards or spelling bees in the lobby, filling the last seconds of companionship with rote memorization, I desecrate their knowledge props with dive-bombing precision.

Halfway through my juggernaut, I catch myself, a mini-blackout, recognizing that I am smiling and holding an imagined remote control, that I do not own the Multicopter Power Tree Pruner with dual eight-amp power saws. Lieutenant Misch watches me from the guard station. I do not know how long I was out, or if anyone saw, and this is what disturbs me about the Luderica. It has dug up something feral inside my mind, perhaps closer to my gut, a possibly unholy and morbid realm that is as much a part of me as my understanding of meteorology, my love for my children. It was meant to find my buried playfulness and joy, but there also exists buried resentment, buried fear, buried alcoholism and gambling and vice, buried tribes of animals. Buried terrorism. Buried irrationality when it comes to protecting my family. There is a reason we humans limit our sins, push them deep where they are hidden, and to unearth one is to chip away at the foundation of things we do not want shown.

I am dressed in a gray and purple zip-up Gopa sweatshirt, which I wear over my suit each morning to show school pride. Many parents do the same. I love the capital G and lowercase opa, as if we are more than just a meaningless acronym full of oversized letters, but a community of students, parents, and faculty with an identifiable notation. Gopa is not even the correct acronym for the Gifted and Purposed Academy, which would be Gapa. We are often mistaken for the Gifted on Purpose Academy, as if our children had been chosen by a higher force to walk through the marble archway. This misunderstanding comes mostly from parents who could not get their children enrolled here, which causes us to be scorned by the larger private school community. All our shirts and bags and jackets and hats are monogrammed with the Gopa pride, the merchandise available on VillageShop at a discount, and it is impossible to gaze upon the word and not smile at another parent, shaking hands and kissing cheeks and sterilizing hands to know we are one.

The school occupies the old Trembley building on the Lower East Side, an Italian Renaissance style hospital that was once used to house, and shock treat, the city's sexually depraved. It transitioned from a hospital to a warehouse to a storage unit, and was on the verge of being gutted and turned into condominiums when self-righteous neighborhood purists were contacted by Gopa's leadership, and a for-profit school was born, the building sold at a ridiculous value of what developers would have paid. There is a full pool in the basement and nap room on the seventh floor.

A middling Tuesday in April brings a different vibe to drop-off. One of the mentally challenged bunnies bit a first grader and the parents are threatening a lawsuit if the entire population is not exterminated. This has brought a cackle from the animal rights purists, who insist the bunnies are not dangerous, and because of birth deficiencies were born without teeth and some without eyes. It would be impossible for them to physically bite a child. Instead, one of them probably gummed a finger too hard, which should not result in murder. The consensus is that since we pay $40,000 a year to send our children here, we should be able to afford bunnies that are cute and cuddly with regular eyes, and not fucking or dying by the bushel.

On top of the bunnies, one cannot turn anywhere without hearing the name Russ Haverly. He has been missing for more than a week, and with the big game only two weeks away, the lacrosse season is in jeopardy. The pride of the athletic staff, Russ was recruited from a private school in Darien, Connecticut, years earlier, having just taken the squad to the state championship. He is handsome, a determined coach, a mentor of young men who want to grow up to be just like him, except wealthier, not working with a bunch of snot-nosed athletes, or living on a boat. The junior class advisor, he was voted by the parents to sit on the committee choosing the eighteen students to participate in the ECI. Along with Heather Pace and Thomas Turk, director of talent, Russ seemed like a solid choice to tip the scales toward the Slancy families.

Worse than harboring our lacrosse aspirations, I am beginning to understand Russ's wider role in the Gopa community. He is a drug dealer for the nannies and parents, quietly and safely providing illegal narcotics that we might otherwise have to obtain from nefarious strangers. My stash of Luderica has dwindled, and, according to the whispers, the same thing is happening in households from Chelsea to Westchester. It is an inconvenience because we count on Russ to win games and advise the juniors, and I think he teaches a few algebra courses. But also he keeps us chemically sane and properly medicated, and his disappearance is an incomprehensible pain in the ass.

I was up much of the past two nights combing through the Moveable Museums business plan. I am furious with Harry and Allie, but mostly with myself. We have called an emergency meeting of our investment club for this evening, at which point Harry has promised to talk us through any concerns.

This morning everything irritates me. Iliza runs through lines from *Our Town*, an admirable endeavor for a high school girl, Tungsten her reading partner. And yet I cannot help watching my teenaged child and her friend, and loathing their existence the very moment they peek up at me from their pages, watch me too proactively, and whisper. Iliza has done something. I know she has done it. She knows that I know. We do not discuss it. Tungsten's subtle smirk solidifies my suspicion. Gus is congregating with the nannies that pinch his cheeks; he is dressed in antiquated layers of cotton and wool. He is flunking everything but some mysterious writing program that only offers two grades, pass and fail.

Look for a smattering of clouds and tense moments of insanity for much of the afternoon, a violent uprising somewhere peaceful and morbid that will cause the sports broadcast to be delayed. A chance of light rain and low winds, and war to the east. Today "14 Ways to Make Facial Hair Cooler" is trending on LustFizzle. The subject of this week's Cooperative Marriage email is titled "Spring Feelings." I hate my phone. I am one with my phone. To look away is to reenter this sphere of exhaustion and expectation. I have correctly predicted the weather for thirty-seven days.

Laura was introduced to my tribe's indignation this morning, a rant about Moveable Museums and Ray McCrutchen and the perceived

American dream we are carving out on the isle of Slancy. My mood spreads like a pandemic, Laura calling Ray with my point of view, who shared it with Olivia, who called Allie. I was quickly on the phone with Jackson, who I could hear telling Jason, who thought we already knew. Jackson promised to sort it out with Harry, but the damage is done. Even two doses of Luderica is not enough to find the joy on this Tuesday morning when black patches in honor of Russ Haverly have crept up among the lacrosse players and parents. I glance at my arm to notice I am wearing an RH patch that I do not remember donning.

Once at Gopa, we remain silent about the collective conniption. Laura stands next to Allie, who stands beside Olivia, who stands beside Harry and Ray and Jason, who is next to Jackson, all of us civil and smiling, sanitizing and pretending to enjoy each other. Jackson is to my right, completing the circle, and he appears to be remarkably diffusing a dispute I am not entirely sure I entered into voluntarily. The man's name escapes me, Rick or Dave or Topher, and he has a kid on the lacrosse team, Ayden or Jayden or Topher Jr. He dresses like a banker, a black patch like mine, a Gopa lacrosse hat that has been removed or knocked to the ground in what I am guessing is a tussle, a hopeless spaghetti-ness to his haircut, a few strands manipulated into an identity.

The father touches my shoulder, telling me he read on the Gopa website about school security visiting my home and the possible misunderstanding with the Dalton boy. As a father, he understands my plight, but as a supporter of the lacrosse team, there is a better way to address the situation if I do not want trouble. Ray and Harry are also lacrosse fathers and know this man. They are stuck in the middle of what, it occurs to me, has become known in the lobby as "my disagreement." I think about weed whackers, not the one I own but the one I borrowed from Jackson, a 1.6-horsepower two-stroke engine with a fifty-inch steel shaft that could make quick work of Topher's haircut. It was not my intention to mention the whacker aloud.

He's shouting. "Are you threatening me?"

"Is this about the ECI program?" I ask, casual. "Because I don't think it's responsible to bring that up over this dispute."

"You touch my kid like that and you'll know a thing."

"I don't even know your kid." I glance across the room to see the lacrosse team watching, Rhen Sedlock and Doug Whorley and Toby Dalton and other arm-patched lookalikes. "I know *of* your kid I suppose. Self-entitled, lacrosse some kind of messianic pardon..."

Security is involved, Misch's hand on my shoulder. We are hustled out the marble archway to the front sidewalk where we are broken into two camps. Harry and security restrain Topher, Jackson and Ray are on me. Ray is explaining a four-step process for dealing with conflict, which was outlined in his near-bestselling business manual, *Best Road Ahead*. He recites phrases like "cognitive dissonance" and "constructive behavior" and "attraction redemption." I notice the bike strap and the oversized three-wheel trike. It strikes me as hilarious, a grown man on a tricycle. Ray means well. He truly yearns to be a sunshine breeze in a field of decomposing cadavers. He believes his own bullshit, that optimism gives him dominion over an uncontrollable universe, and I have to respect that every morning, regardless of the ethnicity of the blood spilling on his TV, he comes out of the shower chanting, "Everything happens for a reason, stay positive."

Deep down where we differentiate alliances, far below the ego of whether or not my wife favors his cock over mine, I like Ray. He wishes to teach me something about the world and I understand what Laura sees in him. If we could airdrop Ray into Afghanistan or Syria, countries with continuous warfare, send him off to disputes in tough neighborhoods and seedy bars and devout protests, we could accomplish civility.

"Why are you smiling?" Ray asks. "This is serious business."

"Knock it off, Pisser," Jackson says. "You're just aggravating the situation."

"I wasn't going to bring this up, but it relates to your aggression toward me, toward everyone lately." Ray explains my role as a kind meteorologist and father that this aggression is not to my nature. "Aggression, just like kindness, is contagious. It begets further aggression. Do you hear me?"

I laugh too hard to make sense, but I explain to Ray and Jackson that I am changing, that there are mammals growing inside me that they cannot see, primitive war chants echoing in my guttural chambers that are seeping out of my pores, a tribe of derelicts stabbing my heart to sip the warm gore. It sounds poetic in my forehead. Through the laughter it is much less beautiful to security and bystanders.

"Stop laughing, Pisser," Jackson says. "You're not making any sense."

Ray takes me by the shoulders. "I found a dead chipmunk chained to my trike this morning, a roadkill necklace. Is there something you'd like to say to me, Pisser?"

Topher is tearing off his sweatshirt. He wishes to engage me in a fistfight. I return the embrace, two hands on the back of Ray's neck. "'Church bells are ringing for those who are easy to please.'" There is so much I want to say to Ray as I stop laughing to lick the sweat molecules from his cheek. "'And the frost on the ground probably envies the frost on the trees.' Jason Isbell, off his *Southeastern* album. You think about that a minute, Clutch."

Economic Benefit Of Dead Kids

THE SEDLOCKS' HOUSE SITS on a slight bluff just north of the East Bridge leading into Slancy. The front yard has open views of lower Manhattan and the Brooklyn Bridge, a wraparound porch that eavesdrops on millions of tiny worlds that call this metropolis home. The backyard opens onto the bicycle path. It is a lovely home designed exactly like every other house in Slancy, but the bluff gives it an edge over the rest of us, a superior landmark status that I cherish. When I cross over the bridge and see the single-family craftsmanship, the rooms lit up with a tawny glow, I am certain we made the right decision to set down roots and purchase a home we cannot afford. I feel privileged to share this journey through parenthood and adulthood, through Gopa and life knowing we are doing it with people like Harry and Allie Sedlock.

More than smart entrepreneurs, they are gifted shoppers, which as a mobile-shopping addict I appreciate. Harry has an eye for clever pieces of yard equipment he might use only twice a year, but which adds to his impressive shed that bears museum-like organization. Allie is responsible for the interior design. Every piece of furniture, every sculpture and photograph and candle holder has been thoughtfully placed so that the doorknob in the front entrance has the same shade and grip as the bathroom fixtures and the cabinet handles, a deliberate message that what people will touch should have an interconnected feel. They get more deliveries from VillageShop than even we do, the trucks stopping at the Sedlocks first. I know the male delivery personnel just want to see what Allie wears each day, but there is a level of respect that the Sedlocks command. Everything about them—from their belongings, to their clothes, to their manners—is better than what I have, better than how I do it. The only entity in which they finish second is the school play, Tungsten the understudy to Iliza, and only because Allie suggested her daughter take up theater to juice her resume.

"Admissions officers like that sort of thing," Allie once told Laura, regarding the hundreds of hours Iliza's invested into acting classes.

I'll be the last member of our investment club to arrive, with the exception of Russ. Whitman from work put together a video of catchphrases he would like me to adopt. "It's wetter than a paper man at a scissor party" and "Windy as a barroom door at last call." My style is not to make the weather the main portion of the broadcast, but rather a sideshow to the digital destruction of news and traffic. Nevertheless, we had to try out a few, which caused the delay.

I shower, change, slip the BB gun into my waistband, and as I am heading out the door I notice a fresh delivery of boxes at the Hendersons. I have a mobile-shopping addiction that is as bad as alcohol or gambling, my love for the anywhere-anytime-nonverbal nature of the transactions. Outside of my children and my backyard, nothing in the world completes me like sitting down with a phone to browse VillageShop for hours. The logo sets me off, the smell of cardboard and torn postage tape, the way young children feel about brightly wrapped toys. Laura hates the boxes. I know seeing them will cast a pall over our already hectic marriage, so I spend ten minutes miraculously tearing into them wondering what kind of trouble I have ordered. It is nothing dangerous, some propane tanks for the grill, Tiki torches for the backyard, several spools of cable wire rope for which I have no need, though I am impressed I had the foresight to order. I dump the equipment in the shed and get rid of the boxes, then hustle down to the Sedlocks.

My hope is to blend into the room without sanitized handshakes and kisses. Instead I wander into a dire beginning. Tungsten's therapy dog, Muggly, has taken exception to Jason, who is sitting where the dog usually naps. From the foyer, I hear it yipping. By the time I reach the living room, a grown man stands on the sofa to escape attack, terrified and pleading with Allie to intervene. Rhenium is filming this, which the Sedlocks find hilarious—Rhen is the prince of the household, and Harry and Allie eagerly approve all of his decisions. Jackson chases Rhen around the living room, while everyone looks on horrified, expected to enjoy this large black man and small white boy and medium-sized homosexual and therapy canine mashup, a multicultural evening. I snatch the phone from Rhen's hand and shutter it. All charisma halts.

Muggly forgets about Jason to growl at me. The room seems disappointed at my appearance, even though it was my rant that inspired the meeting. Rumors of my marriage failure and disputes with both Toby and Topher make it difficult to look me in the eye. On top of this, everyone has been told to be kind to me since the breakdown. I have deflated the evening. Surprisingly, Laura seems relieved to see me, assuming I would forget altogether.

"Good, Pisser's here," Harry says. "Let's get started."

The Sedlocks have transitioned their media room for tonight's presentation, a projector flashing images onto a screen that is slightly larger and nicer than the one in my backyard, a cart with coffee and liquor and beautiful standing pancakes. Allie has joined Harry at the front of the room, their shadows blocking the bar charts. Everyone is upset with the Sedlocks, an emotion with which we are least familiar, but looking at them, I only feel forgiveness. Harry wears jeans and a blazer, professional but blasé. Allie wears a red dress that stops just above the knees, a pendant necklace that draws eyes to her breasts and neck, her hair tied up in a floral scarf. How could we be angry with them?

"First things," Harry says, head bent. "Allie and I would like to apologize. I know some of you feel we've been less than forthcoming with our plans, but I assure you it was unintentional." He seems genuinely upset at our fallout. "This entire project came together in the past month, then this thing with Russ..." He fights back sudden emotion. Russ is close with the Sedlocks, old friends. "Look, we just want to put all the cards on the table so everyone is on the same page."

"That's right," someone says. I turn to find the Sedlocks' attorney who has snuck into the back of the room. Or rather, he was probably always here and I did not notice. I was the one who crept.

His approval sparks something in Harry, who shifts direction. "I should mention, before we get started. Legally, there is nothing suspicious about the timing of the strategy pages you've all received. I asked Dan Mathers here tonight in case anyone had questions. He'll be available after the presentation."

It is unsettling to have Dan Mathers at our investment club. He does not live in Slancy. He is not one of us. He sits in my blind spot, and I have concealed the BB gun in the stern of my waistband, making it impossible to get a fluent kill shot if it comes to that. I have no questions for Dan Mathers because Jackson has already spoken to his own attorney, who I note is not in the room, and who agrees with Harry's assertion of legality. The Sedlocks were up front with us, claiming there would be a new round of fundraising but that they could not divulge the nature of the expansion. We were free to hold our investments until more information was available, but we trusted the Sedlocks and saw big returns the first time and we wanted to be part of the new endeavor before the opportunity vanished.

Harry walks to the back of the room to work the slideshow. Allie stands alone at the front. It is a strategic decision to let Allie do the talking, a natural congeniality that puts everyone at ease. Furthermore, she sips wine, which is a relief. She is not pregnant, which implies I am under no pressure to produce a sample this week. I turn to see if Laura notices, but her refusal to look at me is nondescript.

Allie begins with a summary of Moveable Museums and recounts bike tours and adventure hikes through remote parts of the world, how we are, quite literally, changing the nature of what it means to vacation. Moveable Museums is for people with an active lifestyle, intellectuals who crave fitness and knowledge and do not want to sit on a beach or eat at buffets on vacation, which is what I like to do on vacation. She does not say it in these words, but we have invested our hard-earned money into vacations for people who are better. People like us. Except for me.

There are bar charts and line charts and pie charts showing us how our investments grew. She stealthily jumps into the new tours and how they will work, the number of tour guides, tour directors, a fleet of buses, contracts with national hotels, contracts with local communities, county officials, lawyers, a security force, an extensive marketing campaign that is due to kick off in a month. A new set of charts illustrate the latest round of fundraising, and we all reposition ourselves in our plush chairs, gaping at the numbers.

Can this be accurate? We are due to earn a fortune. Laura and I have tripled our investment in the latest round, and should everything go to plan, we can pay off the house and the credit cards, pay for college, turn the Standcake idea into a national business, and there will be enough leftover that I will never work again. Goodbye Channel Fourteen. Goodbye cold fronts and humidity and Whitman and Lustfizzle. We thought we were investing in raft tours down rivers, bike expeditions through pristine lands. This is heavier.

"What is a museum?" Allie says, her hands pushed together so that her breasts prepare to catapult from the red dress. "Is it a stuffy building where no one can speak or touch anything? Or is it mountains, communities, outer space. Our investments are redefining the concept of museums."

Fresh charts hit the wall. Allie has moved into a future round of fundraising, in which we will sit intrepid vacationers on the tips of rockets and fire them into space. It sounds so rehearsed and thoughtful, I have to mentally remind myself why we are here—this round of fundraising, the critical one, that will call into question our ethical flexibility and make us all wealthy, the big break everyone awaits. We have invested in vacation excursions that will allow foreigners obsessed with American violence to tour the black stains of our culture. At a hefty cost of $15,000 per couple, what people spend to travel to Italy or Hawaii or Belize, they will be bused across our continent to visit the sites of our worst shooting massacres, an emphasis on the schools. They will learn the history, stand in the very offices and cafeterias and kindergartens where the bloodshed happened, speak to the survivors and parents of the gunmen and teachers. They will be led by trained tour guides through the escape routes that the survivors took, speak with retired faculty who were there and listen as they recount the fateful minutes, driven to the shooter's neighborhood and home and playground where he spent his fondest hours. Then, once that is finished, they will hop on luxury buses and head to the next location with stops at hotels with pools and restaurants with cheeseburgers.

With the new tours, we are tapping into a massive population of murder culture enthusiasts, and there is no better place to tour carnage than America. A series of beautifully synchronized charts proves it: bigger than parents that want the perfect beach holiday, than the baby boomers who enjoy resorts, than bike and raft misogynists hoping to conquer the world. We have more than two thousand preregistrations before the routes have been finalized, the marketing campaign rehearsed. Harry and Allie Sedlock did not come to us, their "friends," with this opportunity. We are their Ponzi scheme, the stupid money. They groomed us to believe in them when no pragmatic bank would offer up a loan, regardless of the financials.

Laura shakes her head, sad, in need of some Ray McClutchen literature to feel good about things. Jackson is quiet. Jason excuses himself for fresh air. "It's unethical." The words incense me until I realize they came from inside, my tribe.

"For once I agree with Pisser," Ray says. "We're parents, for gosh sakes. What does this say about us?" "Gosh sakes" is Ray's worst curse. He has been rubbing his hands and arms since Allie began talking, having torn the button off his left cuff, this entire concept not jibing with his philosophy.

"There's nothing unethical about shining a light in dark places." Harry has joined Allie at the front of the room, casually disemboweling a pancake man over a tiny plate. "Gun control is an international discussion. People want to know about it, experience it, stand where the victims stood. It's not like we're killing anyone. These shootings are part of our history. Part of who we are. And if we don't do it, someone smarter will."

"We're exploiting it for monetary gain," Laura says.

"Absolutely," Jackson says.

Allie shakes her head and breasts. "We're not exploiting anyone. That's the last thing we want."

"It's worse than the media," I say. I should know. Every time we get a whiff of a mass shooting, we go straight to national coverage, the reporter on the ground. Forget the weather, forget local sports, forget Melanie Trotter and a pileup on the Cross Bronx. Our viewers crave bloodshed. Our highest ratings come on our country's most infamous days. "Allie gave a wonderful presentation. But in the end we're earning money from dead kids."

"It's not all dead kids," Olivia says. "Lots of offices, public places, teachers, administrators. Parents would want to know. I'm interested just listening."

Harry points the end of a pancake at her. "That's what we think."

"Not one nickel," Ray says, despite his investment having already funded it.

Jackson's arms are crossed over his giant chest. "My goodness, Harry, what are we doing?"

"It's my money, too. And I'm investing." Olivia turns to Dan Mathers. "I read something about 'nonrefundable.'" Back to Harry. "Our investments were nonrefundable, weren't they?"

Allie hugs herself. Harry shrugs. Laura stands to pour a glass of red. Dan Mathers clears his fat throat. "The money's been spent. If anyone wants to back out, there will be a significant penalty."

"How big?" Laura asks.

"Eighty-five percent."

"Gosh sakes," Ray says.

"Fuck," Jackson adds.

"Five percent back now. Maybe another ten when we start earning." Harry holds out his arms. "It's the best we can manage, Ray."

It means walking away from the investment, which for Laura and I will be financial ruin. The end of the Standcake business, selling the house, bankruptcy, divorce. I suspect the same is true for Jackson and Jason. Ray has his books and speaking seminars, but that line of income would take a hit when it came out he was an investor in this. Ray is bent over, praying into his hands. My wife rubs his shoulders. Olivia checks her phone.

"Come on, Clutch, don't do that," Harry says. "We've dotted the I's and crossed the T's. Lawyers, contracts, we've flown all over the country giving this presentation to school districts, county legislators, good folks, many of who see the truth in this. In six weeks we're flying in the world's premiere journalists covering murder culture, taking them on the tour, letting them draw their own conclusions."

"They'll hate it," Laura says. "I can't even listen to it."

"They won't hate it," Allie says. "They'll understand. They'll go home and write about it. And once this becomes the most popular tour in the world, we'll look back on tonight as a victory."

"How is this any different than the millions of people who visit Auschwitz every year?" Olivia asks.

I groan. Allie smiles. Harry snaps his fingers. "It's called the 'Moveable Memorial Tour.'"

"I love that," Olivia offers.

"A percentage of the profits to the victims' families?" Jackson says.

Harry, "Already in the works. Two percent annually. More when we can."

"Or the September Eleven Memorial," Olivia says. "Or any memorial. It's not like we're inventing a new sin."

"That's precisely right," Allie says.

"Fucking cunt."

They have hacked into my voice. The words slip in through my ears and I discover I am the source, the harsh tooth into lip and the whisper ending. Allie gasps. Laura's mouth falls open at the word. Harry sighs. Something occurs to me when I hear Olivia McClutchen speak, and I am not proud of myself. It comes from the darkness within me, the dust of which has loosened as my tribe bandies forth. I have discovered Olivia is the one person on the planet I am certain I could stomp to death, her miserable bluntness. We are all guilty, but Olivia is unapologetic. I am to blame for my marriage falling apart. But on her side of this mess, she pushed Ray into the timely predicament of Laura's loneliness. And I hate her accent.

Olivia stands, dramatic and offended. "What did you say?"

I pace the floor, the metal of the BB gun cool against my skin. Jackson has my back. I know Laura was on my side momentarily. Ray is ready to step between us if it gets physical. "This is a horrifying thing you are justifying. Completely unethical."

"Ethics now?" Olivia points into my face, the accent gone. "This from the asshole killing innocent animals so he can sit in hot water." *Whatah.* "The homeowners association knows, Pisser. They're sending a letter."

"Olivia, drop it," Laura says.

A communal sigh, our present dilemma much worse. She turns to Ray, and then Dan Mathers. "Did you know he's living in his backyard? Like an animal."

I am not a violent person. But I maintain it is not me as I move toward her, the mechanics of my jiggly frame unprepared, the weapon sliding from my waistband. It tumbles to the floor, a taut crack into the hardwood. Olivia has sucked me into a petty brawl. My hatred is so pure I cannot help myself. And because I have been roaming my neighbors' lawns at night with a measuring tape and a power saw, I know I have the upper hand.

At some point I have bent over to retrieve the gun, and I point it at the ceiling. Everyone knows to treat me kindly, what with the breakdown and splintering marriage and suspicious nanny departure. No one wants to be the first to tell me, perhaps, that I should not have a gun at the investment club. I am shouting about chipmunks and treehouses and school shootings and the use of the word "cunt" as a descriptive noun and aiming the gun into the air as I holler at her stupid, pouting face. Olivia falls to the ground, weeping. Ray and Jackson are on their feet. Jason returns to the room briefly until he sees me brandishing a weapon and disappears again.

This comes out of my mouth. "Why don't you tell everyone about your treehouse, Olivia."

Her sobs are breathless, dramatic. "He's insane. Someone call the police."

The treehouse is made of recycled wood pallets and PVC piping, the kit purchased on VillageShop. Ray hired someone to put it together. The homeowners association states that artificial items cannot be placed in trees. Furthermore, it was built too high above the ground, an eyesore for other property owners. The trees in Slancy do not have decades of roots that intertwine underground. They cannot support heavy structures. I relay this all in polite detail while pointing the BB gun at the ground as Olivia covers her head, Jackson urging me to stop.

"I'm sending a letter to the homeowners association as well," I say.

"Please, Pisser," Jackson pleads. "Get a hold of yourself."

"We built it for Maddie." She sobs into her arms. "It was a birthday gift."

"Well, it's illegal." I shrug, put the gun back in my waistband. "It needs to come down. One good storm and it could take the entire tree."

Most of the room is quiet, appalled. Allie's hand is on my arm, her fingers tanned and warm. Her other hand is on my waist and I let it creep toward the gun. Inexplicably, an erection materializes. She grabs the weapon and hands it to Harry, who shoves it beneath the tray of Standcakes. "The Hendersons have the same treehouse in their yard. They built it for the grandkids. Duffy O'Neal as well," Allie says, pronouncing each word. "He recommended it to Ray and Olivia."

"Then he's also in violation of the ordinance. It's coming down. And all those fake tree cell phone towers— violation. They're coming down."

I feel good about this breakthrough until I face the room. My friends stare. Laura has helped Olivia off the ground and settled her with a glass of wine. Jackson tugs me into a chair and keeps a protective hand on my neck. Whatever support I had when I first spoke has dwindled. The tired lawyer is hunched over a plate of half-eaten pancake men, eyeing me tenderly. Laura will not look at me.

"Maybe we should reconvene another night," Harry says.

"No." Jackson is adamant, his hard hand on my neck. "What about Russ? Does he know about any of this?"

Harry turns a chair and sits. "I was planning to speak with each of you personally to hear your concerns, but then we called this meeting. If Russ were here I believe he would be largely supportive."

It means Harry and Russ spoke about the new strategy. There is a foggy image, shadows dancing over moving water that I cannot summon into focus. A memory of Russ and me talking about this topic near liquid. I try to grab it from my mind but it is not there and Jackson's fingers are hard and the chair I sit on grinds into the wood that connects to Laura's chair, and I send back to her feelings of apology and longing and love, but still she does not look.

"His shares," Olivia says, now recovered. "What happens if he doesn't turn up?"

The miserable bitch. A flicker of a smile on Allie's face, a nod from Harry, and they know they just won a majority. If we put it to a vote, which legally Dan Mathers would say is immaterial, I am certain of the results: Laura, Ray, and myself opposing the investment, Harry, Allie, Olivia, and the Jays supporting it. Despite his fear of animals, Jason is ruthless when it comes to money, and Jackson is ruthless when it comes to Jason.

"Worst case for all of us," Harry says, arms raised to God. "If Russ were to not return, his earnings would be divided among the other members."

Free money. Cherry on top. We move forward into something vile and untamed.

Breakfast With Tungsten

I AWAKEN TO BRANCHES snapping as I come out of the tent, a nymph scampering through my backyard. I am holding a new BB gun. I have six more still in the packaging, hidden in the shed, in case I have to ditch a weapon in a trash receptacle during a foot chase, or if I lose it during a blackout. Like many Americans, I feel I require constant armed protection, and yet my fear of guns forces me to stick with innocent projectiles. The morning intruder seems dreamlike until I recognize an entirely naked Rhythm Ferris from next door running through my woods. She chases Clint Eastwood, trapping my cat beneath the shed where it has pushed itself into a dangerous, quivering ball, hissing at the large girl who laughs and swings her paunch in the April morning.

"No," I call. Rhythm's neck snaps toward me. I am shirtless. And pantsless. My only accessory is the gun. She crosses her arms over her large, white breasts but leaves her bushy crotch exposed. I hold up my hands. "The cat. Be careful. It's dangerous."

"Mister Pickles was chasing me," she says. "Now he gets a tummy rub."

She has issued my killing machine a frivolous moniker, but the playful smile and obvious joy are beyond my capacity to explain. Scampering to my right, busted twigs and heavy sighs, as Clint Eastwood makes a hard dash toward the golf course. Rhythm squeals and gives chase. Suddenly Jackson and Jason are standing in my tree line dressed in rain gear, hollering at Rhythm to stop, their tired gaze coming to rest on my withered manhood. It is a strange moment for everyone.

"It's not supposed to rain today, fellas," I say, but they have disappeared into the woods after Rhythm.

I leap into the Jacuzzi and submerge into the hum of the motor and a final prayer from the bubbles. It is a chilly dawn, the chemical entrance singeing my skin. There are no dead chipmunk bodies floating, my head and shoulders smoking as I rejoin the morning, the taste of spring and the sound of warbles and the smell of coffee. My eyes adjust to Tungsten Sedlock sipping from my mug, a painted toenail testing the water.

"Morning, Tom."

I spit water. "Is that mine?"

"Laura said to leave this. You were busy drowning so I figured I'd wait."

Tungsten rides the shuttlebus to school each morning, but she has breakfast at our house where she and Iliza run lines. My guess is that she only comes here to smoke weed before school, and if caught could successfully blame it on me, the neighborhood recluse. Rumor has it I pointed a loaded gun at Olivia McClutchen in her parents' living room, so marijuana is not out of my wheelhouse. My daughter's best friend is dressed in a rain jacket, suggesting my neighbors do not watch Channel Fourteen for their weather, and a uniformed skirt that is too short and which no mother should allow. She hovers over the water, legs spread, and casually inches lower to set down the mug. Tungsten will one day grow into her mother, but for now she displays a fraudulent smut, an uncoordinated whorishness devoted to an inventory of male attention. I have no desire to fuck Tungsten; I only crave my wife's fondness. A reflex inside me yearns to reach out and grab her tiny ankle, and tear her into the surf, drenching any screams and killing the demons that compromise my daughter's innocence.

There's lipstick on the mug. I keep my eyes low.

"You were looking."

"No, I wasn't."

"I saw you." She laughs, tries to encourage me into collusion. "Rhythm was running in the backyard, and you were staring at her fat ass, you old horn dog."

"She's not fat." Jackson has confided in me about Rhythm's obesity, and his concerns about body image. Jackson, too, is overweight, and blames himself for his adopted daughter's girth. They are quietly dealing with her exhibitionism and do not want to make her feel she is doing anything wrong. This is how we handle non-traditional behavior in our sect—we do not encourage it, we do not discourage it, we just allow it existence out of the direction of our peers. "Just a bigger girl."

"So you were looking." Tungsten grins down at me. "It's okay, we like what we like. I'm into college boys. You like fat girls."

"Knock it off, Tungsten." She has a casual familiarity with adults that I dread. In any situation not involving naked teenagers frolicking in my backyard where I am also naked, I would take this complaint to her parents. "Go back inside."

Tungsten, from nowhere, "Iliza and I talk about our parents' sex lives all the time. My parents aren't having sex either, thank God. But their lack of sex is from financial anxiety, whereas yours is due to impending divorce. It's weird you keep semen in the freezer."

"That's none of your business." I'm explaining my habits to a teenager. "I only keep it there for a few hours. At the most."

"Accidents happen." She makes a pouty face and then feigns vomiting. "The McClutchens aren't having any sex, but you knew that. And I hear even the Jays aren't doing it." She giggles at her cleverness. My arm shakes with the coffee, drizzling the bubbles in brown condensation. "Seems like the only people fucking these days are Ray and Laura."

That's Mister McClutchen and Missus Pistilini, you little shit. I do not know what Iliza tells Tungsten, or why Tungsten is telling me, or if any of it is true. I stand suddenly, my shrunken cock exposed over the water line, and hurl the mug. It bounces off the back of the house, coming to rest in the yard near her feet. She does not flinch, bursting into laughter.

"Relax, psycho." She kicks the mug toward the patio. "This is why you keep getting in fights at school."

I cover up in the water. "I wasn't looking at Rhythm. It just happened."

"I won't say anything." Tungsten heads inside, nothing left to entertain her. "Besides, if I was planning to divulge secrets, naked photos of Channel Fourteen's weatherman would be much more valuable. Don't you think?"

Sailors Lost To The Seas

EXPECT OVERCAST SKIES THROUGHOUT the morning with heavy fog over the shorelines. A school shooting in Indiana has newscasters gushing, the fourteen-year-old wounding a vice principal before offing himself, but still a gratuitous taste of murder midway through the work week. A serial groper is roaming the subway system in search of young girls, the police not able to identify the suspect despite cameras everywhere. Most meteorologists are forecasting rain, but it will not rain today, tonight giving way to heavy clouds and light winds out of the southeast. Trending on Lustfizzle is "19 Cooked Eggs That Resemble Famous People." On the Gopa website, Jacuzzi_Dad authored a blog post about school prayer, along with an eleven-minute video of a sphincterotomy that plays continuously when someone clicks the post.

I am calling for a morning prayer to begin the school day, not suggesting it be intended toward any specific God or allegiance, but instead a general peace offering to whatever is out there to watch over our children. If parents intend to read and dispute my proposal, they have to do so beneath four gloved hands slicing apart a red anus, the atheists and non-atheists and semi-religious proctors leaving death threats in the comment section. Expect moody thoughts with a mass killing somewhere with escalators toward the weekend. It has been thirty-eight days since I incorrectly predicted the weather. I already know that it will rain ten days from now, though from the dress of my neighbors and Gopa peers, umbrellas and ponchos and boots, no one pays attention.

Gopa is in a state of chaos when we arrive. Nannies and parents congregate on the front sidewalk, gaping at the media vans parked in the drop-off zone, causing the traffic to snare several blocks as security personnel argue with drivers. There are only three, but their presence causes havoc for taxis and SUVs idling toward the curb. The Channel Fourteen logo is on one van, but I do not recognize the reporter, young and affable, recording footage of the school, just-in-case filler, a follow-up to last night's news.

Laura and Iliza distance themselves when we arrive. I cannot blame them. Since the scuffle, I have been asked by Lieutenant Misch's people to wait near the front windows, just past the security desk, a special section where noncredentialed drivers and part-time nannies with oversized strollers congregate. Topher cannot go inside either, not until the bad vibes settle, and we keep to separate ends in Gopa purgatory, careful not to make it worse. Gus sticks by me, his geriatric impersonation so pure I am certain he will be mistaken for one of the part-timers.

Across the room, Allie weeps near consoling moms who squeeze generous dabs of antibacterial gel into palms. Harry and the lacrosse dads huddle, each with one hand pursed in the other elbow, a hand over the mouth, carbon copies of strategy and sobriety. Russ Haverly's boat was found seventeen miles south on a Staten Island beach, having drifted there from the Lower Bay. There was no sign of foul play. Investigators believe Russ got stuck in a current and was taken out to sea. The theory is he had possibly been drinking and fell out of the boat. The body is still missing. The school issued a statement last night just after I received a call from Lieutenant Misch with more questions. Where does he dock the boat? How does a high school lacrosse coach afford it? When was the last time I was on the boat? I have not mentioned the phone call to anyone, the media vans and security officers arguing over the sidewalk real estate.

Everyone fears the worst. The children check Lustfizzle on their phones. We wear black patches with the initials RH, all we can do in the perishable state of our constant recuperation. I feel self-conscious about my patch, as if Topher and the others realize I only wear it to fit in. The biggest game of the year against Darien is coming up, an event that has virtually no impact on my life other than I must drive there to deliver the Standcakes and show Gopa unity.

In the lobby, I discuss sunscreen and parenting methods with a mother of triplets who has hired three nannies, the seven of them causing a logjam. She wears a hat to which an umbrella has been cleverly attached, which she lowers via a remote control tucked into her jacket. The umbrella hat and jacket with remote control retails for $280 on VillageShop. A modern weatherman could use one of these. I stare lustfully at the contraption as she tells me about bingo therapy.

"...and checkers therapy and quintessential Monopoly and the studio is planning to offer Twister meditation in the autumn."

"I don't believe I would kill my nanny, if that's what you heard."

"It's a way to blend the homey-ness of board games with the madness of civilization without having to get your hands dirty and play board games yourself because who has the time anymore. They have certified college students who engineer the games and the kids just adore..."

"They're infants. The necks don't work. I might have killed her, I don't know for sure anymore. She was stealing from us, opened up a credit card on VillageShop. She was having the stuff delivered next door, to the Hendersons, who are never home, long story, and reselling it online. How can they follow what's happening with a board game?"

"Oh they know. Trust me, they know." I have offended this mom and she is lowering the visor via remote, making eyes at the nannies that are discussing me in a foreign tongue. "Board games instill gamesmanship and skill. Why would you say something like that?"

I am constantly shocked at how much of an advantage other people have over my parenting skills. They are forever finding innovative ways to prepare their children for the broader world, whereas I carry a BB gun to bruise the skin of any would-be rapist or groper or critter. The Millers found a new studio in Brooklyn where Christopher goes to play in a controlled scrap heap, boards with nails jutting out, old PVC piping, broken pots and dishes. Rehabilitated felons, who sing and strut about their experiences, run an improvisational tap dance course in the East Village. I have the kids in kickboxing and wrestling and chess and theater and therapy for Gus and a math tutor for Iliza. But am I doing enough? Are other parents gaining a leg up on me while I stand in the lobby insulting what's-her-name?

"Remedial Candy Land has proven benefits. Why are you smiling? Stop doing that. I'll have you reported."

Here come the worthy: lacrosse players, cellists, softball moms, banker dads, the honor students, the faculty, all of us parading forth. I enjoy my perch near security since everyone must pass, front row to our faux affection. We are a juggernaut of shared sanitizer and sunscreen and moisturizer, half-consumed water bottles, leftover spittle on bronzed cheeks, of collagen-infused lips colliding with perfect skin, of useless selfies of a random morning, of darlings and sweeties, of promises of Hamptons and cocktails. All the moms touch and kiss when they converse, the dads shake hands and bump fists and rub necks, collaborative foreplay.

I pick up a few juicy morsels. The committee announced the first child selected for the ECI program on the Gopa website this morning, a boy by the name of Rory Stokes. His father is Iranian, a supermarket billionaire who donated funds for the library—not that Rory did not earn the selection on his own merit. His mother, Vichian, who friends fondly refer to as "Vicious," is complaining to other mothers about the media vans and the buildup in the lobby and the fact that there has not been an official verbal announcement about her son's designation.

"He was the first selected," Vicious complains loudly. She's Malaysian, or Vietnamese, a beauty pageant winner of a forgotten geography lesson who does not wish to be lumped into an ethnic designation. "Am I just being bitchy or isn't it important?"

It is important, the other moms confirm, kissing and handling her, because we are all frightened of the size of her lips and the rumors from the nanny chain that she once pitched a delivery boy down her front stoop for staring too long at her large feet. The nanny chain embellishes. It is important, we reason without discussing it, because her husband purchased their shitty kid a spot in the ECI program, which means there are only seventeen spots left for children without supermarket moguls in the family tree. Vicious is a customer of Russ Haverly, weekly deliveries of barbiturates and marijuana that billionaire moms are not supposed to possess. His absence is having similar effects for Vicious that I, too, am experiencing: night sweats, bad moods, perpetual hangovers—she probably does not get the painful erections. She wears dark glasses and her normally glowing skin seems patchy. There are many parents, I notice from the security lounge, suffering from lacrosse coach withdrawal.

The bunnies are a minor theme this morning, a new one born with oversized ears, pictures of the adorable critter on the Gopa website. But what the pictures do not show is that the bunny is too weak to pull its ears around and it just sits in the corner, waiting to be photographed or euthanized. The ears smell faintly of rotten basil and feces, and the one child who held it cannot seem to get the smell off her hands. Daily, a half dozen rabbits succumb to birth defects, but because we have not dealt with the problem, an additional half dozen new rabbits are born each week. The birth rate is worsening as we stand around discussing the politics.

I contemplate all this while staring at my reflection in the window; slight shadows to my creatures that I know are there, passengers who would like a turn at the wheel. A new problem drifts into the gateway. There has been a terrible accident, a man bleeding from his forehead and arm, his raincoat badly torn, the black RH patch intact. I stare at his wounds, the patch, neglecting to identify the victim who I would like to tell—it is not going to rain today.

Ray McClutchen sports a worried scowl, the trike hanging over his parka. The Jays are suddenly in my quarantined sector, as are the Sedlocks and Laura, Gus shaking his head and inspecting the damaged wheel. Clutch is popular with the lacrosse dads and all the mothers who read his self-help nonsense. A huge gust of "what happened" and "get him a towel" is made over these injuries that the nanny chain claims are a product of a car-bicycle fender bender.

"It was no accident," Ray tells security. "I keep my bikes in pristine condition."

Because of the third wheel, the proper designation is tricycle, though Ray never mentions this. A back wheel loosened this morning and he veered out of the bike lane into traffic, swiping a vehicle and landing hard against the pavement. He watches me. I shake my head and cross my arms, mime, *What can you do?* I cannot stop smiling. My erection is doomed to join the morning.

"Someone tampered with my bicycle," he says. "Pisser, you were outside this morning. Did you see anyone?"

My neighbors are aware I am sleeping outdoors. Everyone awaits my explanation. Jackson and Jay were also hunting for their naked daughter this morning, so we all know who was present. "It's a tricycle, Ray."

"Beg your pardon?"

"Stop begging." I put a hand on his shoulder to explain. "You said someone tampered with your bicycle. It's not a bike. It's a tricycle."

Ray is not his usual positive, noncombative self, the gash in his forehead having scabbed. A school nurse works balm into the wound. "It's an urban trike, Pisser. I'm asking if you saw anyone this morning who shouldn't have been there."

I examine the trike, savages chortling inside, strange arrogance as I watch the blood. "A grown man on a tricycle, Ray." I click my dry tongue too many times. "You need to start taking the shuttle with the rest of the adults."

Nine Out Of Ten Demographics Are Not Your Demographic

THERE ARE MORE PEOPLE at the Channel Fourteen offices than usual this morning. Whitman is in the control room with Charles Kreb, the news anchor, who is doing his first show in twenty years without his desk mate, Allison Lovato. He will be joined by Emcee Dough, a barely nubile hip-hop artist who will be rapping about the Syrian refugee crisis, stock fatigue, and ninety thousand gallons of oil that spilled in the Gulf of Mexico earlier this week. Everyone seems excited about the new format except for the traffic reporter, Melanie Trotter, who climbs out of the makeup chair and falls into my arms.

"It's awful, just awful." She means the departure of Allison, but it drifts into a complaint about Whitman and millennial creatures. Melanie has been weepy for weeks, and this morning makes it impossible to get her makeup correct. The smudged mascara and red eyes are the perfect look for a traffic reporter, the emotions of anyone stuck in gridlock.

I tell her everything will be okay even though I know a truck carrying mannequin parts jackknifed on the BQE causing mass confusion about fatalities, and everyone will blame Melanie when it turns out to be fiberglass. Even though I see Whitman and Lustfizzle more each day, the way they hover over the decaf coffee and green mint tea and fruit bars, and nod victoriously as they greet each other. I do not want to despise the youth movement of our organization. I accept that they are smart and energized and all types of witty. But it is the terminal optimism that shards me, the perpetual Kumbaya-ness of their message, a satirical renaissance they hope to deliver to smart phones with each digital breath. And while rapping the news might be savvy and fresh, I believe news is serious and dire and should be spoken not sung.

I fist bump Whitman and two others I have never met and take a call on my cell phone, Bill Chuck, the head of Slancy's security. One of my neighbors filed a complaint this morning, claiming I tampered with his bicycle.

"It's a tricycle, Bill. Not a bicycle."

Bill sighs. "Yeah, I know. He sent pictures. Just protocol that I have to interview the accused. You don't know anything about it then?"

"Grown men shouldn't ride tricycles. It's a traffic hazard to drivers. I can put the traffic reporter on to explain." My other pocket buzzes, Tug's phone. Melanie weeps loudly while a transgender kid fixes her hair. "And I'm busy, Bill. I can't be bothered every time some nitwit falls off a bicycle."

"A tricycle you mean." We do not laugh, but we both like it. "Sorry to trouble you, Tom. Last thing. You heard about the boat?"

"I did."

"Anything more you can tell Misch, probably help down the road. Not that I think you had anything to do with it. Just that people talk."

My pocket buzzes and Whitman waves and Melanie howls. I am vaguely aware something important is happening around me as I lean into the phone. "Something I heard the other day," I say. "Russ Haverly. Might have been dealing drugs at the school."

"No shit?" This excites Bill who has a bland job watching security cameras. Drugs and murder he remembers from his precinct days. "What do you got?"

"Mothers. Nannies. I don't know much, just something I heard. You didn't get it from me."

We hang up. I answer the other phone, Angela from VillageShop, raspy and impatient. She has a new list of items that were ordered on Tug's phone and sent to the Hendersons: a power saw, a termite colony, some ibuprofen, a bicycle repair kit.

"You sound sick," I say.

"Picked up the flu. It's going around." We've lost the playful banter. "Do you own a bicycle, Mister Reynolds?"

I do own a bicycle. I just have no idea where it is. "What's this about?"

"The bicycle kit you had delivered to the address. It's near the house of a member of a VillageShop school community who was injured in a bike accident this morning."

It was not a bike accident. It was an urban trike accident. "Was anyone hurt?"

"A bit, yes." Whitman and the others are trying to get my attention, a raucous across the room. "It could have been serious. We need to meet," she says.

"I'm afraid I have to run, Angela."

"How's tonight work?"

"Not good."

"Your place after dark."

"No, that won't work at all." Why would she even suggest my home? Do minimum wage retail employees make house calls? Things are strange enough without my VillageShop representative wandering around the backyard. "I'm afraid you've got the wrong idea."

Angela raises her voice. The distraction across the room perseveres into my realm. "I know who you are," she says. "I know where you live, Tom."

I want to be stunned but there is no time. A strange phenomenon has enveloped the Channel Fourteen newsroom. When I reach the epicenter, Whitman and the others smile and encourage me to step forward to the source of the disruption. She is introduced as Penelope Garcia, my new weather assistant, and this is how I know my career is nearly complete. Penelope is clothed in a pink dress so tight it holds her remarkable breasts and buttocks perfectly still, a pose learned from a pageant or runway. Regardless if she read me last year's weather or the wrong answers to tomorrow's crossword, I would hang onto every syllable, as will our viewers, morning therapy before the workday. Worse, she poses in front of my weather center that has unironically been renamed, in neon blue letters, THE PISSER REPORT.

"What do you think?" Whitman asks. Everyone waits for my response as though this Columbian woman is a gift for me, new golf clubs, a handsome washer-dryer combo. She is, in a way, a retirement gift.

"The girl or the sign?"

"I'm Penelope Garcia," she says in perfect pitch.

"Everything." Whitman ushers me onto the stage. "See, Pisser, the weather is changing. Strange patterns, dire expectations, events with no historical basis, end of times. You dig?"

"I should mention I've correctly predicted the weather for thirty-eight straight days. I'm sure if we checked it would be some kind of record."

Whitman waves it off. "No one watches our weather report. Besides, I'm not talking about accuracy. I'm talking about shaking things up. Making the weather an event."

"An event," I say, staring at the sign with my nickname. "It seems vulgar for a news segment."

"Pisser is a colloquialism for a rainy day."

"As in, 'It's a real pisser out there,'" someone adds.

"That's one of your catchphrases. She won't be able to use any of your catchphrases," Whitman says, reassuring me.

"I'm Penelope Garcia," she reminds me.

"Twenty-nine percent of our viewership is Hispanic," Whitman says. "With her background and your predictions, this will be the go-to place for weather events."

"Hispanics." I slap him on his weenie back and try to contain my hatred of my own evolution, that Whitman and Penelope and all of them will forget about me moments after I depart. They do not need me. They need and want this twenty-two-year-old reading cue cards of weather patterns plagiarized from more knowledgeable reporters, posing in front of a graphical map of Manhattan. Melanie weeps inconsolably, which means we'll be delaying the traffic report again. Whitman offers a sympathetic hand on my shoulder that feels suspicious.

"I'm excited, Whitman," I say, clapping my hands. "Let's really shake things up."

Here Comes The Fan Club

I ENJOY CHECKING THE mail, the domestic coordination of a synchronized world knowing where I exist and conjuring the mechanics to communicate my participation in global debt and retail discounts. Today is an exception. There are several bills, including a past due notice from Devin Brenner who is charging me to oversee the Cooperative Marriage, along with an informal letter from Duffy O'Neal letting me know a formal letter is due to arrive. The informal letter is meant to be friendly. The formal letter will contain the same language and will be signed by my neighbors. This is the homeowners association's first step in ousting my family from Slancy's gated inclusion. It could go the other way, the friendly letter points out, if I maintain a low profile, make amends for my transgressions, and get rid of the feral cat.

In the past few days, Clint Eastwood has widened his patrol staking out the Jays' yard to the north, the Hendersons to the south, and making a sand trap on the seventh fairway its official litter box. He attacked a female golfer who landed her second shot in his shithole. He scratched up a foursome of bankers. He went after the Murphys' nanny who doused the cat with pepper spray she was saving to ward off perverts. I owe the Murphys a canister of rape spray, which comes in a convenient package of four at VillageShop. Overall, the chipmunk epidemic has improved, though I fished two bodies out earlier this week and one of the light fixtures was destroyed.

Laura wants to fight about the informal letter along with a comment I made that I am halting use of toiletries, specifically shampoo and deodorant. I convince her that we should hold off on the fight, outlying a three-point plan for how this disagreement should proceed. Otherwise, we will duplicate our squabble—once for the informal letter, again for the formal letter. She is furious with this agenda and initiates a fight about my miscomprehension of the letter's importance. Technically, we are fighting about my approach to the impending fight, though I think it is all the same fight, and for good measure I let fly Penelope Garcia and Lustfizzle and whether or not I will have a job to pay for the lawyers if our homeowner dispute continues. This turns into an argument about responsibility and marriage, and eventually bickering over what we are fighting about, which proves my point—that we should have waited to have one, defining fight.

Laura, exasperated, retires to the bedroom with a glass of wine. I take the bottle to the backyard, light a fire, and shake out one of the last six Luderica that I wash down with the Bordeaux. I am aware there is someone sitting in my chilly yard near the shed, watching me work the fire pit. Once settled, I discover Josey Mateo, the Gopa secretary with the inked out skin who volunteers with the drama department. It takes a moment to click. My VillageShop representative, Angela, who threatened to visit this evening.

Josey holds my cat and strokes the mangy fur. "Tug."

"Angela."

She carries her chair closer to the fire. Josey is Dominican, her brown skin speckled with ink drawings of animal totems she composes in bathroom mirrors. Rumor from the nannies and theater parents is that she has a mental tic that incites the animal drawings when she experiences anxiety. Despite the hobby, she is known as an organized and digitally sophisticated employee, and a sufficient addition to Gopa's administration, which is forever floundering under the caustic expectations of private school parents. As an afterschool volunteer, she has been a strong supporter of *Our Town*, especially Iliza who has relied on Josey's feedback this spring. It does not hurt that Josey has a crush on me, which has permitted me stray conversations to learn the things my daughter refuses to relay.

She sneezes. "Just a cold going around school."

"I already had it."

"You're lucky the cat is alive. If you harmed it, I would have handled you differently." She extends a hand. I offer the bottle. "So what *did* happen to your nanny, Mister Pistilini?"

"I didn't kill her. Don't believe the rumors."

"I heard she was stealing from you."

"She might have been."

"So you killed her."

"I didn't kill her," I say, snatching the bottle. "At least, not that I remember."

She rubs the cat. "A white, yuppie, private school shithead like you—if there was even a chance you did it, the police would have nailed you for sure. Dealing with rapists and meth heads all day, you'd be a white whale. The fact you are not in prison proves your innocence."

"How can you be sure?"

The ink drawings climb across her skin to pursue my eyes, her animals staring into my own primitive chambers. "Because you're a good person. A good father. You want to do the right thing, even when the right thing seems impossible. The best weatherman in the whole city, nearly forty days perfect."

"Thank you."

"I know everything." She shifts closer until I smell the rank of my unwashed cat, myself, Josey's illness. "I know about your shopping habits. I know about your marriage. I know about Moveable Museums." She reaches for the bottle. "We have some things to discuss, Mister Pistilini."

"Call me Tom."

I should not trust her. I signed a confidentiality agreement. The way the nannies would spread the gossip and distort even the unforgiveable aspects make it a necessity our news does not get out before it is time. But as I sit near her, the inky specks of morphed animation, there is a symbiosis, her inscriptions and my chemical tribe. I am certain I will tell Josey Mateo everything I know about Moveable Museums, about my marriage and children, about the cat and the chipmunks and Ray McClutchen's tricycle, which I do not recall tinkering with but probably did.

She rubs the fur, cat fast asleep. "What's the cat's real name?"

"Clint Eastwood. Like I told you."

Josey's attention drifts into the trees. "Clint Eastwood is pregnant."

Part Two

A Walk Down Murder Lane

ON JUNE 23, 1986, Kenneth William Walls walked into his place of employment, the US post office in Mirth, New Jersey, and gunned down seventeen employees before turning the weapon on himself. Known as pleasant and soft-spoken Kenny to his colleagues, he was the furthest thing from a madman, right up until the shooting. Afterward, news shows dispatched reporters to Mirth to speak to the townsfolk, each time another neighbor or colleague or long lost cousin coming forward with innuendo that the signs were there all along.

Forgotten in the annals of mass shootings in the United States, "Going Postal" was the phrase that office workers feared in the late eighties. It was not the angry, bossy, irreverent colleagues that were the concern, rather, the quiet ones, the heartbroken, the slump-shouldered weaklings who came to work each morning for thirty years, going about their routines, allowing the rage to build until it exploded in irrational whodunit.

Mirth is a landlocked town of 2,500 residents, fourteen miles to the nearest lake, and twenty-two miles from Slancy. People never leave Mirth. They are born there and live out their days remembering the massacre of Eighty-Six. Three decades later, everyone has a story.

Everyone is connected to someone who was there, or knew someone who was there, or can relay a lucid account of what contributed to Kenny Walls' uprising.

Harry suggested at least one member of each family should attend. I take off the day, as does Jackson, and we load a bus along with the Sedlocks and Olivia and head for Mirth. A young man who looks like a miniature version of Tom Petty is our tour guide. He pops up as the bus rolls across the town line and does not stop talking for two hours. We visit the old post office, now a fenced-off memorial that gets mowed weekly and painted every five years. We wander the property, blood and gore removed. The guide talks us through how Walls entered that day, his cubbyhole, where each victim met their end. He points out scratch marks at the base of a door that the carpenters neglected to conceal. We drive to the high school Kenny attended. We meet old neighbors. We ask unrehearsed questions to Vernon Shaw, who probably has a career and family and identity, but is known in Mirth as Kenny Walls' bowling partner, and that is who he is. Vernon answers kindly, thoughtfully, telling stories about Kenny that make him seem so human even thirty years later we cannot believe he was capable of the crime. "Used to buy chips and grape soda from the vending machine on bowling night. Not much of a drinker, Kenny."

We load the bus and drive to 17 Hickory Lane, Kenny Walls' home, where his widow still resides. She invites us in for a look at his room, his "stuff" still in the basement that brings to mind the hoarded junk of a teenager—baseball cards, train sets, a poster of Elvira, a mild fascination with outer space. Tina, the widow, sits with us for thirty minutes and snaps off one-liners about her notoriety that was never sought but now has become her retirement fund. I believe Harry paid her just enough to keep her hands from shaking for a day, a back counter littered with empties. Jackson slips a few bills onto the counter when we leave.

On the bus back, we contemplate the hell we just toured. Harry is on his feet, fidgeting, calling for feedback. Olivia's accent has grown hazy from the excitement. Allie sits next to me rubbing my thigh, not any sexual attraction but a diverse hysteria that she does not know what to do with her hands. It really *was* an intriguing tour and we can all sense the good fortune coming our way. This is how we pay for colleges and mortgages. This is how we expand our pancake business. This is how we make marriage work.

"What do we think?" Harry says. "The widow? Too much, or does she play."

"I thought she was excellent," Olivia says. "So believable."

"That's because she's the real widow," Harry says. "And now an employee of Moveable Enterprises. And the length? We need to trim it back to ninety minutes. Was Stephen too long?" Stephen is the Tom Petty doppelganger who is sound asleep.

"Stephen displayed such energy," Olivia says. "The length was excellent."

"I believe it could use a shortening," Jackson says. "Especially for older clients. Can't be on their feet that long. But otherwise excellent."

"Excellent point," Harry says. This is called workshopping, he explains.

Everything is excellent, Allie is talking so quickly I am slightly aroused at how pleasant it must be to live with someone like this, a bus ride summoning the emotions of a wet, horny teenager. I am certain the Sedlocks will return to Slancy and disappear into their perfect house to fuck like life-sentenced felons before the kids arrive from school, and then Harry will whiteboard our feedback over a bottle of Chardonnay. I pop a Luderica to extinguish the mental sadness, a cathartic eclipse that something dark and perplexing has passed between my neighbors and me.

There are various tours and price points. Harry explains the complicated algorithm. Moveable will begin the regional expedition at a hardware store in Midtown, where four people lost their lives, stopping at a shopping mall in Staten Island, the post office in Mirth, New Jersey, and capping the day with the crown jewel, the Sandy Hook massacre in Newtown, Connecticut, where twenty-seven people died.

We will run six tours a day for starters. In the first year, a second route will be added, the Premier Route, which will cover mass shootings along the Eastern seaboard—from Binghamton, New York, to Sandy Hook, to the intriguing murder of five Amish girls in West Nickel Mines, Pennsylvania, to Virginia Tech where thirty-two people were killed. There are three-, five-, and seven-day options, with stopovers at great shopping and food. There will also be a national tour for diehards who can afford to spend eight weeks on the road, crossing the United States, visiting sights, drinking craft beers, stopping by places like Columbine, Orlando, Parkland, Las Vegas, and Oklahoma City, and snapping selfies of our national conscience.

How To Create A Standcake

PLACE THE NONALLERGENIC, GLUTEN-FREE ingredients in a bowl. Mix thoroughly. Cook the pancakes. Let them cool. Place one on a flat surface. Roll loosely until it is about an inch in diameter. The little pancake person should not be too fat, thus disrespectful to obese customers, or too thin, in which case it will not stand properly. The proper thickness is roughly the distance of the top half of the thumb.

Once rolled, place the pancake into a Standcake holder, which come in two, six, and twelve hole sizes. Push the pancake person in firmly so it does not unravel, but not so hard that it crushes the pancake "legs." Pancakes can be decorated in one of 1,400 possible scenarios (see the Standcake manual for instructions) using the fruit-based frosting (see manual for recipe).

Do not deviate from the instructions. Even a small misstep will result in listless pancake people, hunched over so they cannot be decorated. This process was developed by a man and wife over the course of two years, during which they sacrificed social lives and marital commitments to transform the basic element of a comfort food breakfast into a trendy, edgy snack that can be consumed at any time of the day by children, ensuring parents will not feel guilty about feeding their kids junk food. Also great for birthdays, weddings, and bar/bat mitzvahs.

Some Kind Of Record

A COURIER ARRIVES AT the Channel Fourteen newsroom with a package. Inside is a lone lacrosse ball. This follows a similar incident from a week earlier in which a parcel was left incorrectly at the Hendersons, and again at the Jays, Jackson opening it to reveal another of the round projectiles. He delivered it to my backyard to find my Jacuzzi littered with beer bottles and cigarette butts, issuing me a terse lecture about responsibility and feuds and how I need to get my pill consumption under control, which I have cut back on, mostly because my stock is running low. I suppose I did not expect Toby Dalton to go away quietly after I strangled him in the bathroom. It feels like an organized assault as opposed to lone intimidation by one insignificant teenaged miscreant. Perhaps he has engaged the entire lacrosse team in our dispute, taking away from valuable practice time, and that I, Tom Pistilini, might be the most fearsome competition the Gopa Worthy face all season. I contemplate the complexity of youth athletics on the Sunday morning I arrive from the backyard to find the letter on the counter, the homeowners association having made good on its promise.

Laura has read the first of what will be ten official letters, a legal technicality, signed by our neighbors and fellow barbecue patrons, detailing my offenses. The feral cat. The backyard landscaping for which I did not ask for, or receive, approval from the homeowners association planning board. The designer chipmunks native to Slancy, their nut allergies, and my purposely poisoning them with gallon-sized jugs from VillageShop. For each chipmunk corpse found near my property going forward, I will be fined $1,000. The association is sending Head of Security Bill Chuck to confiscate the BB gun, which is not illegal though I was seen brandishing it at a nearby residence by several witnesses. The letter does not mention the crossbow, the power saw, or the arsenal of BB guns still in the packaging I have hidden in the shed. It does not point out that I have been wandering my neighbors' yards at night, awakening mid-blackout on strange porches, fairways, the East Bridge. Nor does it reference the savages clawing their way into all of our futures. It is my task to remove the cat within thirty days. After that it will be removed by force.

"Don't you see, Laura?" I am guilty of every infraction the letter outlines. My only defense is to make Laura feel she is not seeing the big picture, not understanding the conspiracy afoot.

"We could lose the house, Tom."

"We're not going to lose the house."

"We could lose the business."

"We'll hire a lawyer," I say. "We'll fight these accusations."

She swings the letter around until it gets caught in a gust of exhaustion. The edges make crackling noises that trigger my playful button, and I suppress a painful smile. My indictment is a paper airplane zooming through our kitchen; the only thing missing is the sound of a pretend engine from Laura's mouth.

"Everything in the letter is true. We don't have money for a nanny. How can we afford a lawyer?"

Laura is right, of course. We own the land and pay the mortgage, but at any time the homeowners association can vote to rescind our access to the gated community. We would be paying for property we are not permitted to use, a situation we could fight, but it would be expensive. It happened to the Parkers two years earlier. Regardless that his yard was not zoned for it, Tim Parker was building a helicopter landing in his backyard to improve his commute into the city. They voted out the Parkers and turned the property into a driving range. I know there are plans to expand the golf course, and the positioning of my land would give them an eighth hole, one away from relevancy. Everyone on this island, including Laura and myself, adore regulation, the idea that while we cannot control the world, we can regulate our slice of it in Slancy.

The bigger concern is Standcake, our ethical pancake business that has blossomed into *the* trendy dessert—"disruptive dessert," Laura calls it. Everyone loves the pancakes and that they are made from ethical ingredients, by ethical parents, decorated with smoothie syrups and frosting made with real fruit that customers adore. Lawsuits cost money that we need for pancake batter.

"An organized, systematic attack," I say.

"Who is attacking us besides you, Tom?"

"Everyone."

"Who is everyone?"

"You just don't get it, Laura." I rattle off our enemies. "The homeowners. The lacrosse fathers." I grab the letter to show her a name. "Even the McClutchens."

"Don't bring Ray into this." Laura is brilliant, smarter than me. If there were a conspiracy she would sniff it out early. She walks close and looks over my shoulder, guilty in our own home. She's in a ragey whisper that summons an animalistic scurry through my ganglia. I want to tear off her panties with my teeth and let them dangle from a fang while we argue. "I heard a rumor the other day," she whispers.

"You said you didn't want to know."

"I don't want to know." She pauses, thinks. "It's out there, Tom. Pictures of girls."

"Iliza," I say. "From the nannies."

"They don't always get it right."

"No one knows for sure."

We whisper over the counter. This is the closest I have been to my wife in weeks. When she is not busy planning and strategizing, scheduling our lives and returning emails and setting orders, she can be downright cuddly. I want to touch her hand, throw her naked body in the place our children eat their breakfast, cover her in syrup, devour.

A subtle transition back to Gopa mom and business owner. "You could go away again, Tom. Let everything settle. Say you need more time."

"I'm not going anywhere."

"We're in trouble. Why not disappear for a bit?"

"Forty-two."

"What does that mean?"

"It's been forty-two days since I made a faulty weather report."

Hands on hips, trouble. "Are you fucking kidding me?"

"It's some kind of meteorology record. Most people don't even know. Our society has become so complacent in our meteorologists' faulty calculations that we do not hold them accountable, like a shortstop that gets a hit once every four times. So, of course, there is no official body recording how well…"

She is not listening as I rattle off the reasons I cannot disappear to take a second whack at baptizing myself into a friendlier, playful version. I have a chipmunk infestation in the backyard that my pregnant cat cannot handle alone. Despite my resurgence as a weather prognosticator, I am about to lose my job to someone less qualified but possibly perfect to make random guesses about chaotic weather patterns that will impact property owners in the coming years. My son is transitioning into a nanny. My daughter has strayed. My wife has likely moved into the second phase of her affair with the optimistic weenie. I disappear for the darkest moment to imagine human hair and bloodstains and busloads of burning orphans, which is a sign my chemical composition demands another dose of Luderica, which I must conserve. When I return, Laura is weeping.

"I have to get ready," she says.

"For what?"

"Geezus, Tom." She unbuttons her blouse and heads for the stairs. "We have our session with Devin and the McClutchens."

"The marriage cooperative," I say.

"It's a Cooperative Marriage, Tom. Start fucking cooperating."

I am trying to cooperate, to maintain zeal for this diplomatic adultery, but my savages are not. They are there against their will, refugees streaming out of genocidal lands, just like the bunnies caged inside Gopa's elementary science center where the first graders stare dazed at their disreputable anatomy. "I'm not available this evening."

"You promised to try," she says from the stairs.

It feels like one million savages are stabbing pitchforks into my conscience. "This is my trying," I say, but she is gone.

Cut One of Us Do We Not All Bleed?

IN THE BACKYARD, I discover $5,000 in chipmunk parts that Clint Eastwood left near the waterfall. The trees show blossom as a blind world of butterflies and birds, mosquitoes and earthworms practice genocide on each other. Besides the hum of golf carts beyond the junipers and the buzz of the cell phone towers decorated as trees, my backyard paradise is silent. I loathe the cell phone trees. Not that they are most likely weakening our molecular components, allowing radiation to infect us with cancer. But the subliminal meaning that they tie our children's palms to a world we cannot control, all of them streaming Lustfizzle and pornography and instructions of how to build bombs.

I get dressed in my bathing suit but forget to take a dip, the Jacuzzi bubbling as a movie plays overhead. The film is *Vision Quest* starring Matthew Modine as Louden Swain, a high school wrestler who yearns to fight a stronger, more agile opponent. I purchased the movie for Gus hoping to inspire him. Louden is talking to Elmo, the cook, played by J. C. Quinn, who has just taken off a day for the first time in his life to attend Louden's wrestling match when he says,

"I was in the room here one day…watchin' the Mexican channel on TV. I don't know nothin' about Pele. I'm watchin' what this guy can do with a ball and his feet. Next thing I know, he jumps in the air and flips into a somersault and kicks the ball in—upside down and backward…the goddamn goalie never knew what the fuck hit him. Pele gets excited and he rips off his jersey and starts running around the stadium waving it around his head. Everybody's screaming in Spanish. I'm here, sitting alone in my room, and I start crying. That's right, I start crying. Because another human being, a species that I happen to belong to, could kick a ball, and lift himself, and the rest of us sad-assed human beings, up to a better place to be, if only for a minute… Let me tell ya, kid—it was pretty goddamned glorious."

Everyone at the fire pit is weeping. It is just me, alone in the yard, appreciating the touching scene. The pit and all-purpose starter were purchased as a combo item at VillageShop, along with the brick kit that encompasses the structure. I put it together myself, including the pizza oven we never use because we do not dine together, and the space below to store firewood, although I did something wrong with the brick chimney that results in occasional thick, black smoke streaming out of my yard. It's a chilly night and the fire rages, my tent lit on the far side of the lagoon.

Relaxing in the chaise, I open my phone intending to browse the online retailer for some sod and driveway sealer, the members of the Cooperative Marriage pouring drinks and kissing hello in the kitchen. I can hear the house creak and settle, Devin Brenner standing at the backdoor, trying to decide if he should coax me into the living room or leave it be. There are twenty emails from the Gopa website, which means a conversation has sparked an uprising. I click into the site to find the epic blog post that has led to the firestorm. A parent uploaded a document outlining all the offenses, both minor and serious, that members of the junior class have been associated with in their time at Gopa.

Minor offenses of demerits, warnings, detentions, tardy arrivals, forgetting Gopa IDs; infractions such as cigarettes, bullying accusations, using a cell phone during school hours, caught making out in a bathroom stall, fashion that does not conform to the Gopa uniform; more serious issues, behavior that a teacher has to discuss with a principle, parents contacted, suspension considered; extreme issues involving the school's attorney, drug use, fighting, fellatio, bribing a teacher or principle, sneaking off school grounds. This information is recorded by the administration and meant to be private, but here it is, in all its shit-storm glory, for public enjoyment.

It was uploaded by a parent with username Gopa_Sally, a handle I recognize. This is about the ECI program. If parents are planning to drag children through the mud, it should be fair and partial and we should drag *all* the children. Gopa_Sally has removed infractions by members of the lacrosse, rugby, and fencing teams, perhaps thinking the rest of the parents would not notice. The lacrosse players are barbarians. At least one each year is brought up on sexual assault charges that are always dropped in exchange for money. They are constantly bullying students in the lunchroom, spending ample parts of their morning in detention, and running the student lounge like a prison commissary. According to the nanny chain, students can purchase anything from cigarettes to drugs to pornography, all of it run through a meaningless, but slightly dangerous group of adolescent boys.

I do what every rational, obligated parent with an anonymous username would do—I go straight for the comment section, bursting into a rant that runs two thousand words before I hit the maximum limit, a Shakespearean jumble that "we will not live in fear of your princes, not be hectored or tormented by your wallets and attorneys, for our struggle is the struggle of all parents with an eye toward the future, far beyond you who are not even hallow enough to call yourselves our enemy. Our enemy is invisible. Our enemy is called unfairness and brandishes keystrokes from anonymous quarters under the tyranny of good deed and..."

Parents are not up in arms that the document was made public. Most of their children are not implicated. We are enraged that the juniors on the lacrosse team have been excluded from the public shaming, a clear indication that a lacrosse mom is behind the subterfuge. Iliza is guilty of minor points: cell phone use, two stints in detention, the subject of a meeting between administrators that is not outlined. Todd McClutchen, a lacrosse player, is not mentioned. Tungsten Sedlock has also been pardoned as the sister of a lacrosse player. Damian Ferris, the tutor mainly responsible for ensuring much of the lacrosse team is eligible to play, has been listed for fighting and tardiness, arguably the most honorable kid in the school. Rhythm

Ferris has been charged with indecency countless times along with several parent-teacher meetings.

The backdoor opens, Ray McClutchen. "Pisser, you better get in here." They have discovered the same document. We are all in battle mode.

"I'm reading it now," I say.

"Awful, just awful. This type of thing cannot happen."

"Don't interrupt me."

"Okay, good," he says, happy to see I'm on it. "I'll leave you be."

"Close the door, Ray."

I hear trudging through my backyard, broken sticks, a stray foot into my eaves trough that loosens a curse. Jackson moves with the efficiency of blind cattle, tripping on hoses and stray edges of my footpath. The reason I installed the rape lights next to the path was so Jackson would not break his neck en route to my Jacuzzi, which he no longer uses.

He's shouting. "You see it?"

"I'm reading it now."

"Completely out of bounds. You saw what it said about Rhythm?"

Jackson is the closest thing to male companionship that I have, so I cannot tell him that if there are seventeen remaining spots for the ECI program in a class of one hundred fifty students, I do not believe his daughter will be rewarded with one of them. She participates in no sports or clubs, is an average student, and has disrobed multiple times on school grounds, not to mention my backyard. Because the Jays are homosexual and Jason works at the school, I believe they will receive unfair consideration for their child. And because Damian is almost guaranteed a spot, I do not think it fair the twins take up two of the nominations.

The flu is going around. I had it, but it spared Laura and the kids. Jason has it, Damian as well. Jackson is on triple duty with work, parenting, and bed nurse. I pour him a glass of scotch and get him situated on a chaise, Clint Eastwood wandering in from the hill to enjoy our agitation. I watch overhead as Louden Swain tosses an opponent around the mat.

"I appreciate you keeping it quiet about Rhythm," he says.

"It's nothing."

"No, it isn't nothing. Hell, you could have blabbed it all over the school. You're a good man, Pisser."

Though we have not discussed it, Jackson and I are in agreement that we have entered into something sinister with our investment in Moveable Museums, and there does not appear to be an exit strategy. We are aligned in our contempt for the lacrosse team, for all the athletic teams really, and he is well versed in the failures of my marriage, what the presence of Ray McClutchen means to my domicile. I would never say a bad word about Jackson or his children, and I know he views our relationship the same.

"Ridiculous." Jackson leans, the chaise etching forward into the bricks. "Big game this weekend, which means Damian had to stay late tutoring the dumb little fucks. Like a game of lacrosse matters, everyone wearing those stupid arm bands—" He stops himself, remembers Russ Haverly who he never liked but still tolerated. "I'm sorry, that was poor of me."

"It's fine."

"Just the way they treat Damian, like he's there to serve them. The way they treat Jason." He points a big, meaty finger at me. "They've been harassing you, too, Pisser. We should go to the administration."

"We can't do that," I say.

"Why the hell not?"

I do not remind him that I strangled a midfielder on school grounds, or mention that Toby Dalton may have incriminating photos of my daughter. "ECI," I say. "Laura and I don't want to rock the boat."

We listen to each other rant and read the comments on our respective phones, the camaraderie ensuring we do not make rash decisions. The scotch and the fire mellow out Jackson, and we watch the flames disintegrate. It is much later, after midnight but hours from dawn, when I come to inside a treehouse. I cannot decipher from the trees if it belongs to Duffy O'Neal or the McClutchens, the world looking small and identical from fifteen feet in the air. I have a power saw, a drill, a claw-tooth hammer, and a canister that feels empty until I shake it out and several bugs crawl onto the wood and my skin. I hold a towel over the motor to muffle the sound. I am drilling holes into the frame where it attaches to the tree, and shaking the canister into them. I know without question these are termites and, if hungry enough, one strong storm will knock this treehouse to the ground.

    I blacked out again, an issue since I've been conserving the last of my Luderica. I have been gone for hours, evidence of my time away visible on the ground beneath me. I climb down to see what I have foraged. One of the cell phone poles disguised as a tree lies between my feet. It resembles the local junipers, although it is constructed out of resilient polyester, the branches and needles made of urethane and polyethylene, able to withstand winds up to 160 mph. Should a hurricane roar through Slancy, all the houses and trees will be destroyed, but these poles will endure, living on long after the fairways and houses and footpath are gone, totems that the gods we sought failed us.

    There is a handle near the trunk. The cell phone tower is lighter than a tree, though it looks the same, and to residents up at this hour I resemble a Sasquatch lugging firewood across their property. The sensation of heaving something unorthodox feels natural to my muscles, labor I have performed in the not too distant past. Another cell phone tree. A tarp of glass clippings and manure, of dark soil and compost. A human body.

Transgenerational Therapy With Gus

SATURDAY IN MID-APRIL. THE Gopa Worthy warriors are ready to defend our way of life, which means our Gopa boys are heading up the interstate to toss a lacrosse ball back and forth more efficiently, we hope, than the tribe from Darien. Our fleet of SUVs and overpriced hybrids are packed for battle, Gopa bumper stickers and seat cushions and wildly obnoxious picnic fare in purple and white coolers, the Gopa tones as we wait for our boys to run onto the field. "Here come the Worthy!" someone will call, and we will explode with pompous laughter and cowbell zeal and one last run to the coolers as the pride of our youth appears, helmets affixed, two perfect lines, the apex of our endeavors. Deviled eggs with salmon, tiny quiches crammed with duck confit and pork belly, mini blintzes bursting with asparagus and short rib, celery sticks, potato nibblers, kale shooters, champagne cocktails, pancakes dressed as lacrosse players for dessert. The Gopa crew never does hot dogs and beer.

I have a busy day, a reminder of my duties taped to the outside of my tent and, for good measure, also to the backdoor and refrigerator. I need to pick up four trays of Standcakes at the main kitchen in Brooklyn and transport them to Darien for the pregame picnic. Laura provides an assortment of the delicacies for free at each game, which always leads to additional sales. We push the desserts on parents of the opposing team under the guise of sportsmanship—"Go ahead, help yourselves, we have plenty"—when in fact we know they will not be able to resist the health benefits along with the overpriced feature that gives Standcake an exclusive feel.

After the pickup, I will drop a semen sample at the Manhattan Cryobank for reasons that neither Laura nor myself understand. I will drive Gus to his therapy session in Chelsea, followed by wrestling practice, followed by his chess club's tournament against the Highline Academy, also in the city. I'll leave Gus there and pick up Jackson in midtown where he is rehearsing a new score with a Broadway orchestra. We will drive to Darien to drop the pancakes and reconnect with the Slancy side of the picnic, at which point I will head back to the city to catch the end of Gus's chess match. It's best that I steer clear of the lacrosse parents, though critical that I transport the desserts to be shoved into their bitchy mouths.

TILLY SOSA WAS OUR nanny for more than a decade. From Ecuador, or perhaps Chile or Paraguay, she helped Laura and I raise the kids while we both worked. She was an atrocious nanny who never cooked or cleaned or bothered with the laundry and who, in later years, took less of an interest in school gossip. Gus adored her. We kept her on long after the children were old enough, even after her vices became detrimental to our financial existence. Two bad knees required her to pop painkillers like gumdrops, prescriptions we covered, typically washing them down with Chablis we purchased by the case. Unable to do much else, she liked to sit around on her phone—the bill for which we also covered—and order discounted merchandise from VillageShop, charging it to a credit card she opened in Laura's name, and then reselling the take online.

The mortgage, two cars, two children, my shopping addiction made worse by Tilly's side business, Standcake and vans with special trays to hold the batter people upright and personnel, Iliza's acting classes, tutors for Gus, it eventually became apparent that we could not afford the luxury of assisted parenting. Also, the stealing and Chablis had gotten out of hand, not to mention we were the last parents to learn about any juicy gossip. We talked it over with Tilly and promised six months severance. She did not take it well. She went straight to the nanny chain to begin a smear campaign. I found her that afternoon in January, drowned in my red lagoon, the two random blood smears on the deck. Cause of death was the most obvious conclusion—two empty bottles of wine, the buckets of revenge dye, an inadvertent collision with the pavement.

"She's dead because I don't know algebra," Gus has concluded.

We do this in Devin Brenner's waiting room every other Saturday. Gus is convinced that the expense of his algebra tutor cut into our childcare budget, and we had to fire Tilly to make ends meet. Never mind she had been thieving from us for years. If he knew algebra, he reasons, we would not have felt the financial strain and fired Tilly, and she would not have had the accident, revenge dyeing my lagoon.

"Gusser, not today. Tilly wasn't your fault. Accidents happen."

"We're an interconnected system of decisions and results. Every thought and action has a repercussion."

It sounds like Ray McClutchen dribble. "If anyone is to blame it's me. I made the decision to let Tilly go."

"You're the father. You had obligations. Work, house, food. You don't realize it, but you have so little control over our lives." Gus wears a caramel colored sweater, slippers, and a pair of twill pants with an adjustable waistband. "We're in charge of our destinies. I should have cared more about the algebra. But I didn't."

I check my watch and roll my eyes at another father, who reciprocates the eye roll, both of us with our fucked up kids waiting to be told how much it will cost. The healthcare in this country is shameful. Not the doctors and medicine and payment plans, but the waiting rooms. We have reverted to third world bus stations and pioneer caravans, our entire system of efficiency thrown off pandering to esteemed sorcerers. Who does Devin Brenner think he is? If anyone in another career brandished such arrogance, forcing customers to wait, the system would grind to a halt. If I decided to predict the weather on my schedule, I'd be out of a job faster than Whitman is already planning. Yet here I sit, my son dressed like a nanny of nondescript ethnicity, arguing over who killed who.

Nanny withdrawal is a serious issue for a child Gus's age, not only facing the pressures of teenage life, but also moving out of the parental sphere. Throw in a savage death and you get transgenerational twists of the psyche, my son wanting foot baths in the afternoon, tea, constant naps. Thirty minutes we've been sitting here, only nine in the morning, and Devin already backed up two appointments. The frustration overwhelms me and I decide to do his job here in the waiting room.

"Listen, Gus. You need to snap out of this shit."

He looks at me with a mousy innocence, one I used to adore and I now want to slap. We do not slap our elderly in this society when they are slow to comprehend, the therapist has explained, we take them to buffets and buy them motorized carts. It permits old age an entitled sheen, incontinence and arthritic knees preferable to the rat race and pressure, and it saddens me that my boy is conceding. His transgenerational symptoms are a shelter, the therapist advises, or possibly a cocoon that he could come out of any day. But I know there are no guarantees. We do not all enter cocoons and come out butterflies. Some of us stay inside forever. Some of us die in there.

"The sweaters, the stooped posture, the five o'clock bedtimes."

"I'm tired."

"You're not tired, damn it." We are not supposed to shout at Gus. We are never to tell him he's pretending. "You're pretending to be tired."

"That's strange," he says. "I feel tired."

He will not fight me. He knows the best way to win is to let me shout and then wait for the apology. "Every other week I drive you here. The same mopey bullshit, Gus. These appointments take time."

"I enjoy waiting with you."

"They aren't cheap, you know."

"I thought insurance covered it."

"Well, it doesn't." This is a lie. "And money is tight these days."

"Exactly what I said. I killed Tilly because I needed algebra tutoring."

I fidget. I itch my arms until they are raw with welts. I need my drugs which I must conserve until…. I don't know until what. Other parents watch my lack of patience, my antipathy for the broken, my unkindness. But I am being kind. Millicent, Gus's alter ego, is creepy and depressing. This is why he has no friends. This is why teachers do not like him, why parents do not invite him to his peers' birthday celebrations. He embarrasses his sister and causes the Gopa community to look at us with dreaded compassion, as if we brood over a dead child and not just dead help. The wrestling coach has pleaded with me to find a suitable sport. The chess club coach suggested Gus quit, that he does not have the talent or speed to move plastic pieces around a board. Devin Brenner and Gopa administrators want to medicate him out of this phase, Prozac and serotonin and other illustrious chemicals that will dig out his youth from wherever it lurks. Only I know that when you dig for something that is not naturally forthcoming, other emotions surface, things that cannot be shuttered.

I am so irritated with my elderly juvenile, with the state of my boy and his inability to fight, that I shake and sweat, tempted to take his half hour for myself, one on one with Devin. I pop one of my remaining pills in the car.

Fucking Annihilate the Pawns

WRESTLING PRACTICE WAS A joke. We missed warm-ups at the chess meet, Gus insistent on accompanying me to the cryobank to drop off his little sister. "Someday she'll sense it—that her life was our priority on the chore list," he says. I fall in love with him all over. Sharon Li, the mom with the prosthetic leg, stands at the entrance of the gymnasium handing out fliers for her annual gala Limbs for Love. Everyone takes one not because they care, but because she hobbles on the obviously fake leg that makes us feel badly about running away from her. Sharon has an implausible peppiness, an irate happiness that causes me distress, and to look at her is to witness the energy that, as a parent, I am meant to possess. She has a stack of the pages and whether it happens or not, I conclude she avoids handing me one, thus disinviting me to her event.

Despite her faux niceties and handicap, Sharon is a Gopa bully, organizing the other moms to sign a petition asking that Gus be removed from the chess team, a petition she does not think I know about; Josey Mateo tells me everything. Gus is slow at chess, his grades deficient, so that he brings down the team average giving the squad the third-highest GPA of all athletic units, behind boys' fencing and girls' tennis. As if it matters. As if anyone outside of gimpy Sharon and her child Whisper and the other chess nerds too inadequate to play actual sports care about grades. Picking up Gus a few weeks earlier at one of these events, I watched the other kids bullying him, the hypocrisy that a chess dweeb and his pimpled posse turned the tables on oppression and were issuing my son a dressing down for his algebra failures. I let them finish, hoping it might do some good.

I snatch a page from Sharon Li. She has no choice but to choreograph Gopa's patented triple kiss and hand touch, after which we share dabs of sanitizer and small talk.

"Oh, so nice to see you..."

"Tom. Tom Pistilini. Gus's dad." She knows who I am. She has two nannies, one for each of her terrifyingly dull children. I read the fucking weather, forty-eight days without a fail. I matter. "Laura's husband," I say.

She moves in for an affectionate shove of my shoulder to convey a secret, her voice low and dainty, a wild transgression she cannot tell even her own husband who must hate her. "I love those pancakes," she says, winking, the closest we will ever come to fornication. "I can't stop eating them."

"Missus Li. Naughty, naughty." I put a finger to my lips, our secret, you fucking animal you. I tap the paper. "You should get some for your event. I'll have Laura call you."

"That would be essential." A political junkie, Sharon Li knows every angle of the Gopa faithful and has purposefully shunned all of Laura's attempts to get her pancakes in front of a new ethnic populace, knowing it is little advantage to herself. I laugh out loud, thinking it was the prosthetic leg that allowed me to snare her in my trap, wondering if this will earn me favor with Laura. But it is only a mild victory as I realize Sharon Li used the word *essential*, and now my tribe has grasped the letters, unraveling the meaning, the Luderica summoning the creatures who do not appreciate the word *essential*. She did not say yes. She did not commit to purchasing pancakes.

"You know what else is *essential*?" I lean, dry mouth returning, my hot breath in her tiny ear, my stench in her realm, other voices. "That we fucking annihilate these little preppy Highline bastards." I hang on the F in *fucking* so the spit I do have bubbles near my teeth. "That we fucking shove the pawns in their sweaty assholes and let them know who the real chess kings are."

She pulls away, an awkward smile, trying to understand if I am unhinged or if this is how athletic fathers talk. "Yes, it's a rather important match."

"Absolutely essential. Embarrass the little shitholes until they're crying snot bubbles to their mommies. Fucking spirit signs over there, dig? Who puts up spirit signs at a chess match?" I know virtually nothing about chess, nor if the spirit signs belong to our side or theirs. "Make it so...so...so they don't even get any of our pawns. We don't just tap their king. We pick it up and snap off the head, light the plastic corpse on fire, and gather around and sing the Gopa anthem. Slam the board with two fists, yes, check mate, bitch, then kick them"—I actually make a karate kick in the air, which sullies my hamstring—"argh, shit...right at the top of their bony frames so they fall over the back of their chairs. Maybe then the parents get involved in the bleachers and tear the spirit signs into confetti and piss all over them, and piss on the decapitated king so it doesn't cause a fire."

I am sweating, unconscious when I finish, fairly certain from Sharon's facial expression that this time was verbal. I am the cadaver representation of Tom Pistilini, Channel Fourteen weatherman. I am a furious land of starving creatures ready for harvest.

"Whoo! Put it there, Sharon Li." I make her high-five me as other parents quietly stream in, nearly breaking off her tiny limb with the force of my slap, another prosthetic that makes me laugh viciously. I shout a few additional curses, then ball up her flyer and put it in my pocket. "Fuck you, Highland," I say, two middle fingers extended toward the quiet bleachers, sweating. "See you in hell."

I join the chess fathers for warm-ups, kids complaining about the lighting in the gymnasium, that it's too cold, moms arranging inhalers and bottled water and mid-match snacks so they do not pass out at the chessboard. I have friends in this crowd, parents who do not have children on the lacrosse team and who know of my recent altercations. I am somewhat of a cult figure with the fathers, happy to have a near-celebrity in their ranks, though I have not showered in a week and am eventually squared off with a Pakistani father who has his own dental practice and gives me a business card for a half-off whitening procedure.

"Unseasonably warm, piano lessons, poor bunnies, dead bunnies, Gopa this Gopa this, speaking of lacrosse did you catch the website last night, the mom who posted the accusations," the Pakistani father asks me, his accent over-pronounced.

"Oh yes."

"Why in the fuck? Am I correct?"

"Terrible," I recommend. "Dark times at the Gopa Academy."

"Yes, Mister Pisser, well sentiment." He pulls me close, offers himself sanitizer and then me. "It is not just me. Indeed these are dark times. Parents fighting for places in this program."

"It is not just you," and then I add, "sir" because I don't know his name. He's a good dad, a caring protector, his bushy mustache the centerpiece of a friendly face, a friendly world. I like this man. His daughter is Mahjeek or Mahbrude. I know because even in her junior year, she already has scholarship offers from the Ivy's, which possibly adds to her father's contentment.

"These lacrosse parents," he confides. "Out to get us."

This makes me laugh insincerely at my friend's concern, his pompous suggestion that the lacrosse parents even know he exists. I put a hand on his shoulder so he knows he is not alone, leaving a trail of liquid, having forgotten to rub in the sanitizer.

"It's me they're out to get," I say. "Do not worry, my friend. They deserve whatever comes."

Something Good This Way Comes

DECIDING ON THE GOPA mascot was a bareknuckle brawl involving parents, teachers, administrators, coaches, lawyers, and a team of ethicists hired specifically to ensure that no entity would be offended by the moniker. Parents refused to name an animal mascot. Personifying an animal was deemed unethical. Anything weather related, such as the Hurricanes or the Tornadoes or the Gopa Volcanoes, was considered cruel to victims of natural disasters. The Gopa Thunder and Gopa Wind were a few alternatives that made a final list, but they were shot down by the ethicists for being unpredictable. We settled on the Gopa Worthy, a term that denoted principles and high-mindedness and respect. For all the good it did in hiring ethicists and not offending other people, we should have called ourselves the Pampered Elitists or the Uncircumcised Redskins. Other schools despise it. Annual newspaper editorials accuse us of elitism and white privilege, even though white students and parents make up only fifty-seven percent of the Gopa tribe.

It actually is a good description of our school community, depending on the interpretation. We are worthy of one another. We deserve to be aggregated into the same class of people. We want the best for each other, until it might impact our children negatively, and then we want the worst. We are all worthy, but each of us is worthier. We undermine each other. We form cliques and team up against other cliques. We move through life with the chaos of an undefined cellular system, peaceful until a cancerous entity disrupts our ubiquity, our worthiness. Like a family, we share rumors and problems, but never with outsiders, other private school parents, the media. We may sometimes falter in our level of worthiness, but the hope is that we are always worthier than others. I am aware that my quadruple association—with the Gopa Worthy, with the gated community in Slancy, with white skin, with claiming to predict the weather—makes me one of the most defined bastards on the planet.

By the time I pick up Jackson in midtown, my mood is in tatters and I am slightly hallucinating. He is not much better. The rehearsal was a disaster, his newest ensemble littered with musicians hired on the cheap to save money. Neither of us feels worthy.

"As if anyone goes to a Broadway show for the acting," he says. I could not care in the least but I appreciate his rage. A southern man with a love of barbecue, also a homosexual and classical music aficionado, his heterogeneity is why I appreciate America, why I adore living near New York City. I let him complain about his job, about Jason, about the kids and Gopa, even me. "Geezus hell, Pisser, you stink."

"I can roll down a window."

He sniffs the car. "No, it's everywhere. On you, me, the pancakes. When's the last time you showered?"

"I bathed this morning. The Jacuzzi," I remind him. "I'm off deodorant."

"It's unbecoming of a father. What example does it send to our children?"

That we are men, feral to the core, primal in our existence, savages at heart that do not require perfume to conform but rather meat and stain and loin. My savages scream it inside my head. I do not say this aloud. Instead, "Maybe you're right. Sorry about that, Jackson."

"Eh, ignore me. I'm in a bastard mood."

We barely listen to each other's grievances, both nodding and accepting imperfection, anything so we do not have to discuss Moveable Museums and our complicity in what will define our children's college education, their inheritance, our retirement lifestyle for years.

"Jason's still down with the flu. Everyone has it. Several members of the lacrosse team, from what I understand."

"That Sharon Li is a witch. A real witch."

"Not sure Rhythm has the grades."

"I bet she has a vanity license plate on all three cars."

"The grades. Everyone cares about the grades. What about the heart? What about Rhythm being a good human being?"

"I have to be better in bed than Ray. Clutch my ass. I bet he's more encouraging, but I have to be all-around better, more perverted, willing to take risks."

"It's not like we're made of money."

"I killed Russ Haverly. The nanny too maybe. Can't prove it, but I did."

"There's something about Spain this time of year. We can't just pull the kids out of school, but I could use the break. From work. From Jason. I love him, but fucksake, he's so tightly strung."

This marks the first time Jackson has opened up to me about the rumors, trouble in their marriage. Their physical appearance could not be more different, Jackson a large man with a deep, baritone voice, Jason thin and bony, effeminate, classically gay. I know Jason does not care for me. The only thing we share in common is that dogs hate us. But I want Jason to like me, and I want Jackson to know it.

We exit from the Henry Hudson Parkway and merge onto the interstate, which gives us nearly an hour to bond, each other's therapy animal. I enjoy speaking to my friend about his problems to take my mind off my own.

"Things okay with you two?"

He shrugs. "We have our issues."

"You can talk to me if you like."

"I appreciate that, Pisser." He shifts to look at me. "It's just marriage stuff. Raising kids. The pressure of...everything."

"I get it." And I do.

"I don't want to change Jason. I just wish he were more..."

"Hard?"

"Not hard."

"More masculine, I mean."

"I'm about to throw you out of this car," he says, repositioning his large frame in the seat. "I wish he wasn't so scared. Of every goddamned thing we encounter."

"Scared," I say. "Like the way he is with dogs."

"Shit, I know you heard. Everyone heard."

"Rumors, mostly." I know the gossip. As we travel north on the interstate, just me and this giant man, the dog issue suddenly seems momentous to progress. "Go on, tell it."

Jackson sighs, shrugs. "School event two years ago. He was chaperoning a field trip to the Met and a dog came out of nowhere. Barking, yapping, something wrong with it maybe. The owner wasn't around. Scaring the kids."

I put the car in cruise control and lean back to enjoy the sound of my neighbor's marital hardships.

"Kids screaming, crying, running away, which upsets the dog more. As the chaperone, Jason instinctively gets between them, trying to scare it off."

"I didn't know about this."

He watches the side of my head as I drive. "Something you should know about him, Pisser. Don't ever fuck with Jason. I know he comes off a bit soft. But if you're ever in a confrontation, give up early. Just put up your hands and concede. He's a slapper, a scratcher, a gouger, dirty little motherfucker."

A bus veers into my line and I react, repositioning the car. "So what happened?"

He exhales deeply. "Dog jumps on top of him and Jason hollers for the kids to run. It's biting him and he knows he's in trouble, so he rolls over to cover his head. That's when it happened."

"What happened?"

"Dog started humping him."

The stress of the morning, along with the bus in my blind spot, has thrown my concentration. I misunderstand the story. "Jason was raped by a dog?"

"No, damn it, Pisser." He sighs out the window and continues. "It just looked like it. And you think all those kids he put his life on the line to save ran for safety? Nah, they didn't. They took out their phones to record it."

"Fucking cameras everywhere."

"Most of the videos were deleted, but one or two still exist. Jason talks about it all the time. He wakes up in the night reliving it, but mostly he knows—one of those little fuckers has video. Really shook him up, as you can imagine."

"No wonder he hates dogs," I say.

Something strange has occurred since we began our therapy chat. The bus that nearly ran us off the road several miles earlier is now in front of us, a rented motor coach with Gopa Worthy insignia in several windows. The bus is carrying the lacrosse equipment which usually follows the team bus. There is no sign of the team, which would have arrived in Darien an hour ago for preparation. This bus is lost or had a flat or possibly a mechanical failure. Certainly something is wrong as I inch closer.

"What are you doing?" Jackson asks.

"Nothing," I say, offended. "What do you mean?"

We follow for several miles at the slower pace, my Subaru Forester close to the tailgate to see inside. The bus driver puts on the turn signal. I put on my turn signal.

"Pisser."

The bus pulls toward the shoulder, a rest stop ahead. I follow, slowing down to give some separation.

"Tom?"

"Maybe there's something wrong. We should check it out."

"What are you up to?"

"What am I up to?" I repeat, shouting, but genuinely interested in the answer. Jackson sighs, shakes his big head. "We are Gopa parents. We have a responsibility to the team to make sure this bus reaches its destination."

At the fork where the cars separate from the trucks, the bus veers right. We go left and park in the center of the lot. The bus lurches to a stop and the driver bolts out the door, a stream of vomit onto the pavement as he heaves loudly.

"The flu," Jackson says. "Everyone has it."

I check the time and then the parking lot. "He's running late. He's separated from the lead bus." The flu has been going around Gopa, and in a brief session of clarity, I see beauty in the transfer of the ailment. I had it the morning I strangled Toby, passed it around to several of the gaping parents in the restroom, to Jackson's brood and Josey, and eventually to this bus driver, the interconnectedness of the universe that Gus mentioned earlier. I get out and check the parking lot again to see if I recognize any parents. No Gopa bumper stickers. "He's all by himself."

Jackson watches me. "What are we doing, Tom?"

"I don't know." Back inside, I close the door and take a moment to consider, Jackson considering me from the passenger seat. "What are we doing, Jackson?"

The bus driver removes a handkerchief and rubs his mouth. Hispanic, in his sixties, I do not recognize him. The Gopa administration loves to keep a balance of minorities on the payroll, which implies investment in the community, goodness, worthy labor practice. He will not lose his job, which somehow matters as I calculate the odds. He begins walking into the rest stop to finish what he's started on the pavement, and I climb out of the car again.

We do not discuss it, but I find myself wishing we would, just so I can plead my case that none of what is about to transpire is premeditated. People do the wrong thing all the time. Hell, myself and Jackson and our neighbors have managed to do the wrong thing regarding Moveable Museums, an ethical bending into which we negotiated our consciences. How can this be categorized differently? The stress of Gopa, of being outsiders, of our children suffering inequities at the hands of the lacrosse machine simply because they do not belong. They tease Damian for teaching them basic mathematics skills. They have implicated my daughter in a way I cannot quite place, though I know it exists. They have used the Gopa website to highlight our flaws. Indirectly, they have caused Jason to step between their brood and a deranged animal, which has infected Jackson's marriage and our level of worthiness on this Saturday. Better that we say nothing. Better that we not talk each other out of it. Besides that, I am not running my machine anymore. To look into my eyes is to see Tom Pistilini, Channel Fourteen meteorologist and father of two, but the savages have taken the reins and are slapping forth my Clydesdales.

"You drive the Subaru," I say.

"This is a bad idea, Pisser."

"So is the prospect of watching those assholes hoist a championship trophy."

"If the keys are gone you get your ass back here." Jackson climbs out of the passenger side and tugs up his pants. I open the backend and grab a putter, our minds in sync. "Watch out for cameras," he says.

"Ten minutes before he figures it out."

"No more than two exits. Find a public place. Another high school, other games, other buses."

"Just don't lose me," I say. For good measure, "Jackson, drive safe. You hit a bump and you'll knock over a bunch of the pancake people."

I dash across the parking lot, an anonymous place where everyone hurries and no one pays attention to hijackings. The bus door is slightly ajar, a camera mounted over the door that points down at the driver's seat. It takes me four whacks to land the winning smash and I climb in to find the bus empty, equipment stacked neatly in rows, medical kits, coolers, duffel bags, cleats, lacrosse sticks. The keys are in the ignition.

I have never driven a bus, although I have ridden one each morning for years, having watched the driver's mechanics, the motion of his shoulders. I am relieved to discover it has automatic transmission. It takes a moment to get the feel of the thing, and while I cannot see anything below me, I manage to pull out of the rest stop without clipping any vehicles. Pedestrians see the giant machine hover toward them and step out of the way, and Jackson navigates the parking lot until he is below me as I pass. I offer a wave. He does not wave back.

On the interstate it hits me in waves, soft flashes across my skin, that I have just stolen a bus. Tom Pistilini is petrified, the creatures undeterred by this world, and we battle over the terrain. I keep the bus at a smooth sixty miles per hour, the Subaru back a quarter mile. I click on the radio to take my mind off the dry mouth, the sweats, the unseemly erection, searching for any station playing Jason Isbell. I cannot concentrate on the road and the radio, and I stop with the buttons once I find a song I recognize. Bob Dylan's kid, the name escapes me, though I enjoyed his music the one time I heard it, his band the expensive entertainment at a Gopa Christmas party. The lyrics are encouraging—*got a good woman by my side, I ain't got much on my mind*—and I roll down the window and blare the music. Here come the Worthy's things. Here come the Worthy's tape and water coolers and destruction. Here come the Worthy's pancakes. A beautiful spring day and two dozen warriors awaiting their armory that will never arrive, the parents nibbling hors d'oeuvres and talking strategy as I shout the only lyrics I recognize at the shuttered streaks of passing cars. *Something good this way comes.*

A Little Rain Must Fall

THE CELL PHONE TOWERS disguised as juniper trees do not burn like normal wood. They contain timber somewhere in the complicated core, a series of polyester and carbonite fixtures that refuse to perish obediently in my pit. They are a nice addition for their aesthetic value. They look like the Yule Logs that burn on television during Christmas, a roaring convulsion to the flames, allowing the regular wood to burn hotter and brighter, a slight blue orneriness to the embers as they tuck peacefully into the beyond. Every so often the cell phone wood gives off the most delightful hisses and twangs, the fiber optics succumbing to the heat, the silica and crystalline sapphires genuflecting to the forces of combustion. There are chemical vapors I cannot see, the collected whispers of my tribe, the calls and texts and emails and photos and shared intensity of our conniptions, and these broken towers continue to transmit even as I heave them on my pyre. My pocket buzzes with Tug's correspondence, the anonymous numbers of people who do not believe the rumors. Tug is gone. Tug is no longer part of the supply chain. I pop one of my final Luderica.

The savages embarked on a reconnaissance mission to find more cell phone trees, swatting down eleven cameras in the process. One cannot just swat at the technology. One must be careful not to enter its vision, the savages creeping on the recorders stealthily and disconnecting the wires, then destroying them with a handheld four-pound sledgehammer that retails for forty-seven dollars. I also ordered some additional razor edged chains from VillageShop, which got the job done, sawing up three cell phone trees the savages have stacked beneath and around the fire pit. It gives the backyard a gorgeous tincture, everyone says so, even my kids who commented on them this afternoon. And the nice thing is that I only have to burn two or three chunks each season, the rest able to stay out all year since the components are immune to the conditions, unlike my real wood that has to be covered with a tarp every winter.

Sunday in April, a day after the latest humiliation in what has been a disappointing campaign for the Gopa Worthy lacrosse team. Their equipment bus lost or stolen, no one clear what happened, assistant coach Hunter Herman begged the Darien side to reschedule. There has been bad blood between the two sides since Gopa stole Russ Haverly from Darien, and the new coach refused. Hunter Herman does not have the clout or blackmail skills of his mentor, and the Worthy were forced to forfeit what would have been a prosperous victory and decent bump up the state rankings. I am told that Doug Whorley and Rhen Sedlock got into a fistfight with Darien supporters as they made their way to the remaining team bus, sore losers, the ride home a series of disgusted accusations about how a bus goes missing. Todd McClutchen was said to be in tears, his father consoling him in the parking lot with packaged wisdom.

The story is all over the news: Channel Fourteen, Lustfizzle, even ESPN did a sardonic clip on what to do when you lose your equipment bus. It was found twelve miles from Darien blending in with other buses near the Shipman Academy, a team Gopa beat by twenty goals earlier this season. Police are calling it a likely prank by private school students, which is the rumor being spread by the nannies. Parents discuss it on the Gopa website, everyone with a theory, even Gus coming out of his nanny swaddle to enjoy the hijinks. We are all in a strange state of schadenfreude and sympathy, even Sharon Li I imagine, apathetically pulling for our Gopa boys with the understanding that they, both parents and athletes, turn into God's little shits every spring when things go well. Humble pie, in the proper serving, does wonders for humanity.

A small band gathers around my cell tower fire sipping a red that Jackson brought, which everyone says is delicious though I cannot taste anything. The lagoon percolates softly, the blue lights offering a seductive glow though none of us are dressed for a dip. Rain clouds pass through, occasionally drizzling us with a precocious mist. Jason Isbell is overhead singing about old lovers and cold nights. The Cooperative Marriage meeting has commenced, my second no-show, though I appreciate the nearness of my wife and potential lover and his wife and their therapist enjoying one another inside our home, not talking about the same topic we do not discuss at the fire pit.

Josey Mateo is quiet, waiting for the others to leave, her skin deranged with fresh markings: a herd of stick mongrels migrating down her neck and arms toward her small breasts. She told me in private she is proud of me even though she would have assisted in planning the thievery more efficiently, had I inquired. She combs out thistles from Clint Eastwood's coat and rubs the heaving belly. Jackson usually hugs me when he arrives, though he neglected to this evening. He is tense, nervous, reminding me to keep my mouth shut. While I might earn a slap on the wrist with the proper legal representation, as a black man the road to purity will be strewn with hardship, not to mention what the Gopa parents will say. He has seen Josey at my fire pit before. Knowing about Ray and Laura, he keeps his opinions to himself. Bill Chuck, Slancy's security chief, stopped by to lodge a feline complaint and accepted a glass of wine. We all thought Bill had come about the bus.

"Took a good chunk out of a golfer's leg today," Bill says.

"What did he do to the cat?" Josey asks.

"She, Miss. And nothing. The cat was sitting on the fourth tee and would not move," Bill says. "Missus Naylor was preparing to tee off and shooed him away."

"Shooed it how? Waving a golf club or hissing or what manner?"

"I imagine that's about right."

"No wonder the cat attacked. Thought it was in danger." Josey sips, rubs, and straightens her glasses. "Golf course. Waste of land."

"I'd agree with that assessment, Miss." Bill points at her lap. "Don't let it wander out of your sight. Feral cats are territorial. It'll attack your cat for sure."

Bill thinks we are talking about a feral animal that is stray and fierce and male, not the oversized kitten, fluffy and pregnant, resting in Josey's lap. He also has not inquired into her identity, a T-shirt on a crisp night, the pen drawings running up and down her chestnut skin so that she appears like every junky Bill had to cuff during his career.

I daydream of sad lacrosse players, their pillows wet from tears, of ruined celebration parties, of athletic scholarships evaporating. Of mothers consoling babies, of fathers consoling each other as they recheck the schedule, wondering where they could squeeze in a rematch with Darien, of angry fingers on dainty keyboards typing their grievances onto the Gopa website. The savages typed an earlier ballad of "lost ships that head to black waters for war and wayfare and never reach their destined coasts and never return to their origins rather drift and bob and soak in haughty seas until they perish in the tide and though a sad day has befallen our lacrosse oarsman do not equate it to the vast tragedies that have ripped heart and hope from our kind through the annals for ours is a gentle ending a peaceful culmination as all the sticks and helmets and pads and coolers returned safely to our shore curbside out front of Gopa." Most parents do not know what to make of it. Several moms flag it as hate speech. The comments are delightful.

"Understand it isn't personal," Bill says.

"It's okay, Bill. I'll see what I can do."

His glass empty, he recognizes it is time to depart. I stand to shake his hand. Jackson left without a goodbye, perhaps assuming I am pursuing sexual relations with the Gopa secretary, exploring her frail and unassuming body in a tent in my backyard. I have never thought of sex with Josey, other than a desire to see if the pen etchings extend over her breasts and flat stomach, down to her pubic bone and inner thighs. The only woman I desire is Laura. I believe Josey continues to return to my backyard because she needs something from me, but it is not sexual in nature.

There is an element between us, an undefined barter that has drifted into the territory of coalition. I have broken my confidentiality agreement and told her about Moveable Museums, the new investment, the school shootings, the money I am due to earn. She was kind enough to not pass judgment, though she disappeared for a week, arriving at my hearth with news of the bus nabbing. She has confided in me as well. The pen drawings help relieve anxiety, a trick taught to her by an ex-boyfriend, Phil. Phil also instructed her in the arts of programming subculture, otherwise known as computer hacking. She and a crew of miscreants refer to themselves as ethical hackers, of which I prod her for detail that she is reluctant to offer.

"We're good enough to hack into Gopa's website, as well as VillageShop, to clean up your mess."

I'm thankful but dubious. "Why would you do that for me?"

"Because you're a good man, Tom. We help good people."

She has secrets, which I admire, and a juiced out laptop on which she can access all the Gopa parents. In addition to deleting the Hendersons' delivery address of orders I placed from Tug's cell phone, she knows all my purchases from VillageShop, both this month and five years ago, how much we spend on tuition, which after-school activities we pushed on the kids, an archive of success and failure. She has passage to the same information for the Sedlocks and McClutchens and Millers and Lis and Tarentellis and Winstons, an encyclopedia of our neuroses and passions.

Josey shares these with me, non sequitur style, and we sit for long stretches staring at the fire mulling the meaning. The Christophers enrolled their son Michael in snow globe assembly because, according to some private testing they paid thousands of dollars to have done, he was slightly deficient in sequencing and urban planning. The Parkers order more granola than any one family can consume. Josey insists they are stockpiling it for end of times, a healthy Armageddon. The Ramuses and Davidsons have their orders shipped to each other's addresses and swap nannies every few months. Josey believes they secretly switched children years earlier. She has all the anonymous handles of parents who post to the Gopa website. For a man obsessed with the site, Josey is better than pornography.

"Did I tell you I'm proud of you?" Someone has not been proud of me in a long time. "And not just the bus. Forty-nine days of perfect weather."

"No one really knows about that."

"They ought to." She types chaotically into the laptop that sits atop a sleeping Clint Eastwood. "If I knew you were planning the bus, I would have gone to the game."

"If I knew I was planning it, I wouldn't have done it."

"To take pictures of appalled moms and shocked dads, wandering the picnic area dazed like survivors of an international tragedy." There are Gopa faculty and parents, similar to Josey, who never played sports and despise the godlike engineering of our social strata. They admire my actions even if they do not post the sentiments on the website. She giggles. "All of them dressed in purple and gold, getting slightly tipsy before the big game."

"The players huddled together," I add, "asking each other how this can happen after all their preparation." I dropped Jackson off but did not stick around for the fallout, just long enough to witness the point when they discovered something was amiss. "Girlfriends weeping in the bleachers, texting friends not there to share the tragedy."

We enjoy the images. My pocket buzzes against the wooden bench. I shift to conceal the noise.

"Why are you still carrying the phone?"

"I'm not really. I'm planning to get rid of it."

"If that was true it would be gone." She sets down the laptop and then Clint Eastwood, who darts for the trees. "Give it to me. I'll destroy it tonight."

I cannot depart with the phone. Whoever Tug Reynolds is, wherever he lives, his existence is entwined with mine. "I'll take care of it. I promise."

"You're stealing from this person, whoever he is. Wasn't that what your nanny was doing to you?"

I forget what Josey knows. "I'm not stealing."

"Two cartons of cigarettes. Four chainsaw chains. A sledgehammer. A Crosshart air pistol with laser site. By my count, you have seven BB guns. Fifty-piece lock-pick set." She pauses to watch the flames crash onto my shores. "What are you planning to do with a lock pick, Tom?"

"I need it around the yard is all."

"To break into your own house?" I do not remember ordering the stuff, but it might come in handy if Ray begins sleeping over and Laura locks the backdoor to prevent me from bashing in his skull with the sledgehammer. "Most buildings now have digital locks, cameras, motion sensors. You can't use tools from VillageShop."

She stands, gathers her bag, readies to leave. She always departs at the same time, always on schedule, the wine glass nearly full, as though calibrating her sips so she does not divulge secrets. I never know where she goes, or how she gets back to the city, if she owns a bike or she walks through Red Hook toward the Brooklyn Bridge. I do not know where home is. She knows so much about me, and I know nothing about her.

"I deleted the order from the account." She puts out her hand. "Give me the phone, Tom. You'll be happy later you did."

Josey is wise, important to me in ways I do not understand, my therapy creature. I hand over the phone, relieved to be free of the burden.

Little Tugger

THERE IS ONE ROAD in Slancy, a giant loop around the perimeter that splits into two paths near the houses and narrows on the eastern side of the island when it wraps the golf course. It is a two-mile loop used mostly for bikers to exercise, with several inclines to get one's heart racing. The McClutchens and Laura, Harry and Allie Sedlock are avid bikers, Allie working those impossible legs past our house twice a day, each morning before dawn and just prior to dusk. It is later on a Tuesday evening when I hear a bicycle that slows as it nears my house. It is Ray and Laura's night out for dinner. I expect Allie Sedlock to arrive in my backyard when Harry appears instead.

"Biking past and saw the fire. Thought I'd say hello."

"I'm glad you did. Something to drink?"

"No, thank you." He holds up his phone. "Trying to take a call from Europe. Can't seem to get a signal. I was biking around, looking for a hotspot."

This is delightful news and I poke the fire, riling a glow that catches Harry's eye. The cell towers look exactly like trees in the darkness, a credit to the manufacturers. I know the answer because I wander Slancy at night. "Seventh hole. The trap just above the green," I say. "Highest elevation in Slancy."

"I'll give it a shot."

Jason Isbell is singing about love songs or fistfights or bliss or strife. I feel like dancing. I have taken a Luderica and have a massive erection, but Harry does not take my advice. He is lying. Harry is not trying to call Europe, where it is the middle of the night. He's come here to see me, alone.

"Terrible thing about Saturday's game," I say. It is all anyone has spoken about. "I imagine Rhen is upset."

"Tougher for the seniors. This is their big year. Rhen's a freshman, so he's got time." Harry sighs. I mimic him with a sigh and a headshake. "All the boys are discouraged. It's been a difficult season. Lots of grownup topics for kids. Russ's disappearance, and now this."

Maybe if Toby Dalton and his teammates and the parents were all-around nicer people, the universe would not be lining up to oppose their championship quest. "Too much for boys," I agree.

He leans conspiratorially. "Your name came up, Pisser."

I already know this from the Gopa message board that parents are aware school security spoke to me about Russ. We men sometimes pretend that we do not care about the gossip, that our masculinity prevents us from setting up anonymous handles to lob barbs at other parents. But I know from Josey Mateo that Harry posts under the name HungryDad, and that he has seen the same accusations I have seen. "How's that?" I ask.

"You were late to the game. Your name came up as a suspect."

I manage the fire and toss the poker, allowing the handmade stainless steel to clang off the rock footpath. I pretend to be appalled at the accusation, hands on my pudgy hips. I have prepared my indignation should anyone mention my involvement, and I have a rock solid alibi. Every minute of my Saturday was filled. I made an impression on the other parents in the therapist's waiting room, spoke to the wrestling coach, a receipt from the Manhattan Cryobank, Sharon Li and the Indian father at the chess meet, retrieved Jackson in midtown, and dropped the pancakes at the pregame picnic. I shook a few hands and spoke briefly to Laura, then was back in the car and at the chess meet in time to see a younger opponent trounce Gus in less than ten minutes. How could I possibly have found time to steal a busload of lacrosse equipment? "I hope you don't think I had anything to do with that."

He waves it off, crosses a leg over his knee. "Nah, of course not. You were late is all. Jackson was with you. I'm not accusing you."

"But someone is."

"Being part of a title team looks good for college, for the ECI program." He waves again, just mentioning it. "Besides, you don't want to get mixed up with the lacrosse dads. Lots of money, lots of rage over Russ. Just putting it on your radar."

It's a nice gesture from my neighbor and investment colleague. We have a lot at stake together. "I appreciate it, Harry."

"Don't mention it." He leans in so I can smell the Clive Christian cologne, see the perfect bounce and part in his hair, no sweat on his brow even though he's been biking. I imagine the Sedlocks get out of the shower and put on fresh clothes and jewelry, makeup and perfume, smelling sexual and presentable to one another before bedtime. "I know you're not pleased with the direction of Moveable Museums, Pisser."

"I have concerns, sure."

"As do Allie and I. But we've come too far to lose our nerve now. We have to stay the course, get this thing over the finish line."

"Yes, but Harry—"

"I need you, Pisser. I need you and Laura to come around. We value your position with Lustfizzle and believe it might do us good. I'm confident if you stick with it, the McClutchens will as well, and Jackson and Jason."

It is nice to be needed by Harry Sedlock, his wingman, a pedestal previously occupied by Russ Haverly. The Luderica has kicked in and my perception is uncanny, each of his movements bearing meaning. The pills allow my tribe to intensely focus on the topic I desire—which should be playfulness—but tonight it is Harry's body language instead. It occurs to me he rarely talks about his missing friend, as if his disappearance is preferable.

"And Russ," I say. "You still think he's a proponent of this investment?"

The name sideswipes him, already thinking of him in the past. "Russ? Sure, of course." The trees and cell phone towers inhale, and the metropolis that glows above our homes shivers irreverently, when it is only Harry Sedlock and me in the world, and we both look into each other's eyes, two mammals who are certain, for the first pure moment, that we are nothing alike, enemies on this orb. "I'm going to confide something to you, Pisser. I'd like to keep it between us. Not even the wives need to know."

"All right, Harry."

He sits back, uncrosses and recrosses his legs boardroom style. "A week or so before he went missing, Russ was out of line with a matter."

"Allie?"

"Nothing like that." He watches the backdoor. "He borrowed money he had not paid back. Which is fine, old friends. But he came around for another loan. And when I told him I couldn't help, he insinuated blackmail."

"Blackmail how?"

Harry shrugs. "Go to the press with Moveable Museums."

"He said that?"

"He didn't say it. He *insinuated* it. Leak out about the new venture. It would have been bad publicity for sure. We would have weathered it." He repositions himself against the fire, watching my face. "But it made an impression. Russ is using again, I'm certain of it. He wasn't thinking straight."

It is this secretiveness that defines our guilt, the crouching out here on Slancy, midnight calls to Europe, cloak and dagger. "We're stakeholders, Harry. You should have told us about Russ."

"I knew he was bluffing. He would never do anything to hurt me. And just like you and Laura were, we were counting on him to get Tungsten into the ECI program. I didn't want to rock the boat."

Were we encouraged by the Sedlocks to elect Russ Haverly as our representative on the ECI committee? I try to reach back for how it happened, but the memory has faded. Laura and I were not counting on him in the way we were counting on years of hard work and extracurricular activities, and one hell of a kid in Iliza.

"Did you tell this to Lieutenant Misch?"

"Of course not. If I said he was using drugs, the administration would fire him for sure."

"They've been asking me questions."

"I heard. Last one to see him alive or something."

"You mean assuming he's dead." I wonder what a handmade stainless steel fire poker would do to that head of hair if smashed repeatedly into Harry's temple. Would his head make a clanging noise or a soft rotten pumpkin *ploof*? I am slightly high from the Luderica and sleeplessness, my mouth dry and heavy, and I am not certain if we are arguing. "I was at the club, one of ten people to last see Russ. I don't have a motive, like being owed money, or trying to keep Russ quiet about controversial investments."

"Pisser, it's nothing like that."

"Harry, did you kill Russ?"

He waves his arms savagely. "More than likely, Russ is sitting in rehab somewhere in Arizona, and he won't resurface until things smooth over. It's happened before." Harry wanders the rock patio, turns his back to the house and watches the woods. "Something about Russ not a lot of people know. We grew up on the same street. He went to college with my little brother, longtime friend of the family. But he was a huge fuckup before I got him the coaching job at Gopa. Arrests, some rather serious, stints in rehab. Staked my name on it, and Russ came around."

Harry is straight and temperate, enjoying a glass of wine or scotch after dinner, but never overindulging. His passion, his vice, is money. Harry has no idea Russ Haverly was doubling as a drug mule for the Gopa parents and students. Russ never came around. He just learned to dress like the rest of us.

"I'm sorry, Harry. I shouldn't have accused you."

"We're all on edge." He rubs my shoulder and watches the fire, and mentions the name that triggers it. "Despite everything, I still love the little shit. Little Tugger."

My neck shoots around. I stare at Harry with incomprehension.

"That's what we called him," Harry says. "Always tugging on our sleeves growing up, trying to be included. Little Tugger."

Cold Blood Or Just Cold?

THE NICKNAME DIGS IT out of my mind, a key passed on to the tribe who unlock the safe and stare at the missing documents. As soon as Harry departs I go for the phone that is gone, passed along two nights earlier to Josey, who promised to toss it in the river. It does not matter anymore. I remember everything. Russ Haverly is Tug Reynolds, his drug dealer alter ego named after his childhood moniker.

Russ and Tug are dead. I killed them.

The Monday before the Toby Dalton strangling, which chronologically makes sense. Or is it a Tuesday? It is early in the school week, I remember, when I tend to accept any meetings or chores that get me out of my house. Russ calls the office and says he has something to discuss. I assume it's my prescription. A cool day in April, I suggest an early round of golf, for which he does not show. A late season squall blankets the fairway in a layer of snow that will be gone by morning. When he arrives to the clubhouse that evening, he is jerky and intoxicated, nervous. He asks to speak in private. He does not own a car due to a driving arrest years earlier, something about barbiturates and a police cruiser. His only mode of transportation is a motorboat that often doubles as his sleeping quarters. He puts it in the water in late March and keeps two slips, one in Slancy, the other in Weehawken.

We do not know enough about Russ Haverly who has burrowed an important designation within our Gopa lifestyle. Whether an office building, a school community, or a government organization, every association has its own version of Russ Haverly—someone with a dark streak and mild underworld connections to cover the sin that keeps our world faithful and productive. *Lacrosse coach* is a respected role within the school, though it does not offer the salary someone entwined in our lifestyle needs to function; high school coaches cannot afford motorboats. Rehab, arrests, old friends, a passing understanding of how criminal networks operate—all have instilled Russ with the credentials to be a buffer between our society and the other side.

A reputation of being an incredible recruiter, he lured the best players in the New York City region to Gopa Academy, athletes who have gone on to Dartmouth and Princeton and Syracuse. He also is a man who knows how to obtain pharmaceuticals for which parents cannot or will not ask a doctor. I do not know where the Luderica comes from, or how he manages to obtain pills that are not yet available for doctor prescription. I am not the only Gopa parent who takes meetings with Russ Haverly. Cocaine, Valium, mescaline, marijuana, codeine, fentanyl, oxycodone, Percocet and Vicodin, poppers and uppers and downers and sex stimulants. Along with Luderica, there are other drugs awaiting FDA approval. Quisquelo, for weight loss. Rugamal, for tighter skin. Cogataline, some type of sexual stimulant that allows the user to hallucinate scenarios with imaginary creatures. Most folks can obtain one prescription, but they require Russ's complicity to complete their sanity. In the supply chain of drugs to drug dealers to responsible parents raising well-adjusted children who go on to fine colleges and become productive adults and raise their own children thus coaxing forward evolution, Russ is an important cog.

On the evening I permanently undid the supply chain, I leave the clubhouse with Russ and walk him down to the pier. A chilly night, windless and desolate, the moon is quartered and low over the bashful water that stubbornly accepts a yellow reflection. A security camera has been leveled, the innards hanging from a suspended pole and twisting in a heightening breeze. The upper bay is typically choppy, though it is docile, exhausted from winter's torment. I set the golf bag down because Russ is weeping, apologizing to me for reasons I cannot understand involving money and photographs and a party. He cannot go to the Sedlocks, Russ says. He claims if Harry knew what happened, he would lose his job. He'd be asked to terminate his investment in Moveable Museums. "It'll be huge. We'll never work again," he promises, lightening the burden. "Both of us, Pisser." He owes money to something named Capra, a drug dealer I surmise. A boy named Toby Dalton, I recognize the name as one of his players, is blackmailing him.

What any of this has to do with me is unclear, his ranting more a confession than a plea for financial assistance. Russ is a distant friend, the classification that exchanges money for drugs with a sprinkling of social etiquette. Toby Dalton. The name sticks longer than anything else, his father a GPS mogul living abroad, no mention of a mother. An exceptional lacrosse player in his junior year, he came from another private school, the nanny chain claiming he was enrolled in Gopa through Russ and his father's doing, the last school that would have him. The nannies say he lives in his father's Chelsea condo where he regularly hosts parties for the Gopa student body. Everyone has heard about the festivities. Iliza and Tungsten have been ordered not to attend. Other than knowledge of who Toby Dalton is, they run in different circles.

He keeps on about a party. "What were you doing there, Russ?"

Snot and whimper, exhaustion, his body flailing as we shiver. "Toby Dalton. I'm the kid's dealer."

"Fuck, Russ." This involves me, something about the Luderica perhaps. "He's the captain of your lacrosse team."

"Don't you think I know it?"

I breathe in the surf, the chill of the April water stinging my nose. I am not wearing a jacket, a vest instead, dressed for a round of golf.

We've both had too much to drink and I ingested an extra Luderica, hoping Russ would restock me this evening. The news and the wind clear my head, a shifting tide from the north from somewhere far away that implies cold fronts though I suspect sunshine in the morning. I make a mental note to mention the warm front shifting into the region on tomorrow's broadcast, and then come to grips with the worst: Russ Haverly is dealing drugs to parents *and* students. According to the Gopa Ethics Handbook, I am required to notify the administration of this wrongdoing. Except I am one of his clients.

"These are kids, Russ."

He laughs, rubs away snot. "They aren't kids the way we were kids. You should see these parties."

Russ lights a cigarette, which soothes him enough to stop the tears. He is late on payments to the Capra entity, up to a month, though he does not know the amount. He places himself at about $40,000 in the red; roughly what his star player owes him in drug money. It is a drop in the bucket for the Daltons, but after his latest expulsion from the Hortimer Academy, daddy Dalton has put a freeze on Toby's assets. He gets an allowance each week, enough for a rich kid to eat. To augment his lifestyle, and for the thrill, Toby sells drugs to the Gopa student body. But he is a dealer lacking the ethical understanding that he must pay Russ for the narcotics, who will then pass it along to Capra, the way drug pipelines have been operating amicably for centuries.

Toby has photographs. If Russ gets him into the ECI program, Toby can show his father he has turned things around, made a real effort, and perhaps his dad will loosen up the purse strings. Only Russ cannot get him in. The other two members of the committee have said as much, and because there are only eighteen spots, all the Dalton money in the world will not buy Toby access. The more looming issue: Capra wants his money.

I am outraged that the drug pipeline we parents always fear will one day burrow a hole beneath our tutors and extracurricular activities and preparatory testing, instead exists out in the open, from the very source where I obtain my illegal fix. Selling to parents and nannies is one thing. Russ brought it into our school. And he was willing to pawn off one of the ECI slots to pay the bill. "I can't believe this, Russ."

"I'm in bad shape, Pisser. I'm using again."

"We voted you in as a trusted advisor to the ECI committee. And you lobbied for Toby Dalton."

"That's not the point."

"Sure, I thought you might put in a good word for Iliza and the others. These are good kids who you know. Instead you used your clout to stump for a pompous little fuck. How could you?"

Russ smokes his cigarette, watches me dangerously, an arrogant prep school dad missing the larger contours of our collusive unwinding. He needs me badly. He could never truthfully outline this request to Harry Sedlock. Rhen is on the lacrosse team. Harry would turn him into the administration. But it is not Harry that holds my concentration, gets my tribe stretching and sharpening spears and handing out war paint. The question of why, of all the people at Gopa, Russ Haverly is standing on a dock confessing to me.

I turn to Russ and understand him in the manner I know storm systems off the coast of the Carolinas making their way north, computer models of faraway winds, in ways I can predict that rain will be falling an hour from now but can still practically suggest a warm morning. He sees that I have snapped to the point of our meeting, a new round of tears.

"The pictures, Russ."

He shrugs, speaks through the mewling. "I don't know. Toby showed them to me fast, but I couldn't tell for sure. I don't remember anything from that night."

"What do you remember?"

He inhales, nods. "I was naked in a shower. Bad shape, Pisser." Snot bubbles in his right nostril and he wipes it away using the same hand holding the cigarette, sending a spark off his face into a fierce wind picking up charisma. He's sobbing again. "There are girls, high school girls, in the shower with me."

"Fuck, Russ." I know it cannot be stopped. Russ Haverly will be fired, arrested, placed far away from high school children. He is the thing parents avoid when they decide to pay tens of thousands for private school.

"I promise to pay you back."

"I don't have that kind of money, Russ." With the investment and Standcake and tuition, we have emptied our savings.

"Listen to me, Pisser." He inhales deep, lights another cigarette, and walks down the dock. "*You* do not want these pictures getting out any more than I do."

When the Luderica touches my tongue, the saliva begins to fragment the pill into chalky portions that become a liquid and get absorbed into my blood stream. From there they find the nervous system, specifically the gamma-aminobutyric acid, which slows everything and loosens my tension. Typically my eyes go blurry and stop working for a few minutes. I often drool, and once I pissed myself. My mouth goes dry and my penis gets extraordinarily stiff, although I cannot feel it blossom in my pants because most of my body is numb. After a few moments, my heartbeat quickens and I feel an itching that starts in my feet and moves up through my solar plexus and races through my spine, eventually into my brain. It is an itch I cannot touch, and it is where I know the Luderica is attempting to dig out the playfulness, but this is why the Federal Drug Administration has not approved it yet. This, and the massive erections, and also the blackouts, and perhaps the laughter. The pill digs into something unnatural, but it is not playfulness. It is native hostility, indigenous temper, the feral state of man.

Russ is still talking, blabbering an explanation for the photographs that are my concern as a father. At some point, I have bent down and retrieved my four iron, which I hold like a club, something else in charge of my mechanics and muscles. He does not see it in the darkness, apologizing and pleading for kindness.

"The girls in the shower," I say, face toward the wind.

Russ shakes his head. "I don't know for sure."

"Iliza?"

"Toby says so. But I don't know."

I'm hollering, my voice erased over the black water. "Was she there, Russ?"

"I'm so sorry, Pisser. I never meant for any of this."

He never meant to deal drugs to children and shower naked with my sixteen-year-old daughter in a luxury apartment in Chelsea. I do not ask if he's having regular sex with her, how many people fit into a Dalton-sized shower, because none of it matters. The iron comes naturally, mechanically, and crushes his left temple, opening a four-inch gash that quickly covers his face in blood. The collision knocks his phone to the deck. Russ puts a hand in the air, as if attempting to hush the river that has grown wild during our dispute, a rain from the east of the metropolis creeping toward Slancy.

I hit him again and he tumbles into the water, the still-lit cigarette afloat, a tiny lighthouse. According to an accurate model of water temperatures in the North Atlantic in April, we are looking at swimming conditions anywhere from thirty to forty-five degrees with a chance of warmer temperatures near the shoreline. While a conditioned athlete like Russ Haverly could survive easily for fifteen minutes, enough to get to shore, he is heavily soused on pills and liquor and spouting blood from two gashes in his head. Also, he does not know how to swim, a discovery I make after he's in the water, paddling for life. I innately leap in to rescue him.

The water hits my body and instantly sobers me, allowing me to transition from my crime. I read somewhere that cold water is excellent for conditions inside my testicles, and I could mention to Laura that this late night swim has produced some fine sperm for future progeny. I grope through the darkness until I locate Russ. His face is covered in blood and he's unwittingly drowning me with his attempts at survival, chaotically slapping at the icy water until I am submerged beneath his weight. Survival, kindness, safety, warmth, he has seen my daughter naked. It is the last thought that emerges victoriously, and I pull his head underwater by the back of his coat then use my legs to drown him. I do not let up until he is motionless in the surf, until I am certain he is dead.

Once on shore, the body is wet and heavy, not moving, neither of us. I am exhausted, freezing, cannot catch my breath. I am not physically fit enough for murder, but the tribe mobilizes. The rain and tide cascade toward Staten Island, and I am on my feet dragging Gopa's esteemed lacrosse coach over land, below the clubhouse and the first tee, to reach the far end of the harbor where the tide will hopefully catch it and push it toward another shore. I pull the corpse by an arm through tall grass and litter and sewage, white bubbles shedding their peace as we pass, my adrenaline and heartbeat motoring us through, the muscles in my back and neck stretching and awakening—this is what it feels like to haul death, to participate in murder. South of the harbor, I walk it out until I am submerged to the waist, then push the corpse into the tide.

My cell phone is ruined, the screen a vague set of advice. I feel emptier knowing it is not my ally tonight. The flashlight works. I walk back to the dock and check for blood, but it is too dark to know what is blood and what is water. I retrieve Russ's phone from the boards but I cannot turn it on, the battery dead. The boat and the golf bag are immediate concerns, and I am left furious with indecision. Why does Russ own a boat if he cannot swim? Why do I own golf clubs if I cannot golf? In matters of survival, neither of these items suffices. I toss the bag into the watercraft and struggle with the mechanics until I ignite the motor. It is my first time captaining a boat and I do not know what to do, I only know that it cannot be found near Slancy, a place where good people exist and do not deserve intruders like Russ Haverly preying on our children and turning up murdered. I am a good person. I have to drop off my kids at Gopa Academy in the morning. I am part of a Cooperative Marriage. I sit on two committees: Gopa Parents Think Recycle and Gopa Parents for Trees. I am a Zenith Member at VillageShop, in the market for a chess set and some petunias that will make the edge of my backyard pop.

The final memory is drifting away from the dock toward Staten Island. I have no idea how I eventually made it home or where the cell phone came from or what I have done, the night concealed in a blissful, pharmaceutical blackout. My last recollection of the evening: the things we do for our children.

Adjusting To Our Reckoning

DAWN BREAKS OVER THE East River as I climb too quickly from the tent, my blood making oblong attempts for order as it rushes through my cerebrum. Clint Eastwood has arranged the bodies of four chipmunks and a small bird in a circular pattern, a Stonehenge of carnage. A truck crew from the cellular company gets an early start, the beeps and hums of the motorcade assessing the damage to its towers. Steam rises from my coffee at the edge of the patio. The motley sky suggests my mug arrived an hour ago when Laura and Iliza left for a breakfast at the school, yet the fumes seem new. I am dropping Gus this morning and sticking around to hand out *Our Town* flyers with Iliza, a father-daughter bonding event both of us are dreading.

The coffee settles my vision. Behind me, Rhythm runs naked through the yard. Clint Eastwood makes a beeline for the shed. "Naughty, Mister Pickles." Jason watches from his back patio as Allie Sedlock coasts past on her bicycle, slim legs against peddles, a wave, her dinging bell the Slancy version of an air raid siren. The Hendersons' house that borders me to the south is empty, the yard accommodatingly quiet, the way it always is, except for the cameras that whir as they capture our distraction. Everything in Slancy is in its natural order, other than my recollection from a week earlier—I bludgeoned and drowned Gopa's former lacrosse coach. I have not shared the updated version of that night with Laura, who deserves to know.

My tribe stretches, my hand shaking so I cannot get at the hot liquid. It is not my implication in a murder I know was deserved, one I am not ashamed of and would do again if called to task. Instead, a mysterious shadow lurks inside my house. Iliza and Laura are gone.

Gus roams the kitchen. I focus on the foreign body. Toby Dalton is inside my house, Gus gawking as though the greatest celebrity of his nubile world has materialized to serve him breakfast. He sits on a stool, sipping the same coffee he poured for me, entertaining my transgenerational recluse.

"Morning, Mister P." His cheery voice as I arrive half-dressed from the backyard. "Left you a mug on the deck."

"What are you doing here?"

"He came to give Iliza and Tungsten a ride to school," Gus says. "He didn't know about the theater breakfast."

Toby lifts the mug. "I didn't know about the thing. Gusser let me in."

"I let him in," Gus says, beaming.

Toby smiles, handsome, his shoulders broad and fit. Alone, I do not have the strength to strong-arm him, but the creatures that inhabit me do. "You came all the way out here on a Monday to take the girls back to Manhattan?"

"Beautiful morning for a drive."

"I love a good drive." Gus is dressed in knit pants, a floral top and a shawl, with worn-out slippers he never removes. He is psychologically stretched to play the part of a dead nanny, but he cannot disguise his eighth-grader thrill to be in the company of Gopa royalty. If he had any friends, he would brag. "You want another cookie, Toby?"

"Nah, little man." He smiles. "Gusser has been feeding me cookies for the past half-hour."

"Gus, go get ready for school."

"I am ready."

"Go brush your teeth."

"I already did."

Gus is not leaving. Toby and I stare across the kitchen.

"Where's your car?"

"Visitor lot."

"You don't have a pass. They wouldn't let in a stranger."

Toby shrugs. "I talked my way in."

"He talked his way in," Gus says. "He's giving me a ride to school today."

"Both of you, Mister P." I don't blink. "I thought it would be nice to chat."

"We're taking the shuttle bus."

"He's got a convertible," Gus says.

"We're taking the bus," I say louder. "Go put on a different shawl."

"But dad."

"It's okay, little man." Toby sets down the mug and rubs a hand through my son's hair. Regardless of what it takes, the lacrosse tribe will learn to keep their filthy skin off my children. "Another time. I just remembered. I have an errand before school."

He issues a series of snaps and handshakes, all of which Gus knows well enough, a promising development in his socialization, all things considered. Toby's careful to exit without being left alone with me for even a minute, enough time to push the BB gun muzzle into his aorta and snap off twenty shots, a wound to drain that arrogant smile. At the front door, he assesses the other yards, nodding that he might want one of these properties for his next birthday.

"I didn't want to say this in front of the kid, Pisser." He leans close, a sniff. "But you stink, old man."

Forces Of Failure

ON THE BUS, GUS is excited, bouncing off his seat, his boyish happiness a relief as he peppers me with questions. Are Toby and Iliza dating? *That topic is never discussed with me, a mere father.* Will he be coming to dinner regularly? *It's not possible.* How come he didn't know that Iliza wasn't home? *Toby's knowledge of my daughter's whereabouts matters little because something very bad is going to happen if he continues on this course.* On Lustfizzle this morning, "94 Photos That Will Make You Love Carrots." Devin Brenner has emailed a summary of last night's Cooperative Marriage meeting, which I neglected to attend. Expect mostly average feelings during the morning rush hour with anxiety developing midmorning and turning into shades of failure. Wear your sunblock because the murder index is moderate to high. It's been fifty-seven days since I misinterpreted the atmosphere.

I have begun regularly smoking cigarettes again, a habit I have not practiced in fifteen years. I glance down on the bus to see my left hand innately flipping an unlit smoke, the cadence of the activity relaxing. Gus does not mention it and I am able to conceal the cigarette before my neighbors notice. Inside Gopa, things are eerily similar to every other morning: eye drops, hand sanitizer, water bottles, sunscreen, hair gel, children with backpacks connected to ropes so they do not wander toward their own destruction. I am still quarantined in the stroller waiting area with the part-time nannies and drivers, though I notice that Topher has excused himself from our detention to freely stroll the lobby. I am better off in detention where I can eavesdrop on arriving parents. A bus driver smokes a cigarette, a habit I have taken up now that I'm down to just one pill. I join him for small talk, both of us familiar with the mechanics of multi-passenger transport.

"Ever killed anyone?" I ask.

"Beg your pardon?"

"With the bus, I mean. The saying, 'If I get hit by a bus.' It ever happen?"

"Clipped a few cars. Never killed anyone though." No one chats up bus drivers. He is happy to share. "Bullets don't always kill, but people panic when they get shot. That's what causes the fatality. Same with buses. Person gets run over, they think—this is it. Typically, if you get it in your head you can survive, you probably will."

The stolen bus is old news now that the team has dropped three straight games, whispers about the missing coach, the failed season. Many parents are without their prescription supply, looking haggard and jittery as they arrive, jealous as I puff away in the disinfected safety of our building's periphery. There is a subtle thread of interwoven madness that jibes with my frequency, those who intuit what I have done, allowing me to pass winks and nods with parents who return the sentiment.

The Callisters' nanny was anonymously reported to immigration, and rather than hire an attorney to defend their employee of nine years, they are searching for a new one. All the tires on the Babners' SUV were deflated yesterday morning. One of the third graders arrived to school last week with an open book bag, into which a dead chipmunk was deposited. An anonymous parent wrote to three newspapers and the health department, claiming she found rat droppings in her order of Standcakes. There is a French kissing epidemic in the upper school that parents at first were willing to ignore, hoping it would pass. Only now it is making its way through the ranks, infecting some of the honors students. From my understanding, sexual promiscuity is not the concern, but rather the potential spread of herpes and flesh-eating bacteria and other skin-to-skin ailments that might distort our children's appearances. Everyone uses extra sanitizer.

A member of the senior class was rushed to the hospital last week. The parents spread the word that it was the flu, though the nanny chain is telling a different tale that made its way to the Gopa website. The girl, Emily Rosen, overdosed on a peculiar drug becoming more popular with the student body—Luderica, a prescription parents are using for children with stress and depression, and which aids with concentration. There is no mention of the bunnies this morning. A second child was named to the ECI program. This one is no surprise, Whisper Li, his mother being hugged and congratulated as though finally receiving her due for pushing this wonder into the world. She wears a skirt that is far too tight for a woman her age, not to mention one with a prosthetic leg. The beastly thing juts out sideways, her right foot at an awkward angle to the rest of her posture, as though shoving her disability into all our mornings: look at what I've accomplished on one leg, when the rest of you bipeds can only rear mediocrity. She is far too peppy this morning, any morning.

Expecting it was only a matter of time for her son to be named, Sharon Li planned a party for Whisper, which is set for the coming weekend. All the math club families are invited along with the chess community, though Sharon personally called Laura to let her know that an invitation would not be extended to Gus. He makes the grandmothers nervous, and his presence would be a distraction to what should be a celebration of her son's achievement. To show there are no hard feelings, she ordered two-hundred Standcake pancakes despite the rat dropping rumor she read about on the Gopa website.

I have kissed the required cheeks and forecasted enough personal weather reports, that I make my way to the auditorium. The theater parents and students have organized into two groups to raise early morning awareness of the approaching play. Iliza and I have been assigned to fliers. When I arrive, Laura gives a slight wave, late for a meeting. My wife has avoided me for the past few weeks, which has included several missed Cooperative Marriage meetings. With me living in the backyard, bathing in the Jacuzzi, our only point of contact is the mug of coffee she sets on the porch each morning. I do not believe she suspects I was involved with the missing lacrosse equipment. But the stress around Moveable Museums, the rumors of pancakes with rat feces, the humiliation of us being the only parents on the chess team not invited to the Li's party—our distance grows to completion. She is taking the kids for a weekend getaway with Ray McClutchen, not Olivia or Todd or snotty Maddie, or me. She needs to clear her head, discuss things with Ray, keep Gus's mind off the party.

It is six weeks before the spring play, which is already sold out. Still we make calls and hand out fliers so it is known that, along with doctors and engineers and athletes and scientists, we also breed solid thespians that appreciate the historic importance of Thornton Wilder in the context of Broadway theater. Parents enrolled at other private schools will call the box office hoping to get tickets to see what they are missing, only to learn they are unavailable. This will create chaos on opening night with theater junkies and jealous parents trying to score tickets on the sidewalk to what will be an indisputably average rendition of *Our Town*. Iliza and I do not speak as we dangle fliers for passing cars. Tungsten and Allie are halfway down the block, along with parents I do not know, Josey Mateo is on the far side of the street shepherding other students. Drivers do not recognize me as the Channel Fourteen meteorologist, rather just a stumpy father who forgot to comb his hair. Allie Sedlock is the main draw, a skintight dress backing up traffic, while Tungsten smiles and waves.

I wish I were better looking, more dynamic, able to perform a feat that might draw attention to Iliza. I wish I could summon the playfulness of other parents. I love my daughter more than the sum of all my accomplishments, and it sickens me to stand near her knowing what she does when we are not invading her childhood with assignments and ritualistic improvement. Tungsten, the understudy, is elated with all the honking and excitement, whereas Iliza, the leading lady, is stuck with me, a man who would kill for her honor and yet cannot engage her in polite conversation, cannot dance each time a car honks. Iliza checks her phone.

"Don't do that, honey."

"Don't do what?"

"The phone. You have to be engaged."

She sighs. "You can leave. I know you don't want to be here."

"I want to be here." Iliza has picked up on my disgust. "Shall we go down and stand with the Sedlocks?"

"No, we shall not."

"Can I ask why?"

Her shoulders slump. She turns to me with revulsion. "Because you smell, Dad. You need a serious bath, maybe throw out that suit. It's embarrassing."

"I'm getting back to my natural odor."

"You look homeless." A car approaches. Iliza dangles a flier, and when the vehicle does not slow, she tosses it into the air gust.

"Let's talk then," I say, lighting a cigarette. "How are things with the play?"

"Fine. What else did you want to talk about?"

How about Russ Haverly? How about the possibility of a sex tape, your father looking at a terminal stretch of twenty-five to life, but not before I drain your college fund paying off lawyers? How about Toby Dalton in my kitchen this morning?

"You excited about this weekend?"

"Am I excited about being dragged to the middle of bumfuck so that my mother and Ray McClutchen can have an affair without feeling guilty?"

"Watch your mouth." I am relieved to hear she does not approve. I could hug her right here on the street, which would be disastrous to her reputation.

Iliza gives me a tortured look, a long, unpleasant honk, exposing her middle finger to the motorist. "Besides, the only reason I have to go is to keep an eye on Gus who is too weird to be invited to parties and you and mom don't want him to feel lonely."

"That's not the only reason." It's the only reason. "Come on, it will be a hoot."

"A hoot? Christ, Dad." She glances at Tungsten and Allie, beauty pageant contestants to our having snuck in the side door.

"Your mom and I are just going through a thing?"

"This *thing*," Iliza says. "Is she sleeping with him?"

"I don't know."

"Oh, hell. Who would know, Dad? Who should I ask? Maybe fucking Olivia."

"Your mouth, dear, please."

"Why can't you just get a divorce like normal people?"

Because studies show children raised by divorced parents exhibit antisocial and aggressive episodes. They grow up seeking normalcy only to discover that normal is out of their grasp, that their childhood was a sham, that innocence was robbed from them, creating a hard exterior. Also, we cannot afford a divorce, or to live separately, and neither of us wishes to vacate the Slancy home or the backyard into which I have sunk so much time and money. Also, what would happen to me?

"I don't want a divorce."

She throws down her fliers. Everyone watches. "Then do something. Tell mom to fuck off about Ray. She's just doing him to irritate you. Slap the shit out of him for getting involved with mom. Just. Do. Something."

One can fail at an athletic feat. One can falter at career. But there should be a different word for when a father fails his children not by what he did, but by what he did not. It is this essential strength I crave within myself—not playfulness, not happiness, but a feral longing to survive—the very reason I researched medication and took Russ Haverly's offer to obtain Luderica, which has transformed me into a mindless creature with interconnected depths. What I mean to say is that Iliza's accusation, rather than causing me to experience the failure I know I should, tasks my mind on how everything in my Gopa world is interconnected. Whisper Li does not care for Gus. Therefore Sharon Li disinvited him to the party. This incited Laura to take him and Iliza away for the weekend to cheer his spirits and make Iliza despise me. If Ray fucks my wife and impregnates her this weekend, that little twerp Whisper Li is at fault. But we mustn't blame children. Where were the parents?

Flier-less and irate, a Luderica-less stupor, me staring into traffic as I consider the trajectory of the universe, Iliza wanders the block to stand near Tungsten. She receives a hug from her friend, a motherly pat from Allie who offers me a shrug. Alone and weird, I flick the smoke and place a call across the street.

"Hey, Tom," Josey says. "Everything okay?"

"I need a favor."

Prosthetic Spoils

THREE DAYS LATER, DURING the hours when only crime and psychopathic fitness occur in the predaylight metropolis, the mothers of the Upper East Side head to the Excellcient Fitness Center to exercise and swim. Private school moms are incredibly evolved members of our species, organized and prioritized and able to cycle and bike and swim and micromanage on only five hours of sleep and Russ Haverly's assistance. I am there but not there, gliding through the motions, following Josey and her crew of self-sufficient hackers through basements and narrow hallways as they point out security cameras to avoid. She introduces me but their millennial-ness escapes me as soon as I hear it. Which is for the best. These are people who do not wish to be remembered, who are here as a favor to Josey and would prefer never to see my kind again.

There is a large transvestite and a smaller man, angry, with a godlike mullet who seems familiar. Someone named Phil is in charge. They gain access to the fitness center in moments, a series of gadgets and digital readers that pluck the codes from locked doors. Josey introduces me as the Channel Fourteen meteorologist who has delivered a stunning fifty-nine consecutive days of accurate weather forecasts. She tells them I am the author of several clever diatribes on the Gopa website, a forum her crew reads for entertainment. The angry man says he enjoyed my dispatch on physical education, how students do not get enough exercise, that we all end up fat and achy and tired, able to read and calculate equations, but what good are those skills if we lack charisma? He fist bumps me and mentions he does not approve of the way my people are raping civilization, that if sightseers begin loading buses to tour school shooting locales, he will personally burn down my home.

"I've done some sick shit," Phil says. "But your ethics are off the charts."

"We had to get involved because you nearly killed the advice guy by tinkering with his bike," the mullet says. "You nearly ruined everything."

"It was a tricycle," I say, which makes Phil smile, my tribe on edge. "What do you mean: *involved*?"

Josey gets between us, sternly to Phil. "Now's not the time."

"What's that smell?" the transvestite asks.

We all sniff. "I'm not using deodorant or shampoo."

"You smell like you're rotting."

"From your sins," Phil adds.

"We're in a gym," the transvestite says. "You could use a shower."

"Don't listen to her." Another fist bump from the mullet. "I haven't showered in nine years. Your natural aromas will recalibrate. Fucking tricycles, aye?"

"Here." Josey finds the women's locker room and ducks inside, checking to ensure it is empty, all the mothers burning the hell out of hip looseness and buttocks cellulite. She returns to the hallway and hands me a key. "This will open any locker. Move quick but not too quick. We'll watch the doors."

There is no time to rethink the decision. My hands quake, an epileptic fervor as my tribe strains for grace. I fit the key and rattle open tiny doors. It takes me about twenty lockers until I discover what I am after, removing both the main item and a smaller replica. Just before I shut the locker door, I notice the assortment of toothpastes, deodorants, and a cornucopia of pharmaceuticals. There is an entire bag of Viagra and other erectile dysfunction pills that have not hit market. I imagine Sharon Li rations these at home. I recognize the brown containers, unique to Russ Haverly. There are four bottles that I open to be sure. At least two months of Luderica as I pocket all the drugs.

In the hallway, I am greeted by a heavy smile from Josey, confusion from the others who notice my bounty: prescription bottles and other paraphernalia. The mullet smiles. I recognize his features. He looks like a miniature Tom Petty, the Sedlocks' tour guide, a rush of fear crushes me. "Sick, bastard," he says. "I'm starting to like you, Tom Pistilini."

"That's what we came for?" Phil asks Josey. "What the hell is it?"

I hold up the prize. "A prosthetic leg."

We Shall Know It By Its Meaning

LAURA AND RAY'S WEEKEND trip has arrived, for which they will cart along my children but not his. They will attend the lacrosse game in Rye, New York, then continue on to a charming Connecticut town north of the Long Island Sound. My hope is that Gus's weirdness will ensure they never get the opportunity to desecrate their marriage vows. It pains me as I look over the Doppler that they will be greeted with pleasant skies and intermittent clouds, the perfect climate to sip wine and suck down oysters and stare into one another's eyes, consider how nice it is not to have me lurking in the backyard. If Clutch McClutchsky gets a look at her breasts, that's the end of me. After two kids and years of suckling and enough lump scares and needle biopsies, Laura's breasts remain magnificent, which will keep Ray addicted and devoted. He has more money and zest and all around positive vibes to sustain life's setbacks and come out a perkier geriatric, a point about Ray I respect.

My weather assistant has obtained instant celebrity status in the Channel Fourteen newsroom. Penelope Garcia's outfits have grown smaller as her laughter grows louder. She is constant merriment, throwing back that head of hair, her youthful tits bouncing at a chuckle per second, which everyone enjoys. In only a few weeks, Penelope has garnered an impossible following on social media, sending out my PISSER REPORT to millions of fans. My lack of proper bathing, combined with general fatigue, makes me look like the understudy of our broadcasts, the camera focusing more on Penelope and the ass. "Look at it," a homosexual assistant tells me. "It never moves when she walks, like concrete." It's a subtle shift, one he could deny if I called him on it, but I know. Whitman knows. Penelope as well. She is complimentary, treating me as the guru of our strange collaboration, pushing on everyone that my forecasts have been accurate a remarkable sixty-one days. She knows about it because of Josey Mateo, my marketing department, who updates the number daily, sending correspondence to Channel Fourteen and our competing news organizations.

"Oh my, oh me, he do it again!" Penelope screeches—explosive energy sucking the magnetism from the room. She pinches my cheek. "This man is *asombroso*."

It is not me. It is not even the Luderica any longer. I am at war internally, my natives restless for validation, their instincts honed without the use of computer models or radar. I can stare at the sky for a moment and know about wind speed and ultraviolet rays, cumulus clouds and atmospheric pressure. I enjoy the savages, my opposing forces, and would eagerly work out a truce. But there is only so much Tom Pistilini to go around, and they are tiring of the weather besides. Which is good, because the weather is tiring of me.

My days are numbered. Even as my descriptions of the atmosphere grow crisp and flawless, I sense viewers no longer wish to hear flawless weather. They want playfulness mixed with their disaster, meaning weaved with five-day outlooks. Penelope and I yuck it up and holler across the PISSER REPORT stage, and she hoots and claps and does timely dances when the sun shines or the rain gallops or we come to the bridge where weather and pop culture meet. There is always a bridge, Whitman has explained, a way to make weather and culture and philosophy one, and our playfulness must find it.

The Luderica has dragged out playfulness from my psyche, even more so once I am restocked with Sharon Li's supply. Her pills are newer, the chemistry more advanced, as if Russ was pushing the beta versions on me and saving the quality stuff for other parents. I have altered my chemical composition so many times that occasionally the cloud coverage evaporates, erasing my default doom, allowing me to enjoy the cathartic cynicism of Lustfizzle, an ability to relay the world's murder with a wink and an elbow. But I no longer wish to summon the playfulness that daily headlines, even the PISSER REPORT, require. A father of two children, I am obsessed with the dangers in the world, fraught with worry at each new broadcast.

A shooting in a Kansas office, my mind immediately moves to the Gopa lobby, remembering the emergency exits, the location of the back stairs, the sturdiness of the guard's desk, and whether Lieutenant Misch will be steady enough with the ammunition once the gunmen materialize. A flood in Nigeria, and I wonder at Slancy's shores, built at a higher elevation but constructed of sediment and miscellaneous dust from illegal construction sites. I find every tormenting headline an attack on my children, a conspiracy to steal their innocence and complicate their lives, and Whitman expects me to snigger with meaning and verve. The UV index is off the charts this month, and my children are defenseless against the sorcery of starlight because I do not want to be one of *those* parents applying sunscreen in front of their peers. Even though I am one of *those* parents, the worst kind. Most parents claim they would kill for their children if it came to it. I did kill.

From my phone, I spend long hours Googling other parents who have taken this difficult course. The Texas father who came across a man raping his five-year-old daughter and promptly beat him to death with a skillet. An Australian man who discovered a convicted rapist outside his daughter's bedroom door, breaking his neck just for thinking about it. The Indian dad who invited his daughter's rapist to dinner, then removed his genitals and strangled him. I load all these vigilantes to the Gopa website, the comment sections irate and supportive.

I cannot blame it on the Luderica. It led to several blackouts, which occur with regularity, but I was there, in tribal form, and I killed Russ Haverly with my four iron. You find out what type of man you are in those situations, whether you will kill or be killed or run screaming into your cell phone for the authorities. I am glad to learn I belong to the other animal, the ones who run toward the violence. The pills found it in me. "That's what combat used to find in men," a blog post from Nadir_ Father I do not recall writing, "a feral life behind the cloak of safety, but then combat, for much of the population, was replaced by sports: the Yankees are going to war tonight against the Red Sox, the Rangers will take no prisoners at the Garden, the Gopa Worthy must win at all costs. Now even sports are flimsy versions of teamwork with participation trophies. Manhood these days is about being positive and sunny, not dwelling on the bloated hardships of the world, smiling and keeping the chin up and finding the silver lining when some fundamentalist blows up an ice cream truck in Times Square, scattering children and sprinkles all over the spray-washed pavement."

"Good set today," Whitman says. He bumps my fist then twists my hand a bit. "If I can bend your ear a minute."

"I know everyone else in the city is forecasting rain. It won't rain in the northeast. I'm on a streak."

"I know about it. Fifty days or something."

"Sixty-one."

"This is about the other weather. Existential weather." The kid can turn a phrase. He stops me in the hallway where we are alone. "Have you given any more thought into why you showed me the Moveable Museum portfolio?"

"I told you. It was an accident."

"I think you left it there on purpose."

"Why would I do that?"

"Because you want my help. Or for me to talk you out of it. Something." Whitman stares me down. I cannot escape judgment. "See, the universe has stuck us together, you and I. How else can you explain our involvement?"

"If you tell me you've read Ray McClutchen literature, I will quit right now."

He moves close, talks low. "I hate my job, Pisser. I hate the..." he searches for it, "...shallow minisculality, that nothing we do lasts, overrun by the ensuing seconds of interruption and fatigue. I read somewhere that due to the constant influx of data, millennials are suffering midlife crises earlier."

"At what age?"

"About twenty-seven."

"How old are you, Whitman?"

"Twenty-seven. Don't you see? I am here to help you through this episode. And you are here to help me through my crisis." Another kid to worry over, just what I need. "Let me in, Pisser. Let me help you destroy this tourism cell. There is meaning in this endeavor. Real, true meaning."

I am saved from Whitman's reckoning by our ubiquitous cell phones—his for Lustfizzle matters, mine for Laura. I take it in my office. Laura and I go through the usual niceties, how are the kids, have a safe drive, my Saturday chores involving yard work and masturbation. We dance around the finer points, the room situation at the hotel, whether a naked Ray McClutchen will be lying on top of her at any point, if Olivia McClutchen will be at her son's lacrosse game.

"Something you should know," I say. "The other morning, at the house, after you and Iliza left. Toby was in the kitchen with Gus."

"Toby Dalton?" There's only one Toby in our lives. "What was he doing there?"

"Out for a drive. Said he stopped to offer the girls a ride to school."

"Out for a drive?" It's a foreign concept for Slancy residents. "Did you..."

Strangle him on the kitchen floor, in front of our son already suffering psychological shrapnel from a death that occurred on the property? Spoon out his eyeballs? Knock him unconscious with the coffee mug? "I told him to leave."

"This is very unsettling." It pleases me to know this will impact her weekend. "We should speak to someone, the police maybe."

Laura knows, as well as I do, that it would be a horrific idea to speak to the police. Working with Lieutenant Misch, the police are following up on a coach who went missing in Slancy, Misch likely sharing his investigation opinions with colleagues. They would not look favorably on my dispute with a teenager.

"Are you okay, Tom?"

"Yes, I'm fine."

"You'll be safe tonight. And not drink too much."

"I'm planning a quiet night in the backyard, a soak and a fire." I cannot resist some psychological torture. "You and Ray just have a nice time. Don't think about me."

I head home after work to shower and change and admire my new trophy that is displayed in my shed. It looks beautiful hung between the sixty-volt cordless hedge trimmer and the heavy-duty two-cycle leaf blower, completing my collection of manliness. The backup leg I carried around lower Manhattan earlier this week, searching for a homeless man in a wheelchair I saw months earlier. He was still alive, still legless, and happy to receive the prosthetic leg even though he was not sure how to apply the contraption. We both agreed that now he only needed one more prosthetic leg to make him whole, and we parted with a handshake, the two of us feeling good about class relations.

Drinks With Parents

THE PARTY FOR WHISPER'S acceptance into the ECI program is this evening. While Gus was uninvited, Sharon Li never officially rescinded the invitation to the rest of the Pistilinis, and I arrive to show there are no hard feelings. Dressed in jeans and a tailored jacket over my unwashed physique, I even brought along a gift for the troubled genius, a pair of chess gloves made of breathable fabric so the pieces do not slip out of his nerdy fingers. I stuck a dead chipmunk at the bottom of the package and wrapped it myself, which I later regret. Gus has a birthday party next month, and since he has no friends, we'll probably have to invite the Li's.

The party is being held at an arcade and cocktail bar in midtown, children dashing through the neon lights while the adults enjoy drinks and appetizers and threaten their offspring to stop running, that they may injure themselves in the shadows. Sharon Li ordered two hundred pancakes for the event, a reward for Laura's unconditional surrender regarding Gus and the party. She is surprised to see me. Seated in a wheelchair, a blanket over her legs so other parents do not have to avoid staring at the stump, the immortal peppiness finally tamed. Congenial and social, the theft has ruined the party for her, a smaller version of me behind her ready to push the chair when she demands locomotion. This is the husband, to whom I do not introduce myself.

"Sharon," I say, taking her hand, my tone offering neither condolence nor celebration, just a record that I remember her name in spite of our falling out. The BB gun grinds into my back when I bend to greet her.

"Tom," she says, surprised. "Tom Pistilini."

"Sharon." I place the package on her lap. "We could not be prouder of Whisper."

"Well." She glances around for her husband, steel-eyed and waiting for a directive. "Thank you then. Will you stay for a drink?"

"Of course, I will." This surprises her more than the gift. Mothers gawk and whisper. Fathers purse their lips. A nanny darts for her phone, eager to get this encounter onto the Gopa website, the scoop of the weekend.

I help myself to a pancake dressed as what I imagine is Whisper Li and guillotine the head. The tangerine ones are my favorite, a smoothie ooze crashing the shores of my tribe. I sip whatever drink the husband was sent to the bar to procure, smiling at the other mothers and delighting in their discomfort. I am surprised to find Jackson and Jason at the party, and recall that Whisper is in the honors program with Damian. Having heard about Gus's uninvite through the nanny chain, Jackson avoids me until I approach. Jason shares with me the gossip that no one dares mention.

"Stolen from her gym locker. Are any of us safe? It's hor-*rib*-le," Jason says, over pronouncing which causes me to chuckle. I am not laughing at her missing appendage. I have previously laughed myself into apathy over it. But rather at how dramatic Jason finds the theft, how he equates it back to his existence, the safety of his children, the way all of us do with extraneous news from the far corners of the world. A capsized ferry in South Korea, hundreds missing: should we double down on swimming lessons? How does Sharon Li's missing leg impact Jason? If anything, Damian should have been the first, maybe second, student selected for the program, so this party should be an abomination to the Jays' parenting skills. "It's not funny, Pisser."

Jackson smiles covertly. "It's not funny, Pisser."

"I'm more surprised than entertained."

"You shouldn't be surprised or entertained," Jason says.

I am not in control of my reactions, I want to say. I am not directing Tom Pistilini's operations any longer. I am on my third drink. I think it is an Appletini, or maybe a fruity beer. It's a terrible party, everyone morose and crowding around Sharon Li, who sits forlorn as though she just lost the actual flesh leg this morning. Jason excuses himself to make nice with the moms, leaving me alone with Jackson. We still have not discussed our felony.

He turns his back to the moms and gives me a serious reproach. "What are you doing here, Pisser?"

"It's a party. I was invited."

"No, you weren't."

"*I* wasn't uninvited."

"Laura and Gus and Iliza were invited. No one thinks to invite you to anything." It is true, of course, though it makes both of us feel badly. He grinds closer. "Something about you, Pisser. You've always been strange, but you're getting stranger. The stolen bus. Your trouble with the parents. Items I'm reading on the website. You smell awful."

"You stole the bus, too."

"Careful, Pisser." He places a giant hand on my shoulder and squeezes the back of my neck. It feels good, this human contact. "And don't for a minute think I don't see it coming."

"See what coming?"

"Another breakdown. I don't want to be anywhere near it when it happens." Even closer, into my ear. "I'm willing to bet you know something about that missing leg. Come on, Pisser, why'd you really come?"

"For camaraderie. To chat with other parents."

"Or to look at them. To enjoy someone else's misery." He runs his hand down my back to the gun handle and slaps my fat, indicating he has not abandoned our friendship entirely. "This the Ray and Laura weekend?"

I nod. The nannies again, or maybe Jason. Hell, everyone knows, probably even Sharon Li, both of us not pitying one another.

"Tough times. How you holding up?"

"I'm doing okay."

We sip our drinks and watch the parents who stare viciously into the blinking lights looking for signs of their children. The arcade is full of pedophiles and drug-dealers and sex traffickers lurking to steal our youth, and at any second one of the moms will dash from Sharon Li's side to defend her young who brushed too closely against a clown's arm.

"Did you and Jason find time to talk?" He knows without me suggesting a topic, but I do it anyway. "About Moveable Museums."

"Argued mostly. It's all we do anymore." Jackson shrugs. "I've been doing some research. Most of what Harry says is true."

"How so?"

"The money. The returns. If it wasn't us starting this business, then someone else would." He shakes his head, which has grown sweaty beneath the alcohol and lights. "I don't know what the answer is, Pisser. Jason and I cannot afford to lose this investment, not now."

I have spent enough time with Jackson to know his past, the courage of a Southern man marrying a Protestant teacher for whom no one much cares. The struggles they have been through. His dream of running his own orchestra, having the talent and drive to do that, but falling short and training Broadway musicians because that is where the money exists to pay the bills and nurture his dreams. I have failed in my own dreams as well, and glancing around the arcade, the smell of fried food and chemical cleaner, the arcade violence of war and sport and space vengeance, the Americanish of all of us, I cannot help but feel defeat, a metaphorical checkmate.

"What happened to us, Jackson? Where did we go?"

"We became parents."

Don't Call It A Comeback

THE SECOND LETTER FROM the homeowners association arrives. It is the same as the first letter although they have upped the rancor with bolded headers and, if I'm not mistaken, a slightly larger font. On the shuttlebus ride into Manhattan I order a foldable weatherproof storage bag that regularly retails for $400 on VillageShop but is on sale for Zenith Members for $175. I do not need a storage bag, but it was one of the bestselling items and I could not pass up the discounted price. Hours ago, a terrorist in London detonated a bomb in a crowded tourist area, making us hug our children firmer. Seventy girls were kidnapped from a Nigerian school, several of whom were reported murdered hours later, resulting in a blog post and comments on the Gopa website questioning school security.

On Lustfizzle, "17 Ways to Sculpt An Avocado Before Eating It" has garnered over four million views.

    No one speaks on the shuttlebus. I review a Gopa post I wrote about the merits of having your child quit an athletic team so they are not accidentally murdered during practice, their neck snapped like a twig by a more evolved student, a lacrosse ball bursting their sternum, a freak flesh-eating rash. The volleyball crew, as if anyone cares about volleyball, has gotten together to flag Nadir_Father for profanity, even though I only used the word "cocksuckers" once in the comment section. Several rugby dads are suggesting I am fostering a culture of failure. Some mothers who despise the sports teams are soft proponents of the post, although they prefer the word "decease" to "murder," so we argue the semantics on the commute.

    Gopa's world-renowned daycare program is a waste of personnel and space that could be better spent on older children, namely mine. I consider this from the stroller penalty area where I blow smoke over the mothers who furiously sanitize and cover the wee ones with blankets. The penalty area is open air on one side, which means I am not breaking any laws by smoking, or carrying the BB gun in my jacket, because I do not actually step inside the school. I receive a firsthand look at the Gopa Method each morning; a system that fluctuates with what the experts claim is trendy. One minute, we address the toddlers with baby talk, making them feel adored and special. Months later, nannies and parents and teachers speak to the rubbery dwarves like adults. No cooing, no fawning, no pretend voices, rather monotone directives, none of which the children understand.

    Ages one to three, parents spend the same amount of money to enroll these sucklings into rolling and napping and diversity etiquette, assigning one teacher to every three kids, a ratio unheard of in private school curriculum. The little fuckers take up two floors of prime real estate that could be transformed into a second gymnasium or science labs. They have their own manners studio. There's an allergy-free ball pit. They have a tumbling room I am told resembles a giant pillow, though no parent has ever set foot inside. Not one of them appreciates this gift, this elaborate purgatory into the real-world hell of kindergarten in which children must understand complicated addition and dual languages.

"Is Teddy having a bad day?"

Teddy is wanting nothing and expecting everything. Teddy is a manufactured elitist who should sit in his stroller and patiently await entrance into a world where my children have already laid down financial roots. In my pocket is a two-week old sample that later this morning I must deposit into the Manhattan Cryobank, actually harnessing another parody of this thing called civilization.

"Ah, what's a matter Teddy?" I dab a finger at his snotty chin. He reacts with a blind scowl, and the mother smiles dubiously as she measures the temperature inside the cradle chamber, not sure whether the friendly Channel Fourteen meteorologist hovers near her child or if word of a madman is accurate. Was my nanny really fished out of my Jacuzzi? Did I have something to do with the missing coach? Did the police help me cover up the murders because I'm a mild celebrity in the Gopa livestock? Did I really steal a busload of lacrosse equipment and a prosthetic leg?

She apologizes for Teddy's manners. "He's been grouchy today."

That's because he's a little asshole. I can sense it in his pampered posture. As I stare at Teddy's soft features, I know I want six more of my own. I cannot even protect the two I have from ungodly humanity, but I crave a third and fourth Teddy.

"Whats-a-whats-a-whats-a-matter with little Teddy Weddy Woo, huh?" I cannot remember which end of the spectrum we have settled on this month, cooing and fawning or adult sophistication. I do a bit of both. "He just needs a bout of tumbling, don't you young person?"

"I'm sure that's it." The mother turns the stroller away and hands him a rice cookie, which he deposits on the floor.

Teddy's mood is all of our moods. The body of Russ Haverly was pulled out of the harbor last night, drifting in the opposite direction of the boat. The sidewalk is filled with flowers and candles and placards of remembrance for Gopa's unsung drug dealer. Despite the harsh murder conditions worldwide this morning, a dead body in the Hudson earned decent coverage, news vans stretched across the street watching the mourners stream in for the day's education. Bill Chuck and Lieutenant Misch came to the house last night to tell me the news. Awful, just awful, I kept repeating, Misch asking me the same questions. Even though they have not said as much, as the last person seen with Russ Haverly, I am a suspect. I have an upstanding reputation as a meteorologist and a fairly adequate record as a father. I also have intuition, brought on by consumption of the new Luderica pills, that Lieutenant Misch has warmed to me. He does not give a damn about Russ Haverly. He despises our elitism, our people living on a manufactured island, a golf course in the backyard, foldable bicycles and lagoons and private school. He knows by now Russ was dealing drugs, that the underworld connected its sticky tentacles to our constituent, and one of us, perhaps me, had to slice it off.

A small shrine has been assembled in the lobby. Candles, lacrosse balls, a jersey, photographs, white boards markered with nostalgia. I try to recall the moment things flipped and I crushed his skull with a four-iron. Did I intend to kill him? Because a jury will want to know. Did I leap into the frigid water to rescue him or to finish the job? How did I steer the boat without maritime skills? How did I get back home to Slancy? Was it justice or an overreaction, backlash from the very chemical enhancements Russ Haverly was providing?

For the lacrosse community, their worst fears have been realized. When the boat washed up nearly a month ago, only the most ignorant optimists could believe Russ Haverly had swum to shore and would crawl back into our lives to put together a winning streak. Everyone hugs and cries, the tragedy pulling us closer. The lacrosse season has been canceled, which is just as well. Under assistant coach Hunter Herman, the Gopa Worthy have dropped their last five games. It is a relief to be able to blame everything on death, which many are calling a homicide even though the police have not made that designation.

The atmosphere is too much for Harry Sedlock who emerges from the lobby to wander the sidewalk. He has lost more than the rest of us, an investor and an ally at a critical juncture, a childhood friend with demons Harry knew too well. I join him, placing the non-cigarette hand on his shoulder and pat it twice.

"Appreciate that, Pisser." I offer him a smoke, but he declines. "Shitty thing is I knew this was coming. Soon as he went missing."

"Sad day." I blow into the sky, letting the pining May sun ignite my skin. The trees have a mystical look, branchy faces screaming at the heavens, yelping over the smoke and congestion and fumes, begging something out there to send backup. "He was one of us," I say.

Harry's eyes are tired and red, tears and late nights, also worry and panic and planning and devotion and financial trembles. He only thinks about one thing these days, Moveable Museums, all our money tied up in it, our homes and children and lifestyles. The Luderica, coupled with the nicotine and caffeine, often invades my hearing so that everything becomes background noise. While my tribe hears Harry speak, his voice is there for convenience, something we listen to while concentrating on the trees. He speaks about our investment, about how sure he is of success as my people watch the screeching branches blow smoke, feel the eyes of the lacrosse parents upon us, wondering what happened. Do they suspect us? This is no time for cowardice, Harry says, we have to pull together as a community, buckle down, not let political correctness corrupt our business sense. Harry is in apparent mourning, which means arguing is poor form. Our investment has little to do with political correctness, we telepathically inform the trees. It is about right and wrong, and Harry is talking himself into the center of things, trying to convince us of the principles of our initiative, the responsibility he and I as entrepreneurs have to educate the rest of the world about the importance of gun control. This is about money, my tribe revolting, and the trees go on screaming, and Harry reminds us of the dozen journalists coming to look at our project. He will not use murder culture enthusiasts on the sidewalk outside the private school where he sends his children, but that is what they are. My tribe beats wooden sticks against the tin floor of my conscience, *whomp whomp whomp*, let us out.

The cigarette burns down to my fingers. My other hand shakes Harry's. My phone buzzes. I am caught in the shadow of Josey's inked frame on the far side of the glass. She watches Harry and I, standing near Lieutenant Misch who tips a chin toward the window. It is clear from their proximity, the familiarity of their closeness.

"Tonight at Mimic," the voice says on a delay, the mechanics of her mouth through the glass preceding sound, a time travel wormhole.

"I have that thing tonight you helped me with earlier," I say.

"After your thing. Bar on Seventeenth. Remember not to drink the wine."

Jammy With An Earthy Finish

HISTORICALLY, UPRISINGS HAVE BEGUN on the doorsteps of power—storming of the Bastille, the jungles of Cuba. If we ever get around to a class war in America, wine tastings are a good place to initiate the first blows. They are equipped with menacing pretension, a caustic exclusionary vibe from people who can afford to sip privilege out of tiny glasses, swirling and admiring and kissing cheeks. Tonight's event is held at the Gopa school, an occasion we could not possibly cancel just because a friend and faculty member was pulled lifeless from a local harbor. I imagine the front wall of windows exploding inward as bandanna-wearing rebels shimmy down ropes, machine guns over their shoulders on straps similar to Ray McClutchen's fold-up urban trike, and me, the only one armed with a BB gun as I decide whether to defend my brood or join the revolution.

The tasting doubles as a benefit for Last Course, an organization that provides dessert for the homeless, a sweetening to the appeal of poverty. Both Laura and I sit on the planning board of this wine tasting, for which I spent much of last night opening and then resealing hundreds of wine bottles. We donate old pancakes to Last Course, which distributes them to the homeless along with crusty pastries, expired ice cream, gelatinized cannoli, and other near-molding delicacies.

Parents have fallen into their proper circles—Manhattan with Manhattan, Brooklyn with Brooklyn, Slancy with Slancy. We island dwellers avoid tense talk around Moveable Museums and steer toward the gentle discourse of Russ Haverly's body. Selections to the ECI program have been put on hold in honor of the coach's confirmed death, which has led to several discussions on the Gopa website. Who will replace Russ on the ECI committee? How long will this delay announcements? Will sympathy skew the results toward lacrosse players, Olivia offers, and if so does it speak well of the minority players? She only speaks of one minority benchwarmer, her boring kid Todd, who is only half minority.

"I expect Damian will get in," Jackson says. "I'm less certain of Rhythm."

"She's made great strides," Jason says. "Why are you so down on Rhythm?"

"It's because she's white," I say, uttering what Jackson would never relay to a diverse crowd. I am referring to a post I read on a message board, which I wrote, that says white students have a disadvantage in the ECI selection because of a communal burden to conform to political correctness. "Jackson is right. No way Rhythm gets in."

"Fuck you, Pisser," Jason says.

I have angered Jackson as well. "Yes, Pisser, fuck off. You're ruining the evening."

Personally, I would prefer that all eighteen spots be filled based on merit. Rory Stokes, Vietnamese or Malaysian, was a bullshit pick because his father likely funded the entire program. Begrudgingly, Whisper Li earned his spot, although I feel he was chosen ahead of more capable students, including Damian, based on pressure from his mother's clique. Mostly, I just want to get under Olivia's skin and see if I can eradicate that accent.

This conversation creeps up often enough, our skin color conflicting with our tribal goal as parents. Typically, I bring a stable of rehearsed arguments, only to be overrun by firmer policy from Jackson and Olivia. That was before the Luderica made me crazy brave. Before the savages raided my innards as I try to sip wine and simultaneously contain this war. My creatures do not want a class war. They do not want a race war or a nation war or a religious war. They are the worthy. Their desire is a war of the reputable versus the fallen, and they have taken me hostage. I often wonder why I carry a weapon. It is to protect my family from people like me.

"I would expect a remark like that from you," Olivia says, sipping, pronouncing it *re-mahk*. "You don't know what it's like where I come from—"

"You come from Long Island. Private schooling. Country clubs."

"—having to prove yourself day in and day out," she says, threatening a weep, accent gone, "to Neanderthals who do not understand the white privilege they inherited simply by being born into a lottery."

"You've never worked a day in your life," I say

It escalates quickly. One of the lacrosse fathers has wandered over to take Olivia's side, consoling her along with Devin Brenner. Ray stays out of it, as does Harry. Allie offers Laura a squirt of disinfectant and they concentrate on their hygiene. Others watch from their circles, eager to see if this is the culmination when someone finally gets physical with me. Up until this point, we parents have been stabbing each other silently on the Gopa message boards, but I feel their licks elsewhere. Boycotts of Standcake. Rumors that I do not understand meteorology and plagiarize my prognostications. A petition, intercepted by Josey Mateo, to have me banned from school grounds. It is the reason I snuck in to the school last night, and, along with Josey and Little Petty, opened two-hundred bottles of wine, spilled out the top inch, and filled each with enema discharge. The things I have done for these people. They talk about defending their children. I have murdered for all of our children.

"...living off the tripe your husband passes off as inspiration."

The lacrosse father. "You are out of line, sir."

"...white men account for seventy percent of the suicides in this country."

"Someone get security."

"...blamed for constant injustice by pushy liberals who want everything handed to them and when they don't get it, it's the white guy's fault."

Laura now, "Tom, will you shut up please?"

"...the things I've done for you people. All you people."

"The weather?" Olivia looks around our circle for support. "Hah!" If she only knew.

"By gawd, he smells." Another lacrosse father, "He's drunk. Get him out of here."

Little Petty is screwing a woman who works at a spa that provides colonic therapy. Not knowing exactly what he would use it for, he told her to preserve some of the enema runoff in gallon milk jugs, which adds a subtle earthiness to the vintage. I left the Malbecs and Syrahs ass-juice free, and up until now I have been concerned with ensuring Laura does not ingest the cabernet. The bottle I am holding was the end of Little Petty's batch, when the concoction grew flaky.

"Perhaps I was overserved." I put up my hands, admitting defeat, and pour Olivia another glass. Devin sticks his glass forward, as do Harry and Allie. "A toast," I say.

"Yes," Harry agrees. "To all of us and our investment."

"To Last Course," Laura adds.

"And to the children," I say. "May they all know a friendlier tomorrow."

We sip. Devin examines his glass. Olivia swirls her nectar, shoving her nose into the goblet. "It's nice," she says.

I top her off. I am less agitated now but it's too late, a parent having pointed me out to security. It's just as well. I have someplace to be.

"And stay out," one of the lacrosse fathers mentions at the door. "Take a shower why don't you."

Imperialists Of Youth And Idealism

THE ESTABLISHMENT IS IN the basement of a gaudy hotel that caters to a subculture of bleached hair and questionable fashion. It sells tacos to tourists during the day, and at night is transformed into a dive club without bouncers or velvet ropes. A single bartender manages eight feet of real estate, a small scaffold that serves as a stage. Two musicians belt out cover songs that sound oddly familiar to the music emitted from behind Iliza's bedroom door. The man, handlebar mustache, plays a guitar while the girl dances and hums into a microphone. The band's name is The Elevators.

Josey is seated at a corner table with her crew, about which she has leaked few details during our evening fires. I met them before, during our theft of Sharon Li's prosthetic legs. It appears from their postures that they already do not care for me. I am the opposition—a privileged homeowner, opposed to their youth and rectitude, which permits living rent-free in an abandoned grocery store. Linda is the large transvestite of unknown ethnicity. Little Tom Petty seems on a perpetual diet or bender. Phil is in charge, an ex-boyfriend of Josey's who may or may not be working himself back into the rhythms of her affection. He strikes me as a Harvard graduate posing as a rebel to complete a doctoral thesis. He has small eyeglasses that age him, a T-shirt that reads *Words*. He conceals a condescending procession of eye maneuvers, though I have a teenaged daughter and speak fluent eye roll. Phil is trying to rough me up with gesture.

Linda stands in line for a living. She runs a service where people can text her to wait outside clubs or theaters or shoe sales hours before an event begins and, for a fee, can show up just as the doors open and swap spots. Phil is a mechanic at a bowling alley. Currently, Little Petty earns a meager salary as a tour guide where he spies on the Sedlocks and Moveable Museums. "Horse bones make the hardest knives," he explains, showing me his weapon and asking for a look at my BB gun, which he does not return. They pool their wages for living expenses and to support various initiatives, which until this evening Josey has been kind enough to exclude me from.

When life falls out of balance and order and discipline transform into lawlessness, you permit the universe to commit resources that fill the failure with chaos. Human beings depend on chaos to develop. Every great feat or invention was born out of failure, out of a need to fill the void with pandemonium. In my case, the transformation comes from Josey Mateo. She is not an ally who enjoys me because I read the weather properly, though she did send a new round of correspondence to Channel Fourteen earlier this week mentioning the unprecedented sixty-plus days of perfect weather coverage. She is not a theater junkie interested in taking my daughter under her wing. If she likes Iliza, it is a secondary notion to her involvement in my life.

Josey and Phil and Little Petty and Linda are activist hackers, cyberterrorists in certain circles. Having graduated from hacking the websites of hate groups and religious movements, into infiltrating banks' emails and making the findings public, they have settled on a new campaign. Word has come out about Moveable Museums' foray into a mass shooting tourism business. Their intention is to destroy it and anyone who gets in the way. Quiet, Dominican Josey covered in therapy ink to seem pathetic and lost, is nothing of the sort. She is calculating, having taken the job as an administrative assistant at Gopa to gain access into our lives—the Sedlocks and McClutchens and Ferrises and Pistilinis. She studies our spending habits on VillageShop. Watches our interactions on the Gopa portal. Knows our marriage banters, fallouts with faculty members, how often we visit the Manhattan Cryobank. Befriends a member of the Moveable Museums investment club, dopey, sad me, to report back to her crew.

"No compromise. We will destroy this business no matter the repercussions." Phil tells me this as he sips a ginger ale. "You will lose your investment whether you help or not. If you go to the police, or tell the others, it only prolongs the inevitable."

"Tom won't snitch," Little Petty says. He spent nearly a year infiltrating the Sedlocks' trust, their most loyal employee. "Tom wants a way out."

"Tom will find certain police friendly to him," Josey says, eyes on her skin as she inks a giraffe with a lion's face. "Tom needs friendship."

"We weren't planning to approach you, just let you rot like the others," Phil says. "Then you nearly killed the advice guy with that bike stunt. We think he might be an ally, even if he is fucking your old lady."

The clouds lift, my role clear. They may not know the extent of my involvement with Russ Haverly, or Toby Dalton, or the photographs of my daughter, or if I was trying to kill Ray McClutchen or just maim him. I am certain one of these people leaked the details of Moveable Museums to Lieutenant Misch, and his reluctance to investigate me is a result of my cooperation. My heartbeat is too rapid. I can feel the blackout approach. I need Luderica, water, something wet, an escape. The tribe bellows from my throat, slamming pitchforks into moist fields, the scents of feral wretchedness in my perspiration that sully my composure. Phil blinks. Josey draws on her wrist, eyes avoiding mine, as though she has accidentally seated herself at the wrong table. I check over my shoulder for a waiter, but a cocktail is not forthcoming.

"I'd like to explain."

"There's nothing to explain," Phil says. "We don't like you. The only reason you're sitting here is because Josey believes you are of value."

"Why would you think that?"

She raises her eyes momentarily. "You didn't hurt Clint Eastwood."

"That's the basis of my credentials?"

Josey takes a sip from Phil's ginger ale. "You're a good person, Tom. You didn't know what you were getting involved in. You've said so yourself, it's not too late."

"To betray my friends? To bankrupt my family?"

"You're already morally bankrupt," Linda says. She is not angry, shuffling a deck of cards with one giant hand and then spilling them in an avalanche of aces and jacks. "You'll lose your money either way. Be on the right side of history."

Phil transitions into a soliloquy that is both critical of my existence and beautiful in its dispatch. My kind is the roadblock for humanity to grow into a new dimension. We are an allegory of what is broken in the world, a pathogenic microbe gaining on the charisma and vigor of our species. We spread the religion of capitalism, controlling the world through modern-day slavery of baristas and retail schleps. We spin false remnants of a glorious civilization so that when distant creatures discover us ten thousand years into the future, unearthing our indestructible microwaves, our waterproof hiking jackets, our luxury sport utility vehicles we drove a mile to the supermarket, they will assume we were happy and friendly and valued each other. We are imperialists. We are colonizing their youth and virtue, all that is good about them, and using it for our gain.

Too often we equate the Whitmans and Joseys of the world to vapid inexperience, a digital promptitude that is impersonal and unmannered. These are my teachers, not those I have taught. When Phil finishes, my body is covered in a layer of cool sweat. My neck aches from nodding. I excuse myself to gather my courage and purchase ginger ales and something stronger. When I return, the table is empty.

Clint Eastwood's Latest Rampage

THE FIRE GLOWS BESIDE a bubbling pool, festive music, escaping charisma of a follow-up gala in my own backyard to which I was not invited. I am hopeful to find Iliza waiting up for me, maybe even Laura, anyone to discuss the night's revelation, to put my mind at ease that I have not, in fact, failed at every possible attempt at worthiness. I sense something significant occurred during Laura's weekend away, which she has been reluctant to discuss. It is Jackson instead. On the giant screen, the digitally remastered *Commodores Live!* DVD I purchased for his birthday last year. It ruined the celebration, Jason calling me a racist for pushing black culture on Jackson who prefers classical music. I only purchased it because Jackson once told me his father loved Lionel Richie. Beneath the glow of the Commodores crooning about love and change, somehow all of their lyrics about missing Lionel who is beside them on stage, I notice the outline of a leg in my pit. Jackson discovered my trophy.

I sit without addressing it. Jackson is kind enough or inebriated enough not to scold me. He does not offer any of what he's drinking, which I am happy to see is not leftover wine from the gala. "Have you done anything about the cat?"

"I took care of it the other day," I lie.

"It attacked Jason tonight after the event. When he was taking out the garbage."

"Damn thing must still have a few more lives in it." I am a series of bad jokes, an endless epiphany of disappointment. "Sorry to hear it, Jackson. Truly, I am."

"Chased him down the street to the McClutchens' treehouse."

"Why would he climb into a treehouse?" Jackson does not answer. "Cats are magnificent at climbing trees."

"Pisser…"

"Those treehouses aren't regulation," I say, changing the subject. "He could have been seriously injured if—"

"Tom, stop talking."

I try for sympathy. "Clint Eastwood is pregnant. Things are complicated."

He shrugs, not his problem, having been sent here by his husband to address our neighborly dispute and getting caught up in a 1970s drift. A spark from the cell phone tree ignites the fire, illuminating a tear track on Jackson's cheek. We watch the leg smolder, the crackling of Sharon Li's mobility giving off a bluish hue. I have interrupted something meaningful by coming home too early. Five more minutes, the Commodores would be bowing and hugging and heading to their next venue.

"Can I ask you something?"

"If it's about Moveable Museums, you may not." Jackson shifts in his chair, not wanting to leave but unable to stay longer now that I am here. "We have no decision," he says, hovering over my chair. I think he's going to hit me, but when I stand he offers his hand. "Just remember I was good to you once. Whatever you're up to, whatever shit is going on with the other parents, leave me out of it."

"Jackson."

"Say it, Pisser. Say you'll leave me out of it."

"Of course." We shake hands. "Is Jason okay?" I call.

He disappears into his yard. "Just take care of the fucking cat."

Sex Lives Of Dead People

ON MY WAY HOME from work today I passed three leashed dogs, two of which clotheslined passersby to dash at my legs, not to bite me but to lick my skin. I stopped to pet a third, a large Siberian husky, which took a seat on the sidewalk and allowed me to rub its neck. In the past, dogs would nip and bark and tug their companions, teeth gnashing for flesh. They can smell my natural odor, intuit my savagery, and know that I have returned to a primordial version of myself. The owner seemed pleased to see me. "Sixty-five days. Must be some kind of record."

I arrive home early with plans to make dinner for Laura and the kids. Since her trip with Ray, Laura has been more aware of my existence, intrigued by my backyard occupation and evening rituals in spite of my tellurian aromas. The kids as well. We have not eaten a proper sit-down family meal in nearly a year; I remember the exact dinner—a chilly December night, departing a Broadway show, we saw the steam-harried windows of a pizzeria and ducked inside to enjoy the warmth.

A cool May evening, I ordered several bags of charcoal from VillageShop, which as a Zenith member I had delivered this afternoon.

I expect to find the loot waiting on the front stoop. Instead, the boxes and packing peanuts lay crumpled on the walking path, my favorite pastime disemboweled. I detect the smell of burning coal, the shit revelation of Toby Dalton drinking a beer, his feet in my Jacuzzi, several empties lying in the grass beside his lacrosse equipment. A new BB gun against my waist, I arch my back to feel the handle.

"There he is." Toby smiles, old friends. "I'm in a lacrosse league in Red Hook on Thursdays. Thought I'd swing by. You know there's a fucking wild cat back there?"

Had I returned to find a dead cat, I am certain the creatures in my larynx would have beaten Toby to death with a brick and burned him over the charcoal, sorting out the legal matters another time. Most judges will be lenient to fathers involved in revenge murder if their children are injured. Do the same principles apply to therapy animals? A mental note for a blog post on the Gopa website: should we all begin arming our children with therapy animals to cope with modern anxieties for when we are not present, and how will that impact morning drop-off?

I light a cigarette, watching my problem step out of the water. Six schools. That is how many expulsions Toby has been through, and Gopa will be no different. Only that his old man has set terms: make it work this time or the Daltons wash their hands of him. Getting into the ECI program would have been a way back, but I ruined that option with my four-iron. Lacrosse season has ended early and Toby has other things on his mind besides education. He has nothing else to do but play pickup games in Red Hook and haunt me. The two of us have been brought here by divine decree—Toby for blackmail, my tribe and I to eliminate the dirty urgencies that might poison my child.

"Where's the phone?" he asks.

"Gone."

"No, it isn't. You should have thrown it out, Pisser. Soon as they found the boat. It would have put an end to it." He winks at our dilemma. "Now he keeps calling and calling, and you keep answering. He wants his money."

Someone keeps answering, but it is not me. I check the woods for Doug Whorley or others waiting in sabotage, expecting to see a gang of helmeted minions with Worthy insignia descend from my trees brandishing sticks. My tribe is ready, the fire in their lungs. The woods appear empty, the slight buzz giving Toby adrenaline he might need. From my mind's eye the chain goes something like this: students purchase their drugs from Toby, who was supplied by Russ Haverly. Russ's supplier is a thing named Capra, a Persian living in Canada. For some racist reason that defies logic, I am relieved to be dealing with a suit and tie criminal from the friendly border. Along with Toby, Russ was supplying the Gopa community with illicit drugs, a lucrative connection for everyone. Once Capra knew the phone was live, he investigated the chain of command, which led him to dipshit Toby.

"Ask your father for the money."

"I can't." He tosses a can in my yard, and I sail a nicotine projectile in that direction. "Or rather, I could. But it would be my final request." He cracks another beer, which spills over the edge of the can. He has not offered me one. "You're going to help me, Pisser."

"I don't have any money."

"Bullshit." He looks around the yard at my house, my woods, the sound of spring golfers whiffing over the bluff, a paradise lagoon, a wife with a blossoming business, two kids enrolled at Gopa Academy. He does not understand that we are mortgaged through the eyeballs, living here as impostors, that our savings is responsibly invested for the future so that tourists can enjoy how Americans kill innocent bystanders and school children in hails of gunfire.

"I don't have sixty-thousand dollars to give you, Toby. Even if I did, why would I help you?"

It was closer to forty grand a month ago, so I'm ball parking. He lifts his eyes at the number, surprised that I am paying attention.

"You owe me, Pisser. Coach was getting me into that program. Now I'm fucked." He snarls, aggressive, slightly intoxicated as he crosses my yard to show he is not scared from his last strangling.

"I can't do anything about that. But I can make sure Capra doesn't kill me. And I can make sure your daughter gets booted out of the play and ECI."

"The photos," I say.

"Who said anything about photos? Find my money or the video goes public."

We gulp, all of us at once, a collective swill that drains my being of moisture. "What's on the video?"

He smiles, the little fuck, leans in to have a smell. "Geezus, Pisser. You killed him, didn't you?"

He's hoping I spill it. "What's on the video, Toby?"

"Russ came to you for help and you killed him. Over a video." He smiles, sips the beer, laughs at our complications. "I go down, you go down. Easy."

The thought of my daughter in Toby's possession, even as a digital image imprisoned in his cellular data plan, is a concept that makes this a delicate discussion for Toby. It killed Russ and summoned my tribe of savages—my streak of feral urgency to rain down justice on my fellow Gopa parents. Did I allow a predator into my daughter's world? I have to see to know for sure.

"Let me watch it, Toby."

He tries to gauge my reaction, a dangerous time. Russ Haverly could not describe what was on the video, too stoned to recall the evening. If the images are bad, it could summon the rage that ended Russ's life.

He takes out his phone and clicks buttons. He tosses it to me. My eyes race across the illumination, an expensive apartment that I deduce belongs to Toby's father. I recognize a number of faces, all Gopa students, my heart and rhythms galloping as the camera winds through a smoky room, an inebriated vibe. Toby has taken the time to pan in on all the faces, teenagers performing teenage transgression, blackmail in case he needs it. There is beer, cigarettes, most likely marijuana, a physical game around a Ping-Pong table where a group of kids has congregated.

The camera winds upstairs, different music from a new floor. My mouth is dry, my neck tightening. A door opens into a bathroom, steam and promiscuity, the sound of water and laughter, the wickedness rushing up my arm into my shoulder, a sharp pain as if whatever emerges from behind that shower door will kill or heal me. The shower is larger than my den, two spouts of water. Inside, there is a tangle of legs as a voice calls out "Coach," and a naked and inebriated Russ Haverly turns to the camera, red-faced laughter at his cameo. He is behind the girl who is bent over at the waist, trying to manage a glass that has fallen onto the tile. I cannot see the face hidden in her sopping hair. It looks like every girl Iliza's age, tiny and soft. She picks it up, drops it, picks it up again, no face. She drops it, laughter, Russ hollering at the camera and Toby.

"Say something, Coach."

He leans, squints; the girl intoxicated. She could be Iliza who I have not seen naked in a decade. "Let's have a great season, guys," he slurs, the girl shrieking as he turns, partially numb, to see the blood.

She has cut her hand on the broken glass—Toby laughing, Russ laughing, blood from her hand streaming down her breasts and legs, still no face. "Hold still," Russ is saying. "Hold still." The camera moves into the shower for a look at the wound, the girl slapping at the device playfully as her face emerges. Tungsten Sedlock, the bloody hand, fucking her father's friend and investment partner in a strange shower. I stare into the trees, breathing for the first time, sweat dripping down my nape.

"Hold on, there's more," Toby says.

Back out of the shower and down the stairs, a congregation of students around a table covered with miscellany into which Toby focuses the lens: a bra, car keys, several pill bottles. In the living room I discover my failure, what no father wishes to see. Iliza is bent over the table inhaling a line of what I can only imagine is an illegal pharmaceutical, her face rising stoned and vacant, a breast nearly hanging out of a shirt I've previously ordered her not to wear. Pill bottles litter the table, the same brown hue, the euphoric wander of her gaze as she studies the tremendous architecture in the ceiling, children snorting a dead man's Luderica. As Toby pans in on her features, I would be relieved to see marijuana or vodka, any sin other than a hard cock in her hand, kids these days.

"Say something, girl," Toby calls.

My child awakens, her eyes rising to meet the camera, the boy holding it, of which she was, and possibly still is, enamored. She seems lost and torn, but elated and enjoying herself, a child navigating the complexities of youth. She smiles and gives a tiny wave, too delirious to understand she is surrounded by predation. Of the one hundred fifty students eligible for the ECI program, this video eliminates at least thirty if it goes public. My daughter is one of them.

I regain my composure and toss the phone to Toby. I killed a man for the wrong reason. The task was worthy, though it belonged to another father. Someone else's daughter, someone else's penance. I'll deal with the guilt another time. I'll deal with Iliza soon. I'll tell Harry and Allie what I know.

"Why come to me?" I point across the yard. "The Sedlocks live just over there."

I already know the answer. Harry is an acquaintance of Toby's father, their sons members of the same team and Gopa hierarchy. Blackmailing the Sedlocks comes with risk. And, as Toby has gathered, I know what really happened to Russ Haverly.

"You're my guy, Pisser. You could have saved us both a lot of heartache if you dumped the phone."

"You won't show it. It won't just be bad for Iliza. It'll be bad for all your friends. It'll be bad for you especially, Toby."

He shrugs. "That's a chance you won't take."

He turns to leave. I am eager for his departure, but my tribe has other plans. Toby is in my yard, my domain. Like the helpless, parentless chipmunks, he has nowhere to go, a prey in my wilderness.

I race into his path. "Why would you do this, Toby?"

"This is no time for lectures, Pisser."

"Iliza is your friend. I thought you liked her."

It is not the shrug that does it. It is the bitchy smile. "She doesn't put out. Tungsten, now that girl fucks. But your daughter, she's just kind of in the way."

My hand is there quick, my army cocked and ready. He underestimates for a second time our rage, the muscle of my people, and we have him in the Jacuzzi in one push. We land on my feet, up to my waist in water, but Toby has tumbled over backward frantically kicking as we drown a creature for the second time. This is how Russ went. It is possibly how the nanny went as well. Only this time, I am present. This time I enjoy the bubbles and fury, the sight of his legs kicking against the wall. We grip his neck and realize, in spite of the drug use, we are oddly proud of Iliza. She will be punished, but at least she was raised properly enough not to put out for this filthy fuck.

Behind the tree line, Clint Eastwood screeches and races for the waterfall ledge. Rhythm is naked and chasing the cat through the yard. Which means time has passed. Which means school is out. Which means I have to get the steaks on the grill and toss the salad and set the table. Which means we have loosened our grip on...

Toby climbs out of the water, irate that he's experienced near death a second time from Channel Fourteen's weatherman. Out of breath and wet, he reaches for his lacrosse equipment in the yard and mops his dopey face. "A month. That's how long Capra gave me. That's how long you get."

He disappears around the edge of the house, voices inside, my family returning, me standing in a wet suit. From the back porch, a set of eyes hover as I emerge from the Jacuzzi. Tungsten Sedlock is staying for dinner.

Dark Tourism

Tonight is the consummate meeting of our investment club. Since her return from the weekend with Ray McClutchen, things have been different with Laura, better—several chats about the kids and Standcake, my record weather prognostications, and the third threatening letter from the homeowners association. They have added "tent structure" to the language. Residents are allowed to build treehouses in weak timber, but according to the bylaws I cannot pitch a temporary habitat in my backyard for longer than seven days. Laura and I smile over the legalese. I miss talking to my wife at night, after the kids are in bed, our phones put away for the day. I have no intention of corrupting this streak with discussions about Toby Dalton, or what I plan to do about him.

We gather at the Sedlocks on a Friday instead of our regular Monday appointment, our congenial beginning hampered by the presence of new guests. We barely manage to get in our hugs and triple kisses, Olivia making a wrenching face when it's our turn—"Pisser, you need a proper bath." The Sedlocks' attorney is seated in the rear, along with Connor Mack of the Mack Strategy Group. A former lobbyist for the National Rifle Association, it will be his task to cram this aberration down the throats of critics. There are two members of the media who write about what Harry has referred to as murder culture. In a few weeks, they, along with a dozen of their constituents, will travel to sites along our tourism route. This will begin the publicity push for which the Sedlocks have hired a public relations firm out of Los Angeles that specializes in getting out front of what might become negative reviews. In preparation for tonight's discussion, I have popped two of Sharon Li's Luderica along with a tumbler of scotch to steady my nerves.

A man named Pietre Graeme—*Grim*, I hear—writes for an underground German publication called *Leichenbestatter*. He is excited to speak with the investors behind the Moveable Memorial Tour. He looks like he is personally responsible for decapitating and hiding the bodies of several prostitutes in his lifetime, and he sniffs his cognac before every sip. A Danish woman, Hansa Schultz—*Shank*, I hear— writes for *Voldtage*. She looks nothing like the goth and emaciated character I would expect to write about murder culture, her blonde hair and spring colors more attuned to lifestyle journalism.

Something has come to pass between Olivia and Ray, or maybe between Ray and my wife. Last week's Cooperative Marriage meeting was canceled, no follow-up email or explanation. The three are sitting in isolated parts of the room, ignoring each other and concentrating steadily on their phones. Jackson and Jason are no more cordial to one another, all of us a convocation of one man gangs listening to Pietre Graeme explain the history and wonders of murder tourism.

"Classically it's referred to as thanatourism. After the Greek god Thanatos, who was associated with death. He wasn't as popular as Hades. Most people have never heard of him."

I hate Pietre Graeme in ways that improve hatred. We are not reinventing the wheel, Pietre tells us, setting down his cognac to issue us air quotes with both hands. People enjoy death. The end of life is a mystical phenomenon that human beings have always valued. Haunted houses, dangerous rollercoasters, ghost tours, graveyard walks—all have transformed from macabre activities into traditional leisure events accepted by the mainstream. Tours of medieval torture sites bring incredible numbers around the world. People flock to Hiroshima and Auschwitz and the September-Eleven Memorial, places where mass death occurred. Chernobyl, the site of one of the world's most devastating nuclear disasters, brings in tens of thousands of visitors each year.

"Catacombs of Paris, celebrity murder tours in Los Angeles, Roman Colosseum," Pietre says, smiling, sniffing. "I could go on."

And then he does. Sites of genocide. Penitentiaries where prisoners were electrocuted. Cambodia's killing fields. Aokigahara, he says in a strange accent, the Suicide Forest in Japan where hundreds of people take their lives each year, and where tourists come to whisper and buy souvenirs and snap pictures they post to social media with bucket list verve. Haunted castles. Haunted barracks. A haunted bowling alley in a town I cannot make out through the accent. The site of a clown convention where years earlier a man dressed as a jester gunned down eighty-seven other clowns, and where each year tourists, dressed in brightly colored garb, rent hotel rooms and eat shitty chain food and revisit the massacre. Ford's Theatre where Booth took out a president, group rates for the JFK Assassination Tour: the grassy knoll,

Jack Ruby's apartment—the sixth floor of the book depository where tourists can crouch in the spot Ruby prayed, even aim an imaginary rifle out the window at regurgitated history.

"I've been to it twice," Connor Mack says from behind us. He holds up two fingers so we get it.

Hansa takes over. The Lizzie Borden House. Pompei, where two thousand years ago a civilization cooked, and people still pay to be photographed with the ghosts. Alcatraz. Al Capone's Saint Valentine's Day Massacre. The sites and methods of various serial killers organized into two-hour increments and guided by an hourly wage historian. Tours of current and past war zones, adventurers not satisfied with the media's version and willing to travel into danger zones to witness firsthand civilizations shredded for historical satiation.

"Tours of America's slave trade," Allie says. "No one finds the Underground Railroad to be in poor taste," as if taste needs to be defended.

"That's exactly it," Hansa says.

The women are taking sides with Hansa in ways we men never did with Pietre, a sinister gender politics at play. Harry nods quickly, satisfied; if the moms can come together, we can all get on board. Dan Mathers reads his phone. Pietre sniffs his glass. I notice an alarming tattoo on Hansa's ankle, which in the shadows looks like an infant kebabbed on a spear. Laura stays out of it, the way Jason and Jackson and Ray and I stay out of it, subtle whisper of shifting alliances. The recent appearance of Russ's body hanging over our congeniality; we inhale darkness and exhale guilt.

"There's precedent here," Harry says. I blacked out for a bit and can tell from his rhythm that he has been at it for some time, reviewing what was already said. "Our society has long consumed murder and disaster as entertainment. The Moveable Memorial Tour is no different."

"It's different and you know it's different, Harry." It is my voice I hear suddenly litter the room with anger. I am not sure where I summon the courage to speak, but now I am the opposition and I own it. "Otherwise, why hire a publicity firm?"

"There's an historical balm that comes from this type of tourism." Connor Mack is brilliant when he speaks, his car sales pitch refined into selling drug addictions and sexual assaults and accidental murders to a hungry public. "We recover, as a society, from past negligence by learning about it, making it more obtainable for the public." He holds a thumb over his fingers, hand held out, body language that former US president Bill Clinton patented. "Coping. Understanding. Getting better."

"We're selling tickets to places where children were murdered," I say.

"It's not all dead kids. There are several mass murder sites on the national tours at which no children perished at all." He turns to look for a pamphlet to prove it. "Some will see dead kids. Others will see resiliency."

"It's not just us," Olivia says. "Without tourists there would be no necessity for our business. They share the blame."

Connor Mack is quickly in the center of the room, hovering over Olivia's words, Harry as well. "Whoa, hold on here. No one said anything about blame. This is not about blame. Let's get that straight."

I stand. The BB gun in my waistband grinds into my skin. "We have children," I say. "We cannot be a part of this."

Harry is shaking. "Solid perspective, Pisser. Let's talk it out."

"Other parents will feel the same."

"You don't know that," Olivia says.

"It's common sense."

"Economics always conquers common sense," Pietre says, holding up his glass, a toast. "This venture will be prosperous. A responsibility to shine light into dark spaces. This is important work. Never forget that."

From beneath the Luderica and my lofty observations, I cannot decide who is more repugnant. Pietre or Connor. Or maybe Olivia or Hansa. Or Allie and Harry. Or possibly it is me. The way Pietre and Hansa casually discuss murder, and how they have wrapped us all inside the responsibility of our endeavor. Have we come too far? We all need the money. The only thing I consider, as Pietre rips into another retelling of the intrinsic value of murder tourism, is how much I love my children. Dead or alive, they are not a tourist attraction.

I owe it to my kids. I owe it to myself. I owe it to my wife who is quiet and removed from the discussion. If there exists even a fraction of a chance my marriage will survive, I will fight my way back.

"I've heard enough." This quiets Pietre. Allie rubs her arms. Harry hangs his head. Dan Mathers glances up from his phone long enough to shake his head at my financial ruin. Jason clutches a pillow. "Laura and I are out. We don't want any part of this."

Dan Mathers sighs. Connor Mack pumps a fist into a palm. Ray McClutchen appeals for our cooperation. "What about you, Laura? We didn't hear from you tonight?"

"I'm in agreement with Tom. It isn't right. You all know that." Once my wife makes a decision, there is no deterring her. She is a flood, a raging fire, a gospel of conviction. "We cannot support this."

"Let's find a solution," Olivia says.

Ray is broken. "There isn't one," he concedes. "I hate to say it, but I'm in agreement with Pisser. There's nothing positive about any of this."

Allie's fists grind at her hips, her tongue beating a tirade into her cheek. Harry places a hand on her shoulder. "We're sorry to hear it. Honestly, I'm just really surprised at the both of you."

"Our investment," I say, though I know this is not the time.

He shrugs, hands shaking. "We'll see what can be done about returning…a percentage. I have to caution, as I said before, there will be a significant loss."

We cannot afford the fallout my words have created. I am less concerned with the money and more intrigued with the state of my marriage. Laura just nodded at me, a partial smile, proud for a change. Despite the state of our financial situation, we are in this together the way we once promised. Olivia says she and Ray are staying in, a house in the Hamptons, another for her parents in Arizona, nanny wages; despite Ray's lucrative book sales and tours, they cannot afford to lose the investment. Jackson and Jason are staying as well. Laura and I are no longer members of this investment club and we excuse ourselves. Our neighbors avoid our eyes as we exit, Harry asking me to the backyard for a private word.

In the foyer, I find Laura's coat and help her into it, letting my hands rest gently on her shoulders as I fit her inside the warmth. "Shall I wait?" she asks.

"No, get home. Check the kids."

"You're sleeping in the backyard tonight?"

"It's for the best."

She kisses my cheek, and my insides fall apart, the scent of this woman conquering my civilization. "Don't be long, Tom."

Seventy Percent Chance of Vengeance

IN THE MANNER I sense weather patterns, I know about the backyard conversation before we exit the foyer. Overcast moods turning to clenched fists, high of pointed fingers and flying spit with a chance of middle-aged wrestling. Harry is six foot four, a business casual addict, his gray, floppy hair godlike when he arrives in a room. Only now it has fallen into his eyes, his neckline pulled lower by an extra button. He runs a hand across the back of his head, shaking, perspiring. He is upset, he tells me, discouraged. He thought we had an understanding. He confided in me about Moveable Museums. He trusted me.

"I understand it might take time to return our investment."

"Fuck your investment." The phlegm I forecast on my way to the backyard finds my cheek. "This isn't about money. It's about perception. When one person loses his nerve, others follow. And we were counting on your relationship with Lustfizzle."

"Ethically, I just don't—"

"Ethically?" He's in my face. "Don't talk to me about ethics, Pisser."

The Luderica dries my mouth, makes me sleepy, part of me anyway. It dulls the tribe living in my wilderness, squatting on my plains, and hunting my woods. Harry has awoken them. They are arming their warriors. They are ordering their women into underground bunkers with the children, but the women are not vacating. They are flashing teeth and slapping horses.

"Step away from me, Harry." We pace the yard until there is sufficient buffer. "Don't talk about ethics? What's that supposed to mean?"

Harry laughs, his lips hard against his gums. I have never noticed before. His teeth are fake. "Russ Haverly."

"What about Russ?"

"You and Toby Dalton. The nannies get it right most of the time. Tell me," he says. "The nannies talk about some photos. Do the police know about the photos?"

"You don't understand, Harry."

"I could give a shit about Russ." It's soft but I hear it, the growl, his own monsters. "All the times I bailed him out. You know, I'm actually glad not to have to clean up his mess anymore."

"There's video. Something you need to know."

Harry sighs, talks to me like a dad. "Iliza. I know the rumors."

Russ never told his friend because he knew what it meant—the end of Gopa, the end of his coaching career, the last hand that would offer assistance, the cessation of his investment in Moveable Museums, more than likely drug money he was laundering. It's on me to deliver the news. "Iliza is in the video, that's true. But so is Tungsten. In the shower. With Russ."

I cannot halt his momentum across the patio, a larger man with more rage. He goes for my neck, but I am prepared. We tumble against the house. He smells wonderful, like summer in the Florida Keys, a whiff of rodeo. I smell of homelessness, deer entrails. "Say it again, Pisser. Say what you just fucking said."

"I saw the video."

"You're lying." He tries to punch me but I'm holding the lips of his collar, the worst fight in the annals of male testosterone. "You killed Russ. Everyone knows it."

I know better than to confess anything to Harry Sedlock. I hold the stare and he pounces to the far side of the patio to straighten his collar. A thick hand through his mane, he comes around for fresh negotiations.

"All right, this is how it is." He walks close, calmer now, too exhausted to punch out my teeth. "I don't want trouble, Pisser. Russ gone is a blessing. I'll keep quiet. You'll keep quiet about Moveable. These things happen in business."

"I'm sure they do."

"Laura's Standcake interests are tied into the Gopa community. She has reasons not to piss me off." If I'm not mistaken, Harry just threatened my wife's occupation. My neck tingles, the tribal lords lifting their weapons. "But you, Pisser. I never liked you. Strange, a man sleeping in his backyard, the way you smell, the way you mope about. Can't trust a man who doesn't have his house in order. I associate with you because our daughters are friends. Were friends. That ends tonight."

"I'm not lying about the video, Harry."

"You'll pull Iliza out of the play. You'll do it this week."

The world stops spinning. The island goes silent. The cell phone trees hiccup a ballad of descent and ire and then doom. Somewhere Clint Eastwood rests her paws midway into a kill near a freshly raked bunker, an idiot chipmunk out for a stroll only to cross the pregnant cravings of gnashing death. I feel the Luderica break down and mist against my cells, the chemicals suffusing into my blood and rolling along my ganglia. There is no wind. The hum from distant Manhattan takes pause as existence centers on the Sedlocks' backyard. The steel from the BB gun grinds into my skin. My mind replays his last sentence as I step toward Harry Sedlock, a second threat to my family.

"We were counting on Russ to get Tungsten into ECI. That's over now. Playing the lead in the play is a credential she needs." He transforms from extortion to business. "Come on, Pisser. Small price to stay out of prison."

"Iliza worked hard. She needs the credentials as well."

"Iliza's father killed someone." He shrugs, renegotiating our neighborly boundaries here in perfect, mirthful Slancy. "I'll tell the police. I'll tell the lacrosse fathers—both about Russ and the stolen bus, which I'm certain you had a hand in. I'll make Gopa a living hell for your kids." A third threat. "Pull her out, Pisser."

"That can't happen."

"Blame it on trouble at home. Difficulties with studies. The fuck do I care?"

The tribe is irate, begging for eyeballs, to hoist his testicles on a spit, cook it over fire, and serve it with chocolate and graham cracker. Tom Pistilini, Channel Fourteen meteorologist, has righted the ship. Tom Pistilini is doing his best to appeal to higher moral ground, following Ray McClutchen's advice, seeking the positive. "Let's sit down with Allie and Laura, the four of us talk this out."

"Allie?" He laughs until he moans. "She wanted me to force this weeks ago. I said no. I appealed to her business sense. You know what I said? 'The Pistilinis are neighbors,' I told her. 'Laura and Tom are on our side,' I said." He shakes his head at me. "You want to fuck my wife. I see how you look at her."

I reach around my back, my hand on the gun.

"She's not as nice as she looks." He growls again. "She's worse than any Gopa mom, ruthless. And sometimes moms have to be ruthless."

My hand shakes. My neck heaves sweat down my back. I imagine aiming the gun at his greasy face and unloading terminal BBs into his eye sockets until his veins explode from the tiny steel orbs. The tribe demands it, winning out over my patience. I pull the gun and fire off a round into his thigh, which does nothing. I unload a second round that tears through his pants.

"Fuck, Pisser."

"Come near my family, Harry." I shoot him twice more—once in the shin, another in his left shoulder. "I'll kill you. And I'll fucking destroy your business."

He massages his leg, checks the fabric to see if I ruined his outfit, then skips into his house as though he's being hunted. He slams the door and yells something through the glass, but it only sounds like a mumble as I unload the gun into his face, the door cracking and speckling as Harry disappears.

Marriage Is A Strange Institution

THAT EVENING, IN THE solitude of my backyard, I submit to the forces I can no longer tame, a lineage that has existed dormant too long. The part of me forced into silence and sensitivity and order and teamwork, everything it takes to be a successful parent in the complicated world of Gopa Academy. We played by the rules. We did what was required. We joined clubs and hired tutors and employed nannies and volunteered for committees. The system failed us. Everyone failed us except the awakened creatures that I have done my best to contain. Only now I need the creatures to survive, need their instincts to guide me. A part of me, the portion associated with fatherhood, is clinically insane. I have conformed to conceal it from the world. The Luderica liberated it. My actions, while criminal, have summoned my savagery, which may ultimately save my marriage.

A rustling outside my tent that I suspect is my cat returning home to watch the last of the music video, Clint Eastwood having become a Jason Isbell fan. Instead Laura climbs into the nylon, the scents of shampoo and meat and survival. The rapidity with which she enters implies danger, the children are dead, their throats slit by a madman, potentially me. She wears a sweater and underwear, wrestling into the sleeping bag until I am thrust against the estranged nostalgia of where I belong.

"The kids?" I ask.

"Inside. Asleep."

"Are you?"

"Drunk? No. Some wine. Lots of wine." She reaches down to undress herself. I am quickly erect. I am relieved to find that my wife is ungroomed, which means sex with Ray McClutchen is not occurring.

"Are we having an affair?"

She tenses, then laughs, the situation more erotic that we are clandestinely fucking in a backyard tent. I maneuver inside Laura, the familiarity of her outline and odor, and I feel my composure wane, thinking of anything to prolong the sex.

"What about the cryobank?"

"Shut up."

"Moveable?" I whisper.

"Don't. No pancakes. No homework. No Iliza."

Less than a minute, Laura breathing heavy on my chest, my heart beating into her ear, listening to the cell phone trees hum, the singer pining over faith in a girl and prayers for daylight, the darkness as it shifts into a morning when everything is different.

Part Three

Memorials For Drug Dealers Are Like Normal Memorials

THE DOUCEREUX LINE OF rainwear is made of breathable acrylic camel hair that has been specially treated with waterproofing chemicals. It is available on VillageShop only a few times a year for Zenith Members. We purchased a matching set that sits in our closet for much of the calendar year owing to my previous penchant for poor forecasting. Occasionally, a wet commute would find Laura accusing that she should have had the Doucereux jacket and matching umbrella that morning, a sly piece of passive aggression that, like most conniptions left unquarreled, leveled our marriage in ways I could never have forecast.

We are the only parents dressed properly for the memorial service. Unseasonably cool temperatures are expected for much of the Eastern seaboard, the latest models showing readings seven degrees below normal and, most likely, a series of fast-moving showers that could turn heavy at times. The models changed overnight, and since many of the lacrosse parents attended a private memorial to which we were not invited, they arrived sans rain gear. Laura wears a black suit and boots with a blacker umbrella, the various shades of darkness inspiring fantasies of throwing her on the wet turf to fuck her gracelessly in front of our children. I wear a large Doucereux camping poncho that could fit seven other parents. A floral umbrella, Florida retiree muumuu, and oversized sunglasses, Gus is dressed like a fucking idiot.

Iliza wears jeans, a Gopa sweatshirt, and a scowl. She does not stand with her friends because she is grounded until I decide to speak with her about the charges, which she damn well already knows. She insists on explanations of my anger, but I cannot properly address her discretions without implicating myself.

"Don't look at me like that," I begin each interaction. "I will wipe that glare off your brow."

I have informed Laura about the video's contents, and while we are relieved, all things considered, we are appalled at our daughter's drug use. Making moods worse, the revelation came on the heels of Gus's fourteenth birthday party, for which none of his "friends" showed. We knew the attendance would be shoddy, but there were a few strays that rarely get invited to parties we hoped would attend out of desperation. None of the Slancy neighbors came. A rumor out of the nannies is that Olivia McClutchen made reference to a rabid cat living on the property, which sent the sanitized and virtuous into ritualistic distress, lobbing elaborate excuses of truancy. Three hundred vertical pancakes, a dozen pizzas, and a showing of "Mary Poppins" on the big screen, Gus's choice, all for naught. He did not seem sad as the four of us hunkered close on a chilly May night, the fire pit wild and gregarious, as Julie Andrews made a mockery of the heartaches of childcare and I contemplated vengeance, a destructive blow from my enemies.

"Don't even think about looking at that phone," I intermittently hollered at Iliza. "This is a goddamned party."

The memorial is held at the soccer turf on the East River that doubles as our home lacrosse field eleven days of the year. Off to the south, if you crane your neck, you can get the general direction of Slancy without actually seeing home, the edges of Governors Island and the Brooklyn shipyards blocking eyesight. Here come the Worthy's fifth grade girls, done up with makeup and short skirts, and who seem positively whorish in their rendition of "The Star-Spangled Banner." The song is an odd start to a memorial, but we all feign patriotism and sympathy even though the singers' mothers painted their lips hot pink and are obviously treating this as a hired gig for their resumes. Because we rent this turf, even the memorial seems transient, the passing boats a wayward reprieve as we bow heads and try to remember what Russ Haverly meant to us. Lacrosse coach. PTA ambassador to the ECI program. Recreational drug dealer. Pedophile. The beginning of the end, really, of our Gopa community as our federation has unwound into affluent warfare.

Like many wars, we do not know how the fighting began. Lacrosse parents will claim it was the stolen equipment bus that initiated our strife, but other parents will nod further back in our history at the various privileges and misdeeds that are associated with the sports teams. Perhaps the dead coach launched our squabbles. Or maybe, for those privy to the footage, our pampered coach should not have been fucking teenagers in showers at high school narcotic buffets. What we can all agree on is that even at Gopa there is a deficiency of raw materials needed to build the perfect human, which in our case comes down to the last sixteen spots in the coveted ECI.

The Jansens' nanny was deported. This came after a series of checks by immigration, which was tipped off to illegal employees working under the table at our school. Rumor has it the Youdles' housekeeper was bribed to provide dirt on her family and, even though she refused, the Youdles fired her anyway. She was compromised and would expect a raise for her loyalty, and they could not have that sort of thing around the children. The help has long been off limits when it comes to family disputes, in the way that mob families did not pick off each other's landscaping crews. That has changed in the new ECI conniptions. The nannies circle their wagons.

My seventh handle this spring, Cloudy_Dad9, has been revoked from the Gopa website even though I only commented on, and did not post, the blog entry about rumored lesbianism on the girls' volleyball team, which everyone knows about.

"It's more of a trendy sexual romp, not one based on actually appreciating the pussy, but rather the stigma of being told licking pussy is wrong. If we all just back off and stop making an issue out of what is, essentially, fairly mild and unhygienic foreplay when it comes to what these kids are capable of, it will cease to be an issue. Do you know they stick things in their assholes, record the most outrageous items, and share it on social media? It's a thing. It's called 'assholing.' I've included a link to LustFizzle's '41 Things You Don't Have To Stick In Your Anus Because Someone Already Did.' Which begs the question: how much of our children's behavior is a product of our eagerness to overcompensate for our own failures at relevance? Digging into our kids' sex lives is a reaction to our own miserable sex lives. We demand perfection in their studies because we are consistently stupid creatures. Our shock at kids doing drugs and drinking alcohol is because we know, in some small sense, that we depend on these features more than we like."

Another student, a sophomore, was taken out of Branding Shop class in an ambulance. The parents spread the word that it was complications from a juice cleanse, but we all know it was drugs. The nannies claim Luderica is again the culprit, the pills provided by the mother, although this time the child was going through withdrawal. I have tried to reach out to Sharon Li, warning her that children should not ingest the medicine, but foreseeably she will not take my calls.

There was a slapping fight last week at a spinning class between two moms. They both claimed later to their respective circles that it was over the last bike, though everyone knew better. The website is rife with accusations of child abuse and quiet affairs between various family members, faculty blunders, and foiled plots. Mothers are randomly uninvited to lunches. Fathers are kicked off committees without reason. Cliques are reimagined. Loyalties changed. There have been subtle repercussions for Standcake: orders canceled, nothing large enough to spark our paranoia, but enough to send a message. We spoke to an attorney and went over the paperwork. With the certainty that we will see no return on our Moveable Museums investment, every pancake counts, every morsel and dab of cream, every ingredient and box and fork. Wedding season is here, and this is a make or break year. The Ferguson wedding, a major springtime event scheduled to take place at the Slancy Clubhouse, must be preserved at all costs; Laura making weekly, often daily calls to the bride, to the mother of the bride, to the cousins and wedding planner and father of the groom, all who express continued excitement over Standcake's participation in the nuptials.

The lacrosse parents have it in for me, rumors that I strangled their star face-off player, ordered a hit on their coach, and planned the heist of the now infamous bus. They associate me with the bad luck that abruptly terminated their championship season: Tom Pistilini 1, Gopa Worthy 0. The Gopa moms have also turned, a phone call from Josey Mateo warning me about the fallout. A man who resembled the Channel Fourteen meteorologist was spotted near Sharon Li's health club the morning of what Gopa moms refer to as "the assault." My image was not captured on camera. Someone ratted. Thoughts drift to Jackson, who I dismiss as a neighbor and a confidante, and who I have not heard from since the last investment club.

Lacrosse parents and mom cliques go about things differently. The lacrosse repercussions are mostly psychological—fathers staring me down too long, shaking their head disapprovingly at my oversized parka. They will go to their phones and cowardly comment about me on the website. The moms are blunt, cohesive. Someone contacted the Channel Fourteen news desk and asked to speak to my manager. Whitman is an idealist, calculating, too arrogant to let viewers dictate who will call the weather. He strangely takes my side, the two of us united in what he perceives as solidarity.

"They're coming for us, Pisser," Whitman whispers as we watch the morning lead-in, waiting for my set.

"I can feel it."

He is in awe of my superpowers. "You feel it? Like the weather?"

"Not like the weather, Whitman. Stronger than the weather. Forces of the soul at work. Good versus evil."

My struggles give him meaning. "I feel it as well."

"Lieutenant Misch." We never discussed it. "You talked to the police about me."

"Only to help. I'm on your side. So is Misch."

"Josey?"

"I stole her number from your phone. I thought you were having an affair."

"I'm having an affair with my wife."

"What about the semen?"

"I don't know. It just sits there, next to the ice cubes. I don't know what to do with it."

"I meant the stuff you store at the cryobank. What happens to that?"

It's an intuitive question. What will happen to the millions of children I am storing for our future? "You should stay away from Josey," I advise my young boss. "She's not what you think."

"Not now that I know she's out there. The ink. Those animals. That skin."

The *Today* show has asked to do a segment on my weather prognostications, which have gone on a remarkable seventy-one days. Other stations have delayed their meteorology segments toward the end of the broadcast, which means weather reports in the New York City region have been increasingly accurate the past two weeks. Lustfizzle's lawyers and *Today*'s lawyers cannot work out a proper arrangement with Whitman worried I will jump ship if the right opportunity arrives, despite the fact I have not shaved in weeks, my mane an untamed mess of ramshackle and fatigue. Complicating matters, Whitman also has bosses, who have heard the rumors of my malfeasance and enjoy watching Penelope Garcia as much as the rest of our viewers. If I could just whisper the weather into her perfectly contoured ear, an atmospheric Cyrano de Bergerac.

With my guesses and Penelope Garcia's talent, our ratings have soared. The entire Channel Fourteen crew arrives for our show, many confiding that I am their favorite weatherman, that my impossible streak inspires them vocationally in ways that a college education never did. Joe DiMaggio's fifty-six game hit streak. The Boston Celtics' eight consecutive titles. Tom Pistilini's forecasts.

"Bring an umbrella. Put down your phones. Watch the sky trickle, showing us how we shall know better days." Twenty words is my forecast today, and everyone smiles and nods. "Over to Penelope Garcia. Quick, Penelope, tell a story about the rain."

"Oh, geez, oh my, oh well, back in Cuba." Penelope is quick on her toes, her mind and body built for television, her lovely buttocks bouncing in trampoline fits. She pronounces it *Koo-bah*, the accent thick and gamey, even though I know she is not from Cuba. She is from Columbia. But research shows that there is renewed interest with viewers for Cuba, so we produced a Cuban weather girl. "When it rain it come off the muddy hill behind our houses and form a creek through town. Kids sit in the hill and it carry our bodies, dunking us in the muddy water all the way to the bottom. Oy vey."

I know the viewers the way I know clouds. Who would not want to hear a story about Penelope and her consummate breasts covered in mud and water, trying to maneuver the contours of some fictional Cuban hillside? It is why Penelope Cruz is taking over Thursdays. This, and rumors that I assaulted a crippled minority. Melanie dabs her eyes with a tissue, the beauty of weather. Several of the interns hug.

"It's all connected," Whitman says as I exit. He is witness to something ethereal, though he cannot say what, and is preposterously tormented by the possibility he is not doing the worthy thing with his life. "The threats. The weather. Moveable Museums."

"I feel it, Whitman. I see it as well."

Adultery Talk, With Ray McClutchen

ROCKY V IS AN underappreciated film in the Rocky canon. His fighting days behind him, he returns broke to his old neighborhood to pick up the pieces. It's easy to appreciate the films when Rocky is busting up

Apollo Creed and Ivan Drago, and running up the symbolic stairs. But to be a true supporter, one must be down in the trenches with Rocky and Paulie, living hand to mouth, training young boxers even though the viewer must accept that no amount of training can prepare Tommy Gunn to be the type of fighter that Rocky was—the grit, the determination to stand up no matter how severe the beating. Rocky is us. Rocky, like death, is a reminder of the sanctity of life, the wonder of children, the fortune of having problems with which to contend. Once problems cease, breath ceases, life terminates.

The cell phone trees give off a glowing ambiance, a quiet flicker without the corporeal crackle, proving that technology cannot improve on the campfire. Overhead, Rocky and Adrian argue in a dark street, and I turn down the volume to listen to the city. Laura and Gus joined me at the fire earlier. Josey was a no-show. Ever since our meeting at the bar a week ago, things have been strange. I put it together: Whitman talking to Misch, Josey to Whitman, all of them conversing behind my back. Slancy's security chief, Bill Chuck, has been a regular in my backyard. Tonight it is only me and my mortal enemy, Ray McClutchen, who comes bearing a bottle of wine and heartache.

The frown is an unusual ensemble for Ray. Regardless of bad news or terrorist explosions that cause the rest of us to purchase more life insurance, Ray thrusts onward. His books about inspirational thinking and positive visualization, while a pebble into the rock pile of self-help manuals and law of attraction bunk, have earned him a comfortable living. DVDs, mugs with clever inspirational sayings, T-shirts, calendars, speaking engagements, retreats. *Clutch Thinking*, *Best Road Ahead*, and *Like, Now*, while all essentially the same wimp-osophy, have been described by critics as essential reading for modern tension. "Chin up," "tarry forth," "do not let it ruin your day"—all catchphrases I have heard Ray mutter in the Gopa lobby, except he honestly means them, clenching a fist to show he's there should the shit go down.

In truth, I did, and still do, respect Ray McClutchen for maintaining the silver lining. I am a trine loophole of personalities—mediocre Tom Pistilini, which everyone expects; the savage tribe occupying the terrain somewhere between my esophagus and colon, which everyone fears; and Ray McClutchen doppelganger, expected to keep the spirit with a multicultural bent and pleasant nod. A man who came up similar to me, the same challenges and responsibilities, the same affluent pressures from Gopa, and through it all he was able to keep a healthy optimism. I have to believe it is not easy living with Olivia. Maddie is a trying child with her array of inhalers and influenzas. Todd, while a nice kid, reeks of a mediocrity that no one could wish on another being. Through it all, Ray has preserved a positive attitude, or at least he pretends to. Often I consider whom I would want to take my place if I could not do the job of father and husband. I would not want a tough guy, someone rugged and cynical and armed with paranoia and steel. It would be someone like Ray McClutchen who, just like Rocky, keeps climbing off the mat.

That does not imply I do not find Ray irritating or his dropping by suspicious. He shows up with a bottle of wine, which means he is hoping to share it with Laura, only to discover the front door locked. Upon checking the backdoor, he encountered my *Rocky* marathon, pretending he had come to see me all along. I am weaning myself off them, but I ingest a Luderica hoping to summon some playfulness so I do not awaken to discover I have chain sawed my neighbor into miniature McClutchens.

"I just don't get it," he says again, after the second glass, mistaking me for someone who cares about his failed Cooperative Marriage. "Everything was going so well. Now she's..."

Now she's fucking someone else, Ray. "Now she's what?"

"Distant."

"Women," I say, turning up the volume to drown out his moping.

"No, not this woman. Laura is special."

"That's why I married her."

"We don't deserve her. Neither of us."

I refill my glass, enjoying the fight scene overhead. "Don't be so hard on yourself. I don't deserve her. But you—you've got a lot going for yourself. Those books, your tricycle. Lot going for you, Ray."

"Then why is she shutting me out?"

"Maybe she didn't know you were coming tonight."

"It's Tuesday. Tuesday is our night. I reminded her earlier."

"Maybe she forgot." I know Laura. She did not forget. If she wanted to sip wine with Ray he'd be sitting on my sofa looking at her breasts. "Maybe she's busy with work." I fucked her, Ray, not more than twenty yards from where we sit. "Sometimes when she gets her mind on work, she can't think of anything else." I have an erection just thinking about her fingernails tracing fuck slits in my flesh.

He leans forward, an idea. "Can you let me in the backdoor? Maybe she's still up and didn't hear my knocking."

"Can't do it, bub. Don't want to get involved if there's trouble with you two. Remember what Doc Brenner said about respecting boundaries." I turn up the volume another notch. "Besides, you don't want to seem desperate. Give Laura some space. That's my advice."

He sips the wine. "I appreciate it, Pisser."

"Don't mention it."

"I really like her, you know? I sometimes get strange feelings."

The Luderica sets in, time for a blackout. "Hmm, like what?"

"Like Laura is sleeping with someone else. Something about her lately."

"It's not like Laura. Once she settles on something." I do not finish.

Ray talks and I doze and listen and watch the stars as Rocky beats the piss out of Tommy Gunn in a street brawl, a scurrying behind us I take for Clint Eastwood who settles beneath my chair, and I try not to move so as not to disturb my cat, passive therapy, whatever works. Ray is a heartbroken man, as damaged as any of us, and only another heartbroken man can understand his worthlessness. He is also dubious about Moveable Museums, feels that we are wandering toward a dark frontier, his trajectory through the cosmos having shifted, that maybe he is not a motivational speaker after all. Maybe he is one of my tribe, having escaped from my thoughts to wander the cold, hard world.

"What do you say, Pisser?"

I tell him something I read on the Gopa website by the author ndr_cnstrctn, who is no longer with us. His postmortem quip from weeks earlier was left in the comment section of a blog post about the prospect of a prophylactic machine in the student restrooms. The comment had nothing to do with the topic, only that "all of us are bumbling around, concentrating, making lists, investing in four-oh-one-ks, buying insurance, taking vitamins, minding the rules, avoiding doom when doom is inevitable, doom is all there is, so if we must face doom—and we must—best do it with a smile. The smile is the test."

My mouth is dry when I finish. I am not sure if it sounded sane to Ray but he smiles, and pours us another tumbler; two drunk dads watching the stars writhe across the island.

"Thanks, Pisser. I needed tonight."

Juice Of Broken Dreams Makes Sad Wine

DURING ONE OF MY blackouts, I cannot determine a time frame, I came across Duffy O'Neal walking his dog. This was prior to the transformation, before I stopped showering and using deodorant, when dogs despised me. His poodle mutt strangled itself attempting to ingest my flesh while Duffy explained the religious features of canines. A Catholic, he talked about heaven and hell and reincarnation, though not the traditional variety. His dog hated me, he explained, for something I had done in a past life, which animals can sense, although the past life was occurring right then. There was no past or future or present. Everything was happening at once, all the tenses, with one man's heaven—an actor on break from her latest blockbuster enjoying a condo in Barbados; watching another man's hell on television, genocide in Darfur; while unknown purgatory occurs elsewhere, a New Jersey man, adequate apartment and job, rolling his eyes at the flat screen while he awaits the entertainment report. The past did not exist, Duffy insisted, nor was heaven a distant pursuit. It is here, a simultaneous juggernaut, and it is up to us to determine how we belong.

"What about God?" I asked.

"Oh, yes. Many."

"I thought you said you're Catholic."

"Don't get snippy. I'm just telling you how it works."

"Are these gods here with the rest of us? What about mass shootings, kids with cancer?"

"I won't get into it with you. I was trying to teach you something about why dogs hate you." Duffy picked up his mutt, scared I might crush it with my heel. "Get on out of here, Pisser. I catch you urinating in my yard again, I'll have you fined."

I am reminded of Duffy as I walk down a city street passing treats to dogs. The furry critters adore me. They come out of shops, wander on their leashes from owners, notice me across desolate avenues in the late-morning spring just as the sun crests the East River and climbs cautiously to observe the dirt and prosper with equal disregard. I carry biscuits in my jacket and offer them to each hound, *coo*ing as they nibble and chomp, depositing drool on my hand and sleeve and sniffing at my dander. A large collie follows me to work, gaining entrance to the studio and interrupting a segment. It leaps its forepaws onto my chest and balances there as I speak about clouds, and it occurs to me—I am this animal's deity.

"And bones. And lice. And detritus. And food carts. And foreign hair. And myths. And bullied children. And used baggies. And expired milk. And discount cookbooks. And the man who cannot find a lost valuable, checking his pockets on the sidewalk on which you just passed—not your problem, no idea what became of his evening. All these are connected. All these are valued. These are to be appreciated on cloudy days."

The segment seems staged, the dog on my torso, tongue out, me smiling and continuing the report, even Whitman uncharacteristically without the turn of phrase.

"Wow, Pisser. Just, wow."

Six weeks remain in the school year. With Russ Haverly planted in his hometown, the ECI embargo has lifted, the names expected to come quickly. Laura and I have been called to a meeting this morning with the Gopa administration. It can mean only one thing, the news we have awaited for months, the butterfly of our unceasing cocoon—Iliza has been accepted into the program.

As soon as we enter the room, I know this is not the case. Something unholy has transpired. If I did not just see my children three minutes ago in the lobby, I would assume one of them has been murdered, shot execution style in the back of the head, trampled by a maniacal police horse, an accidental death no one can explain and for which Gopa has arranged an official apology. Laura takes my hand. I bow my head and squeeze.

Gopa's director, Heather Pace, is charged with delivering the message, but it is the duo of attorneys that ruin our composure.

"Tom, Laura, I'm terribly sorry to be the bearer. A video involving Iliza has come to our attention."

I gulp, squeeze Laura's finger, shift to contain my tribe.

"Legally, we have little choice. We have to ask Iliza to step down from her role in *Our Town*." Heather pauses. We look at each other and leave it there. I have not shared with my wife the things I have done. She deserves better. It will kill her to actually witness Iliza on the video, a failure of parenthood, even though it was not our child naked in a shower with a Gopa faculty member. "To be clear, we have not seen the video," Heather continues. "But we can speculate on the fallout."

"What fallout, exactly?"

"Illicit drug use." She does something with a hand. "Other things, from what I hear."

"What things?" Laura says.

"I know this is a shock. Gopa's morality clause is clear." This from a woman who was getting regular deliveries from Russ Haverly, who claims they engaged in sex during the pill exchanges. "If this comes out in the press during the play, it will be worse to deal with then. We'd have no choice but to expel her. Our decision, while difficult, is the only one."

"She's worked so hard."

"You have no proof," I say. It sounds like a lie as it leaves my mouth. My daughter is guilty of exactly what she's being accused. But without the intercession of other entities, there is no validation to the charges.

"Others have come forward," Heather confesses. "There is pressure from the parent community."

I hear Laura gulp. We know what we're up against: the money, the machine, the organized vitriol of the Gopa community. This is payback for the bus, for Russ Haverly. The role in the play is just the start. The ECI program, applications that took months to fill out, college essays, extracurricular activities, volunteer posts—all of it fizzling like a stabbed balloon. This is the Sedlocks, the lacrosse parents, Sharon Li and her brood, the Gopa network pressuring the administration.

"I know Iliza," Heather says. "She's a nice kid. But it's for the good of the school. We're here to assist in whatever help she needs."

"Who will be playing the lead?" Laura asks. It's a cold question, direct and cutthroat, why I love and fear my wife.

"The understudy, I suppose."

"Say the name, Heather."

Heather Pace has been sent here against her will. "Tungsten Sedlock."

Through childbirth and bad nights, premature fears and sad afternoons and funerals, our marital woes, the fights and accusations, Laura never wept. As the tears build, I can sense she is ready to fall apart. It is time to go, to gather my wife in my arms and get us through it. Yet my tribe will not vacate the seat. I am their God. They are my descendants. I should be able to command their actions, but they are not listening.

"I know you were fucking Russ Haverly. In exchange for drugs," I hear myself say, growl really.

Her mouth falls open. She looks to Laura for an explanation, covers her teeth to stifle a gulp, then appeals to the two lawyers for intervention. The male lawyer, homosexual, young, reaches to touch my arm, a gentle suggestion to retreat. I punch him in his forehead. He plunges to the ground. The other lawyer, female, maybe Jewish, bends to assist him.

Laura, weeping. "Tom."

"What are you doing?" Heather asks.

Laura watches as I shove the desk out of the way, Heather Pace twisting her legs toward her chest to protect herself from what I can only assume she believes is certain retribution. She has had parents threaten her position and career, sic lawyers on her. She has never had a parent physically assault her.

"Admit it," I say. "You were having sex with him."

"I don't..."

"It was my idea to harness the administration to the structures during the save the trees benefit. So you could enjoy some wine without injuring yourselves. I suggested it even after I knew you were fucking Russ." I pick up a chair and start swinging it randomly, at lights, wall mounts, lofting it at a window, breaking glass that ignites an alarm, my reflection in the other panes appalling, unbathed, hairy, wild. "Admit it and we'll leave."

Breathless, weeping, the lawyers hugging on the floor, Heather covers her face. "It was just a few times. I'm not married. There was nothing wrong about any of it."

The phone is ringing, the security desk locating the window and calling to interpret the emergency. Outside the office, I pop one of the Luderica that I am trying to quit. Laura does not mention my outburst. We make our way through a quiet hallway where Josey Mateo waits. Her arms and neck are red from hard ink, her eyes tearing and ornery beneath the lights.

"We'll get those fuckers." She spits, her fist clenched, muscles tight. It scares an already terrified Laura who has just witnessed me dismantle an office. Josey wipes tears from her own face and then from Laura's. "Iliza's a good kid, Missus P. We'll get those fuckers for this."

On the far end of the hall, our children wait for the news, Iliza buried in her phone, Gus staring hurriedly against a wall. For the first time in months, Gus is not dressed as a nanny, donning his purple and white uniform in honor of his sister's day. Dressed in her Gopa uniform, Iliza spent longer than usual in the bathroom, ensuring her hair and makeup were perfect, her shirt cinched into an ornate style. We were expecting different news, all of us having tried so hard.

I shake, furious. My arm bleeds from something I do not remember. Laura takes my hand and we watch each other. "You look like shit," she says, wiping my lip. "Have you calmed down?"

"I'm at war. Harry will pay for this."

"It isn't Harry. This is Allie. She always wanted it for Tungsten."

"We can ruin them," I say. "Don't forget where I work."

"If you talk about it, they'll sue us for everything."

Laura is right, of course, possessing the same business sense that Harry displays. The friends we still have would abandon us. The Sedlocks would send Dan Mathers for as long as it took. We would lose the house. We would lose Standcake. We would declare bankruptcy.

"Besides," she says. "Iliza did it. She might not deserve this, but she deserves repercussions."

I grab her in both arms and kiss her forcefully as I summon some Ray McClutchen. "We'll survive this. No matter what. Do you believe it?" Laura nods. "Take Gus to the lobby. I want to be the one to tell her."

Arrows Of Outrageous Fortune

I CROUCH IN THE tree line that runs adjacent to the seventh tee bunker, the highest elevation in Slancy. I am dressed in black, the crossbow I promised Jason and Jackson would never leave my shed lying in the grass. From here, I have access to the bicycle path as it extends along the length of our neighborhood and condenses into a walkway that encircles the golf course. I have had enough target practice with the BB gun that I know a steady posture is key to striking a target, though, because of my neighbors, and a dearth of arrows, I have not practiced with the bow.

My intention is not to kill Allie Sedlock. A neck strike would be devastating to my reputation, and because I have been sleeping in a tent a hundred yards from this spot, an alibi is out of the question. Instead I am aiming for the meaty part of her tender thigh, just before gluteus meets hip, flesh that can absorb a bolt, leaving the shaft sticking out to let her know the battle is only commencing. I assume she will crash the bike and ruin that pretty face, maybe scuff her pink skin against the pavement. But if I miss, just a fraction higher than I intend, and it strikes Allie in the face, and she goes over the handlebars and smashes into the pavement to leak brains all over Slancy's sole path—well, then, that is the main argument against fucking with Tom Pistilini's children.

There is constant humming at this hour, the sound of New York City's churn, the cell phone towers waiting, the warblers awakening and preparing to relieve the fairways of plump worms. The decorative chipmunks are still idle, pondering their fate, if they will survive the day or be torn to shreds by the pregnant she-beast. I hear the bicycle in the distance. Allie Sedlock is right on time. Dawn has not broken, taking its time behind the Long Island suburbia, but there is enough light to catch her as she approaches, and I find her long legs through the tactical scope. The optics are precise, they cost as much as the bow, and she does not notice the red dot finding pavement and then her left thigh, her headphones blasting a ritualistic anthem that leaves her oblivious to danger—who would be crouching in the weeds, at five o'clock in the morning, aiming a weapon at her?

She peddles furiously, working up a sweat. My concentration drifts to Allie Sedlock's wet asshole grinding into the bicycle seat, the laser on her torrid thigh, my body steady as I follow with the bow, finger on the trigger. It will give a little kiss when it enters her epidermis, the sensation a smack as it travels back and forth to her brain until her eyes look down and she realizes—what have I done, what freak lineage have I crossed? I begin the countdown as Clint Eastwood scatters through the tree line, having followed me to the bunker and now aware of the approaching bicyclist. Warblers warble. The horn of a barge explodes, announcing itself to the metropolis before everything falls silent and we are alone. My finger bends and just at the point of turmoil, an odd scampering to my right. A nymph, naked, chasing Mister Pickles. It happens quickly.

The red dot bounces from Allie's thigh, to the ground, back to her thigh, to the handlebar, her forehead, the thigh, I hope. The arrow races out of my grasp and strikes metal, a crisp *ta-chink*, the handlebar most likely, and Allie Sedlock swerves. It ricochets into the trees as branches wisp and then a firm *thwack* and the crackle of leaves and sticks, a groan. I think: *I just killed Clint Eastwood*. And then, relieved to see the cat scurry toward the fairway, followed by a disturbed: *I just killed Rhythm*.

Allie stops the bicycle to check her equipment. She removes the headphones and watches the trees. I stay crouched in the bunker, wondering whether to reload. Spooked, Allie quickly turns the bicycle for home. I stay where I am, listening. A moment later, Rhythm is on her feet, a wounded deer running. In the morning light I can see the arrow protruding from her bare buttocks, the girl assuming she's fallen onto a stick, and how to explain this to her anxious fathers. I try to call to her but no words come.

Out of breath, scared, there are no lights on in my house when I reach the yard. I hide the crossbow in the shed and duck into the tent, pulling my sleeping bag over my head. I wait. Because if I am sure of anything, if I am absolutely guaranteed of one action, I know that someone is coming for me, either to alert me to the accident or take me to prison. I hear things: slamming doors, an argument, weeping, Jackson's voice followed by Jason's. "That sonofabitch. That crazy sonofabitch." A shed door. An engine, the Ferris's golf cart. If it were serious, they would not be driving the golf cart to the parking lot to get in their car. An ambulance would be summoned. Instead they are doing what I would do: disappearing to a hospital upstate where no one has ever heard of Slancy or Gopa, where if anyone asks about their daughter's exhibitionism, word will not reach the nanny chain. A drive suggests the injury is not life threatening, the realization causing the strangest thing to occur. I fall soundly asleep, peacefully, and dream of refugee chipmunks, duffel bags packed, hauling possessions and children over a war-town fairway that once had so much golf and promise and now is a symbol of tyranny and all they have lost.

Cells Must Fuse To Grow

LYING IN MY TENT, the midday sound of golf balls and wildlife, I am aware I will awaken to this temperament each morning once they fire me. I have slept through work. There is no sense arriving this late. There is a note next to the coffee pot from Laura. She tried to rouse me, both her and Gus, but they were late. I check the street, nothing peculiar, the Jays' house empty, the whisper of a car's engine echoing through the silent morning. There is only one car in Slancy. Bill Chuck's black sedan. In the passenger seat, Lieutenant Misch, who rarely leaves his post during the school day.

I assume the worst. I am the main suspect in a murder attempt, and in my paranoid haste it does not occur to me they would not send school security to investigate. It has been ongoing psychopathic behavior, first the nanny, followed by the coach, the equipment bus and dead chipmunks and cell phone towers and poor Missus Li's leg. They will have been to the hospital, obtained fingerprints from the arrow, taken statements from all parties. They will ask to see the weapon, my whereabouts earlier this morning.

"Sorry to bother you, Tom," Bill says. "Lieutenant Misch here needs a word."

"Of course." Always happy to help.

"Tried you at the office." He's apologetic, nicer it appears. "Your guy, Whitman, said you were out doing field research today."

Unshaven, unbathed, pantsless, T-shirt. "Coastal temperature readings."

The shrug seems choreographed. "Won't take long. Ever heard the name Antonio Capra?"

I know half the name. "Doesn't sound familiar."

"Didn't think so. Associate of Russ Haverly." He is not writing any of it down, ignoring that I have come to the door in underwear with muddy knees.

"You think this Capra had something to do with Russ's death?"

"It's possible. The more we know, it seems Haverly was a major dealer."

"Major?"

"Kids. Parents. And not just Gopa. Throughout the private school community."

"As far north as Connecticut," Bill says, smiling. "Big drug ring."

"Huge." Misch whistles, which for the first time makes him seem human. "You hear anything that might help, you'll let me know?"

I try to seem like an insignificant weather troll with two kids and a wife, who has seen enough police dramas to understand the protocol. But my tribe has latched on to a sentiment, an idiosyncrasy in their postures "Why would you think I might hear something?"

Misch and Bill exchange a look. It's subtle, two old cops who know it when they see it. "I was wrong about you," Misch says. "You're one of the good ones, Tom."

"Worthy ones," Bill adds.

Misch taps the side of his head. "I hear things."

"Things," Bill says. "Like how you told Sedlock to fuck himself."

Bill did not come here to ask about Russ Haverly. He came to join the tribe.

"How do you know about that?" I ask.

"I'm security around here," Bill says. "What do you think I do all day, just watch the bridge?"

Mish leans close, a scent of aftershave and bacon. "Sandy Hook thing a few years back. You remember."

He mentions the main stop on the Moveable Museums Memorial Tour, when a deranged gunman murdered six adults and twenty children all younger than Gus. The Sedlocks do not want to start the tour there, preferring to warm up sightseers with an office building in downtown Manhattan, where in 2002 an employee littered the cafeteria with grenades, injuring thirty and killing eight. I nod that I am familiar.

"I helped on the case, the both of us," Bill says. "Certain law enforcement aren't too fond of tourism in these parts."

"You think you're a hard man, a hard cop," Misch says. "Right up until you see a dead seven-year-old. Then you ain't shit."

If they know, others know. That it has not been on every major news channel is a combination of luck and Connor Mack. Without the publicity giant, there would be cover stories, exclusives by the morning shows, intrepid reporters harassing the Sedlocks for details, Tom Pistilini, Channel Fourteen meteorologist, the public face, something at which to direct the hatred. The tribe has honed in on a detail I neglected. Harry Sedlock was counting on a fall guy.

"Anyway," Bill says. They pull back.

Misch hands me an envelope. "You probably knew this was coming. You need assistance, you let us know."

"Of course." We shake hands. There's a momentary intuition, a parting of the universe religious folk might say, when everything lines up, and I know there will be redemption. It only shows itself for the faintest moment and then disappears, and I am left with the aching feeling that I nearly murdered a child this morning.

Later that evening, after the houses have dimmed and the children are in bed, and no one came to accuse me of assault with a deadly weapon. I come in through the backdoor that Laura left unlocked. I find her naked in our bedroom and I do not ask permission. Where the Luderica was meant to discover playfulness, it discovered savagery instead, my odors chasing her perfumes and laundered sheets. It is this sentiment, my inner tribe, fucking my wife greedily, rolling her over to hear her squeal, passing her around our cavern like a massive feast. I have become a religious man, more than I admit. There is desperation to our lovemaking, something mythic about our resurgence, and in that redemption I remember. It comes back to me in a flash, the portions of my life I lost in the pivotal blackout. After I hit Russ Haverly with the golf club, drowned him, and dragged his body below the clubhouse to the western shore of Slancy, I drove the boat two miles south before finding shore. I pointed it toward the ocean and ignited the motor, jumping into the water and swimming to land.

I was freezing. That was how I got sick. I walked until I found a payphone and placed a call to the person I trust most. Laura picked me up and took me home, and listened as I explained what Russ Haverly told me about our daughter.

Her pragmatism against my lunacy. "Are you sure he's dead?"

"He's dead."

"Iliza wouldn't do those things. What if you're wrong?" Pacing, late at night, I could not get my body warm. "You could go to prison. Both of us. The house. The business. Do you understand, Tom? You cannot talk about it to anyone. Not even Iliza."

"I was protecting her," I told Laura.

"You need to protect all of us. Don't say anything to anyone. Not even me."

Break A Leg

NO PHONE. NO TELEVISION. No after school activities. Seven o'clock curfew. Computer use monitored. No sleepovers with friends. No weekend plans. Family dinner every night. No skirts. No dresses. No tight clothing. No T-shirts with witty sayings that might contain pop culture references Laura and I do not understand. No sex. No thinking about sex. No boys at the house. No undermining our home with cleverness. No kindness. No weakness. No fair. No justice. No end to our hypocrisy. No mention that I murdered someone. No discussion of the cover-up. Prisoners have more freedom.

"And wipe that pout off your voice," I say.

"You brought this on yourself," Laura adds. We do not look at each other for fear we'd be ashamed.

After explaining the meeting with the Gopa administration, I let Iliza know that not only will she not be in the play or accepted into the ECI program, forcing her to spend another year with us, but that I will not be permitted on school grounds for the remainder of the year. Mostly the punishment validates Laura and I, makes us forget our failures, gives us confidence that we can still dominate our children's lives and they will not disappear forever to Hollywood or Miami, or just across the river. Destroyed. That is the word for Iliza. She worked hard for something and was failed by her friends, our friends, the Gopa factory. I have told her the Tom Pistilini lies. We do not do drugs in this family. We do not bring drugs into this house. We do not associate with people who do drugs. I have even relayed the Ray McClutchen lies. This will make you stronger. Harvest the positive. This will make you larger hopefully without making you harder. I am out of lies.

We have not been to Gopa Academy in three days. Laura and I remain at odds with the administration. Also, Heather Pace filed a restraining order against me that Misch was kind enough to deliver in the envelope without a lecture. We keep Gus at home with us. He is despondent and sad, wondering how to make his sister smile. He wears his nanny cloaks and awakens in the same state, rushing through the house emptying the dishwasher and offering to fix Iliza smoothies. Laura works from the den. I occasionally wander into the backyard to pull weeds or check on Clint Eastwood. This is our boycott. This is our nonviolent protest. There are entities demonstrating against sex trafficking and racism, nuclear annihilation and mass shootings, the destruction of the environment and gross corporate misconduct. Our battlefield is the private school theatrical production of *Our Town*, our Gandhi moment.

Three days in the desert, cut off from civilization. Without a nanny, our lifeline of gossip and communal parenting is gone. Two more kids have been selected into the ECI program, none of which matters anymore. Iliza is out for certain. No one from Slancy phones to check on our existence other than Bill Chuck. He is how I know that Rhythm was injured in the woods, a stick or contusion, and the Jays had to take her upstate for medical attention. It does not occur to me to phone and check on her, just as it did not occur to Jackson to check on my daughter. We have devolved into secular tribes, hunkering down in our caves to make sure no one steals our meat and fire.

We still have the Gopa website on which we can enjoy the bloodshed. Two fathers were charged with disorderly conduct for punching each other over a parking spot during drop-off. Someone took a mallet to the Carters' Porsche. In the middle of the day, cement was dumped in the bicycle parking center. It congealed around the wheels and spokes destroying dozens of bikes. Most of the exterior cameras in the school have been tampered with, security at odds on how to address the vandalism. A child was elbowed while riding a scooter to school, the mother who did the elbowing claiming he was budging. A parent accused another family's driver of sexual harassment for excessive leering. A blog post under my new handle, Feral_Tribe, referenced last week's offsite brainstorming about whether sixth graders were too young to witness nude models during art history. During the discussion, I spiked the communal punch with Sharon Li's batch of Viagra. One father was rushed to the emergency room, the nannies claim. Lifetime associations dissolve. Cliques grow more assertive. Parents settle in for battle, all over the ECI program. Administrators have called an emergency meeting next week for parents. We are neither predator nor prey, forgotten by the Gopa community.

Bill Chuck and Josey are with me tonight. Bill is a bulletproof veteran who has seen it all and stomped it all and come out with bruises. It was his job to remove Clint Eastwood, which he never did. While he may be retired from the police force, he can never absolve himself from right and wrong. Foes have been revealed. Sides have been drawn. Bill Chuck and Lieutenant Misch are in my camp and, by extension, are Josey Mateo's allies. My backyard fire pit has become the planning ground for an insurgency to defeat Moveable Museums. Laura has joined us, slippers and a glass of wine to make it appear that rational adults have gathered to discuss politics, or the latest movie, or even the weather. The rest of Josey's crew stays away. We are going after the Sedlocks' property, first the office building they quietly lease in New Jersey and then, if it comes to it, the house.

Josey runs the meeting. "Laura, you should make nice with Ray McClutchen."

"That's not a good idea," she says.

"He likes you. He has valuable information."

Josey is not aware that we have renewed our conjugality. We have glossed over the Cooperative Marriage without ever discussing whether Laura and Ray engaged in sexual intercourse. In the manner that a family forgets moments after passing roadkill that did not impact their minivan's bumper, we do not utter the word "McClutchen" in our domicile. A suspicious voice within my tribe volunteers for the assignment. "I'll speak to Ray," I say.

"Laura would be better," Josey says.

"We have an understanding, Ray and I."

"Laura has tits."

"I should distance myself," Laura says. "For the kids' sake."

Josey nods. Bill adds another log to the fire despite the eternal vigor of the cell phone combustion. "Dirty fucks. I know a dozen retirees. Good police. Be happy to get their hands dirty when the time comes."

"The time is coming." Josey carves a bull on her thigh, her dark skin scarred and flaky, in need of moisturizer. "We should be going."

"This late?" Laura asks.

"Distance," I say.

We do not discuss where I go, what I have done. For the good of Standcake, for the sanctity of our family, my association with Josey and Bill and all my vengeance must occur discreetly in the confines of Laura's ignorance. I have ingested two Luderica, not because I want them, but because they help me overcome my rote cowardliness that I am brainwashed to believe is acceptable. "We are a demographic of default coward," I type into my phone during the short drive, the comment section of a blog post about ethically farm-raised cod served in the school cafeteria as opposed to wild cod caught under dubious fishing laws. "War is a reality show. Terrorism is good for ratings. We turn off genocide, ignore stories of babies used for target practice by creatures that loathe us. We donate to causes and say the right things, but the blackness of our hearts grows larger with each despondence, casting algorithmic shadows over a future we have worked perilously to disinfect for our children. Instead, let's teach fight. Let's teach roots. Let's teach the value of dying for what is right. Let's teach different than we are."

I move in and out of the blackout freely, a Zamboni driver choosing the scratchiest path to cleanse. When I come to, Josey is dismantling a camera at the kitchen entrance of Gopa Academy. Bill Chuck eats a hot dog through an open window in his sedan. Little Petty wears a Bruce Springsteen tank top and bulky pants, a tool belt to complete the ensemble. He picks the digital lock with a cell phone. We are inside.

"That's a Roger," Bill Chuck mumbles through the window. "Check in soon."

Two hours later, we have filled the theater and props with dead bunnies, bloodied machetes lying in a pile at the edge of the stage. We hacked off the legs and heads and ears, spilled their entrails over the sets and rubbed the carcasses on armrests and doorknobs. We do not slaughter any bunnies. We take the ones that already perished, having succumbed to whatever disease found them.

Little Petty is sweaty, blood on Bruce's forehead. "What about the other bunnies?"

Josey shrugs. "Leave them, I guess."

"Well." It comes out of the blackout, my dry tongue, my tribe.

"What?" she says.

"They sense it. The death. Imagine us here, talking, and on the far side of that door a bunch of elbows and chins. We would know."

Josey clenches, her ink people opining. "What do you propose?"

I've enjoyed the evening, the rush of hacking through bone, my golf shirt mahogany. "Take them to my place."

No one disputes the solution, the defective bunnies inheriting both their freedom and a golf course utopia to live out their existence, the furry bodies deposited into the backend of Bill Chuck's sedan. Slancy is where they belong, living in the filth and confusion of artificial extravagance. I do not know how Clint Eastwood will take to them, but the approaching reality intrigues me—the adorable, laboratory refined chipmunks getting a look at these gargoyles, their swollen faces and purple noses sniffing over a shared food source.

Storms We Cannot Forecast

"THERE'S A HIGH OF entitlement in much of the tristate area through Wednesday with only a seventeen percent chance of class war. Rioting takes planning. Rioting takes money and energy," I say, ignoring the virtual background of the metropolis. "Much of the minority base that would benefit from revolution is too busy and angry to carry it out. We moved away from running around with pitchforks centuries ago, folks. My kind—I'm not talking the white variety, nor the male variety—is being evolved out for a more multicultural whimsy so expect the weather in most of the country to sound playful. Look for accumulations of social justice in the evening hours, a trendier socialism and taxing the lower class into a middle class. Tomorrow, chance of rage and stress with a high of passive aggression, more school shootings and racial profiling and nationalism for much of the area and don't even think about leaving the house without your umbrellas. Whoops, did I say umbrellas. Sorry about that, folks. I meant guns. Don't leave the house without your guns."

The PISSER REPORT is experiencing a transition. I have not researched the weather or checked models in weeks, and yet my reports, when I bother to read them, contain a perfect description of the environment. Our ratings are constant; viewers sticking around to hear Melanie Trotter with the traffic, or listen to Channel Fourteen's hip-hop vibe to the news. Penelope Garcia is petrified of my odors and chaos, leaving the set before we finish.

"That was interesting but psychotic," Whitman says. "You never mentioned the weather."

"The globe is crumbling, Whitman. Refugees are scurrying in remote lands. Bombs are exploding in kiosks. Whenever it happens every parent thinks—thank God it's not my kid. How can we talk about weather?"

"Do it again. This time mention the rain. More temperatures, less class war."

"What about the blood, Whitman? Should I mention the blood?"

He tugs me toward a corner. Suits nearby watch our exchange. Whitman's job is on the line, along with my own. "This is about tourism. You almost did it. You almost talked about it on the weather report. Does Josey know?"

"Why are you speaking with Josey?"

"She said something's coming." Whitman looks at me that way, young and irritating and wanting to matter. "Let me inside your head, Pisser. I can help."

"You don't want to be in there." I lean close, my scent reaching me as it ricochets off his organically dry-cleaned shirt, his millennial goodness. "There's a storm coming, Whitman."

He digests the meaning. "Are you talking physical, as in an actual weather system, or metaphorical?"

"Yes," I say.

Tonight is the emergency meeting at which administrators are expected to address the havoc that has imploded the Gopa community. Someone (not me) roofied a children's birthday party a week ago, the culprit sprinkling nuts onto a display of Standcakes that sent two kids to the emergency room. It would have been worse if a discerning mother had not waved her Digital Nutfinder XP, which retails for $250 at VillageShop, over the snack table, locating the contraband nuts in the gluten-free frosting.

"This is personal." Laura was outraged upon hearing about the pancake nutting, just before I fucked her in the backyard. "They will not screw with Standcake."

A parents' roundtable on the college application process was hit two nights later (this was me, in retaliation for the roofied pancakes), the seltzer water roofied with actual roofies. Myself, along with other anonymous parents, regularly post gossip, much of which is invented, onto the Gopa website accusing others of adultery and domestic violence and threatening each other's nannies with video we claim to have of them beating the children. Worst of all is the lingering murder and mutilation of dozens of bunnies, their tender limbs strewn across the theater stage.

Heather Pace has applied to twelve other private schools in Manhattan (also me), most of which were not hiring, the rumors reaching the nannies and eventually the parents and board of directors that the head of Gopa is jumping ship. I am a destroyer of reputations, a conqueror of marriages. Other private school parents have heard the rumors and are enjoying the schadenfreude: that the Gopa Worthy community, which everyone secretly loathes, has kinks in its armor, falling into disrepair the way mortal schools are destined.

My restraining order has been pardoned for the meeting. Heather Pace will address the misunderstanding—she is not, in fact, leaving Gopa Academy—and will discuss the attacks and shameless rumors that have dominated the message boards for the past month. Everyone knows this is about the ECI program, the administration appealing to our sense of decorum to overcome our antagonism. I take Laura to a burrito joint, where we talk about everything other than work and kids and school and illicit videos. She wipes sour cream from my lip with a napkin, smiles, and I am sheltered by the realization that my life has inklings of perfection. Here, with Laura, my chemical makeup is not faulty, my neuro synapses unsullied, my tribe meek and curiously playful. Laura is my drug. If only I could liquidize her and insert her into capsules.

"Behave," she says, a prelude to the evening. "We don't need any further drama."

Ray And I On Wives

THE GOPA LOBBY BUSTLES. Parents sanitize and hydrate, lubing up for the night's politics. The lacrosse parents hover near the cocktail bar, ignorant that someone else might want a glass of wine, holding the space for their contemporaries who arrive wearing Gopa windbreakers and sweaters, their bulging stomachs colliding against each other and the wives, an orgy of cholesterol and failed calisthenics. The theater crowd ignores us completely, people with whom we dined and hugged at fundraisers, moms and dads who told us too haughtily and sadly how wonderful an actress our daughter had become. The noble parents are situated toward the auditorium entrance, eager to be the first inside once the doors open, which will put them in proper seats, the armrests onto which I smeared bunny gunk. A few mothers give me eyes. I pucker my lips and air kiss them across the room.

"Stop that, Tom." Laura straightens my shirt. "I have to speak with the Fergusons. Stand here and do nothing."

I have no intention of interacting with anyone. I am eager to keep our animosity stranded on the Gopa message boards, where it belongs. I begin a blog post on my phone about the unfortunate lobby vibe, from right there in the lobby, when I am interrupted by Ray McClutchen. His terminal smile and processed gait have disappeared. He sweats, slightly tipsy.

"What was that the other night at your place anyway?"

It takes me a moment to understand what I like about this version of Ray: he smells like me. Ray has not showered or shaved, one shoe untied, food hardened into his jacket's fabric. He's referencing something I might have said at the fire which I cannot recall.

"You were talking," Ray says. "What was it about?"

It was about our failure. Not as parents or workers or citizens, but as men, as husbands, as fathers and warriors and brothers. "Listen to me, Ray. I need your help."

He slurs, "Just so happens I need your help."

"If you want to know what's going on at my fire, you pull up a chair and stop sulking on the porch. We are talking revolution. We are talking worthiness." I lean in close. We sniff each other like wild dogs. "I'm taking down Moveable Museums. I need information: money, meetings, the things no one talks about."

"No, no, no. Listen to me." He takes a drink from an empty glass, the ice rattling against his yellow teeth. "Things are not good at home. Not good at all. This fallout between Laura and us—she won't return text messages." *Thext mattresses.* "I can't think. I canceled two speaking engagements. And what's this about Moveable? You and Laura need to make it better with Harry and Allie, put the team back together."

"Just stop it, Ray. You're acting hysterical."

"She's sleeping with someone. We have to combine forces and get to the bottom of this."

We glance around reflexively and both lay eyes on the Sedlocks hovering somewhere between the lacrosse and theater crowds. They watch me while pretending not to watch, knowing what I know, Allie's smooth skin without any shaft intrusions because of my goddamned therapy cat. It pleases me to hear that Laura is giving him the cold shoulder, and that his motivational nonsense has evaporated. But I pity Ray McClutchen because he is me, the two of us trying to control the uncontrollable.

"Listen up, Ray." He watches with big doe eyes, his lip quivering, and I know in that instant I can tell him anything. What he needs more than redemption is truth. "It's me, okay."

"What's you?"

"I'm fucking my wife."

He gulps, nods. "Okay. Just one time then? I can understand that. Olivia and I had sex a few weeks ago. Rage sex. If we don't fuck out the hate we might harm each other."

"I don't want to hear about sex with Olivia."

"So it was an accident." He laughs uncomfortably, willing me to fill in his interpretation with the proper benediction. Months ago I would have nodded, kept quiet. But I have noticed the immaculate clutter returning to my home, the lack of Ray McClutchen titles taking up space on ledges, the disappearance of good luck totems and gaudy crystals. I have crossed over to savagery. I am my shadows.

"It wasn't one time. I'm fucking her plenty, see. Can't get enough of her wet pussy, Ray."

Other parents move into hovering range. Like a child, Ray holds his hands over his ears. "I won't hear this talk."

Now the tribe is involved, casting blue words on the overhead screen of my mind, hacking the busted synapses to reach my communication center. "I bite her ass, Ray," I say, removing his hands. "Do you hear me? I slap her thighs and she likes it. The other day, I found her cooking chicken. She was home alone so she took off her pants and put on an apron. Panties and an apron. I pinned her head onto the breakfast bar where we all had scones that one time, with that shitty maple jelly Olivia canned and insisted we would love, remember? The chicken was burning and smoking and the fire alarm was going off and she was wailing and I believe I was shouting things, just fucking, Ray."

"You attacked Laura?"

"It was more animal, more wilderness. Technically, it would have been an attack if she hadn't submitted. I couldn't stop when I saw those panties and apron, what an outfit." I whistle at the memory, erect as I tell it to Ray. "We're having an affair, Ray, and it's weird and hot and I know this sucks to hear, but that's the way it went. I don't want to hate you, Ray. I want to know you. I want to speak to you like a man. No more cowering behind therapists and etiquette. You want to fuck my wife. I want to strangle your wife. Let it be. Let's you and me evolve."

Ray is shocked, one hand holding himself against the front windows of Gopa adjacent to the security desk where two of Misch's men notice.

"I want in," he says.

"In to what?"

"Whatever is happening in your backyard. I want in."

The Beatings We Deserve

A LOVELY TRANSFORMATION BETWEEN neighbors is interrupted by a phenomenon developing behind me. Loud voices, struggle, a large man holding back a ferocious Jason, the two tangling and not tangling, keeping their voices low. Security is not watching Ray and I. They are watching Jackson, a hand on Jason's chest, trying to calm his husband. Jason has seen me and does not care for the image soiling the white lobby. I broke the silence and sent flowers from VillageShop. I typed a nice message, wishing a speedy recovery for Rhythm and asking for an audience to explain my side of the hunting accident. The Sedlocks complained to Bill Chuck, who confiscated the crossbow with a tongue click and little verbal exposition. "Shame about the kid. You probably had your reasons." Jackson and Jason said nothing to anyone, transporting Rhythm upstate for treatment and returning as though their exhibitionist daughter was not shot in the ass by a vengeful lunatic.

Ray is still talking about membership into an organization that seeks to ruin his financial investment. Jason and I lock eyes. There is little the larger man can do to dissolve the situation. Jackson is not an ally. I know he leaked the details of the stolen bus, downplaying his role, along with the prosthetic leg, which is what set the parents and administration over the edge, costing Iliza her spot in *Our Town*. I don't blame him for using leverage. I blame him for being a coward. I approach and offer my hand which Jason punches away, and Jackson says something into his ear.

It's too late. I have it coming. All the rage and frustration and anxiety of the past months, all the heartbreak and emotion and failure of everyone in the room—it comes to a head when Jason spits in my face. I wipe away the fluid, as if I expected it, and in the same motion produce a cigarette that I light, ready for my sermon. I am incapable of mounting a proper defense, either verbal or physical. First, I am in the wrong. Second, there is nothing to be gained by punching a homosexual father of two adopted children, a man who has the upper hand ethically and philosophically, parents who do not even know Jason siding with him in our dispute simply because his people have been socially maligned for so long and we, the Gopa community, are better than our past. And third, this is not Toby. I do not believe, in a fair fight, I stand a chance against Jason. He is smaller but determined and works out six days a week, and he is about to unload on me the anxiety associated with parenthood and emergency rooms and the dreaded ECI program.

What ensues is a vicious attack that lasts as long as it takes Jackson and a security guard to pull Jason away, but what seems an eternity. The slaps come windmill in consistency, Jason winding up and sending open hands at my face and neck—*crack, clap, thwack*—and with each contact an *ooh* and *ahh* from the lobby, parents ashamed of such violence but unable to look away. They wish to be doing the slapping themselves, eager for the feel of my red skin against their sanitized palms. He has gone crazy, arms swinging haymakers and spit falling from his purple mouth, and somehow I am able to hang on to the cigarette. He curses, but some of his slaps hit my ears, and the ringing in my head prevents me from hearing his insults. I think I put my hands up to stop his arms, though it does little good. I am bleeding from my lip and nose, a nasty scratch on my neck. My right eye is swollen. Somewhere I hear Laura plead for assistance.

Suddenly, I am on the ground, on my back, the lit cigarette in my swollen lips as I inhale and blow a thick puff into Josey Mateo's ratty skin. Laura cradles my neck and hollers at Jackson. Jason weeps as other Gopa moms console him. Security is requesting that I put out the cigarette, that we are a no smoking community. Ray holds both hands over his mouth. Olivia has maneuvered to the front of the crowd, standing over me with a frown that in my condition I still understand is upside down. The bitch grins as she films my heartache.

I have been ejected from the lobby for getting my ass kicked. Josey and a security guard help me into a cab, a crowd of Gopa parents gathering in the front windows to watch the Channel Fourteen weatherman depart. Laura directs the driver toward Slancy, and once out of site of the school, breaks down in the backseat, weeping into my shoulder. My phone buzzes in my pocket, the first from what will be a series of anonymous calls, all from Gopa parents, reminding me what transpired. "That faggot really whooped you good. Haven't seen a beating like that since…"

I crave solitude with my wounds. Once I get Laura inside, I retreat to the backyard, hopeful for a long soak. I have no idea what time it is. Primitive compulsions, to bleed and to shit, cloud my lucidity, substances needing to escape my anatomy quickly. In the backyard, I am greeted with the destruction. My overhead screen is destroyed, bricks through the canvas. Empty cement bags lie in the grass, which means the cement is at the bottom of my lagoon. I know the culprit before Gus tells me, The Commodores concert DVD missing. He left me Jason Isbell.

"Mister Ferris just going nuts," Gus explains, dressed as Millicent, which seems comforting. "I was going to record it. Then I decided to hide in the closet."

"You did the right thing."

"Was this because you tried to kill Rhythm?"

The news is out, the nannies quick these days. "I would never intentionally hurt Rhythm. Just like Mister Ferris would never hurt you. Adults sometimes have disputes."

Gus sighs and we look at the bubbling lagoon. "Lot of tragedy in this yard. Maybe the ghost is trying to tell us something."

I assume he means Tilly. "What ghost?"

"Theodore Slancy," my fourteen-year-old says. "You should read about the history of our property. Fascinating stuff."

I cannot blame it on the Luderica or lack thereof, but perhaps on the combination of the drugs and my injuries, my anger and rage and because I cannot see out of my right eye. It cannot even be called a true blackout, though when I come to my senses I find myself squatting in the center of Jackson and Jason's driveway, shitting into the blacktop that was sealed last September. It occurs to me as I bend—why do we have driveways if we do not park our cars here? What we need is more grass, lovely trees, gardens in bloom. One of the kids watches from a window, Rhythm I believe, which should be enough to shame me into moving ten feet into the grass. Instead,

I let out a screeching howl that melds with the moonlight for an image that will remain with her forever.

Existential Weather

Despite the flawed decisions that have brought me to this point, wounded and limping across an abandoned golf course in the early morning searching for a pregnant feline, I am overwhelmed by a thought: how another cat was able to get close enough to impregnate Clint Eastwood. One of the fiercest creatures with which I have ever come into contact, my therapy animal will not allow me near it. I have not seen Clint Eastwood in days. If it had been living beneath the shed as I suspect, it would have scattered during Jackson's rampage. A loose calculation based on when I kidnapped and uprooted her from the graveyard, I believe she should give birth shortly.

I abandon the search when a white orb nearly bludgeons me, gliding beyond the tree line, crackling several twigs, and coming to rest near the Tomlinsons' porch. The first wave of golfers in their ridiculous outfits traverses the fourth fairway. With my swollen eye and limp, I cannot chance an encounter with members of the homeowners association who have now issued me seven official letters and would add my nefarious appearance to the next dispatch.

Inside the newsroom, I notice hands over mouths, curt glances. My odor, which as Little Petty predicted, has developed into a natural redolence, along with the red eye ensures no one approaches for explanation. The assumption is that whatever beating occurred was issued on my way to work, which I do little to correct. These are mostly kids, along with Melanie Trotter who calculably weeps, and an executive I do not recognize who studies my injuries as if watching an old racehorse trot into the newsroom.

Today at Lustfizzle, "17 Pickles That Look Too Sad To Be Eaten" is trending. A fourteen-year-old in South Carolina, Gus's age, shot his parents before taking the semiautomatic weapon to school and killing two students and a teacher. Different levels of problems occurred in Syria, where an overnight bombing clipped a children's hospital. The pickles really do look sad. I am not going on air today, I overhear, something about a meeting. I point out that a segment of a bloodied me reading about sunshine is the recipe for viral success.

"He's right," says a thin-necked boy with jeans and no socks. He holds a clipboard that seems to contain all of life's answers. "Viewers will tweak. We can have the anchors ask him what happened. It'll be a thing."

All of this planning and strategizing and blood is too much for Penelope Garcia who is threatening to quit if she has to stand next to my wounds. "You promise no more," she screeches at Whitman, throwing a full glass of juice that strikes the sockless young man, who cannot stomach this anarchy and tosses the clipboard, promising to quit action news forever.

Whitman smiles. "You look like shit, Pisser."

"I feel surprisingly at peace."

"You can't go on air like this."

I'm partially inventing this, not having checked the radar or a weather module. "I'm seeing a suspicious pattern out of Canada, combining with a mass shopping spree sweeping across the Great Lakes. Ever heard of thundersnow?"

Whitman likes storms, Mother Nature filtered through a camera and spit out into his ratings. He does not budge.

"Typically occur in March, but this will be a clipper with pockets of thundersnow. Very rare. The snow suppresses the environmental acoustics, so the thunder is only heard within the very spot where the precipitation occurs. Intense emotions. Communal distress. Angst in the atmosphere."

"Existential weather." Whitman twitches, behaving the way I imagined he does just prior to ejaculation. "That would be something."

It is not that we are alone, without cameras. Rather, it is Whitman's sadness that allows the pulse of what is occurring to burst onto my perception. The executive suddenly matters, white and crusty, a man who has relied too long on phosphorescent lighting for his Vitamin D. I am being escorted by office security, both myself and Whitman, the BB gun stiff against my tailbone. They place me in a chair and look on from the far side of a table, the executive, a lawyer, Whitman, a pen, a set of papers. The end does not come with a flurry of shouted accusations. Instead, initials on various lines.

"It's not a bad idea, Pisser," Whitman says, ignoring the others. "Existential weather. Theater for the anxious. Hear me out a minute."

"Let's get this done," the executive says.

Whitman circles the table. "It's the weather report but it's not about weather. It's about the state of our national misgivings. Our worries and fears. Feralism, isn't that the word you used the other day?" I don't remember using it. "What does feralism mean, though? We need a new word, something that can be branded. We can probably run an algorithm on the day's news and actually give you a Doppler and some percentages to gauge just how bad the anxiety is out there." He smiles and pants and part of me loves Whitman, his energy and youth. "The Existential Weather Report, with Tom Pistilini."

I tap the pages. Whitman shrugs, defeated by the forces of morality.

"Someone lodged a formal complaint, Mister Pistilini," the executive says. "That you stole a woman's artificial leg out of a health club locker."

"I would never do such a thing." But my tribe would.

"There are photos."

"Impossible." I know there are no photos, no videotape, Josey's crew combing the security for meddling eyes.

"Not of the theft," the lawyer corrects, passing printouts across the table.

Tungsten Sedlock, the clever little bitch. My naked image wandering my backyard, the headline in one of many of Lustfizzle's competitors: "Sasquatch Weather." I do resemble a primitive ape scrounging the woods for protein. Whitman shakes his head. The photos, while poor quality, have been packaged with a millennial charm, a clever wit that has even me chuckling at my messy life. Whitman joins me. The lawyer cracks a smile and then quickly adjusts her frown.

I begin initializing the lines. "Fine then," Whitman says. "Look at it as gardening leave for the summer. Everyone forgets about the pictures and fake leg. Then you come back. We'll put you on late night at first, remedy your image, lose a little weight."

"That's not part of the agreement," the executive says.

"So we change the language."

"The boycott," the lawyer advises. "Our female viewers."

He waves it away. "Something else will be bothering them by then."

I sign my name and hand them to the lawyer. My string comes to an end at eighty-one consecutive days, though I will go on with my uncanny predictions on the Gopa website. Whitman raises a fist, a manly bump goodbye, but I tug him in for a hug. We do not hug enough anymore, not the people we love, certainly not the strangers we fear with their grimy diseases and concealed weapons. If there were such a thing as an existential weather report, hugs would be our umbrellas.

"Moveable Museums," he says into my ear. "I'm still in."

"Stay out of things that do not involve you," I say.

Whitman squeezes. "Just like the weather. It impacts all of us."

Video Footage The New Achilles' Heel

BY THE TIME I reach a computer it is too late. Hecticmom14, Olivia McClutchen no doubt, posted a video of my beating to the Gopa website, parents clicking on it in droves, quickly forgetting last night's rebuke by the administration. The beating is followed by several photos of me wandering my backyard naked, along with more controversial footage that many have passed off as myth. The final insult is Josey Mateo's doing. Had she asked my blessing, I would have notified her that I deserved the beating, that I nearly killed Jason's daughter, that he had every right to attack me, rendering retaliation unjust.

The footage is dated, but one can make out the Gopa students, wiry anatomy running from the dog as a slight man enters the frame to distract it. There's an admirable intensity to the faceless man's courage, which quickly turns to violent lewdness once the dog gets the better of my neighbor, Jason. Confused by the testosterone and fight, the animal begins thrusting itself into the fallen man. The same children who moments earlier feared for their lives intrinsically turn to watch, a few reaching for phones to capture their survival.

I quickly dial Josey. "What have you done?"

"He had it coming." Her voice is soft, impassioned. I imagine her skin a ruthless parade of stick animals bobbing their young and tirelessly marching across the plains of her tendons. "He's one of them."

"This doesn't help my situation."

"Your situation?" Things have shifted between Josey and myself, boundaries and allegiances, a submissive administrator I thought once sought me for adultery now acquisitive of bedlam inside my languishing paradise. It is not clear if Josey Mateo and her people are my allies, or if I am being blackmailed into serving as their stooge. "He humiliated you. In front of Laura. In front of the parents."

"I didn't know the dog rape video existed." The phones that captured the footage were confiscated, videos deleted, but Josey has her ways. If she was able to obtain this footage, the Zapruder film of the Gopa community, I find it impossible that she cannot get her hands on the video Toby possesses. "You knew about the video, the coach in the shower. You knew it wasn't Iliza. Why didn't you tell me?"

"I didn't think you were going to kill him, Tom. Besides," she shifts the phone, types into a computer, a casualness to her manner that feels deplorable. "Russ Haverly was a bad person, a cancer that had to go. He's the reason we spared you, why we didn't bomb any Standcake shops, which incidentally I despise. Pancakes are meant to lie horizontal, prone, relaxed. It's what makes them comfort food, not standing up all jittery and decorated. Don't tell Laura that. I'm fond of her." She giggles. "It does kind of look like the dog is raping him, doesn't it?"

I watch it again. "He saved those kids."

"You need to come to terms with the mission, Tom. I'm sure if we bothered to calculate it, all your neighbors would exhibit shades of goodness. We don't care if they do occasional good, or that you sit on committees, or that your children volunteer during Thanksgiving to collect cans of pumpkin filling for the homeless." She repositions the phone. "We care that the roots of the creature are worthy, wanting of redemption. Our religion opposes your exponential homogeneity, your default gluttony. Your neighbor, like you, can save himself, the same way he made a choice to save those kids; all your neighbors can. They have to walk away from Moveable voluntarily. The same way you and Laura did. If they don't, we will expose them. We will hit them in the only place that matters. Their wallets. There," she says, shifting the lecture. "I took down the video of your beating and the photos. You need to lose some weight. The dog rape video stays."

Bill Chuck's cruiser is parked out front of my house when I arrive. He takes in my bruises meticulously, an old cop tying it together. He has likely heard about my misfortune from Misch and shrugs that beatings are inevitable. Bill's retirement involves sitting in an oversized office inside the Slancy Clubhouse monitoring screens hooked up to wireless cameras stationed all over the island. His only job, as Slancy's security man, is to hunt down the vandal destroying the cameras. He probably realizes by now that I am the vandal, or rather a tribal version of me, but my opposition to Moveable Museums is my saving grace.

"You shit in the neighbors' driveway last night," he says. "Security camera picked it up."

He points at the house next door. The Hendersons purchased the property for the novelty, its proximity to the golf course and Manhattan. Wealthy, they spend most of the calendar year golfing in exotic locales. I never noticed the camera before.

"I tried to hose it off to save you the hassle, but it's on their good."

We watch the Jays' driveway, trying to see if we can spot where a grown man relieved himself. "Tell them I'll have it repaved."

"Probably not necessary," Bill says. "Camera also had footage of your neighbor dumping concrete in your Jacuzzi. That'll cost more than a driveway."

"Same camera?"

Bill nods. Something about this conversation troubles me. Bill Chuck is not leaving, and I am loosely coming to grips with the reason. The Hendersons' security system is a series of high definition weatherproof domes disguised as birdcages that retail for $15,000 each on VillageShop, four different mounts capturing every angle of the property. Bill does not have access to the videos. From a remote location, they monitor their property from the cameras, occasionally phoning Bill if a faulty delivery is made to their property, or a neighbor defecates publicly. While one birdcage captured me in the driveway, another is pointed directly into my backyard, witnessing Jackson dismantling my oasis.

"How long those cameras been up?"

"Since the Hendersons moved in I'm guessing."

"And they record everything?"

"Imagine so. Missus Henderson saw you in the driveway. She called from Ireland. Claims the neighborhood is going to hell."

"You think they'd let you look back through the archives."

"Anything I'm looking for in particular?"

"January. Around the time of the accident."

Bill was the first police to the scene of Tilly's death. He phoned the coroner and authorities. "I'll delete what I find."

"That's not what I'm asking." I turn to Bill, who seems mysteriously willing to overlook minor transgressions, such as emptying my bowels in the neighbors' driveways, and perhaps murder. I need to know what I am capable of doing during the blackouts, if, as Josey says, the roots of my creature are good or if I am just pretending. "I'm going through strange times, Bill. Transformation I guess you could call it. There are...lesser attributes of myself I believe could be destructive. I need to know what I did."

Bouts Of Insomnia

SLEEP WILL NOT HAVE me, my mind replaying the day's events, our finances, my discussion with Laura that I am no longer employed as a meteorologist. The severance package will keep us afloat for the rest of the year. After the money runs out, we are technically broke, vegan-cyborg pancakes our only method to keep the lights on, the children fed, the therapy bills paid. We will get through this, she says, and she believes it because she does not know how deep I am, the extent I will go to finish what I have begun. She thinks Josey and her people are community activists, not urban terrorists who will not cease until they have established victory on their terms.

My tribe is still hungry at oh-three-hundred when I emerge from a blackout to the howling, the brutal hours of paranoia as I clutch a BB gun expecting retribution. A feline's tantrum calls to me from the rough of a fairway glistening with sticky dew, a yellow moon low over the earth to cold open on a bloated Clint Eastwood. The late May chill gnaws at my neck as I fight exhaustion and arthritis and other fresh aches I have inherited from my insatiable tribe, their gripes and terrors deposited into my bloody creeks. I brought Clint Eastwood here, to this artificial Eden. My therapy creature belongs to me the way normal people have pets with names and habits and personal toys.

If I harbored sentiments that I would turn Clint Eastwood into a needy kitten, docile in my embrace beneath a Christmas sweater as we pose for our annual holiday card, that is not us. Clint Eastwood belongs to the land. She will make it in this world with or without my assistance. She will starve in pain in a deserted hollow to protect her young, and in that we are in agreement. I am ready to die to protect mine. I have white privilege, and class privilege, also father privilege, husband privilege, human privilege, the privilege of knowing right from wrong, the feral creatures summoned through a chemical birth to inspire my path. I know what I must do. I have dreamt of it. In the manner I intrinsically know what the atmosphere will spill forth before each sunrise, I can sense the destruction. There is little difference between myself and the terrorists bent on godly honor. In many ways, I am more dangerous and undeserving of postmortem generosity. I went looking for my God and did not find her, and I operate with my own creed and spirits: one dead by four iron and strangulation, one possibly dead for reasons unknown, too many chipmunk souls to tally.

The Angora rabbits flourish in their new home, having habituated to the Slancy tree line near the fifth tee where even the chipmunks and Clint Eastwood did not realize that an underground rivulet had woven itself into the sediment. It is cooler there in the shade of trees, and they thrive in their own lifestyle, ignoring the other creatures native to this island and going about their tasks with a spontaneous playfulness they never knew in the Gopa cages. They have become a photo sensation with the golfers, many noticing from a distance the furry white balls grazing on clover, assuming the universe has planted them there for significance, good luck, vast fortunes, a hearty tee shot. It is only when they get close they notice the strange faces, rabbit lips where they ought not be, curious placements of eyes, a puckering that grows fiercer. The golfers discover there is something wrong, something malfeasant on the course, and they wander back to their golf bag to arm themselves with steel and beer.

Operation Touristcide

CHILLY TEMPERATURES WITH A high pollen count, chance of felony conviction: sixty percent. I am sullen in my Subaru Forester and the situation. The corporate headquarters of Moveable Enterprises are tucked away in an office park in New Jersey. The planning for this mission began months prior to my involvement—the reason Josey Mateo took a job at Gopa. I am driving domestic terrorists to New Jersey to vandalize what I partially funded, while their purported leader, Phil, criticizes my satellite radio stations as bourgeoisie and mainstream.

The buildings look identical, two stories with the same number of entrances and windows, a loading dock, a parking lot, lawns that are cared for by the same illegal immigrants who unironically refer to this as the American Dream. The buildings house commercial businesses, an import-export operation, hotels, travel agencies, technology startups, all stationed along an unspecific corridor off the parkway. This is where the Sedlocks have invested our money, two new buses, office furniture, fresh paint for the lobby, several wall posters depicting the routes, other posters cross-selling bicycle and kayak trips through picturesque valleys. There are no lights on in the building, no sign at the entrance, an anonymous pile of real estate devoted to the working class. Lights in other buildings suggest the park is not abandoned, late-night go-getters or indifferent janitors, a security car that rolls past once an hour.

Josey and the others dress in black pants and stolen Gopa sweatshirts, bandanas over their faces, each of us issued a two-way radio purchased on Tug's phone. Bill Chuck visits the guard station, friendly former NYPD, arriving with fresh coffee, just passing through and making faux inquiries about job opportunities in the business park. He can only bullshit for so long, buying us fifteen minutes. Josey is the eyes, seated in a darkened building across from Moveable Enterprises with views of the roads. Linda manipulates an oversized body with the skill of a marine, gliding through the property until she locates the loading dock, picking the lock and signaling. Whitman is with us in the ether, stationed near the parkway exit, his task to notify us if police cruisers approach. I am better suited for his job as watchman.

"Nothing on my end," he says into the radio. "How's Pisser holding up?"

Pisser is a wreck of nerves and paranoia, of jittery ganglia craving Luderica. Pisser has gone cold turkey. Pisser is jealous of their idealism, of their camaraderie and purpose. They have identified a cancer in the suburbs, and they will quietly destroy it not to earn glory, but because it must be purged for the worthiness of the future. Despite a job that pays him well, Whitman wants to be one of them, one of the worthy. So does Pisser, who is timidly preparing to go on three.

"Go on three." Josey's voice finds me crouched in bushes, tiny lives skittering past my knees, my heart thumping as I steady my breath, and my tribe thunders forth. And then we are sprinting across the business park, Phil and Little Petty and myself, the two getting ahead of me even though each hauls a canister of coyote urine while I lug hoses and spray nozzles. Note of pop culture phenomenon: one can purchase coyote urine on VillageShop in both small increments and canisters as large as propane tanks. Mostly used for rodent deterrent, Phil tells me strategically spraying this in an office setting can lead to headaches, nausea, complex dreams, low self-esteem, impotence, and an overwhelming need to depart work early.

Phil and Petty man the coyote urine while Linda secures a tank to my back, this one filled with actual propane. She outfits it with four feet of hose and then a buttoned torch that I am cautioned, for a fifth time, not to press until she advises. She wears her own tank, lovelier than I do, and we crouch beneath the buses, igniting the wheels, which turn from black to soft blue. If we are careful and not overzealous, the torches will give the rubber wheels a slow burn, a chemical sweat that will destroy the underside of the vehicles and creep casually toward the mechanics. Linda has already drained the engines of gasoline, benevolent terrorism, making it safer for the local fire units to salvage what will ultimately be an insurance dilemma: arson or accident? Linda blares music out of her phone, a 1967 version of "This Wheel's on Fire" by Bob Dylan and The Band. She explains the significance over the liquid fire emitting from my hands.

"Six minutes," comes Josey's voice. "Tom, get the sub."

The sub is my Subaru Forester that has sixty-seven thousand miles on it, and which I have been thinking of trading in but which now, as I sprint across an empty business park somewhere in Edison, New Jersey, strikes me as a utilitarian vehicle with a wide payload able to accommodate multiple tanks of coyote urine, or up to five-hundred

Standcake delicacies, while at the same time blending in with local workforces and suburban roads.

"Tom." The invisible voice. "You've got company. Stop moving now."

Whitman from the highway, "Do what she says, Pisser."

"Everyone stay put," Josey says. "If we have to, we leave him."

"We can't." It's Little Petty, sticking with me. "He has the keys."

Of course I do not stop, my heart clawing for an exit. Nor do I notice the large dog, German shepherd in force, running beside me at a steady clip to monitor my retreat. It has not attacked, a positive sign. There is no security in sight. If the animal changes its mind, nothing will prevent it from finishing the task.

The dog emits a low growl as it sidesteps, unsure how to assess my relation to its world. Most likely it is the scent of coyote urine keeping it at bay, but, in the way that men can embellish their control over nature, I believe the tribe I have uprooted from my core has garnered the respect of this killing beast. I stop running and make a fist and hang it over the dog's nose. It turns, wanders a few steps, turns, growls, inches closer to sniff my offering. After a moment I am able to pat the dog gently, ferocity neutered. I give the dog a sophisticated rubdown as the radios erupt.

"Is he dead?" Whitman asks. "Is that why you're all so quiet?"

"It's time," Josey says. "We have to go."

From the maps on the walls, Moveable Museums has confirmed the national routes. They use the building to train tour guides, one being our very own Little Petty, otherwise unsophisticated college graduates with no other job prospects willing to travel the country to brief foreigners on our most flawed days. The unfortunate tales consist of second amendment privilege and destruction that forever alters lives, but the Sedlocks have used my investment money to hire storytelling experts to teach the guides to deliver the anecdotes with suspense and vigor and rationale and tearless explanation. We have spray-painted warnings onto the ivory walls and ceiling and desks, but it will not deter the Sedlocks, who have studied the analytics and demographics and can be breezy and positive about their convictions.

There are people who will hate the shooting tours the way we do. Connor Mack will convince enough of them otherwise, tickets and word of mouth and heartbreak making Moveable Enterprises a viable business model.

At a diner, later, we celebrate. "Don't forget Edison," Phil tells us, toasting over ginger ale.

I raise my glass to them, to Josey who would have left me behind. She accepts my stare without flinching. "To Edison," I say.

"To Edison," Josey agrees. Whitman clinks her glass.

Little Petty, "Ever noticed how similar the words are: tourist and terrorist?"

To protect Laura, I have not discussed my involvement, that my rebellion does not cease with abandoning our investment. I have not told her that Edison is only the beginning. I do not like keeping things from Laura, but protecting my family eclipses marital loyalty. Also, I am certain my cohorts, if they suspected I was bragging about my involvement, would hide a bomb in a Standcake location to make a point.

"Bombs go off all the time," Little Petty mentions between bites. "It's the new broken shoelace."

My Unborn Are Taken Hostage

LAURA WORKS FROM HOME, frantic over the two thousand standing pancakes decorated like wedding guests that were ordered for the Ferguson nuptials, an important function for Standcake. I, too, am "working" from home, mostly Googling Channel Fourteen and Penelope Garcia. I track the storm no other weather outlet is reporting, a gale on which I have staked my deteriorating reputation—the viewers having long forgotten me. I post my daily forecasts to the Gopa website, my streak of eighty-four days intact.

"Fog early in some of the lower altitudes with crisp winds out of the south and mostly sunshine. Expect periods of jealousy and intermingled rage but look softly at the moment and know there is something more vital lurking on the inner mesh. Mellow with instances of goodness, but carry a weapon."

We meet at the counter when the mail arrives, both of us avoiding vocations to inspect our bounty, my face healing beneath the scratchy beard. Today there are bills, a magazine from AARP, and several letters. Laura and I each have a similar envelope, updates from the Cooperative Marriage. I set mine on the counter as she carefully peels the edge. I tear into a letter from the homeowners association, my tenth and final, revealing information too important for computer correspondence. Someone had to type it and address it and track its delivery to our home. The written notice informs me that legal proceedings have initiated to terminate my living arrangement.

The list of infractions is impressive. I have exterminated chipmunks that are not considered rodents, but instead designer creatures native to the local ecosystem, their likeness a branding initiative for the autumn, a calendar that will raise money to thwart erosion: "The Twelve Months of Slancy's Indigenous Chipmunks." I harbor a feral cat, the concept impossibly thrilling to see in ink. I am suspected of setting loose a population of deformed bunnies on the golf course, which are attacking the chipmunks. I own weapons, though the letter does not outline the projectiles I have fired at neighbors: Allie Sedlock, whom I missed; Harry Sedlock, who I struck; Rhythm, who was the unfortunate recipient of a wayward arrow. I tampered with Ray McClutchen's tricycle. I cut down cell phone towers and shit in my neighbors' driveway causing a black smudge that still has not been remedied. I believe I had reason for all these infractions, though reading them now in an official letter makes me feel badly. I am *that* neighbor. In order for there to be happiness, my family and I must depart. No one knows about the treehouses.

Laura smiles, and then weeps. She holds her hand over her face, waving her fingers to dehumidify the tears after a confusing few months through conjugal politics. She sets down her letter, the drama enough to well my interest in my own Cooperative Marriage update. It was most likely typed by Devin Brenner's secretary, though the signatures at the bottom are from both Brenner and my counterpart in the mess, Olivia McClutchen. For ethical reasons, they have decided to excuse themselves from the Cooperative Marriage for the rational explanation that they have been having an affair. There is a long, psychiatric babble about when the attraction occurred, subtle blame aimed at the arrangement itself, which has the effect of shifting this situation onto Laura and Ray, and subsequently me. I know that is what goes through Olivia McClutchen's head as she lays on white pillows in Devin Brenner's Manhattan apartment, where she will reside until divorce or a more bizarre arrangement has been established, joint custody of her kids and bank accounts and real estate—that I am to blame for her diaspora out of Slancy.

The last letter is unstamped and addressed to neither of us. Inside the envelope is a single photograph, the inside of a freezer, three glass tubes with a milky substance. These are vials of semen, presumably mine, which I should have deposited at the Manhattan Cryobank in the past month. I rush to the icebox, empty, which causes Laura to cover her mouth.

"Tom, what?"

"Abraham and his siblings. Someone is holding my sperm hostage."

"It's not funny." She smiles and then loses the grin. "It's Olivia. Stay away from Moveable Museums or else."

We contemplate the scenarios she could create with my semen—scatter it on her pillow, a child's pillow, turn it over to the lacrosse parents and let them imagine my destruction.

"I'll talk to Josey," I say. "She'll know what to do."

"No." Laura puts the letters into a drawer. "I'll handle Olivia."

Economic Benefits Of Sex Tapes

AN OLIVIA-DEVIN AFFAIR WOULD typically be endless gossip, an excuse to have dinner with the Jays and Sedlocks to discuss the McClutchens and all the ways it will affect our own livelihoods. We barely see our neighbors anymore, all of us keeping our doors shuttered and children sequestered in their tasks of becoming more lucrative adults than the neighbors' brood. On the morning shuttle to school, we engage in antisocial busyness: typing, tapping, swiping, sending, reading the same blog posts on our mutually beneficial collaboration, avoiding eye contact.

More broadly, the Gopa community has again erupted into shameful behavior, parental cliques annexing other cliques to combat foreign cliques, all of us enemies. The dead bunnies instigated the new round of trouble. Police were called. The administration blamed an anonymous group of pet loving parents that had been sending letters for months and threatening legal action if the mammals were not removed from their children's biology lesson. The Jays are suing the administration for releasing the video of Jason being sexually hampered by the dog, which has led to an investigation into how the video was leaked. Jason is on mental health disability for the remainder of the year, presumably watching his driveway to ensure it does not suffer further exudation.

Parents have made donations to radical political candidates and controversial charities in the names of other parents, their surnames arriving at the top of lists as Blue Chip Donors. Other parents share the lists on the Gopa website to publicly shame the intended, who deny the allegation without condemning the virtue. They neither support nor oppose Planned Parenthood; they are proponents of gay rights but libertarian on gay marriage; they do not support or despise a candidate for State Senate, Jeffrey Rears, who wishes to sterilize the homeless and felons. Like other Gopa parents, they toe the line. They are neutral. They are not getting involved in affairs that do not concern them.

The parents have put pressure on the chess coach, who has found reason to "bench" Gus. He has been placed on the injury list, something to do with carpal tunnel that was explained to me briefly in a gymnasium a week earlier, and to which Gus agrees because he hates chess. He wears a sling to the matches and sits with me in the bleachers, where I stare angrily at Sharon Li and her wretched disability. I had Josey hack the website to learn who GopaGirl9 was, Maria Sherwood, after she began a rumor that Iliza is dating a lacrosse player, presenting further intrigue to the Pistilini-Lacrosse confrontation. In turn, I accused Missus Sherwood's daughter of spreading gonorrhea in the upper school, only to later learn the child is only six. My latest username was revoked soon after.

Fully flowered petunias arrive from VillageShop, most staying alive through the shipping, and the colors are bright and mirthful and, dare I say, playful planted in my backyard. The chipmunks, now properly attuned to survival of the fittest, have learned to steer clear of my flowerbed and lagoon, even though the concrete damage bears a price tag I cannot meet. I water my plants. The cell phone trees hiss. A golfer whiffs, curses. The dimpled projectile plonks into wood and scatters brush. A bicycle approaches. A moment later, Allie Sedlock is in my backyard. It is late May, too early for the tank top and tiny shorts, her legs impossibly tanned for this time of year. She holds a cactus that she tosses onto my porch, shattering the pot.

"Peace offering," she says, crossing the wet lawn. "Harry's idea. He sent me in this fucking outfit. Said it would soften you. Or harden you. I don't remember." She smirks, hates the hell out of me shoeless and bearded with water shooting out of the hose. "Let's talk, Pisser."

After we destroyed the Moveable office, no one came to interrogate or arrest us. There was nothing about the damage in the newspaper. As far as Bill Chuck could ascertain, it went unreported to the police. The Sedlocks did not mention it a night later at an emergency investment club meeting, according to Ray, although most of their employees quit, with the exception of their prized tour guide, Little Petty, who they know as Steven. Which means the terms are clear—we will handle this how it is meant to be handled by entities engaged in dispute, no media or authorities.

I shut off the hose and reach around to check the BB gun. She reaches for a hoe.

"You shoot me, I'll bury this in your neck. Everyone will assume it was self-defense."

"What do you want Allie?"

"The offices. You aren't clever enough to do it yourself, but you know who did it. Olivia wants to hire someone to cripple you. I'd say things are out of hand in our tiny paradise, wouldn't you?"

Olivia McClutchen: harlot, semen thief, hitman.

"We're prepared to offer you and Laura your full shares, along with eighty percent of Russ's investment." We meet eyes, the tricky business of murder among neighbors. "He was Harry's friend, not mine. You did more good than harm getting rid of him."

"It's too late, Allie."

"Do you hear yourself?" My inability to barter shatters her sublime illusion of capitalism. "You have no job. Your life savings is tied up in this venture. Harry will see to it that you are reimbursed first. All for doing nothing."

"I'll have to keep my mouth shut."

"Sure."

"Which I can't do. You've crossed a line with me. There's no coming back."

Furious, the beautiful Allie Sedlock begging in my backyard, near a cement-ruined Jacuzzi he and his wife refuse to enter because I may have killed an old woman here. "Think about Laura. Think about your children."

"I am thinking of them." For the first time in years, my wife respects me. I have begun looking my children in their eyes again. I watch Allie, see how willing she is to make amends. "Pull Tungsten out of the play," I say.

"You know I cannot do that."

"I wouldn't ask it of you, Allie. I don't want it for Iliza anyway. It's a steep repercussion, but one she deserves. I was just wondering how sincere you were."

I wander to the shed. Allie follows. "In two weeks, the most influential names in murder culture will arrive to take the first tour. Whatever they write will set the stage for the rest of our lives financially, vocationally, even where our kids go to college. It'll be huge, Pisser. We cannot have this..." She waves a jeweled hand at whatever I am to her, "...bullshit continue. You tried to kill me with a crossbow. I know it was you."

"You released naked pictures of me."

"You ruined the lacrosse season. You know how important extracurricular activities are for college applications." She runs a hand through the petunias to see if they are real. "Despite everything that has happened, we want you back. There will be a media storm. It's unavoidable. It would help to have a public face on TV."

"I don't work there anymore."

"Harry knows people. It won't be a problem."

Harry could have told me this himself. He is wise to send Allie, and also slightly afraid of me. She goes for my pants, cigarettes in the front pocket. We light one and listen to the waterfall and die a little.

"Thank you," she says.

"For what?"

"Russ Haverly. Someone should have thanked you long ago. He was a shit toward the end. I was surprised you had it in you, Pisser." Allie smiles, blows smoke, passing this information informally, two neighbors discussing recipes.

"Allie, there's something you need to know about Russ."

"I know about the video." Her voice is lavish with irritation that I even bother to mention it. "Don't make this about that damn play. We're not pulling Tungsten out. You put us in this situation."

I puff rabidly at this accusation, the tribe sucking its share of the nicotine and distributing it equally. I put the Sedlocks in the situation of having to blackmail my daughter out of her role in the school play to better their own daughter's chances of getting into the ECI program. I did this by killing the man captured in a video fucking their daughter at a high school party and providing illicit drugs to my own child, along with dozens of others. I am a folk hero, a goddamn Davy Crockett of the private school community. They should erect a statue of me in the Gopa lobby.

"You'll have no choice to pull her out if Toby Dalton releases the video," I say. "That's exactly what he intends."

"No, he won't."

"How do you know?"

"Because I bought it from him." Allie smokes angrily, watching my reaction. "I'm releasing the tape myself."

Harry Sedlock is not the spirit behind Moveable Museums. Allie is. She is polite, always smiling, her hair in a perfect ponytail, a juggler of motherhood and perception to which every mom aspires. But she is cold and determined, a mother who has scaled the Gopa ranks, and who no one sees coming. They have strategized about the video, asked the advice of Connor Mack.

"Why would you do that to Tungsten?"

"Not to Tungsten. For Tungsten. She's a victim, not ingesting drugs like other girls I won't mention." She checks her phone, shrugs that this is not personal, the things we do for our children. "Timing has to be right. Just before opening night would turn our little school play into a national event. A private school teacher—a dead private school teacher—assaulting a teenager in the townhouse of a GPS mogul. Geezus, Pisser, think of the lawsuits, the hush money. An entire news cycle devoted to a high school play." She points the cigarette at my left eye. "That's attention you cannot buy."

"She looks like a little slut."

"Watch your mouth, Pisser." She's disgusted with my review of her child's sex tape. "She's only naked for a few seconds. It's mostly her breasts," she continues, willing me to agree.

"She's in a shower." I recollect the critical scene, which alerts Allie that I have seen Tungsten naked. "Her hand is bleeding. She has a man's penis inside her." I toss the cigarette. "What about Iliza?"

"She shouldn't do drugs." Allie watches her phone. "Besides, my daughter is naked. I hardly think anyone will notice poor Iliza."

"I noticed."

"Of course you noticed. You're the father. It's your job to keep your daughter out of rooms like that." She shakes her head, sighs, transforms into loveable, enviable Allie Sedlock. "Poor Harry. He feels just awful. People will assume he killed Russ. And rightfully so." She smiles at me. "In some circles, he'll be considered a hero."

It is this moment in my backyard, contemplating the economic benefits of sex tapes, the failures of fatherhood, the hijacking of my worthy contribution, that it occurs to me that we, as a community, have lost our way. I am more like Allie Sedlock than I admit. She would do anything to enhance her daughter's distinction. I would kill for my own. And if Allie does not vacate my backyard, my tribe might do it again.

"Get out, Allie."

"Think about it, Pisser." She taps my ass as she passes. "Let's be an example of collaboration in the face of adversity. For our children's sake."

Hypocrites Anonymous

TONIGHT IS ILIZA'S DRUG prevention class. It is held in Brooklyn Heights, in an unremarkable neighborhood where other students in the private school community who have been caught using drugs can attend clandestine lectures on the perils of addiction. The place is easily reachable from Slancy, though we take a ferry into Manhattan and two different trains. I want her to experience the monotony of addiction, the cost in both time and patience that comes from abusing narcotics, the waste of life. The C Train is filled with chaos, commuters and vagabonds vying for dirty seats, odors of perspiration and fast food combining with the rickety shake as the cars pull themselves through the moil of urban existence. I do not believe Iliza has a drug addiction. But I want her to forever associate this experience with abomination, the embarrassment of being accompanied by a parent to these lessons, the knowledge that I am judging her in every effort I pretend to ask about her day. "How was school?" I silently play back my daughter snorting drugs on a sofa that belongs to Toby Dalton's parents, exhaust of recreational euphoria exploding behind hair I once ran a hand over through retellings of Mother Goose tales. "How is physics?" I killed a man because I thought he was raping you when he was only raping the neighbor's daughter, another father's felony. This is how you love something over which you have no control. This is how you protect a child who you gifted life, who you cannot stop loving, who in two years will be a woman and will do whatever she chooses regardless of my judgment.

I sit in the hallway of a public school, a chair too small to contain my girth. I can smell my being, feel the failures of open combat on my healing face. This is therapy for my own addictions. While it has been several days since I used Luderica, my tribe has not disbanded, hanging around to mentor me through my unwinding. I wait until the drug counselor has exhausted his threats, until my daughter is sufficiently broken. Even though she just wants to go home and climb in bed, I insist on a milkshake, a ritual we once enjoyed and which now reeks of imposter and bribery.

"Try mine," I say, part of the ritual. "It's delicious."

"No, thank you."

"You love peanut butter." I hold the straw to her mouth, the end brown and ready to drip. As a child she loved to share, and just before it reached her mouth, I would tap the end on her nose with the wet cream, causing her to burst into laughter.

"I'm okay."

"Just one taste."

"Dad, stop." We sit at a counter that looks onto a crowd of young people, freedom my daughter craves. "You're going to stick the straw on my nose. It was funny when I was six. It's embarrassing now."

"I won't. For real this time. Take a taste."

Iliza does not trust me, the beginning of an agonized smile that is more exhausted than enjoyed. She leans, her pink mouth open as she goes for the straw, and at the last moment I tap her nose with the moisture. It is a risky endeavor for sure, but it works, the evening's tension perishing into laughter.

"You jerk. I knew you were going to." Iliza emits a rare heave of levity. "I really wanted a taste."

"Here." I pass her the milkshake. "I don't want it anyway."

"So what are we doing here?"

"I wanted to talk. Like old times."

I shove my stool close and ask about school. About friends. I inquire into rumors of a boyfriend, and she brushes me back to my side of our lives. About the play and how angry it makes her, that in many ways it is a relief because she no longer enjoys pretending. She has no one to talk to, not me or Laura or Tungsten any longer, no outlet on which to unload except Josey Mateo, who is a proponent of not pretending any longer, too much reality to occupy our pursuits. It occurs to me that in our eagerness to raise a pragmatic and independent daughter, we neglected to equip her with a faith system, a God to whom she could reason out the confounding illusion of control. Real estate is hard to come by on the island. Slancy lacks a church of any denomination, a sacred dwelling to get us through the rough times. We thrive on our secular savvy, our smarts, but we are missing something vital that other people call on in times of duress. "Religion is feral to us as creatures, God an unblemished source of survival and renewal," I will later write on the Gopa message board, inciting an argument with the parent body that will cause yet another handle to be revoked. "We do not need lectures or milkshakes. We do not require further testing or additional committees to discuss the merits of our children's school day. We need church."

"Can I ask you something?" Iliza says.

"Of course." My daughter has access to the same nanny chain. She is familiar with rumors that I bludgeoned Tilly, which she does not believe; that I had a hand in stealing the equipment bus, which she dismisses as insanity; that I may have lost my job for swiping a prosthetic leg. "Ask me anything."

"It's embarrassing. I heard it from my friend Amanda who said it came from the nannies." The muscles in my neck strain with anticipation. "Are you..."

Guilty of murder? On the verge of bankruptcy? Planning a terrorist attack on the neighbors? "What is it, honey? Just ask."

"Are you and mom having sex again?"

Sometimes the nanny chain gets it right.

Thundersnow

It arrives on the final week of May, the storm few news agencies predicted but nonetheless claim as their own for the few hours it corrupts the commute and makes global warming a fanatical topic. Lustfizzle ceases publishing articles about "24 Men Who Painted the Tips of Their Erections" and "The Most Intriguing Torture Methods of the Last 100 Years," instead sending intrepid reporters into the squalls armed with raincoats and cameras. From our bedroom, Laura and I watch the storm on television as we listen to trees split, the lack of decades old roots felling our woods, an effortless gale of giant fingers flicking toothpicks into shreds. We dwell on the wedding, if the Slancy Clubhouse will be in any shape to host four hundred guests in another week. Until it is too late, the radar never revealed this storm would climb out of the Atlantic and combine with low pressure systems out of the west and north, biting into coastal regions. The result is a massive heap of fog and anxiety, moisture and sirens. Many weather outfits reference my prediction as a guess, having mentioned the possibility before reliable models were available. I could sense it was there, the way Clint Eastwood knows to hunt and will never starve because of it.

It is my cat, my therapy animal, that has me wandering through dangerous conditions in the black dawn, clouds of orange and purple malfeasance illuminating the wet island. I can do nothing to prevent Laura from accompanying me, our argument awakening Gus, who will not be deterred from the hunt, dressing quickly in a poncho, scarf, and, strangely, a helmet.

"We have a cat?" he asks.

Clint Eastwood is an important cog in my therapeutic transformation, I explain to Laura as we trespass through neighbors' yards. It rains and snows, not enough to cause accumulation, but still an incredible phenomenon so close to summer. Every cracking branch makes us clinch our necks, Laura and I reaching to cover our helmeted son. A falling tree will take wires, electrifying the ground, and there is little we can do to protect Gus. We grip one another at a sudden crash, the McClutchens' yard, where a branch slices in two the treehouse that hangs sullenly from a maple.

"What was that?" Gus asks.

"Termites." From thirty yards away, I sense the bugs scurrying. I drilled the holes and purchased the insects on VillageShop using Tug's phone. It seems so long ago, a tender period when the McClutchens were my only enemies. "They get into the wood and rot it out."

"Not that. Listen."

"I hear it," Laura says. "Like a rumble."

We cannot see anything above the tree line, the precipitation making the sky heavy and somber, black in places where first light should arrive. It is an indecisive weather pattern, cold and warmth vying for skin.

"It's called thundersnow. When a cold front passes over a warm front it drops precipitation as snow. The snow drowns out the acoustics of the thunder, which is why it sounds so intimate, directly overhead. It will start hailing soon."

Gus clutches himself inside the poncho. "Will I have school today?"

"It'll be over in an hour. The sun might even shine."

"Is it dangerous?"

"It's unusual so close to June." I listen for branches. "We should get indoors."

"What about Clint Eastwood?"

It would be nearly impossible to capture the pregnant cat without being clawed half to death on a normal morning. In this weather, bloated and exhausted, we might encounter the feline's last stand. I am certain she has found shelter to wait out the storm. I take a final look in the woods. There are no chipmunks, only several of the sopping rabbits dashing through the mulch, this cataclysm preferable to the Gopa cages.

"We'll come back tonight. After it passes."

Messy Commute

A LACTEOUS RESIDUE COVERS the city as the storm slinks quietly north. Garbage cans and branches scatter across roads. My backyard is in relatively good shape, although the golf course took a beating, much of it under a deep soak. The morning commute is delayed. Gus and Iliza are furious that school is not canceled; I am also disappointed. I was looking forward to all of us hunkered inside the house, a giant afghan concealing us in musty warmth while we watch on television as the world has its way.

The Gopa lobby is excited and distracted, parents having dug out the winter clothes to dress their children, everyone swapping stories, embellishing close calls, exchanging hand sanitizer, and hydrating children with eye drops and spring water. Another student was rushed to the hospital, having overdosed on Luderica, although this time it was lethal. Rory Stokes, the first inductee into the ECI program, had been taking the drug for nearly a year by his mother's recommendation. Not only does Gopa have a serious drug problem, but also it appears an ECI spot has been vacated.

"Nearly lost power and her boots don't fit and this weather feels anxious," we tell each other, all of us prognosticators, "the city is on edge and my nanny says someone was named to ECI, although it's probably the teacher's kid because of what happened..."

Lower Manhattan and Brooklyn were hit harder than the Upper East Side, with some moms claiming they were not even aware there was a storm, as if the thundersnow made its decision based on status. We separate into our respective circles, Laura finding the Fergusons to assure them everything is set for the weekend, Iliza and Gus merging into the stream of excited students. Due to the restraining order, I am not permitted on school grounds, though I can drop off my kids and wait on the sidewalk, where one of Misch's men keeps an eye on my cigarette. Ray McClutchen arrives with the trike over his shoulder. His pants and jacket are wet, a nasty tumble.

"Too many puddles," he says, out of breath. "Had to walk it a mile."

"You shouldn't be riding in this weather. Stop being proud and take the bus with the rest of us."

"Car exhaust causes global warming. Global warming is why we have weather like this. It's why I bike everywhere."

"It's a tricycle, Raymond."

"Urban trike. And call me 'Clutch.'" He has an edge to his voice as he reaches across and takes the cigarette, shaking loose a puff before he flicks it onto the street. "What's happening with you?"

We both fidget. "Everything is fine."

"I mean with Moveable," Ray says. "I want to know the plan."

Ray has provided valuable intelligence on the investment meetings, information to which Little Petty, in his tour guide role, was not privy. But I cannot separate that he was trying to fuck Laura. I also believe Ray is undecided about how to proceed with Moveable. He could easily be reporting back to Harry whatever I tell him.

"Ray, I want you to listen closely." He fancies himself an important man, a homeowner, a respected public figure. I know because I was him weeks ago. Ray has a career that he enjoys. He has a wife, for now, and two kids he loves, but it is a love that has not cost him something essential. He might rebel and join me. He might keep his head down and live off the profits of his investment and optimism, make nice with Olivia, write a few more books, even marry someone more pleasant. He does not know what I know. He has not shaken hands with the man who sullied his daughter. Jason Isbell sings about losing the things that matter. *There's a man who walks beside me, he is who I used to be, and I wonder if she sees him and confuses him with me.* We do not shed our old selves like snakeskin. They follow us around, waiting to reenter the sepulcher if we neglect to mind the door. "You keep asking about something you do not understand."

"Make me understand, Pistol."

I point into his chest. The lacrosse dads watch, hoping for a fight into which they will throw their support for Ray, a fellow lax dad. "It's not a game, Ray."

"I know it isn't a game."

"I need information. When do they arrive? Where are they going? How many?"

"The murder writers," he says. "Fine. But I want to know what you're planning."

Nannies and moms arrive, another slow rain. From the sidewalk, I look through the windows into the lobby. Doug Whorley, Todd McClutchen, and Rhen Sedlock are surrounded by girls, one of whom is Iliza. The nannies are huddled near the coffee. I lean into Ray's neck. "We'll warn them to stay clear. But no one gets away with glorifying school shootings."

"What will happen?"

"I don't know that yet." And it's the truth. In the way I do not trust Ray, Josey does not trust me. "I haven't been told."

The storm and the drug overdose have eclipsed another announcement, that Jackson's and Jason's son, Damian, was one of two students accepted overnight into the ECI program, the first Slancy kid. From the sidewalk, I wait for Jackson to glance my way. It feels unnatural of me to stand here, a grown man ignoring someone I love, someone with whom I have swapped stories in front of a fire and committed larceny. But I am not permitted inside, nor would my friend accept my congratulations.

"Jackson," I holler, slapping the glass. A security guard whispers into a fist. "Hey, Jackson." Mothers pretend not to notice. My large friend glances toward the window, his family sheepish behind him. I hold up a thumb that transforms into a fist. Jackson turns his back.

Pistilini-Dalton Drug Cartel

He waits in my backyard, lounging in a chaise. His eyes are closed, a faith I find satisfying and foolish. Toby thinks we are of the same tribe, teammates helping one another out of a strange pickle, our similar skin color and Gopa sweatshirts ensuring that we do not have to fight and stab deceptively.

"Finally get expelled?" I ask.

"I felt I deserved a snow day." He sits up. "Geezus, Pisser, aren't you a weatherman?"

"Not anymore." I assess the yard. The flowers are likely ruined, though I might be able to salvage some of them. There are several downed branches that I will carve into chunks for the fire pit.

"Good news. I have work for you."

He stands to negotiate. He has a slight cut above his eye, according to the nannies a falling out with Doug Whorley. Purportedly, word of Toby's secret video has gotten around, several lacrosse players concerned about their own cameos. I could knock him unconscious and chainsaw him apart and have most of him buried before dinner. With his parents living overseas, several weeks would pass before anyone would miss him.

Having sold the video to Allie Sedlock, Toby could have done the smart thing and paid off his debt. He did not do that. He knows I had something to do with Russ Haverly's death and he needs a go between with Capra. I am his drug mule.

He hands me a list. "This is for starters. We'll arrange weekly drop-offs."

Like a weather pattern forming in the periphery of my conscience, my tribe is anxious for the task, having already determined the conclusion. "You owe money. He won't give me drugs if you don't pay your debt."

"Look at it as an investment. Float me a loan. I'll get you back next month."

"If you want me to buy you drugs because you're too much of a pussy to do it yourself, pay me upfront."

Toby smiles, shakes his head, the irritation of dealing with a middle-aged father. He turns over an envelope and sits down. "About fifteen grand. It'll have to do."

Fifteen grand. Allie Sedlock bought the video cheap. I walk to the chaise and dump him onto the lawn. "Get out of my yard, Toby."

Feline Bedrest

I LOCATE CLINT EASTWOOD beneath a tree near the seventh tee. Her belly bloated, she is unable to move and has not eaten. She allows me to carry her home and accepts a bed in the shed where Gus runs warm bowls of milk until she falls asleep. Josey arrives with a woman she introduces as a veterinarian, who shakes golden hoops and burns incense, announcing that Clint Eastwood will give birth to four healthy kittens any day. My therapy beast is on bedrest until then.

With the wedding days away, the mother of the groom has gone quiet, Missus Ferguson not returning phone calls. Laura spent most of the afternoon tracking her down, the two thousand standing pancakes dressed in tuxedoes that she ordered already in production. We need the money in the way Capra needs money to survive, in the way Harry and Allie and Jackson and Jason and Ray and Olivia need it, all of us starving for redemption.

"It's not just greed that corrupts goodness," I penned in a blog post, which I recite in front of my fire pit, "but an assimilated greed entwined in everyone else's business, a complete organism. To hold back on personal indulgence means to steal the food from another mouth. Those who earn money and have money enjoy spending money. Those who enjoy food buy food. Those who enjoy toys buy toys. Those who enjoy sex buy sex. Those without money will accuse them of greed, but if they withhold their indulgence, if they do not reinsert the means back into the organism, the organism dies. The organism exists because the beast requires indulgence." Bill Chuck is at the fire tonight. Ray McClutchen is here. Little Petty wanders in somehow, as do several people I do not recognize. We talk about politics and big retail and prostitution while Jason Isbell sings about lost mothers and dusty lands and busted boats. "Indulgence is natural. It is a feral entity. It must grow and eat. But wickedness is also an indulgence. Evil is an indulgence. Greed forsaking goodness is an indulgence. They grow pestilent until they are contagious and infect the future, carve a hole in the bottom of our skiff. The worthy always rise up to contain the leak before the ship is lost."

Tragedy Abounds

The Fire Mouth FM Weed Apocalypse Propane Vapor Torch Backpack and Squeeze Handle retails at VillageShop for $650 with a Zenith Membership. Industrial hose a length of eight feet, dispensing five-hundred-thousand BTUs of flame, it can decimate a motor vehicle in traffic, not to mention the occupants of a city bus, a subway car, or the waiting area of most coffee shops. My chore requires a more direct flame. I have turned down the gauge to a concentrated needle aimed directly at the fuse box, a steady stream of lava that burns the paint and alloys until they drip and erupt in sparks. If not for soldering goggles, my eyes would tear so badly I would not be able to watch the flames catch the wood, which would be a shame. The nice thing about this felony, or rather the surprising thing, is that I did not end up here during a blackout. I am present, of sound mind. I stopped taking the Luderica a week ago.

Laura drank herself to sleep last night, distraught over the Fergusons canceling the order of two-thousand delicacies long after the pancake battalion was complete. We threatened legal action, but it is an empty threat. We can no more afford a lawyer to oversee a pancake lawsuit than we can sit idle while our investment in Moveable Museums disappears. Standcake is stuck with it, the cost of doing business with wealthy degenerates.

Fortunately, Laura has a deranged husband with a tribe of vengeful demons who have not vacated the chemically augmented premises. When I ceased the medication, along with the untimely erections and blackouts, the tribe was supposed to disintegrate into the folds of my subconscious, along with the notion of playfulness that I never discovered. Instead the animals have stuck around, demonstrating the ins and outs of arson. Bill Chuck handles the investigation, the arriving fire chief a poker buddy and September-Eleven alum who has been briefed on my battle with the school tour faction. Earlier, I walked backward down the nature trail toward the seventh tee, then into the Hudson and waded around the eastern side of the island until I reached the clubhouse. The equipment I floated in, a swan raft (nine dollars for Zenith Members) I do not recall ordering, the swan's head complete with a smile and a jerky wink. Once finished, I placed the equipment in the swan and set it adrift, the wind taking it toward Staten Island, the direction of Russ Haverly's final voyage, though the choppy current will ensure the propane tank and torch end up in the river.

By the time I arrive home, the sun creeps east over Brooklyn, the last Saturday in May. I enjoy a cigarette and water what is left of the flowers and listen as Laura calms Missus Ferguson, who is coming to grips with news that her venue is aglow with flame on the morning of her daughter's wedding. It was set to be a beautiful event, a golf course overlooking the Manhattan skyline. She has not inquired if anyone was injured and has no one to turn to but Laura, who is smart and brash with the contacts to salvage the day.

Laura suspects what I have done, although we are bound by our sins and beyond discussing rational reactions. What loved ones did is less fortuitous than what they are willing to do, and a dozen other bumper sticker sayings to adhere to our marriage. We listen to the roar of sirens over our bridge, watch the parade of neighbors make their way to the pyre, imagine the well-planned golf outings that are being destroyed this very minute. Six o'clock in the morning, and already Laura has put in calls to seven possible locations, Missus Ferguson apologizing for the pancake mix-up and offering to pay double for the mistake. All of our former friends are invited, and soon they will receive scrambled calls that the venue has changed. My animals have made sure there is nothing suspicious about the conflagration. Days after the macabre storm, Bill Chuck's fire chief will know the cause: delayed malfunction from a lightning strike that sat dormant in the fuse box, the glitch eventually getting the better of the wiring. A freak event.

Petunias are survivors. Throw a late season thunderstorm at them, freeze them with hail and snow, gusts of wind that would flatten mortal petals. But give them a few days to dry out and douse them with fresh water and sun, and they glow like the cunning offshoots of wedding lilies. Gus watches from the porch, studying my odd accuracy with the hose, which is when I realize I am still wearing the goggles, a cigarette wiggling out of my lips. It should be weird except my son is donning thick slippers, a towel around his head, Laura's bathrobe, his arms crossed against his bony frame.

"What's all the noise?"

"Morning kiddo," I call over the thick, wet stream. "How'd you sleep?"

"Do you know what time it is?"

I nod, shake the hose at him, inhale.

"We're supposed to sleep in on Saturdays."

"Come on out and talk to me."

"The grass is wet."

"Take off the goddamn slippers, Gus." I do not mean to yell, but we are long overdue for a man to nanny talk.

He kicks off the shoes and wanders to the edge to watch the petunias. Since Slancy does not have its own fire department, we contract with companies in Brooklyn. The bridge cannot support the weight of large fire trucks, or rather no one knows if it can. The trucks thunder up to the entrance of Slancy and phone Bill Chuck, who offers conflicting directives. There was no one inside—we made sure of it—so there's really no rush to salvage what is already an insurance loss.

"What's that smell?"

"The clubhouse. It's on fire."

"Oh dear. Was anyone hurt?"

"Nah, it was empty. Want to go have a look?"

By now it is a mass of splintering debris, the flames carving through the four-year-old roof and pushing out a black smoke that hovers over the island. If one concentrates, beyond the gentle whisper of the cell phone trees, one can hear the conflagration spiral. It is a scene of violence and destruction that I know Gus does not wish to see. I slap the porch for him to sit.

Gus is strange, but he is a gentle soul. I have pushed him into combat and logical hobbies, neither of which suit his timid being, hoping to eke out a vigilance I believe he needs in his artillery. Pitted against his peers, there is nothing exceptional about his resume.

And yet he is a kind child, caring, he worries about others—default goodness, is what Josey would call it. One morning in February, a new kid arrived at Gopa, the parents unsure what to make of the lobby or how they fit into our complicated cliques. An innateness to it, Gus approached the boy, introduced himself, and offered to have lunch with him on his first day. The boy took one look at the old lady standing before him and knew intrinsically to decline. Too gentle for this world.

I sense lately that Gus is scared of me. I cannot blame him. I smell like the outdoors. I have a beard and fresh wounds. I rarely wear pants in the backyard. Children are wiser than we give them credit for, and he has heard the rumors. I doubt that he believes I killed his nanny, but even if he does believe it, I hope he considers it was for good reason. I am his father, after all, required to make tough decisions.

"I want to talk to you about something."

"Okay."

I put an arm around him. "Remember what the therapist said about caterpillars and butterflies?"

"How I'm in a cocoon, sure."

"It's time to emerge from the cocoon."

A literate boy, Gus does not enjoy metaphors. "What does that mean exactly?"

"Stop being Millicent. Start dressing like boys your age."

"Emerge from the cocoon." Gus sighs, watches his lap. "I might need more time."

"There is no more time. Emerge, Gusser. Spread those wings and let her rip."

"Let her rip how?"

I have no idea. "Live life. Enjoy childhood. Get after it with other boys your age."

"Get after it." He thinks about the wording. "Like with wrestling?"

"Sure, if you enjoy it."

"Chess?"

"Do you even know how to play Chess?"

"What about lacrosse?"

"Something we should consider, sure." I hug him toward me so hard I could bruise him. Protective gear suggests kids cannot hurt each other, which makes them rougher than necessary. Gus is wiry, weak, but it is his soul I hope to protect from terminal catastrophe. He does not have the savvy or looks to hang with the lacrosse team, an outsider before he is even issued a jersey. Or perhaps, in Gus's estimate, being a lacrosse dad is something I would enjoy, a designation that would lift my spirits even though I know I don't belong with them either. "Look, kiddo, I just want you to do things that make you happy. Don't try things you think will make me happy. What is it that would make you happy?"

Gus glances around the yard, searching for an answer that will please me. He connects with an idea until a smile invades his face. "Rhythm," he says.

"What about her?"

"She runs around the golf course naked. At first her fathers were okay with it. Then later, when other parents found out, they made her stop. I think I'd like to try that."

"Run around naked?" I have been unhappy for a long time. Being unhappy makes other people unhappy, which creates a circular snare of unhappiness. We are bargaining over something I do not quite understand but will later realize is a test. Gus is testing to see if I am true to my word, that his happiness is my profound goal. "If I allow it, you'd take off the robes?"

"I like the Gopa uniforms. The gray and purple work nicely together. Uniforms at our age imply a common pursuit."

"And you'll stop acting like a nanny?"

"Not all at once," he says. "I'll think about it for sure. One other thing."

"Okay."

"You smell. If I start dressing like a boy, you have to start dressing like a dad."

"It's a deal." I rub a hand through his soft hair. "Don't tell your mother about the streaking."

Stealing Back My Unborn Children

SLANCY FEELS APOCALYPTIC BY early evening, smoke mingling in the shadows of precocious trees that sense their near destruction. The island is empty, many neighbors having traveled to the Fergusons' new wedding locale, a Long Island golf course, where they plan to spend the evening to escape the fumes. The fire was the main story on the evening news, schadenfreude to the larger island as entitled Slancy succumbs to its decadence. Laura is gone as well, although she left instructions to sneak into the McClutchens' house and steal back what belongs to me. Bill Chuck chaperones. We enter through the garage door, Bill showing me the mechanics of my fifty-piece lock pick set I will never use again. I do not know when my hatred of Olivia McClutchen began. It was nothing specific, neither of us good enough to sustain our unions, the ugly ducklings of the Cooperative Marriage. If we were different people, it might have brought us closer. Instead our revulsion extends into stolen semen.

I feel badly about what my actions will do to the financial prospects of my neighbors, Jason and Jackson, even the Sedlocks and Ray. But I want to see Olivia McCluthchen's scowl when it sets in that her investment has failed her future, that divorce is expensive, that to maintain a Gopa lifestyle she must rejoin the ranks of the working class. I want a personal association with her defeat when I reach into her freezer—where she keeps Popsicles for Maddie and ice packs for knocked heads—to retrieve three vials of pure Tom Pistilini, the dumb bitch not even bothering to hide it.

Bill eats a Popsicle. "Tell me again why you have frozen semen?"

"We were thinking of having a third."

"Kids," he says. Bill is a survivor of three marriages, three divorces, four kids, two stepchildren, eleven grandchildren. "Used to be easier when all we had to do was fuck."

The burglary lasts moments. We are back in front of my fire pit watching the culminating gasps of sunlight disappear beyond the trees, the news vans losing interest in the Great Slancy Blaze. What began in the basement became a full structure fire, boats from Weehawken summoned to douse the flames from the river. Bill Chuck is eager to discuss his role in the calamity. I am the retirement he yearned for, the apex of a career in law enforcement he entered to make a difference. He knows all the fire chiefs, all the police lieutenants and retired captains within fifty miles of Slancy, a running encyclopedia of badge resurgence.

"Lots of whispers around the island. Plenty of complaints after the storm. Should have left Duffy O'Neal out of it. He knows the tree houses were tampered with."

"They're illegal, Bill. If you did your job, I wouldn't have had to get involved."

He sips his scotch, enjoys our night at the fire. Like Lieutenant Misch, there are people who never retire, but yearn for a worthy endeavor to occupy their angst. "You asked about the Hendersons' security tape."

He pulls out a portable hard drive no larger than his thumb. It contains death for certain, potentially a homicide. Logic demands the object that holds my secrets should be larger. A DVD, an eight-track cartridge.

"How did you get it?"

"Don't ask stupid questions."

"How far back?"

"Enough."

I set my glass in the yard. "Did you look?"

Bill shakes his head. "I know without looking you didn't do what you think you did. But in case I'm wrong, what I don't know can't be used against you."

I take the object and walk it to the porch. My screen destroyed, I point the projector against the house, spotlighting the vinyl siding that offers an added dreariness to the black and white images.

Bill stands. "I'll wait out front."

"No. Stay."

The video begins last spring, footage of my backyard from the Hendersons' view. I fast forward through summer and autumn, and then the alternating scenes of blistery days and twinkling nights until we arrive on January 11. Hours pass in seconds when there is only daylight, the backyard empty, and once night falls I emerge, fat and lonely, depositing myself in the Jacuzzi. I fast forward to January 12.

January was when the blackouts began. My facts are that I was at work on the morning of January 12, a storm system hovering in the Carolinas that I failed to mention was due to hit the region that week. I fast forward until a body emerges, our nanny, Tilly, wandering in the January cold. She deposits two buckets at the edge of the tub, staggering, hovering over the water and looking into the hungry heat. She does it, overturning one of the buckets into the now rocky Jacuzzi, the red dye innocently costing me hundreds of dollars. She stands upright and glances back toward where we stand. Looking at the house, paranoid, she steps opposite toward the woods, an awkward motion that seems significant. I play it back again.

For an instant, I expect to see myself enter the backyard, a hockey mask from VillageShop perched on my brow, slamming a hammer into her porridge head before drowning her in my utopia. Karma intercedes instead. On the playback a chipmunk crawls out of the hill and flitters across the icy patio, Tilly's head shifted so that she watches the house instead of where she steps. At the last moment she looks down, startled by the shadow. She attempts to halt her weight from coming down on the tiny chipmunk, the creature frightening her, the aerobics of old knees and inebriated reflexes colliding with the seasonal irritation of slippery landings. She falls hard against the pavement.

Two spots of blood. The first, her forehead, as the forensics suggested, followed by her unconscious heap rolling into the water. The second, a chipmunk, its posterior crushed, bleeding as it tugs itself toward the woods, smearing its wretchedness onto our crime scene.

"Yes!" I shoulder a fist to the heavens, turning to high-five Bill Chuck for what he always knew was an accident. I grab his head in my hands and kiss the top of his pate. The woman is dead either way, and I want to feel sadness. But she was, in fact, stealing from me. She did dump dye into my tub. And more importantly, just as the police suggested, I had nothing to do with her death. The definition of a serial killer is someone who murders three or more people. While it is possible I will have a hand in fulfilling that obligation before the week is out, I did not murder my nanny.

"To Tilly," I say, toasting Bill.

"And chipmunks," he adds.

Deliveries At The Hendersons

TWELVE INSTADINNER TEN-QUART PROGRAMMABLE Pressure Cookers ($120 each). Three Universal Two-Button Garage Door Remote Controls ($98 each). Four Enermonster Portable Lithium-Ion Batteries ($900 each). Three Wanderlust Oversized Collapsible Picnic Coolers ($54 each). Ten fire extinguishers ($70 each). Four rolls of Multiuse Duct Tape ($9 each). Miscellaneous toys: action figures, marbles, jacks, Legos, Matchbox Cars, Erector sets, copper-coated BBs ($400). Nails, bolts, screws, washers ($200). Terrorism is expensive.

The boxes arrive at the Hendersons in waves, Bill Chuck and I watching the property and quickly shuffling the items into my shed. By Josey's doing, Tug Reynolds's phone number was shifted to a new cost center within the Gopa bureaucracy. Any purchases will be routed from the athletic department, to the faculty, to the administration, to an account Josey set up for miscellaneous expenses. There orders will rest for thirty days, at which point the company will reissue them to be cycled through the cost centers until someone bothers to notice.

"Take this with you," Little Petty says, shoving a knife into my waistband. He is not suspicious in Slancy, a devoted employee of the Sedlocks. He arrives and carts away the material, not offering details of where the equipment is being assembled.

"What for?"

"The blade is made of horse bone. In case they wave a metal detector, they won't discover the knife. I used to wear a small one in my anus. Just in case."

My task is reconnaissance. I am as guilty as the others, although I do not know how to build bombs other than a brief explanation I obtained from the internet. The toys and nails and BBs and tiny projectiles are placed into the pressure cookers, which are packed into the coolers with the fire extinguishers and batteries. Each pressure cooker is connected to a battery and rigged up to the garage door openers, which Little Petty will be holding.

When the power source is turned on, the pressure cookers heat the toys at temperatures of 250 degrees Fahrenheit. Petty has augmented the cookers by removing the steam valves that control the pressure. Once it reaches a breaking point, the cookers will explode, detonating the fire extinguishers, and dispersing the contained objects at speed of 1,500 miles per hour, roughly the velocity of thousands of toy bullets.

Red Herring

I MEET CAPRA IN a coffee shop on West Tenth Street, the horse-bone knife strapped to my ankle. It is June, and the front doors are open, spilling a soft jazz onto a sunlit sidewalk. I am showered and shaved, honoring my agreement with Gus, a clean suit. Capra wears a white cotton shirt and jeans, Louis Vuitton moccasins, dark sunglasses he removes to reveal blue eyes. When he smiles, his teeth are a piercing white. He has an optimistic sheen, as if a descendant of the original Frank Capra, and the same idealism that defined his ancestor's films are vital to his drug operation. He looks like every Gopa father, and he sees the same when he looks at me, only I plan to destroy his life. This man is the source of the poison my daughter ingested.

A man seated at a table nearby stands. As Little Petty predicted, he waves a metal detector across my extremities. No one speaks until the examination is complete. Capra summons a waiter to take my order, coffee. A pit bull with a giant neck lies panting near Capra's foot, and it rises to greet me with a wet mouth.

"Dezzy, be nice to Mister Pistilini."

"Call me, Pistol." I let the dog lick my hand before I drop to one knee and massage his belly. The animal is on its side, my second killer dog in two weeks.

"You have a way with animals, Mister Pistol. Dezzy doesn't like anyone. Do you own a dog?"

"A neighbor's kid is violently allergic. We all agreed without discussing it we would not have pets."

He shrugs at my suburban allegory. "I recognize you from the TV. You say the weather, yes."

"I don't work there any longer."

"A new occupation." He offers a warm smile. I will destroy everything he has worked so hard to build.

Bill Chuck and Lieutenant Misch have researched Capra. Antonio Bernardo Capra, age forty-seven, has long considered himself a musician. Releasing several hip-hop albums in the late nineties that did not achieve sufficient sales, he moved into the production end of the business. He has a stable of musicians, although no one who has broken through the perilous mediocrity of today's musical apex. It is mostly a hobby, a front to his more lucrative occupation as a white-collar drug dealer.

He has developed a unique clientele. Rather than bankers and executives, he services the privileged mothers and faculty and even students in the private school community. He does not dabble with heroin or cocaine or corner dealers, only designer drugs and crooked laboratory workers and dirty pharmacists. The new drug culture. His clients do not go on methamphetamine rages. They seek a controlled buzz, an ordered chemistry. This is polite addiction. He wears loafers to business meetings instead of a Ruger.

According to Misch, he feeds drugs to similar schools from Maine to Virginia, civil places where no one likes to talk about chemical opiates, which is good for business. He has a Russ Haverly in every school, and often several Toby Daltons operating at the student rung. Misch claims drug enforcement agents know about Capra, although he is smart, overly cautious, civil in ways that other drug dealers are not. It is possible he knows that I have been a customer for some time, paying thousands for the elusive Luderica. He is recruiting me to be his new Russ. That his dog approves of me is fortunate.

"I was sorry to hear about your friend, Mister Tug."

"Terrible thing."

"A good associate. I had nothing to do with his departure." No, but someone at our table did. I nod. "The phone, Mister Pistol. Why you keep it?"

"I thought he might come back for it."

The waiter arrives with my coffee. Capra drinks his black so I do the same. "And after the body was discovered, you still thought he might return?"

I cannot tell him that my associates are as dangerous as him, idealist hackers who are using the phone to fund-raise for a terrorist act. "It was silly to keep."

"Perhaps you wondered who was on the other end," Capra says. "Perhaps you were waiting for me." He sets down his mug and moves the chair forward, shoving Dezzy out of the way. "You see, Mister Pistol, I know who you are. I know where you live. You have a wife, just like me. You have kids. Whatever dispute you had with Mister Tug does not concern me other than the money I am owed. Do you understand?"

"I think so."

"We are the same. If you follow my direction, we can make much money together." He takes out a pen and writes on a sheet of paper that he passes across the table. Months earlier, Russ owed this man forty grand. With interest, it is now eighty-five. "You arrived empty handed, Mister Pistol. Our young associate tells me he sent you with my money."

I shake my head. "Toby is mistaken."

"Dishonesty." Capra sips his coffee. "You see my difficulty with your Toby. He is young. He possesses an arrogance that does not coalesce with my operation."

"Toby can be useful." I reach inside my pocket, Capra and the man at the next table watching my hand, which emerges with a piece of paper. It is a list from Toby, a new order, which I pass across the table. "One hundred thousand on delivery. The money you are owed plus an advance. To begin on the right foot."

Capra smiles. He likes that his dog likes me. He appreciates that we have a mutual distrust of Toby Dalton.

He hands the paper to the man, who tucks it into his coat. "Are you prepared to make this exchange today?"

"Next Saturday." He frowns, expecting the answer. "A school near Chinatown. Address is on the paper," I say before he can give instructions. "There will be a black bus. The money will be on the bus."

"We used to meet at a harbor in Weehawken."

"I don't own a boat, Mister Capra."

He considers the location. "School on Saturday. Empty. What else is on this bus?"

"Tourists."

He smiles. "Tourists never know where they are." He sips coffee, enjoying my company. "Where are they going?"

"Red herring," I say, wondering if he'll understand the cultural metaphor. "It has nothing to do with our business."

He nods. The large man stands and buttons his jacket. "Mister Pistol, may I make a suggestion."

"Of course."

"Toby," Capra says. "Perhaps he should be present for the exchange. I believe it does a young man wonders not to take things for granted."

My sentiments exactly.

Gus Murders Millicent

CLINT EASTWOOD GIVES BIRTH to four kittens in the seclusion of my backyard shed, the brood proving the opposite of their hermitic mother and fawning for attention. We each name one. Gus chose the soft brown kitten with a dark eye, Millicent. Iliza the runt, Burt; Laura's choice was Pancake, the brute, which sidles next to its mother drinking milk, stopping only to scratch away a playful hand. One kitten is distinguishable from the others in that it looks exactly like Clint Eastwood. I name her Worthy. Iliza notifies me we are keeping them. I will not attempt an auction. These are not kittens that will appear on fliers attached to telephone poles, or wear cat hats, or sleep in cat beds. They will live in our backyard where they will kill chipmunks and shit in sand traps and avoid cuddling if they can help it.

A Monday in June. I enjoy coffee with my wife while uploading the video of me not murdering my nanny to the Gopa website, a subtle achievement I feel honored to expose. No one doubts I had something to do with it, but in the conversations we are not part of, vindication will earn me points with the nannies. Gus arrives in the kitchen dressed not as Millicent, but in a regular Gopa uniform, his hair combed, shoes polished, an impostor to our morning routine.

He pours himself a bowl of cereal. "I've been thinking about taking a writing course this summer. There are workshops for teenagers in the city."

"Sure, we should look into it." My tribe leaps from my skin, a sonic thunder in my chest. "I didn't know you were interested in writing."

"Miss Mateo talked to me about it. She says memoir writing is a hot topic."

"That's great," Laura says. She contains a similar excitement over the transformation even as we process that thirteen-year-olds do not write memoirs. "What is your memoir about?"

"Some Millicent. Some school. Mostly about being an outsider." Gus explains through the cereal. "It's titled, *My Year As An Old Woman*. That was Miss Mateo's idea."

It is a relief to have Gus back, even if he is taking cues from a terrorist. "Crazy Miss Mateo," I say.

Gus stops eating and stares with his tender eyes, his serious side. "She's not crazy, dad. She just cares too much."

If Our Peace Was Everlasting

"Mix of insanity and greed as we hustle through the work week, an angry, suffocating, comatose slog toward Friday," I write. "Chance of inebriation, seventy percent, the dog meat trade out of Thailand impossible not to consider humane each time I see a therapy mutt riding shotgun in a Gucci crocodile tote. As far as crocodiles, expect mild hatred and distrust toward the species with very few consumer groups advocating for preservation of their hides. Local fishermen will do well to hit the eastern shores of Slancy even though it is a gated community, the water and beaches illegal for most anglers. There's a sixty-two percent chance of God, according to the neighbor attempting to evict me. There is no past or present or future, it is all happening simultaneously, that we are surrounded by Gods, inside and out. Pressure systems out of the subconscious suggest we are all our own Gods. Be a good God today."

This morning on Lustfizzle, "22 Times Penelope Garcia Had an Itch During the Weather," an assembly of just that—short videos of the beautiful newscaster scratching a mild disturbance and distracting the broadcast region. Popular on the Gopa website, a discussion about sexual currency, a number of parents weighing in, both moms and dads, that they would either receive or issue fellatio to assist their child's academic career. We are all on our best behavior about the ECI program. A mother accused one of the fathers of sexually assaulting her in a school elevator when the tip of his flaccid penis bumped against her thigh in the crowded space. It is a claim she cannot prove and he cannot refute because we voted for elevator privacy during last year's PTA, forcing removal of the cameras. Most parents believe the victim is lying to gain advantage with the ECI board, although our inherent multicultural agenda insists we ostracize the pervert. There is a petition to have my family removed from Gopa Academy next year. Posted to the site anonymously, more than a hundred parents have signed the document, which would mark the first time a parent, and not the child, was the result of expulsion.

I concentrate on my cell phone as we make our way to Gopa, the dwindling days of the school campaign. Jackson and Jay and Rhythm and Damian sit toward the front of the bus, ignoring me. The Sedlocks sit behind me, where they can monitor my movements, Tungsten occasionally reading aloud a line in preparation for opening night, and also to bother Iliza. Ray McClutchen has stopped pedaling to work, jeopardizing our civilization's last stand against global warming. Rumors out of the nanny chain are that Olivia McClutchen is pregnant with Devin Brenner's child, and they are deciding whether to abort or announce it. We all have been invited to Maddie's birthday party this week, an invitation that cannot be rescinded or adequately ignored because it is inconceivable to take our grievances out on a three-year-old and her temperamental mucous membranes.

FROM THE HENDERSONS' YARD to my shed, the supplies are then transported to the abandoned grocery store in Chinatown where Petty and Linda assemble the parts. There were three scenarios by which our vengeance would play out, which we put to a vote. The first, Phil and Petty suggested kidnapping one of the Sedlock children, preferably the slutty one, and use her as bait to encourage Harry and Allie to abandon the school shooting tour. I was opposed. As corrosive as Tungsten has been to Iliza's junior year, she is a child and deserving of guardianship. It was voted down four to two. Second, Linda suggested cutting the project off at the head by assassinating Allie Sedlock, a strategy that might have worked. It was voted down five to one, with Linda actually voting against her own proposal.

The third scenario, mine in the primordial phase which Whitman enhanced with ingenious subplots, turned out to be the winner. In a public and loud fashion, we will explode by pressure-cooker bomb the various members of the murder culture syndicate who plan to publicize the school shooting tour. The Sedlocks are paying them for favorable reviews, which is probably not necessary, blood money for kind thoughts they would have offered freely. Each of the fifteen writers has received ten warnings, by Whitman's doing: a campaign of emails, phone calls, handwritten letters, video clips—not so subtle hints to drop out of the visit. By now the Sedlocks and Connor Mack and perhaps the members of the investment club have learned of the threats, dismissing them as mindless jabber.

Phil and Linda and Josey and Little Petty volunteer to carry out the precarious detonation, offering themselves to the rubble. I was able to talk them out of martyrdom, convincing them of the pain and terminality of sainthood. But also, I believe them to be important. For every school shooting tour that gets slain, every illegal backroom negotiation uncovered, every political handout and corporate sin and rueful blunder, there are fifty more creeping out of our deplorable unworthiness to stain our children's future. We need people like Josey and her kind if we hope to survive ourselves.

From the sidewalk, the Gopa lobby seems docile, mourning, no one wishing to compromise the ceasefire. We sanitize and hydrate, exchange air kisses, ask about the kids. Three more have been accepted into the ECI program: Murray Randall, a four-term regional spelling bee champ; Gumption Barr, an artist who uses scabs to create surrealist paintings; and our very own Tungsten Sedlock, specialty unknown. More aggravating is a tidbit that Laura uncovers. Doug Whorley, infamous puncher of my head, is dating my daughter. Further gossip from the nanny chain is that he recently got into a fistfight with Toby Dalton, landing a few haymakers before it ended premature to Toby's brain matter leaking onto a gymnasium floor.

"I don't care what the video shows. It was obviously doctored," a mother tells me about the petition to have me expelled, small talk in the entrance. She does not recognize me without the facial hair or swampy odor, and I quietly smoke and listen to her observation. "That man killed his nanny. And there's no telling me different."

And Many More

WE ARRIVE AT THE McClutchens with two trays of standing pancakes decorated like the birthday girl, sans the snot, a peace offering to our neighbors who no more want us there than we wish to attend. Maddie's third birthday party is a popular event, neighbors from Slancy along with Gopa parents who own a child of similar age and showed the initiative to make the midweek trek to the island. Everyone gathers in the backyard while Ray feigns knowledge of his charcoal grill. The rest of us pretend to care that the allergenic celebrant survived another trip around the sun; sunlight also makes her sneeze. Iliza and Gus dropped out at the last minute. They sense we are not wanted and prefer Clint Eastwood and the kittens to parental posturing.

Lacrosse parents are in attendance, standing in rigid formation with Harry and Allie. Most have signed the petition that would see the Pistilinis ousted from Gopa, a tested theory that if enough of the money complains, the administration will fold. They think they have me, but they fear me and the combined insanity and zeal and fury of my tribal lords. One rumor out of the nannies can be ignored. But a series of rumors, over several months, and I have them on their heels. They do not know what role I played in their coach's death, or how I manipulated the season to ruins. They have seen the videotape absolving me of Tilly's death. And though they have likely studied the tape, played it back, discussed it in private, they can convince one another of my impropriety if they stay determined.

I wander over to the grill, a smoky mess that an aproned Ray is making worse. It is the Smokerbeast LKX Deluxe BBQ Inlet that retails for $7,000 on VillageShop, and which Ray uses twice a year, typically to cook hot dogs. It includes a propane gas stovetop, a rotisserie, and a charcoal pit, which is causing all the combustion. He doused the briquettes in lighter fluid and did not let them burn off before adding the chicken legs, which no one will eat anyway because chicken legs are the new veal, according to the Gopa website. He has a pile of half smoldering bird, part of the coals still black, the others smoking insensibly beneath the poultry. It will take hours to finish.

"Need a hand," I say.

"Eh." He waves the spatula and nearly falls into the fire. Olivia is spreading rumors that she is pregnant just to bother him and her lover is topping off his guests' drinks. Ray is intoxicated over the flames, made worse because Devin Brenner, of all people, has cut him off from the beer cooler. I do the compassionate thing and retrieve him a beer, and commandeer the spatula.

"Thanks, Pistol." He takes a long pull from the bottle, which steadies him. He slurs into surrender. "Don't even ask about Moveable Museums. I've got enough on my plate."

"I wasn't going to. You've been more than helpful."

"Harry is suspicious enough as is."

The only reason I approached Ray at his Cadillac grill is for additional espionage. "But while I have you."

"Shit, I knew it." He bends his chin, buckles in close. "I gave you the names of the writers. What else do you want?"

I've managed to get the lid on the fire, which halts the smoke, and turn on the propane. Once that gets hot, I'll have the food ready in thirty minutes, and then Laura and I can depart. "The location on Saturday. Still Gopa, no change?"

"That's the intent." He drinks angrily. "Tell me what you're planning."

"Better you don't know."

"Is it illegal?"

"Don't be stupid, Ray. Of course it's illegal. What you're involved in is ethically illegal." Ray closes his eyes as if absorbing a slap. What he is involved in, all of us, goes against every bullshit word he has ever written or thought. "The thing I don't understand is—why Gopa? What are they planning?"

Ray does not answer. He glances over me at the crowd, mostly Harry, waiting for someone to make eye contact and rescue him from my persistence. He leans close, voice low. "A school shooting reenactment. Harry says it's important everyone understands the look and feel."

The look and feel, Allie's doing. A school shooting reenactment will highlight the beginning of every tour, both regional and national. In its profound morbidity, it is somewhat brilliant. I don't even have to ask but I do. "Real students?"

"The Sedlocks hired the cast of *Our Town*," Ray says. "There's no matinee on Saturday. Parents were fine with it."

"Why were they fine with it?"

Ray shrugs. "It's a paying gig."

It has moved from unethical to pernicious, involving our children. Making it worse, the purportedly righteous side is staging bombs in the vicinity of where our theater department will perform its most dramatic tragedy. Josey needs to know. Bill Chuck and Lieutenant Misch will have to be briefed.

"One more thing," I say. This is where it gets tricky. "I need a hundred thousand dollars by Friday."

He coughs into a fist, steadies himself on the grill and burns his hand. Yelping, I hold Ray's arm as we lock eyes.

"For what?"

"To pay off Russ's drug dealer."

"What if I say no?"

"He'll kill me. Then he'll kill Gus and Iliza and probably Laura." I flip the meat. "Moveable Museums will become an international phenomenon. You'll get rich. Olivia and Devin will live comfortably with their new kid. Everyone will be happy. Except for you, Ray, and do you know why?"

"Don't tell me. I don't want to know."

"Because you're one of the good ones, Ray. One of the worthy. And I want to be one of those guys, too."

The food taking too long, dusk settles over the McClutchens' backyard. It is past Maddie's bedtime and Olivia skips the traditional order of birthday celebrations, moving forward the cake and presents, her useless husband failing at his one task. Even by three-year-old standards, it is a horrendous party, everyone starving, parents separated into adverse cliques, the hosts settling on opposite sides of the yard. I could not understand why Laura pushed so hard to attend this event; she and Olivia have never been close. And then I understand.

Just before the cake is cut, my wife has a hand on Olivia's shoulder, the two laughing like the dearest of friends. The only other person who notices is Allie, who watches with disdain. Laura's hand disappears below the sea of bodies, and when it emerges, she is holding one of the Standcakes dressed as Maddie, which she offers Olivia. At first there is resistance—no, no, no, I'm watching my figure—and then persistence as Laura pushes the delicacy toward Olivia's mouth. It's like a lesbian wedding, Olivia closing her eyes at the taste as Laura presses forth the erect pancake, actually wiping the gooey fruit smoothie syrup from her lip with a finger and depositing it onto Olivia's tongue. All self-help pop-psychology aside, my wife is a barbarian. I know without ever questioning her that she spiked the upright pancakes, dressed as little children, with the semen that Olivia stole from our freezer. Most likely the frosting as well.

Tonight at the campfire, Jason Isbell croons over the destruction of beautiful things that will have to be rebuilt. The amorphous bunnies have facilitated a pact with the chipmunks, the two tribes coexisting, sharing the creek that the rabbits discovered, too preoccupied with the new supply to drown in my wrecked lagoon. Even Clint Eastwood seems satisfied with the arrangement. Bill Chuck is here, Little Petty, Ray McClutchen who has no place to stay. We are Josey-less, Jackson-less. I revamp an argument I tested earlier on the Gopa website, which caused my latest handle, WifeBanger, to be revoked, after a parent suggested I was a proponent of kidnapping daughters. There is an island 8,500 miles away from Slancy where two warring tribes swapped children to end a land dispute that lasted three decades. The exchange of children, it is believed, would bridge the differences between the people and emphasize their similarities. The example is a metaphor. I was not actually advocating that we swap children every few months to better acquaint ourselves with the plights of our neighbors.

"Give us the princes in exchange for the dweebs. Give us your lonely for the destined that did not require orthodontia. Give us the sad, timid, homely girls, the pale, thin, painfully shy boys, those who have not reached puberty, those with acne and bright smiles and silky hair and cellulite. Let us push each through the grinder of another family's rituals, learn to win and loose from a fresh bedroom, and when we all meet in the lobby, see if we are not better and happier and awake and worthy."

Do Terrorists Kiss Their Families Goodbye?

TODAY AT LUSTFIZZLE, A livestream of people trying to deliver pizza to the wrong address as American hilarity ensues. The delivery personnel come in various genders and ethnicities, one being the popular and always-on meteorologist, Penelope Garcia. The reaction of the customers, who seek only to stare at the television and not participate in germane and clever cultural entertainment, is the point of the clip. Depending on the delivery person, the customer is combative, or angry, or even scared. Several times the authorities are phoned. Pizza arrives at breakfast. Pizza arrives while families are already eating. It arrives late at night, when folks turn on lights expecting a prowler or bad news and discover, instead, warm and gooey comfort. Some pretend they actually ordered the faux pie, that they paid over the phone, accepting the stolen meal. In one clip, Penelope Garcia is eating the pizza when a man opens the door, a skintight dress as she wolfs it down, and when she demands an outrageous amount of money, the customer willingly pays. It is a social experiment of race relations and sexual metaphors and pizza. It is irritating for its grandeur, and because it is impossible to stop watching.

The opening night of Gopa Academy's spring play, *Our Town*. A day earlier, a sex tape was leaked showing what was described as an administrator showering with the play's female lead. The faces of both the now-deceased faculty member and actress are blurred, the footage edited for time, my daughter's drug cameo cut from the premiere. The tape arrived at the apex of the news cycle, as if planted by a professional marketing firm, the media picking up on the significance and inciting a full day of lustful coverage. It was the lead story on Channel Fourteen this morning, a news anchor rapping about private school entitlement and dead lacrosse coaches and civilized rape. Laura and I combed the tape closely, thankful and proud it is not our daughter ensconced in an older man's embrace, even though that very misconception is what doomed him.

Rumor has it the Sedlocks threatened a lawsuit, both against the school and the wealthier Daltons, and the play will go on in spite of the media attention. News vans park outside the school, reporters trying to discover the connection between the dead coach and the actress, already whispers of the father a modern folk hero. It is the most guarded high school play in the history of theater. Gopa's security will canvass the stage, armed guards at the exits and seated plainclothes wardens throughout the auditorium. The school hired a private investigator to tail me on opening night, just to know where I was, which is at dinner with my family. A hankering for pizza, we meet in a small restaurant far away from Gopa. Bill Chuck has a friend tailing me as well, protection against Capra. From my table, I watch the man outside watching me, and Bill's guy keeping tabs on my guy, all of us speculating. It occurs to me to introduce them, which I do. It turns out they know of each other, know the same police, and I suggest they have coffee while I dine with my family.

Tonight, Laura is driving the kids north for the weekend, disguised as a summer shopping excursion. I have revealed to my wife a general strategy that will take place in her absence. She suspects amped up vandalism, just like Edison, and I have done nothing to correct the illusion. It is imperative that if I am caught, or worse, that Laura be able to raise our children without implication. She is scared and sullen, but as a couple we are determined and better and more worthy of loss. I do not know how terrorists say goodbye to their families, but along with pizza and soda and wine, I have purchased gifts. A bracelet for my wife, a book on writing for Gus, a wrapped box for Iliza, inside of which is another box, inside of which is her cell phone that was confiscated last month.

I do not listen to music at the fire this evening, only the crackling of the cell phone trees, the crickets in the darkness, the dripping waterfall, the mewling kittens threatening to open their eyes to participate in this strange terrain. It is only myself and Ray McClutchen, a duffel bag, all of it in neat denominations.

"Will I ever see this again?"

"Doubtful. But I'll pay back every dime. It might take years."

"What if you don't come back?"

"I already thought about that. I want you to take care of Laura, take care of my kids the way you do yours."

This is the time we hug. This is when we grope in the darkness, creatures who need other people. Instead, Ray disappears to his own tent, too proud to weep in front of me, conflicted about which outcome he desires. The house empty, rooms full of beds and couches, we prefer the primitive intonations that dwindle to a whisper as the wind disappears, the fire settles, when all of what we built rests.

I place a phone call. Toby picks up on the third ring. "Took in some theater tonight. Culture, Pisser. Thought I might see you there."

"Brave of you, Toby. I'm surprised to hear you'd go anywhere near a school event that Doug Whorley might be at. Heard you boys had a falling out."

"What do you want?"

"I have money. The handover is tomorrow."

Toby chuckles. "It's called a drop, Pisser. And good for you. I'll be out tomorrow afternoon for the stuff."

"No, Toby. I'll pick you up in the morning."

There is a shift on his end, Toby coming to terms with an arrangement that conflicts with his refined exemption. "Why would you pick me up?"

"You're dropping the money yourself."

"Where?"

"You'll find out in the morning."

"No fucking way."

I let it settle into Toby's shifting desires. "I came through with the money. To square things with Capra, you need to hand it over yourself."

"What if I say no?"

"I know where you live. Which means Capra knows where you live. This is the only time a hundred grand will fall in your lap. See you in the morning."

I hang up and take a final excursion across my lawn to my neighbors' property. It is late but I see a light in the living room. Jackson is a night owl. I gently rap at the backdoor until he approaches, large and shirtless. His shoulders slump when he sees me. He unlatches the lock and softly slides the glass.

"What do you want?" He knows from my stare, possibly my sobriety, that I am here about Moveable. He has spoken to Harry Sedlock. He knows what tomorrow is, the arrival of the murder culture writers who will initiate the onset of wealth.

"You know what they say about bridges, Jackson?"

"Don't burn 'em down."

"The same is true the other way. You can't just give the bridge a little kick in the cement. You have to blow it up."

"Geezus, don't say anything more."

"Take the family out of town. Just get in the car and drive."

Jackson knows better than to ask. He has been with me in felony mode. He knows something inside my cryptic chamber has awakened, something sooty and untamed from a place we do not acknowledge. He has touched this world and turned back to the familiar warmth of wireless convenience and motion sensor luminosity. Already he is calculating the lies he'll need to tell Jason. They likely have plans to be at the location when the bus of journalists arrives, some fruit punch and cookies, summer trousers and jackets, a casual hello. Jackson will have to cancel with the Sedlocks. He'll have to feign excitement, a spur of the moment lifestyle that Jason loathes, be convincing and enigmatic to encourage his husband of his nomadic jaunt.

"Wait." He slides the door and walks onto the porch, where he offers a hand. "Good luck, Pisser. If we don't see each other again."

"You haven't heard." I lean in and hug my friend. "It's Pistol."

Here Come the Worthy

"IF WE ABIDE IT, pretend it does not belong to us, it is the same as performing it. If we choose to ignore it, we condone it. To say it is something else or someone else's is a dull validation, in the manner that litter is not a communal tribulation. To object quietly, in what passes for indigenous prayer, is not enough. Prayer requires intention. Prayer requires grit. I must purge this to be whole again."

The grimy stillness of a Saturday morning in June, when we require more sleep after a long bout of contention, several parents are awake, boosting my post to the forefront of the most read list. Is this about prayer in school, of which WorthyMom28 does not approve, or does "purge" refer to rumors that members of the ceramics club have been vomiting in the girls' locker room?

Today is my tiny offering, my substantiation as a father and member of the parenting sect. In the same manner I chaired the committee that saw the school eaves troughs reengineered so the facilities room did not flood when it rained; or how I sat on the Gopa Parents Think Recycle committee to argue with other concerned guardians about global warming and recycling bins that match our school colors; or attended every parent-teacher meeting since Iliza's enrollment—today is how I give back. My action, while illegal and purposefully excessive so the media must pay attention, is momentous in its resolve. This is a worthy endeavor. This is a silent reinforcement of our species' evolution that we are progressing on the proper trajectory.

Toby rides with me and the money. Josey, Phil, and Linda are in another car tailing the bus where Little Petty will amuse guests with gothic notions of American butchery. "Did you know most gunmen have been linked to antidepressants and processed meat?" he will say, a chuckling head bob. "Did you know blood makes up seven percent of human body weight?" Bill Chuck and Lieutenant Misch, along with a fleet of drug enforcement agents, wait in undercover vehicles surrounding Gopa Academy. Capra is causing the traffic congestion, police agencies eager to arrest a drug trespasser that, up until my involvement, has been untouchable, the Al Capone of the private school community.

The fifteen scribes who write murder culture were given ample warning. Eleven heeded the threats and opted out of the inaugural Moveable Memorial Tour, with four arriving at JFK last night along with Conner Mack. This morning, from Tug's phone, Whitman issued each a final caution, which according to Little Petty went ignored, one man actually boarding the bus with his wife, which by my count tallies six.

"Thirteen passengers." Little Petty's voice is calm through the two-way radio, seated on the bus parked outside the Sheraton JFK. He sounds casual, as if he runs these sorts of tours every weekend. "I make fourteen in case anyone cares."

"I count six," I tell him. They are: Pietre Graeme of *Leichenbestatter*, Hansa Schultz of *Voldtage*, Meniza Perl of *Rebinada*, David Gillard of *Grincer*, along with his wife Tonya, and Connor Mack.

"Harry is on the bus."

"Harry?" The name seems distant. My neighbor, Harry. The man who ruined my daughter's junior year—that Harry. Father of two, husband, the best of what Slancy can become, homeowner Harry. I thought it arrogant that he did not hire security for this event.

Instead he opted to chaperone it himself, which will make an exchange of drugs and money laborious. If Harry is on the bus, it means Allie is with him, which means no one drove Tungsten to Gopa this morning to prepare for her role as one of the dozen shooting victims. The Sedlocks have rented the cafeteria to reenact a school massacre, which will be a mainstay of the tours. Tungsten makes nine passengers. She takes her therapy dog, Muggly, with her everywhere, making ten. Solidarity in numbers, Harry brought along the other members of the investment club who chose to participate. Jason would not be swayed by Jackson, which makes eleven, and my nemesis Olivia is twelve.

"Who's lucky number thirteen?" Josey asks from her radio.

"It's sitting on Olivia's lap," I say. Snotty, allergic Maddie.

Little Petty clicks his tongue. "People make choices."

The route was set days ago. It should be thirty-five minutes until the bus arrives at Gopa, where the passengers will be treated to a continental breakfast—scones, muffins, fresh squeezed juice—along with a simulation of every mass shooting that happens on a monthly basis. The school is empty this Saturday, the administration renting out the cafeteria to the Sedlocks, who hired the cast of *Our Town* to flex their thespian skills, the school brimming with an invisible anticipation that precedes every catastrophe.

The plan is for Little Petty, using his horse blade knife, to halt the driver a block before the school. The exchange will happen and the bombs will explode a safe distance from Gopa, outside the radius of dozens of students expected to be waiting in the glass lobby. Whitman will livestream the fortuitous scene for an insatiable viewing public, which enjoy violence and terrorism on Saturday mornings in the way past generations sought animated superheroes. With Harry on board, things are different. He is directing the driver's route, running ahead of schedule, seated in the first row so that Little Petty, Steven as he is known to the Sedlocks, does not have access to the driver's neck. The bus is not stopping until it parks in front of the lobby.

Inside my Subaru Forester, Toby is giddy, smashing air drums on the dashboard, ignorant of my intermittent radio communication. He is actually excited, having gotten in the car with his lacrosse equipment, asking if I could drop him in Red Hook after we are through, a Saturday intramural league to hone those college skills. He has no idea that he is soon to be arrested for purchasing drugs with the intent of selling them to minors. I am certain his father will buy him out of this mess, although his expulsion from Gopa will be a blow to next year's lacrosse campaign, a subtle fuck you from the departing Pistilini clan.

On the phone, Bill Chuck. "Bus at the Williamsburg Bridge. That's a few minutes ahead of schedule. We aren't ready."

"It's Harry. He's on the bus." I outline the passenger list. "It'll be okay."

Bill disappears, consulting with Misch. He comes back agitated. "Fuck, Tom. That doesn't play. Kids on board, we don't like it. Call it off."

"We're not calling it off." Josey's voice, running the operation. We might not like it the way we did hours ago, but we listen. "It happens today."

Whitman now. "Kids weren't part of this. Pistol, what do I do?"

"Tom isn't in charge," says Phil. "We go as planned."

"Kids, Josey," I say.

"What kids?" Toby asks. "Tell me what's happening, Pisser."

Josey's voice is less sure. "Don't you think I know it?"

"Cargo has to be on that bus," Bill says. "Otherwise none of it works. Which means the bus has to stop like we planned."

Toby taps along to a song. It is the tapping that strings it together. His fingers on his knee draw my eyes to his sneakers, eventually his helmet dangling on an overloaded lacrosse stick. I consult a map of lower Manhattan to find the bus on paper.

Someone, "Fuck."

"There's no way to stop the bus. Let's call it while we can."

Little Petty, "We're turning."

"Listen to me, Bill. That bus will stop. Just like we planned."

"How will it stop?"

"Just have everyone ready."

"On our way," someone calls.

Whitman: "Be safe, Pistol."

There is little time to consider strategy. I turn off the ignition and dial Capra. "Everything as planned. In three minutes." Capra won't go near the bus. Misch's men are following him, and he'll be near enough to arrest when the time comes. It's questionable if Capra's man will make the exchange after he sees what is about to happen. But he has one hundred thousand reasons to board that bus, and I'm counting on capitalism.

I hang up and retrieve the duffel bag from the backseat, unzipping it to reveal all of Ray McClutchen's optimism. Inside, I place Tug's phone, rezip, and toss the bag onto Toby's lap.

"You set, kiddo?"

"I'm just putting the money on the bus. That's what you said."

"That's right."

"And you bring the drugs by later?"

"Something like that." Toby is a child, as green as Iliza or Gus or Maddie. He will grow into an evil, wretched, hungry consumer who will never appreciate his privilege in this world. But for now, he is a kid deserving of my protection, or at least some wisdom. "Listen, Toby, learn something today."

"Yeah, what's that?"

"A teachable moment. Watch what I do. Think about why I do it."

"You're a role model, Pisser." He laughs. "A regular mentor to the youth."

I slap the back of my hand into his face, knuckles into skin as he bounces off the window. My tribe has a misogynistic fascination with inflicting violence on his perfect features. He comes up ringing. "I'm a father. I have a responsibility you will never understand, not for a long time. But hear this, boy. Sometimes the right thing, the worthy thing, does not come packaged neat and honorable. Sometimes it looks like me."

He knows better than to smirk. Toby would like to argue, but there is a bag of money on his lap and I have assumed a leadership role in the Pistilini-Dalton drug cartel. I reach between his legs and wrestle the equipment out my door.

"That's my stuff. What are you doing?"

"Game time, Toby. No matter what happens to me, the money must be on the bus in the next three minutes."

I like the fear in Toby's face, the shape of his mouth, that he has finally tuned in to the proper emotional frequency. He wears a baseball cap and holds a pair of sunglasses, no stranger to crime. "What could happen to you?"

"I could get hit by a bus or something."

"Pisser, what are you talking about?"

"Figure of speech, Toby."

I close the door, leaving him to ponder why a grown man is undressing his lacrosse stick on a busy avenue in Lower Manhattan. There are gloves, shoulder pads, a helmet, a jersey, and a jockstrap that I toss into the street. I cannot figure out the shoulder pads so I toss those as well, fitting the jersey over my swollen frame. It is tight but I manage, the word WORTHY over the number twenty-nine. I squeeze my head into the helmet and slide on the gloves, holding the lacrosse stick like a club.

Weather is faulty. Weather is constantly changing. We can issue calculations based on nifty models and tracking software, but in the end we are mostly reacting to it once it occurs. I know how it looks as I step onto the street, an oversized child where he ought not be. Cars race, bodies in motion. In one of these tin huts Bill Chuck and Lieutenant Misch wonder about their participation. Somewhere Josey tunes in to the shifting pattern, discussing logistics with Linda and Phil. Somewhere Laura and our children are safely stowed. They will receive a call that I have been involved in a traffic accident, but even I cannot predict the weather this time, a fatality or otherwise.

There is no traffic, the morning calm. I hear a wave of revving motors several blocks away, the overhead hum of a city that will barely blink at a traffic accident. From beneath Toby's cage, I glimpse the bus, the black outline over a silver grill that might pardon me death while subjecting me to a lifetime of motorized mobility and mechanical sympathy, three blocks away. From inside the car Toby bangs on the window, confused. Is he worried about my safety, or his lacrosse equipment? Two blocks now, a sense of movement around me, a vague notion that things are happening, Whitman's voice from atop a bench as he films martyrdom. "Get out of the street, Pistol!" My tribe is tuned into the frequency of Josey's worry—*no, no, no*—of Bill Chuck's instincts—*this is it, here we go*—one block, the traffic flowing, the gentle slump of the bus motor as the driver approaches a bend, lets off the gas, giving me a fighting chance.

I gauge the movement at about twenty-five miles per hour, fast and solid but slow for this avenue, taxis racing past. This is the moment courage is either there or fleeting, the ability to step in front of a moving vehicle or gently succumb to the sidelines and live forever with regret. The tribe is with me, all of us summoning the motion that fosters my numb legs into the path at the last second, the bus bearing down as I turn to face my contribution. And then it happens. Tribes of savages, my saving grace. Bus versus man is no contest. Bus versus tribe is different. I cannot help it as my eyes close and I fall away from the impact. The brakes screech. Everything goes silent. A woman screams, Whitman actually. Mayhem.

My knees buckle as the impact spits me forward, a plastic bottle twisting on the pavement before I come to rest near the curb. I lie in a puddle between two vehicles, one leg on the sidewalk that halts my trajectory, the strangest thought: *from whence this puddle, did it rain, did my streak of prognostication cease?* The impact scatters my helmet, which absorbs the cement, Toby's screams drowned out by my Japanese made metal. I assess my condition. I vomited on myself. The wind is knocked out of my gut as I retch on the ground, possibly broken ribs, a dislocated shoulder, a concussion, alive, my tribe bellows, hooting in my spirit. The lacrosse stick is bent in half, a crooked teepee as I hear movement and voices behind me, boots on cement.

"Geezus hell, came out of nowhere," the driver says, assessing the fender.

"Was it a kid?"

"I don't know. One minute it's not and then it is."

"Did you hit a kid?" Harry is shouting. "Where is it then?"

They wander the street as hands slap glass overhead. I listen to the commotion, breathing, slightly asleep. I hear a car door, Toby, in spite of the situation, walking the money through the middle of the confusion toward the bus. From the far side of the street, another door. I turn my head but cannot make out the boots that belong to Capra's man. It happens, both the money and the drugs are on the bus, no one watching the door as they search the street for a child's limp body. According to plan, Petty is on the bus, no one paying attention as he switches the phone from the money to the drugs, making sure the evidence is certified before he powers the pressure cookers. Seven minutes until detonation. Wheels screech. Doors slam. Sirens.

I come around sensing movement, a foot into my side. The trees have blossomed, a nascent shelter for the birds that rubberneck our morning nonsense. *These silly, fucking, bipedal mammals, what are they doing now*? A shadow in the shape of Harry Sedlock enters the frame. He stares down at my WORTHY jersey, a frown, surprised to see his neighbor dressed like his son. I am oddly happy to see Harry, to be alive, and I offer a bloody smile, which causes a second thud, his foot into my stomach.

Josey is over me, talking fast. Capra knew enough to steer clear of the drop, but Misch and his team were following him. Both Capra and his bag man are in custody, the street filled with sirens and familiar boots. "They got him," Josey says. I smile and bleed. "Toby, too. They're arresting him now." Officers have confiscated both bags. Inside the drugs, they will find a phone that belongs to Tug, aka Russ Haverly. After the explosion, they will track it to purchases of all the equipment needed to assemble bombs; sorry about that, Capra, a repercussion for selling drugs to kids, specifically my child. Josey tries to lift me, encourage me to move, but I cannot feel my body as I grab for Harry's leg.

"Bomb," I say. It comes out in breath and spit.

"Fuck you say, Pisser."

"Tom, stop talking," Josey says. "Get up and move."

Harry shoves me again with his foot and Josey slaps him and Phil wrestles her away. Harry does not understand the crime scene.

He mistakes the sirens as police arriving to deal with a fender bender, though what kind of traffic accident summons such a battalion? I wheeze as I explain. "On the bus, Harry. Bomb."

Harry calls to a police officer, pointing out my condition, hoping to expedite his involvement and move the bus two hundred yards forward to deposit his constituents at their destination. The others remain on the bus, having been ordered to stay seated and calm by Harry. That is when it arrives, my tribe's movement. These are someone's parents, perhaps, someone's brothers and sisters, someone's children. The things we do for our children.

Josey and Phil try to help me again but the mechanics do not work, the pain forcing me to the ground. I am a tribe, not one man. On a second attempt, we climb onto elbows and eventually feet, talking loudly. We are not leaving anyone behind, comes our voice. Dizzy, a ringing, I still wear one lacrosse glove, which clutches the bent shaft of Toby Dalton's stick. An officer, his hand perilously close to Harry Sedlock's nose, orders my neighbor onto the bus to sit quietly.

I follow, dragging a limp leg up the stairs, Josey hollering as Phil tugs her into the shadows. The passengers grimace when they see me. My pants are torn off one leg. I bleed from inconsistent ports. The bent stick looks like a weapon. The journalist Pietre Graeme applauds, assuming this is part of the show.

"We need a medic," shouts one of Misch's guys even as he allows me access to the bus.

Petty watches me, knows. "Maybe take a seat, Mister," he says, mustering his best Steven.

"We need to stop it."

He abandons the tour guide gig. "Not the plan, Pistol. We see it through." Allie's neck turns to the prized employee. The Sedlocks get it. "This fucker blows in three minutes whether you're on or off."

Bill Chuck is on the pavement, keeping his people clear. I hear Josey but cannot see her through the windows. I reach out to Petty, unable to take another step. "I can talk them off."

He takes my hand, smiles. I struggle for breath. Maddie sneezes.

"Former investor," Harry says, keeping it light. "Threw himself in front of the bus. That's what this is all about."

I struggle for words. "Harry. Bomb." I find the coolers in the seats, a quiet hiss, the shrapnel cooking. "A few minutes. Before they explode."

"He's lying," Harry says, grasping for their faith. "This man killed our lacrosse coach. He's insane."

It is too late. Three of the journalists leave, not what they signed on for: Meniza Perl, Hansa Schulty, and David Gillard, along with his wife. That leaves nine sets of eyes. "If you don't leave," I wheeze, "you'll be body parts."

Conner Mack follows, eight left. Through the window, I see Whitman on the sidewalk. He has stopped filming, giving me time to get them off before he captures the explosion that will sell more advertising than anything Lustfizzle has ever posted. Tungsten weeps. Harry puts a hand on her head. "It'll be okay, honey. He's lying."

I stand over Allie, drooling. Jason and Olivia watch. "Two minutes, Allie. Get Tungsten off."

Pietre Graeme clapping, "*Bravissimo.*"

Allie nods. "Harry, I'm taking Tungsten."

"I'm not moving. Not for this piece of shit."

"It's over." She stands with Tungsten, who carries Muggly. Jason follows. Pietre Graeme claps his hands and exits as well, the show just beginning. Harry sits.

"You can't do anything about it if you're dead. Think about your kids." Out the front windshield, Allie and Tungsten reach the far sidewalk. "Go to your wife, Harry. While you can."

He curses, bends his neck, departs with a sulk. Two left. Olivia stares at the seat in front of her, Maddie clawing at the fabric with a wet hand.

"Minute and a half," Petty says.

"For Maddie," I say.

She smiles. "I know you, Pisser. You're a coward. You won't do it if she's here."

Petty moves around me, grabbing the child. Olivia tries to hold on, but he tucks her under an arm like a doll. "Minute fifteen. Leave her, Pistol."

Petty descends the steps. On one leg, a minute does not give me much time. I extend my arm. "Come on, Olivia. Think of Todd and Maddie. Think of your unborn child."

She shrugs, scared. "Are there really bombs?"

"There are really bombs."

"What about the investment?"

"It's gone, Olivia."

"I'm not pregnant." She is delirious, heaving in the seat. "I just wanted another nanny in the divorce."

"Take my hand."

I check the windows, the police pulling back the bystanders so that the bus hums alone in the street. Once we hit the concrete, we drag each other to a sidewalk where we collapse. Over the police line I glimpse Josey and Petty and Phil and Linda, watching to see that it is done, the last silhouette of my terrorist days before they disappear. I know it is coming, that the sound will be overwhelming, causing us all to remember this day and hug our children and fear the strange, Olivia weeping into my bloody shirt, Whitman slapping my head, good job, Pistol, as he restarts the camera in three two one...

Cum Laude

WHEN THE INTERROGATIONS BEGAN, I like to believe Harry kept my name out of it because I saved his family. But I know it was fear—of what a man who would step in front of a moving bus is capable of doing. There was whispering in the Gopa community that he had something to do with Russ Haverly's disappearance, in retaliation for the shower video that surfaced of Tungsten, which did not sit well with some parents. With law enforcement aware of his business, Harry Sedlock had little time for me.

Capra suffered most of the fallout, authorities arresting him blocks from the crime scene and charging him with the works—

terrorism, use of weapons of mass destruction, and thirteen counts of attempted murder. In a surprising plea agreement that allowed Capra to avoid life in a federal penitentiary, he even copped to operating a drug ring in the private school community, along with Russ Haverly. Lustfizzle had all the details, a reporter fortunately in the right place recording video of the explosion. It sent shockwaves through private schools along the East Coast, jubilation that the worthy had fallen.

I never spoke with the Sedlocks after we sold the house in Slancy and moved to Connecticut. Moveable Museums struggled on for a few years before the setbacks—computers were hacked, clients' credit card information stolen, Harry and Allie got a divorce. There were television commercials at odd hours. Discerning eyes would recognize the former sex tape actress engaged in travel scenarios, advertising the biking and kayaking tours, but eventually the commercials disappeared as well.

Jason and Jackson are still married, the only remaining members of our Slancy tribe enjoying island life. I ran into Jackson in midtown last year and asked him to a drink—recount the stolen equipment bus for old times—but he made an excuse of tardiness and promised another time. Conflict either rescues or murders friendship. In our case, it was the latter. Olivia married Devin Brenner. They live on the Upper East Side and have twin girls enrolled in the Mayscarf School. I do not know what became of the other Gopa parents and students, or Toby Dalton, but I imagine he is due to graduate from a prestigious college to disgorge his magnificence onto the workforce in a company of his father's choosing. No matter how angry we are with our children, we cannot evade the evolutionary mechanism of parental investment.

Penelope Garcia went on to have a stellar career in meteorology, earning a Peabody Award. I never heard from Phil or Little Petty or Linda, if they were disappointed with me that the bus exploded without bloodshed. Every Christmas I get a white postcard with stick drawings of animals, and I try to discern what message these petroglyph mammals are attempting to disseminate. The postcard sits on the mantle with the other Christmas greetings until we ritualistically burn them in the fireplace each New Year's Eve. I read about it in a Ray McClutchen book, an annual purging of past greetings as a gateway to good fortune in the fresh season.

I meet Ray regularly for coffee. I am paying him back the money I owe a little at a time. We exchange tales of post-Gopa existence that is quieter and modest and undistinguished and noble. He still writes and lectures his brand of fatherly catechism, having discovered why other writers go into self-help: readers have a prophet-ish adoration for people who claim to know what is happening. He is a popular face of self-help lifestyle, and Whitman and I have him on our show a few times a year.

Existential Weather is a twice-weekly podcast that we record in his Bushwick apartment. I take the train in two mornings a week and spend a few hours arguing politics and culture with Whitman, two generations who cannot agree on models and forecasts and who is in charge. It does not pay well enough to afford private school or lagoons in Slancy, but we have a steady following that grows more diverse each month. Whitman has plans to create a radio show, a national audience, a verbal assault on mainstream media. Me, I just need to stay busy.

Iliza attends Trinity College in Hartford, due to graduate with a double major: Education and Sociology. She will travel abroad with a boyfriend name Sigel, who has a goatee and a fascination with communism, the two planning to teach English in Thailand. I miss Doug Whorley. Gus is a junior in the local public school, where he stars as a goalie on the soccer team. He plans to study literature next year, though he is undecided on a college. In the end, it was months of Josey Mateo's involvement, and less of my years harping on applications and seminars, that had the most influence over their lives.

It took us several years to get back on our feet financially, but we managed. Standcake has forty locations in three states, one of the fastest-growing health food chains in the country. Now that Laura can afford a fleet of vans, I am little help to the business, my contributions reduced to homemaker of our Victorian house. This spring, I will paint the wraparound porch and install outdoor speakers so Jason

Isbell and The Commodores can join us in the evenings. There is a room on the second floor I have been reluctant to renovate, owing to Laura's insistence that the ghost of the previous owner resides there. We leave it vacant, which is fine since Clint Eastwood has claimed it as her space, agreeing to domesticity so long as I leave the window ajar. I do not keep tabs on her brood. They appear from time to time, rugged and well fed and often bearing dead rodents, which become Abraham's playthings if I am not diligent.

With my eldest children involved in their respective dogmas, only occasionally asking advice from their father, my main occupation is playing nanny to my four-year-old. Abe will attend the local elementary school next year. I am looking forward to drop-offs and committees and sports teams and gossip. Likely the eldest member of the parenting crew, my experience will provide depth to the younger guardians and foster a sense of statesmanship in the parent-teacher continuum. Most mornings find us at the park as bumper-stickered mini-vans parade past to preparatory classes and appointments, rehearsal and strategy, and I cannot say I am looking forward to the warfare.

My main skill these days is playfulness that Abe inspires, forcing me on monkey bars and slides, up ladders that crack my aged knees and discharge vaporous missiles through my gluteal. Every so often, I will tweak some fiber in a shoulder or ribs, and know it is still there, the scar tissue that the world is a better place because I was run over by a bus. "Come on, Daddy," Abe says, urging me through our sunrise obstacle course. "Hide and seek," he'll say, endless energy crouching behind a tree. Winded and perspiring, I require a park bench to spell my lungs. But there is a hunger in his smile that triggers the tribe sown deep within me, alerting me to the duty, that despite my cultivated patience and age, I still must go to extremes to maintain that joy. I struggle forward. Ready or not. Here come the worthy.

Acknowledgments

TO THE INCREDIBLE TEAM at Rare Bird Lit, I'm honored and fortunate to work with such a dedicated crew: Julia Callahan, Tyson Cornell, Alice Elmer, Gregory Henry, Guy Intoci, Hailie Johnson, and Jake Levens. Thank you to the Gaithersburg Book Festival, my most ardent supporters throughout the years. Thank you to longtime readers for advice and encouragement: Mike Altshuler, Luke David, William Giraldi, and Rena Rossner. A special thanks to friends and family who continue to support me. And to my NYC tribe, Alia, Jack, and Hank, who avoid the writing studio at 4:00 a.m. and keep it free of noise and syrup, somewhat.